Cover art by Jan Falk (thistle-arts.com)

CE by Richard Shealy (sffcopyediting.com)


ISBN 978-1-968767-00-6 (paperback)

ISBN 978-1-968767-02-0 (ebook)

# Praise for Rears & Vices

"*Rears & Vices* is a sexy, swashbuckling adventure full of intrigue, romance, and queer pirates defying empires. It shimmers with marvelous historical detail and sensuous prose. I loved it!"

— FELICIA DAVIN, AUTHOR OF *THE SCANDALOUS LETTERS OF V AND J*

"Full of adventure and romantic in every sense of the word, *Rears & Vices* delighted me from start to finish."

— TJ ALEXANDER, *USA TODAY* BESTSELLING AUTHOR OF *A GENTLEMAN'S GENTLEMAN*

"Avast ye landlubbers! E.M. Caro's sexy and swash-buckling *Rears & Vices* delivers all the passion, intrigue, and high stakes of a thrilling pirate adventure with deliciously modern sensibilities. A bygone maritime era comes alive in Caro's lush, vibrant prose. This book dropped anchor on my heart from the first page!"

— VENESSA VIDA KELLEY, AUTHOR-ILLUSTRATOR OF *WHEN THE TIDES HELD THE MOON*

"*Rears & Vices* took me on a swashbuckling adventure from start to finish. A highly enjoyable poly pirate romp, lush with historical and nautical detail, with a fantastic cast of characters. I can't wait to dive more into E.M. Caro's world."

— EMMA DENNY, AUTHOR OF *ONE NIGHT IN HARTSWOOD*

"Gloriously queer, devastatingly romantic, and unbearably hot. *Rears & Vices* is one of the freshest and most surprising historical romances of the decade—I loved it."

— ALEXANDRA VASTI, *USA TODAY* BESTSELLING AUTHOR OF *LADIES IN HATING*

# REARS & VICES

E.M. CARO

TIDES&TROTH

*For the matelots.*

# ONE

HM Schooner *Netley*
Kingston Harbour, Upper Canada

*HIS MAJESTY JOHN BULL AT FORT YORK:
DEADLY SELF-SABOTAGE!*

Everard glared down at the *Rochester Spy*'s front page in disbelief.

"Self-*sabotage*—? Jesus sainted Christ!"

He threw the thing. But thanks to Upper Canada's lakeshore humidity, the three-year-old Yankee paper was damp, and heavy, too, so it merely hit the edge of his desk with a pathetic, protesting *thump* and tumbled down.

Everard stood from his cot to resume pacing his cabin. It served him right, looking for old gossip about pirates.

But the editorialising! It was just as well he was no longer in printing. He had a mind to—

"Sir?" The ship's boy, from the companionway. "Gig's ready, cap'n."

Right. No need for more newspaper hearsay, anyway; he'd soon see this pirate for himself.

"Presently!"

Everard plucked up his hat, shoved it on. Courts martial were full dress, which meant buttons—eighteen of them—but he had, at least, his own bicorn: satin-trimmed, beaver felt, nonregulation. He hoped someone might take its notice and that that someone might be admiralty, for it was as close as he'd ever get to giving that institution a certain finger.

Everard opened the door. "Jack?"

The boy jumped. "Yessir?"

"Please return these before you take your liberty ashore."

Jack eyed the three crates of newsprint with some trepidation, caught himself, and quickly stared ahead to the panelling. "Yessir."

Everard bit his tongue against a thank-you—it was neither called for nor appropriate, and *please* had been bad enough of a slip—and went above deck. His most recent lieutenant met him at the gangway, saluted with two hooked fingers. Everard nodded in return.

"She's yours for the day, Mr. Spicelay."

The bo'sun piped him off the side with a shrill whistle, and when he'd sat down aft, piped the boat off, too. Everard cast his focus away from Kingston Harbour and across the sealike Lake Ontario. It was hot today, unusually so for June, and the water was calm, waves smoothed and set sparkling by an uninhibited sun. There was a light breeze in from the west, gentle enough that he'd no reason to fear for his favourite hat.

The Lakes Service had few advantages. Water that one could scoop straight into one's mouth was foremost.

Another was that, compared to his saltwater contemporaries, Everard had judged relatively few courts martial over the past three years. Today, though, he didn't have much choice in it. It was 1816, and the wars with the Yanks and the

French had ended. There was a glut of officers. His twenty-four-year career clung to nothing more than a few bits of unwound rope: courtesy, rank, and his lingering—more like withering—reputation. As much as he hated passing judgment on his fellow seaman, obliging the admiralty was unavoidable.

Slowly, the little gig pulled up to the shiny black-and-white hull of HMS *Brigitte*.

Trials were held on the largest deck to be had in-harbour. A fifty-eight-gun, three-masted, fully rigged frigate, the *Brigitte* certainly qualified; she was the biggest freshwater ship left not laid up in Upper Canada.

Everard stood, hand on his sword, and looked up as he waited to be piped aboard. Captain of a schooner he may have been, but still a captain.

The whistle blew for his ascent. Everard couldn't keep in grunts of effort as he climbed the unending hull. His left hand —with the one thumb, two knuckles, and not much else— relied on the strength of his arm below it, and required he wrap his wrist on every pull. Rope handholds were a bit slow going, a struggle some would call undignified. He called those someones fucking bastards.

"Everard!" a voice greeted him as he crested the railing. "About time!"

Everard's two good sea legs were his only saving grace as he stepped down the gangway and untwisted his uniform sleeve.

Preston D'Arcy, Post-Captain, looked precisely the same as Preston D'Arcy, First Lieutenant had: wild, red-brown curls, fashionably cropped and haphazardly greased. Long dark lashes. Just enough French extraction for a profile too pouty to be truly stern. Handsome, and far too aware how to leverage that fact.

They'd been great friends, once. More.

D'Arcy came close, clapped him on the arm. "How have you been, Ev?"

"Just fine, D'Arcy." Everard gave a small, polite nod—D'Arcy and he were not strictly on speaking terms, not anymore—and looked away to eye the line of chairs assembled on the deck. There weren't many; three of six officers' chairs were occupied. "Am I fifth, then?" he asked, squinting against the sun.

"Yes, at minimum today," D'Arcy said. "Hardly anyone left in the Lakes Service, you know."

Everard grunted. He did know. The war was over. "Who's presiding?"

"Johnson."

"Hmm. Best and brightest." Everard swiped his brow with the lace at his wrist. Maybe he ought not to have worn his favourite hat. The *Brigitte*'s deck was sweltering; it would make for a positively miserable forenoon of courts martial. Not that it wouldn't already have been. "Surely by now he'd have lost the posting?"

"You know well why not." D'Arcy brought up his right hand and rubbed thumb and fingers together.

Everard grimaced. "Yes, well, the way of peacetimes, I suppose. We'll be here past supper, do you think? Unless he has got a quicker secretary."

The officers' chairs were situated on the quarterdeck beneath a sheet turned horizontal, which provided shade from the glaring sun. They made their greetings of the other officers, all fellow Lakes Service captains—and sat gratefully.

"Gad, I hope not." D'Arcy leaned in close, whispering for Everard's ears only. "Have a look who I'll miss out on." He shifted back to tilt his chin unsubtly at the upright, red-breasted Marines lined up against the rail.

Everard, not in the habit of sexualising his ranked inferiors —not *usually*—glanced over and frowned.

"Er… which?" he asked.

Not usually, because he had made one—*one*—notable

exception to this rule thus far. The result, of course, being that Preston D'Arcy knew him much better than one probably ought to know his fellow captain.

"They can't be your own Marines?" he admonished.

D'Arcy snorted, though he grinned wide. "You shock me. No, of course they're not mine. Could you imagine? I'd never sleep." He waved. "My lobsters are on shore leave. These are admiralty men, special order out of Halifax."

"Special order," Everard said, beneath his breath.

D'Arcy's single right shoulder epaulette sparkled as he shoved Everard good-naturedly. "And when was the last time we sat courts martial together, Ever?"

As though either of them would forget.

"At least you're not the one gagged this time," D'Arcy continued.

"Oh, don't be an ass." He and D'Arcy—at the time Everard's first lieutenant—had in fact sat their own inquiries after losing a ship—the *Wanderer*—in battle to the Americans, Christmas Eve of '12. But they'd been acquitted honourably, in spite of the surrender and infamous defeat. D'Arcy had even got promoted after.

And Everard, dear God, had certainly not been gagged.

"They gagged the prisoners?" he asked curiously. It wasn't usual, even for violent offenders.

"Well, no," D'Arcy admitted. "Only the one."

"The pirate." Everard's mouth parched suddenly, and he cleared his throat. "I'm surprised the admiralty haven't already pitched him over, had done with the man. Or left him in the hulks. Fewer witnesses, if he was so much fight that he wanted gagging."

D'Arcy laughed uneasily. "You haven't the least idea. As to witnesses..." His voice pitched lower, conspiratorial, and Everard leaned in. God help him, but he did love gossip, and there'd been so little of it on the lakes. "… more charges were brought night "ore last. Barely legal notice."

Everard's heart sank. New charges, last minute? That meant one thing: a sodomy charge.

"Ah." He sighed. "One of those. Any victims?" he asked pointedly. "Statements?"

"None on the docket."

"Hmm." Not likely rape, then, thank God. Most sodomy charges that made it to the courts martial were, though not all. Everard had attended only one such trial personally, and nothing about the relations between the accuser and officer-accused had been equal nor yet consensual. An easy conviction. "Multiple offences and piracy aren't enough for the Lord High?"

"Apparently not." D'Arcy sounded resigned, and no wonder. "This is the fourth I've heard of this year," he muttered. "Halifax calls it an epidemic of moral failing." He sniffed, twitching his fingers over his nose. "I call it a campaign."

Everard put his right hand on D'Arcy's knee and squeezed. "As you are not a rapist," he murmured, very low, "it's nothing doing with you and me. The charge is probably unfounded, extraneous. And it's no surprise they want a pirate to hang, is it?"

"Nothing doing *thus far.* It lacks only their changing the definition to include the consensual." D'Arcy sighed. "I suppose you're right. As usual." A pause. "But how d'you like your *Netley*?" he asked. "Whenever you like, Ever, I could put a word in, get you something a bit larger…"

Everard scowled. Could he, indeed. D'Arcy made it sound quite easy—*whenever you like!*—as though Everard hadn't been petitioning endlessly for that precise thing since the end of the war.

But though he might've wanted it, he knew he didn't deserve a larger posting. Not after the *Wanderer* and especially not after the disaster at York. His *Netley* had hardly seen any action while in the Lakes Service, and had in fact already been reaching too high. The admiralty plainly wanted him to retire. Every week, he waited for the post that would give him notice.

Rightly, he should've retired. Should've taken his injury and his twenty-four-year pension and gone back to printing, or illustration, or even, God forbid, his father's textile mill in Catalonia; anything at all other than continue this grasp at meagre authority.

But in his bones he still felt it: the yearning maw of ambition. He was thirty-six, possessed of an eerie premonition that he had only a handful of years left in him. The barest chance left to yet do something worth being written about—something not flames and death and disgrace.

D'Arcy went on. "I know it's peacetimes, but the Jamaica station—"

The bo'sun's pipes blew again: a new arrival to the ship.

There came a yell from beyond the rail: "Captains!"

A man pulled himself aboard and stomped over: about fifty years of age, grey-haired, with an uncommonly long, jowled face, wearing double epaulettes and the maximum amount of embroidery possible on his sleeves. Everard and D'Arcy both stood.

"Admiral," Everard greeted.

"Blackhand!" The admiral turned to Everard. "Good morning, Captain. But is the sun not horrific?"

*Christ.*

"Sir," Everard replied coolly.

"Blackhand" was the sobriquet that had caught on three years past, after the battle of York. It had nothing to do with Everard's reputation, only to do with the black leather glove he wore over his left hand. In the rightful stead of his long career, it seemed the thing had encompassed his whole goddamned identity.

If he could be considered to have a legacy, that was it.

"Thank you for making five, Anderson," the admiral went on.

*Anderson de Anglada,* Everard corrected mentally, as always. Most Englishmen pretended to forget the Català bit of his surname. Everard pretended to ignore why.

"It was no trouble," he replied. "I was close at hand." The *Netley* had been sailing up and down the Huron, a glorified patrol.

"At hand." The admiral chuckled, glancing significantly down. "Quite."

Everard clenched his teeth. Yes, they undoubtedly wanted him to retire.

The admiral turned to D'Arcy. "What a beautiful lady your *Brigitte* is, D'Arcy! For a lake-goer."

D'Arcy had flushed red all the way to his hat. He cleared his throat, made a short bow.

"Thank you, sir," he said. "We're well aware of the pirate, but who else have they? Surely they've a stack."

"Peacetimes, m'boy," the admiral replied—though D'Arcy was thirty-five if he was a day. "We've a handful of mutineers. The usual deserters and thieves." His eyes gleamed. "Even a *murderer,* I hear. Shall we get on?" He turned with a flare of blue coat and sat in the chair largest and centremost, just beside Everard. He pulled out a pocket watch and observed it haughtily.

A moment later, a harried-looking man came scrambling across the railing, hauling a rickety, brass-hinged lap desk.

The admiral sighed. "Good news, men. I have a new secretary."

D'Arcy coughed. Everard felt his shoulders slump a little in mirth and relief. Anyone would have a quicker hand than the man's predecessor.

Maybe they wouldn't be there beyond supper after all.

# Two

I t was plain: Everard should not have worn his favourite hat.
There really was nothing like a summer on the Ontario.

The ship's boy had made perhaps his umpteenth round of
bucket ladle to the *Brigitte*'s crew audience. They were beginning to show serious signs of wilt; some had even sat down.
Nobody had the heart to tell them otherwise, even the admiral.

Everard thought of the pirate, as yet to appear before
them, and hoped the ship's boy had got round to him at some
point, too: it would be suffocatingly hot belowdecks.

Then he remembered. *Gagged.* It was enough to make him
sit straighter in his chair.

The admiral's new secretary did indeed have a quicker
hand than his predecessor, and appeared to know a good deal
of shorthand, thank God; but everyone was still obliged to
pause, silent, as he scratched down every word that was said in
the proceedings.

Two deserters. A crew of mutineers, five in number. A
thief. Charges proved on all.

Finally it was time for the pirate.

Heat forgotten, the *Brigitte*'s crew revived themselves and stood. Intent. Everard felt mildly sick. Was it that the prisoner was a pirate that had their attention rapt? Or was it the last-minute sodomy charge?

He knew what made the newsprints.

Three marines carried the pirate up through the hatch. This was absurd in itself. One marine had lost his hat, and little wonder: the pirate kicked, though his legs were shackled; he bucked, pale broad shoulders twisting in strain; he screamed and swore, the King's English identifiable from the biting rhythm even through the gag. He was blindfolded, linen tight over his eyes and knotted behind a long rope of braided blond hair that was un-matted and surprisingly clean-looking.

After days in the hold, in this heat, a prisoner ought to have been rendered limp and delirious. At the very least, he should have been resigned to his fate. This man was none of those things. He was spitting with rage. It made Everard's face burn to watch them struggle to drag him, as though he took on the man's own indignity.

The marines wrested the man down, until he fell to his knees with a *thump*, the sound as heavy as dropped cannon shot; Everard winced. They pulled his ironbound, biceps-tied arms back and knotted them to his ankle shackles, so that he was spread out, ribs splayed before them, as though someone would cut out his beating heart to splatter on the decking.

"Jesus," D'Arcy muttered.

Once, one particularly hot summer—hotter than this, even—they'd had to upend a bucket of water over a swooned prisoner to wake him; legally, he had to stand and give his defence. And that had been bad.

But Everard had never seen anything like this.

The prisoner had stopped cursing by now. Other than his harsh breaths, there was a stunned silence.

The admiral cleared his throat and began to read the man's charge sheet.

What pirate had skin so milk-white, untouched by the sun? What sailor, for that matter? Could they have got the wrong man?

"… not limited to desertion, mutiny, sedition, piracy, and unnatural offences against his fellow seamen," he finished.

There it was. *Unnatural offences.*

D'Arcy made a distinctly discomfited noise.

Everard glanced over. Though D'Arcy still leaned lazily, ear to palm, he had recoiled into his chair as far as he could go, and his left hand had shoved itself deep into his breeches pocket, seeking shelter from trembling.

Preston D'Arcy, Post-Captain of His Majesty's Navy, with a fifty-eight-gun frigate-of-war and a crew upwards of 250— some of whom he was obliged to stripe—was far from a squea-mish man.

Everard found he, too had hunched his own shoulders in reflexive sympathy for the prisoner's wrenched ones, and had hands in pockets, though he didn't tremble. His stomach rolled instead, frothing bubbles liquifying his insides.

Even knowing the sodomy charges were likely unfounded, it still turned his stomach. It wasn't commonplace to be arrested for fucking men, especially as an officer, but that didn't mean it couldn't happen. It didn't mean that he or D'Arcy wouldn't find themselves someday court-martialled under the very same charge, just for being the way they'd always been. If the wrong person found out, cared too much, paid a witness…

The admiral, unmoved, waved at his face with a chicken-skin fan, eyes narrowed with contempt and impatience as his secretary laboured over the transcription of the long charge sheet.

At the point where Everard hoped he was near the end of it, the man pitched over the ink pot with a trembling pull of his quill. He groped frantically to stop its roll. And then—Everard opened his mouth to warn too late—the whole stuck-hinged writing desk fell straight over onto the deck, landing with a *bang*.

It startled damn near everybody, but had an extraordinary effect on the pirate: he flinched hugely, went as hunched as he could go in restraints. A pause; a frisson of clear relief shuddered down like liquid over his skin. The braided head slumped for the first time.

It didn't matter that a fallen desk sounded nothing like a shot's echo over lake water and decking; to a bound, blindfolded man it must have been close enough. What mattered were those relieved, trembling shoulders, the strained breathing. Pirate or no, the man had seen gun battle and suffered for it.

That was it for Everard.

"For God's sake, enough," he spat. "Can we not let him have his sight?" He used his most authoritative, crisply squared captain's voice, and pointed to the marine to the right of the prisoner. "You, there. Take off that damned blindfold."

The marine—a sunburnt fellow—hesitated, damn him. "Sir?"

The pirate had gone still.

"*If* you please, Private." *Move your redcoat arse.* Everard had some authority left; he might as well use it for aught.

"Aye, sir." The marine leaned in, and he was the least vicious of the three chosen, apparently, because instead of slicing it, and probably a good chunk of the prisoner's blond braid along with, he carefully picked at the knot.

Admiral Johnson sighed but said nothing. His secretary was still scrambling to reset his desk in any case. D'Arcy shifted in his seat, hands in pockets. And when the marine had the knot nearly there, Everard spoke once more.

"And the gag. He needs must speak his defence."

"Aye, sir."

The broad shoulders twitched again, the strained abdomen

spasmed. The gag was spat vengefully out; the blindfold fell away.

Beside him, D'Arcy inhaled sharp.

Everard couldn't breathe.

It couldn't be. Absolutely, not in a thousand years was it he.

D'Arcy nudged at his knee, and whispered, frantic, "Ev. *Ever.* Hey. You're pale as ash, man."

He meant for Everard not to visibly react, not to obviously recognise the defendant. It was too late for that; he'd felt his jaw go slack.

*It can't be him,* he thought idiotically. *No.*

The secretary had got his desk upright again, and began transcribing Everard's words—his words, championing the prisoner's welfare.

The pirate levelled his teary—teary, oh God—gaze on Everard. His face, in utter contrast to the white chest, was tan and smooth beneath an unkempt beard, with sharp angles all over, and hard blue eyes, too; but the lips weren't hard at all but the most beautiful pair Everard had ever seen on a man—save one. *This* one.

Everard hadn't listened for the man's name in the charges. It maybe wasn't even the same. But he knew it. Knew it well. Had thought of it too often in the past three years, alone in a swaying bunk.

Vitaliy. Vitya. *Vitya…*

"Thank you, de Anglada," Vitaliy Gray said.

D'Arcy cursed beneath his breath, groaning. "God's teeth."

That was about the size of it.

"What?" The admiral shifted himself to glare, hand on a hip. "Anderson," he barked. "You have prior acquaintance of the prisoner?"

*Prior acquaintance.* Did he ever. The problem, Everard thought, was that he in fact had a very good memory. It took no prompting at all to remember the thick, blond-fuzzed thighs pressing close and warm. Not even a glance, to remember wrapping his hands on either side of the tapered waist, to remember marvelling down at pale, furred valleys gleaming with sweat. *Vitaliy Gray.*

An eidetic memory, it was called. While extremely useful for sine, cosine, and tangents, ship's logs, and correcting the purser on the occasional "slip-up" in crew pay—it was also absolutely, positively horrendous when trying to deny one's acquaintance with a pirate and remembering instead the man's prick stuffed inside him.

"Ah…" Everard cleared his throat. What to say?

Captains were recused out of courts martial for conflict of interest as a matter of course. But this morning they were at minimum: five officers. He could recuse himself now, and if he did, Vitaliy wouldn't hang today.

"Anderson?" Admiral Johnson pressed, sounding impatient.

But certainly he would hang, just as soon as another officer could be had and the trial held de novo. It wouldn't take long. A day. A week. Multiple offences and felony sodomy? He'd hang.

He looked up. Vitaliy still stared at him, but his deep-set, dark-blue eyes had narrowed, and those beautiful heart-shaped lips had lifted: the soft smile of expectation.

In calling him out by name Vitaliy had reciprocated his mercy. Everard *could* claim conflict of interest, claim simple recusal, and not have to see his once-upon lover hang. Not have to give his voice to convict him on unnatural—*passionate, sweat-streaked, earth-shatteringly natural*—offences.

Or—or Everard could simply deny it, his captain's word against a pirate's, and the trial would go on.

It was an easy choice.

"Yes, sir," Everard said carefully. "I have in fact had his acquaintance."

Beside him, D'Arcy let out a small, miserable groan.

Everard listened to the scratch of quill point on parchment, testimonial. Every word, recorded. Every word.

"Then do recuse yourself, sir! As is right!" The admiral, in sharp syllables.

Vitaliy raised his chin. *Take it,* he said silently. *Take what I've offered.*

But no. Everard's resolve solidified, lead cooling lumpen at the base of his throat. No decision had ever been easier.

He was about to commit perjury.

"Yes, sir," he said. "That is to say, no, sir," he said, more firmly, as Vitaliy's eyes widened. "I cannot merely recuse myself. You see, this man has served on my ship."

The admiral's fan flapped wildly again.

"The *Netley?* Then it is even more necessary that you recuse—"

"I beg your pardon, sir. On my previous ship."

"Ev," D'Arcy whispered urgently in his ear; luckily, the crowd had got loud again in their consternation. "What in hell are you doing?"

Trying to save a man's life was what. Was it not obvious? Everard glanced right. D'Arcy was the only man there who could refute what he was about to say.

"You mustn't do this," D'Arcy hissed. "Not like this. Recuse yourself and we'll sort it. *Later.*"

Everard ignored him.

"The *Wanderer,* sir," he said loudly.

The admiral was red-faced. "Quiet!" he demanded of the crowd. They hushed, gradually. "The *Wanderer?* That cannot be. His charges—mutiny, piracy—three years ago is out of jurisdiction!"

"Yes indeed, sir. Respectfully, it doesn't matter."

Vitaliy himself was frowning now too, brow furrowed and confused at Everard's lie—no, this was not what he'd meant at all.

But—Vitya, dead and twitching from the yardarm. No, no, no. What was a little perjury?

Everard took a deep breath. "I do formally recuse myself on conflict of interest."

Hushed murmurs shuddered throughout the crew audience, the Marines. The secretary's quill scratched furiously. *Scritch-scritch-scritch.*

"However…"

The admiralty might hang all the rapists they pleased, and with Everard's blessing. They might try to make all sodomy out to be criminal and reprehensible and wrong, regardless of circumstance or consent. But they would not get this man.

"… I feel obliged to make it known that this man should not be on trial at all. And that if he is to be tried de novo, I shall have no recourse but to serve as witness to his defence."

Gasps and disbelieving laughter from the crowd, quickly silenced by elbows. Beside him, D'Arcy had his brow in hand.

"*What!*" Admiral Johnson was beside himself in waiting for the secretary to finish.

Finally: "Witness?" he spluttered. "But the inquiry… all charges were deemed viable! He's a bloody deserter marine—turned pirate! A sodomitical pirate!" he emphasised.

"With due respect, Admiral," Everard began, "I was not present at this inquiry. And I am telling you now the charges are inviable, without foundation. This man is not a pirate, or a deserter, or a sodomite. I've had contact with him these three years past, and he could not possibly have done any of those within that time frame. What we have here, I believe, is a case of mistaken identity."

Everard would thwart all of Vitaliy's charges if he had to do so one by one. He likely couldn't have them dismissed—Vitaliy would not go free on felony charges, not when the admiralty clearly had it out for him—but he could at the very least throw certainty of guilt.

Vitya would be transported, never to be seen again, but he wouldn't *hang*.

Admiral Johnson stared. "That's impossible. Did you not hear who—"

"He's married," Everard said doggedly. "I know him well."

The admiral muttered to his secretary—likely striking whatever was forthcoming from the record—and said, "I don't care if he's your goddamned brother-in-law; these sorts of crimes ought not to go unpunished under any circumstance! You *do* understand me, Anderson?"

Everard understood perfectly.

"Ordinarily," he lied, "I would of course agree with you, Admiral. But in this particular instance, I have some means of proof. In my possession I have three years' worth of correspondence that proves this man cannot have—and would not have—done these offences within the admissible timeframe."

Well, come tomorrow he would have, anyway.

"I trust these will prove more than acceptable to the court, once I have been sworn in properly as witness." Everard stood, put back on his nonregulation hat, set it exactly straight. "I will have them brought you on the morrow. Sir."

# THREE

Three Years Earlier
     King Street
  York, Upper Canada


It was quarter-nine of the morning, on a Saturday, in the midst of the coldest fucking April that Everard had seen yet in York. Arm-in-arm with him on the road, Lieutenant Preston D'Arcy was not only still suppertime levels of sheets to the wind, but also… singing.

"To market, to market…"

In the smack middle of wide King Street. Nursery rhymes, no less.

"To buy a fat p… riiick…"

Worst of all, he was loud.

Everard dug his fingers into D'Arcy's sleeve and resisted the urge to shake the man 'til his teeth rattled. "Jesus sainted, Preston," he muttered. "You'll have us both swinging the yard."

"Admiralty don't hang officers," D'Arcy said. "Not as we're at war with the Yanks."

Everard grumbled. "I don't aim to be the exception."

D'Arcy waved this off lazily. But then, he was gentry. Everard pushed him away so that he was forced to bear more of his own weight.

"And," he added, "you've got the rhyme wrong, you utter sod. It's to buy a penny bun."

He knew he was right, too. Pages appeared, flash-powder white in his mind, as though he held the book in his palms.

*Songs for the Nursery, Tabart and Co., London, 1805. Price 6d without Plates, 1s 6d with Plates, 2s 6d with Plates beautifully Coloured.*

Even without his memory, he ought to know; those particular plates had been his own work. Between wars, children's books had been about the only steady pay for a twenty-five-year-old Navy lieutenant-turned-satirist.

There, plain on page 8:

> *Hey my Kitten, my Kitten… Ride a cock-horse*
> *to Banbury-cross…*
> *To market, to market, to buy a penny bun,*
> *Home again, home again, market is d—*

"Ah!"

D'Arcy had pinched him.

"That's for calling me *sod.*" He whistled, carrying the nursery rhyme's melody on—thankfully now wordless—and they ambled round the corner, nearly onto York's Market Square.

Aptly named, the market was a squarish mud lot near water's edge, at the corner of King and New streets, all edged by a whitewashed fence. Within this neat delineation, one could buy any manner of things: eggs, white, green, brown, or speckled; chickens, similarly feathered; butter and freshly wrapped cheeses; whiskered catfish, yellow pickerel, and rain-bow-scale trout; new spring onions, rhubarb, and last year's cabbages; apple-blossom honeycomb to layer on fresh bread—

D'Arcy belched softly into a fist. "Anyway, they'd never convict you, Ev, on account you hardly qualify."

Everard stiffened, produce forgotten, though they were nearly there. "I beg your pardon. Qualify?"

"Un-*natch*-rul offences," D'Arcy said, in an accent not his usual. "Too uptight. Never any witnesses. Never any *fucking*. Therefore."

Everard couldn't remember the last time there had been witnesses. Well, that was not strictly true. However… "Preston, how're you still this drunk?"

"I'd be less drunk," D'Arcy swayed, "if last night you'd taken proper advantage and proper-*ly* fu—"

Everard stopped dead. "Don't." He looked quickly round, over to the market, to be sure none was close enough to over-hear. But he didn't meet D'Arcy's eyes. He stared at his nose instead. "We've spoken of this," he said quietly. "At length. Our relations were neither appropriate, nor ethical with me as your captain, nor, dare I say it, legal—"

"Oh." D'Arcy snorted. "Legal's the impediment. *I* see — Oi!"

D'Arcy broke the link of their arms and attempted to shove off a man who had run straight into him. He failed, sputtering, "For fuck's— *Excuse* your ar… se…"

D'Arcy trailed off into a sharp breath as their interrupter stepped back. The man was tall, white, blond, in shirtsleeves only, hatless like some disrepute, but he carried himself with the straight spine of a marine at watch, and wore a French musket. He was also—in a word—large. If he wasn't a sailor, the kind that climbed swaying rigging like it were so much solid-rock cliff, Everard would eat his (second-favourite, undress) hat.

"Sir," Everard greeted, hoping that the man would go on his way, and that he hadn't overheard.

But no. The man didn't move. He slung his hands into his breeches pockets and regarded them: glanced over Everard's coat with epaulettes, and D'Arcy's one without.

"Begging pardon," he said, looking not at all sorry. He had a soft, carefully defined voice, and the vowels of a Russian. He saluted briefly, two hooked fingers, and leaned in. "But I hope we were not serious about buying of pricks."

The man had heard! Dear God, D'Arcy had finally gone and done it, his loud mouth would get them both hanged—

The man continued quickly. "Because the sale of one's fellow man I cannot abide, and if that is the case, we will have words." He smiled again, as mild as you please; Everard sensed that words were not the only thing he would have.

"But if it is companionship only you are wanting…" *Vahnting,* it came out pronounced. His gaze focused on Everard, and went up and down, frank and fearless.

Everard almost stepped back. Had he just been propositioned? He, Everard? On King Street, York? In broad bloody daylight, on a *Saturday?*

D'Arcy was faster to recover. He laughed in an airless sort of way.

"Right," he declared, ruefully. "I've definitely not drunk enough for this. Buy me a bird in the market, Ev." He snickered. "If you make it there." Then, with a wobbling spin, he walked in the direction of the coffeehouse.

"Preston!" Everard hissed after him.

D'Arcy waved. "Don't disappoint, Captain!"
*Disappoint whom?*

Everard stared at his lieutenant's blue wool superfine, retreating back, waiting for him to turn round.

He did not.

D'Arcy wouldn't really leave him with a—hatless whomever he was, an unknown—would he? An unknown that apparently wanted—

Wanted him?

"Considerate fellow," the blond man remarked. He came to stand beside Everard, hands still in breeches pockets. "Observant, if loud."

Everard turned.

"I'm… not what he says I am," he attempted.

The man leaned back on heels to regard him. Tawny eyebrows rose.

"Disappointing?" Another look, up and down. "Or uptight? I have doubt of both."

Everard flushed. "A—a man who— Oh, never mind." It seemed useless to deny it; he didn't want to say it out loud. And so Everard, for the first time in a great long while, let himself take a good look of a man.

He was very attractive. His accented speech seemed to perfectly suit him, as sharply defined as the rest of him: from the cheekbones shadowed with curly blond sideburns, to the narrow, chiseled nose, the profile that belonged in a bright, light-soaked rendition of Lucifer—beautiful lips, full and firm and heart-shaped—

Everard was not really an artist. He'd never felt an affinity towards anything more glamorous than pencils, and block prints were, in his opinion, mere technical skill; cartoon, not artistry. But suddenly he felt pencil wouldn't be enough, and even if he could chisel out that face into relief and reproduce it onto a thousand broadsheets…

"A man who…?" the man prompted, and gave a slow, amused blink. There were faint remnants of pitch-black kohl around his heavy-lidded, blue, blue eyes. "No need exchange names, Captain. If you do not want."

The devil knew it, too. Knew that he had only to crook a finger, and a person would nod and follow, consequences be damned. With that beauty turned towards him, Everard wasn't even resentful of it; it was just fact, expected as the sun.

This hadn't happened to Everard before, not ever. No one had picked him out of a crowd like a prize and said, *Yes, I think him, I want him*—unless one counted twenty years past, when he'd been plucked from Barcelona's docks and shoved into a Navy ship's hold.

It was a queer sensation, being so openly pursued. But he liked it. And singing or no singing, the man had taken an extraordinary risk in being so frank. He liked that, too.

"You have no hat," Everard protested at last.

"No," his new companion agreed. "One less thing to remove."

There was absolutely no denying it now.

And it had been a very long time.

*Don't disappoint.*

"Indeed," Everard said.

The man's answering smile was small, but victorious nonetheless. "Good," he said. He pulled free a pocket watch, flicked it open. It gleamed, golden with a glass face, filigreed all over; much too expensive for a shipman's pay, even an officer's.

Knowing hit Everard like a cold thrill. Not just a sailor: pirate. That's what those kohled eyes and lack of uniform said. *Pirate.* He sucked in a breath. Perhaps if he turned away and—

The man looked up, and Everard wasn't walking away, oh, no.

"Nine of clock," the man murmured. "Tell me, Captain… how many hours of shore liberty remain?"

# Four



P resent Day
    HMS *Brigitte*
  Kingston Harbour, Upper Canada

Everard walked across the *Brigitte*'s scrubbed deck and put his right hand carefully on Vitaliy Gray's bare, restrained shoulder. The man didn't flinch, but watched him, unconcerned; Everard leaned in close, as though to offer comfort to the wrongfully accused.

Vitaliy smelled surprisingly clean, like warm sun, golden hair, sweat Everard recognised quite acutely, low in his gut—with a definite base note of fear that made his heart falter and jerk. Up close, he appeared physically unharmed, with few bruises; a relief, considering Halifax's notorious prison hulks. Everard had no idea how long his stay might have been: his prisoner's beard was short and untrimmed, still longer than anything Everard could've grown given five years; no solid indication there.

And any amount of incarceration was too long, even just a

day in *Brigitte*'s prison hold. For anyone, but most especially this man.

Speaking of which. The *Brigitte*: D'Arcy's ship. How *could* he?

And so, "Did he recognise you?" became the first thing Everard happened to say to Vitaliy Gray.

*Did Preston D'Arcy keep you there, knowing your face? Knowing what you'd meant to me?*

Vitaliy blinked. "Who?" he murmured. "Oh, the lieutenant?" He smiled slightly. "No. I doubt so."

Everard felt a rush of relief, both that D'Arcy wasn't a total villain and that Vitaliy would admit it.

"Thank God," he said. "I— You're all right? Hale?"

Vitaliy looked up through eyelashes. "I'm married?" he rasped, very quiet. His smile grew.

There was that queer feeling again in his chest, a crackling kind of—

Vitaliy licked at his dry, abused lips. It broke Everard out of his thoughts. Of course.

"Boy!" he called over his shoulder. "Water for the wrongfully accused Lieutenant-Marine, please."

The marines—still standing stiff to either side of their prisoner—both looked horrified to see one of their proverbial own so lowered. They were definitely new recruits.

But here came the water boy. As the silver dipper was brought up to Vitaliy's lips, and water spilled down his chin and onto the broad, furred chest, Everard removed his hand from his shoulder and looked away.

Behind them, D'Arcy stood in close, casual conversation with the other captains of the court, all of whom seemed relieved the trial had adjourned. D'Arcy shot them the occasional veiled glance but otherwise looked relaxed. He was an expert dissembler, but maybe… maybe he really hadn't recognised Vitaliy.

Admiral Johnson saw his attention and tromped over.

"Captain Anderson," he said. "You've made a devil of a mess for me here. You affirm this is Henry Crause, Lieutenant-Marine of His Majesty's ship *Vittoria*?"

*Henry Crause.* Yet another alias for Vitaliy Gray.

Everard cleared his throat. "It is, sir. Though *Vittoria* was only half-built, before… before York. Mr. Crause served on my *Wanderer* when she was wrecked. We've since been in correspondence."

"*Wanderer*," the admiral repeated wistfully. "Thirty-eight-gun? The recommissioned Frenchie, shot through by the Americans?"

"Indeed, at Christmas '12," Everard added helpfully—as though his fateful defeat hadn't been widely publicised, as though the admiral hadn't put his own voice towards Everard's acquittal thereafter.

"And you've evidence to put forth for his defence on the morrow?"

"Yes, sir. Letters." Letters, conveniently ending in *Yours sincerely, C.* Not *Crause*, not *Henry*, and not many of them, but they would do. The rest he might—might—be able to forge, hand be damned.

The admiral puffed up. "Tomorrow, then, de novo." He looked to the marines, and the marine provost, who snapped up and saluted. "Take the pi—the *defendant* back to the hold." To Everard, he *tsk*ed. "A captain, corresponding with a Lieutenant-Marine."

Vitaliy lowered the dipper and met his eyes knowingly. *Oh, if he only knew.*

Everard said nothing; he'd wanted more time to speak to Vitaliy, make sure he was really unharmed, and the disappointment nearly crushed his throat. But he touched his hat as the admiral took his leave, and, swallowing, turned to watch him walk over to D'Arcy and the other captains. By their expressions, no one was happy to hear they'd be attending courts martial again come morning.

Only D'Arcy looked uncaring. But he bit at his thumb—a tell he hated, the habit of a child who'd had an ever-present someone to ensure their hands were relatively clean—which he did when thinking hard, or was distressed.

Or when he felt particularly guilty.

*Maybe, maybe.* Everard would deal with him later.

He turned back.

The leftmost marine was slowly raising the narrow, tooth-bitten gag up to Vitaliy, looking unsure about applying it.

"Do not you dare," Everard snapped. The marine put away the gag.

But Everard could not stop the shackles going back on, the state of the prison hold below, or another night within it.

"I…" He looked to the deck, ashamed as a boy. "I'll do what I can, on the morrow. It might not—"

"Everard," Vitaliy interrupted him softly. "Enough. You've done enough."

Everard looked up, astonished. Vitaliy hadn't ever called him by name, not even in bed.

But Vitaliy's eyes were closed; his abused lips were pressed tight. Before Everard could respond, the marines frog-marched him belowdecks, back and away and down.

Everard returned to the other captains, amazed at himself for every subsequent step he made without staggering or being sick.

But then, he was on a ship, and on the water he was never sick.

# FIVE

When Everard returned at last to the *Netley*, he found that Jack had obeyed him. The newspapers were all—every single blasted gossip column and cursed satire—quite gone from his greatcabin.

He looked around the neat, clean space, checked the door was latched behind him, and removed his hat with a trembling hand.

It was the last straw. He hadn't recalled the newspapers until he'd been nearly unto the cabin, but now that they were gone and he couldn't look up a single thing more about Vitaliy the pirate, he was… he was bereft.

If he'd been listening at all to the charge sheet, he'd have it there, clear in his mind as a list on papercloth; but he hadn't, because he didn't like having the charge sheets of every defendant he'd ever passed judgment on imprinted upon him for eternity.

And now this God-blessed shred of self-defence could be Vitaliy's undoing, and his own, too.

"Fuck!"

He threw his hat. It *plunked* off the window, rattling the

latch and casing, and he was immediately regretful. The corner fold was probably crumpled to hell. He sat at his desk with a groan and put his head in his hands.

There was a knock on the door. Of course there was; Everard was captain. Some days he was endlessly in demand. It would be one of those, he despaired, just when he most needed a pair of hours to sit and think, read through C's letters, and choose which ones would suit.

He'd just picked up his hat again, and called "Enter," when he heard them from above: the bo'sun's pipes, chirping the call for an approaching gig.

The head peeking around the door was Jack, telling him what he already knew: a captain was about to be piped aboard the *Netley*.

"Now, Preston?" Everard muttered, and dashed up the hatch. He made it just in time.

D'Arcy was still in full dress, like him, except hatless. He gave Everard a big, insolent grin as he stepped over the railing and put out his hand.

"Smile and nod," he muttered, leaning in for a handshake. "Like nothing's happened."

Everard gritted his teeth and obliged him, irritating, correct man that he was. "Captain D'Arcy."

"Been a while since we've been on Ontario together, Captain Anderson," D'Arcy added, loudly. "Good we might do an early supper in Kingston, like old times."

Early supper? Practically a late luncheon. But Everard would play along for now.

"You're kind to oblige my invitation, Captain," Everard said with a nod. "Though I would want a word before we abandon ourselves to liberty."

D'Arcy returned his nod agreeably, perfectly polite. He greeted Everard's first and second lieutenants, who were deboarding on their way to their own leave. He gave the first, Mr. Spicelay, a critical squint that Everard didn't miss.

They went belowdecks to the little officers' parlour.

"Sorry," D'Arcy said, as soon as the doors were shut. "I know it's all backwards. Johnson's taken over the *Brigitte*, my cabin included." He glanced around, checking each officer's quarters to be sure they were empty, and sat. "How have you been, really? I've been so curious."

*What cannot wait until supper?* D'Arcy's raised eyebrows said.

The doors opened again. Jack set down a decanter, a pitcher of water, and two glasses, and whisked himself silently out.

Had D'Arcy recognised Vitaliy Gray? Had he let them shove him into the hot, wet prison hold and keep him there for a day? Two days?

Everard sat, took his time pouring a glass, then slid over the decanter.

D'Arcy caught it and held it steady between two palms. "You haven't returned a single letter of mine, Ev."

Everard downed his drink.

Since D'Arcy had returned to the Lakes Service last year, he had been writing Everard incessantly, spending a small fortune in postage to convince him to speak to him in friendship once more. Everard hadn't written back a word, and not for lack of postage fare.

He raised his left glove, back of hand out.

D'Arcy recognised the gesture in spite of too many fingers. He smirked.

"We both know damned well that hand doesn't stop you from a thing." He pushed back from the table, went to the little parlour bookshelf, and picked up the newsprint lying atop it. It was the *Canada Gazette*, a week old, and nothing in it but the list of deceased, promotions, and *Rags! Rags! Cash and the Highest Price Paid for Clean Rags.*

"Gad, do they even put His Majesty's speeches in anymore?" D'Arcy mused aloud, paging through. "The States, the States… the States are burning… Ah! *Political Miscellany*," he quoted. "Look at that. Good God, but what the Gideons are printing these days, they're going to get themselves arrested for blasphemy. Listen—"

He quipped a few surprisingly faithful sentences from Everard's latest submitted editorial, and then:

"Oh, my mistake. This is hardly the *Niagara Independent*." D'Arcy tossed down the paper and gave Everard a pointed look.

Everard clenched his teeth. "You can't be a subscriber."

"No, but Maud's keeps it in the nightstands." D'Arcy picked up the wine, pulled the stopper, and poured Everard another couple fingers. "Out with it, then. Or d'you need more wine to speak to me at all?" Seating himself on the table, he drank straight from the decanter, finishing it to dregs; at the end of it he smacked his lips. "Well, too bad."

Everard turned to exit the parlour. "I'm afraid I won't have time for supper after all."

D'Arcy stood. "I didn't know. I swear I didn't know."

"*Ignorance* is your defence?" Everard snapped.

"Well, yes. They brought him in with a *hood*, Ever, and as I've said, they're not my usual marines, and by the time I heard about the—the additional charges, it was this morning, and—" He took a deep breath. "I can recuse myself tomorrow, same as you; it'll delay them further. I should anyway, because sooner or later they'll remember what they promoted me for…"

He meant the *Wanderer*.

Everard turned round. D'Arcy's eyes were wide and hazel and sincere.

"… but I don't think it will do much good. They must want this to have as little travel as possible, or they'd have had a tribunal of twenty waiting to give a unanimous death sentence in Halifax. Make no mistake: they want him very, very badly."

Everard sat down heavily. "A hood?" he said. "Why on earth? I don't…" He groped for the wineglass. He knew D'Arcy hated sodomy trials; he always had. He'd warned Everard as soon as he could. And would such unfeeling, uncharacteristic brutality have suited a motive of regaining Everard's friendship?

He thought… not.

"Letters aren't going to do it," D'Arcy said. "Not even *your* letters. You're a damned good forger, but I think he could have Nelson himself as witness to defence and still not get out of this."

"Was," Everard muttered. "*Was* a good forger. I'm not yet sure of my right pen hand, you know."

D'Arcy pulled a flask from nowhere and glugged brandy into Everard's glass.

"I don't, actually." He lowered his voice to a whisper. "All I know is that you continue to write editorials for illegal periodicals and that you are still, if by definition only, alive. Three years, Everard Rubén. Drink, God damn it."

Everard obeyed, sipping this time. "I don't think he's innocent," he said at last. "Not in the least."

D'Arcy laughed. "That's safe to say." He grinned with sharp teeth. "You're sure of the one."

"God. Yes, very sure." Maybe it was the drink affecting him, or the heat of the dining room, but Everard found himself laughing, too. Just a little chuckle into the wineglass at first, and then he had to set the thing down to put a hand over his face; and before he knew it, he had slumped into the crook of his elbow, completely broken down with silent shaking.

Distantly he heard D'Arcy give a patient sigh, heard the assertive clack of high-heeled boots coming closer.

The dining room doors were six-panel windows that looked

straight into *Netley*'s hold, the stairs that went up to the hatch, the crew hammocks; and somewhere just outside, the boy Jack hovered.

Nevertheless, Everard let D'Arcy pull him up and fold him into a hug.

"Soft as syllabub on the inside," D'Arcy murmured, squeezing him tight. "I hope your damned pirate knows that."

# Six

"Sir" came whispered. "Cap'n, sir."

The boy Jack. He was waking Everard with a shake to the shoulder.

Everard inhaled and sat up. But no bells? He shook his head. "What, Jack? No alarm? What's amiss?"

"Nothing, sir," the youth said quickly. "Just as you're wanted abovedeck, like."

"What?" Everard sighed. "A'right."

It felt like he'd only just gone to bed. His head ached, and his missing fingers, too, like he'd used them to write instead of the right hand. D'Arcy and he had had supper in Kingston, and then Everard had come back to his quarters and sat alone with C's letters, to choose which were best to use.

C—for Christian, his first real lover, who had in fact been a Lieutenant-Marine; and as several years' distance had had to pass before Everard could think the man's full name without pain, he was out of practice using it—was long dead. C had obviously not met Vitaliy Gray, but he wouldn't have minded his words used in this way, Everard had thought. And he'd held onto the letters too long. Were their true forms not memorized — written upon his brain forever?

Two strong boiled coffees and many candles later, he had three supplementary letters, creased, stained, folded, and waxed, providing what he thought might give Vitaliy evidence towards a commuted sentence at least, if not a dishonourable discharge. At the very least, they would probably not recommend hanging, not with so much—*forged, false*—evidence to throw certainty of guilt.

Of course it had to be tonight there was some unfixable emergency what couldn't wait 'til morning—

Jack proffered to Everard his banyan, and he shrugged into it.

"Who needs me?" he demanded, sliding his left hand into the stuffed black glove. He reached for his boots, then reconsidered. The weather had been unreliable lately, but it was probably warm enough to go barefoot, he decided.

"It's the cap'n from earlier, sir."

D'Arcy? At—he tilted the clock on his desk into the stream of moonlight—two in the morning? When he had just been to supper, and said he couldn't do anything further to help, but wished him all luck, and he'd see him in the morning?

"Probably not, Jack. You're mistaken. That would be extremely unusual, even for him."

"But sir—he said—" Jack swallowed and squirmed. "I'm not disloyal, sir, nor a thief," he insisted.

"I believe you," Everard said, because if he didn't the boy wouldn't be in his employ. "Go on."

At last, after more discomfited squirming, Jack shoved a hand into a pocket and withdrew something, thrusting it at Everard like it burned his skin. "He said at four bells, bring you abovedeck."

Everard stared at the heavy silver ring the boy had dropped in his palm. No wonder poor Jack was uncomfortable. It was cut sapphire, with a fleur-de-lis imprinted on the band interior, worth five years of Everard's own salary, never mind a servant's.

"Jesus," he cursed.

D'Arcy removed the ring for two reasons, and one of them was something too obscene to do outside of a securely locked door.

Either someone had forcibly removed the thing from his hand and he was dead with someone impersonating him; or he really was on *Netley*'s tiny deck at two in the morning, in desperate need.

*They want him very, very badly.*

"Thank you, Jack." He paused. "Thom," he corrected, because that was the boy's true given name on the muster. As an ex-ship's boy himself, Everard knew what he had risked, taking that ring into his possession.

He opened the door carefully, peering out. He pulled off his sleeping cap, though it certainly wasn't the first time the crew—or D'Arcy—had seen him in such nightwear.

If he were to be unceremoniously knifed as he went abovedeck, he wanted not to be wearing a nightcap. That was all. (The banyan was cerulean silk; he would happily be buried in it.)

The hold appeared calm, hands snoring and farting in usual form.

Everard paused in the doorway. He turned to Jack—Thom. "Stay here," he ordered. "Don't come out 'til I return." He hesitated. "Unless I don't return at all."

Thom's eyes went wide and luminous as he nodded. "Yessir."

As Everard stepped onto the night-quiet deck, the watchman in the foretop straightened and acknowledged him with a faraway salute. Thankfully, it wasn't all that unusual for the crew to find their captain walking the decks at night, especially in-harbour, with half the men on twenty-four-hour shore leave. Maybe two o'clock was a bit much, but he was a known restless sleeper.

Everard took a careful circuit of the schooner, stern to bow and back again, all seventy-two feet of her; it didn't take long. Despite his slow steps, his heart beat drums in his chest. Where was D'Arcy?

All around, lake water lapped, the calm sound undisturbed by the telltale *tap-tap* of a boarding boat brought alongside. A cold, dry fog had curled into Kingston Harbour to sleep; Everard put his finger through frost gathering on the stanchion rail and wished he'd put boots on after all. Such sudden cold after such heat was bizarre for June, even this far north.

Fog or no, there was no gig he could account for at all. And none of the men sleeping between-guns on deck seemed like they'd been disturbed since lying down. But then, not much disturbed a sleeping sailor but guns and the bo'sun's whistle; that was what the watch was for.

Absolutely no boat. Had D'Arcy *swum* aboard?

Everard made another slow pace round, controlling his breathing, wishing he smoked a pipe so as to have more solid an excuse than stargazing. In a fog.

D'Arcy had to have swum it, he decided.

So, where was he? Clinging to a rope? Hanging off a gun port? A schooner had very few hiding places. Everard rested elbows on the forecastle railing and listened hard for the sounds of a man treading water, perhaps scrabbling against an algae-slick hull.

Nothing.

Then: *plink-plunk,* in the water to starboard. It could have been a trout—but no. It sounded like something small and pebblelike had fallen into the water… from above.

Instinctively Everard looked up, to the foretop—and jerked upright in alarm.

D'Arcy sat there on the platform, head slumped back against the foremast, legs dangling through the lubber's hole. Everard spun carefully round the mast, mindful of guns and men, so as to get a better look.

D'Arcy was hatless and out of uniform, soaked through; he looked rather as though he'd had the fight of his life with the water and barely survived. But no, not with the water: beside him on the platform—Good God—a body lay limp and still.

Everard would have gasped, but he was surrounded by sleeping crew.

Instead he leapt to the starboard ratlines, swung himself through, and climbed up and up and up, as he had thousands of times before. He pushed aside D'Arcy's legs and hauled himself onto the platform as quietly as he could manage.

The first thing he checked was that D'Arcy was alive—he was. The second thing he checked was if the other man was dead—he was. By way of the limp garrote still round his neck. The wooden ends of it swung.

Furthermore, he was not Everard's own watchman, the reliably nocturnal Marley; but someone unknown, unfamiliar, and apparently unfriendly. Jesus sainted, foreign agents on his little *Netley*?

"Preston," he said, leaning close, "How badly are you?"

"Ev," D'Arcy said, and giggled. "D'n't recognise me up here? Waved atchu."

Everard quickly covered his mouth with his right hand. God, but the foretop was no place to be delirious with a one-handed man as rescue crew.

He thought, perhaps a hammock to sling him down, and

then imagined the time he'd sat down wrong in one, and flipped arse-over-head—no.

"Ev," D'Arcy said, rumbly against his palm, "… you climb the rattlin's in a *silk banyan?* S'cold!"

"Yes," he said, straight into D'Arcy's ear. "And I'm sorry, you're going to have to climb down."

D'Arcy glared. "I know," he said waspishly, after pulling the palm away. "Been working myself up t'it, s'all. Bast'd hit me. I'm still seeing… birds." He flapped one hand.

Everard caught it, pulled the sapphire ring from his pocket, and pushed it onto its proper home.

"Shoot them down. Let's go."

"Ugh." D'Arcy shook himself, once, twice, and that was all it took.

Everard went first, looking up anxiously every other step, but they both made it eventually; twenty years at sea counted for something. And with no watchman looking over him, Everard gave up all pretence, crossed the decks arm-in-arm with D'Arcy, and pulled him down into the hold.

Thom, bless him, had followed orders. He looked shocked to see D'Arcy so bedraggled; Everard wondered just how long he had been in possession of that expensive ring, if it had been even since before supper.

"Good lad," D'Arcy said sincerely, staggered over to the bunk, and curled up shrimplike around Everard's pillow.

Everard barred the door. "Don't fall asleep, Preston."

"M'not," came a muffled reply. "Smells good."

Everard shot an uneasy look towards Thom.

"He, er… hit his head."

The youth's expression was carefully neutral; probably he was wondering why his captain was bothering to explain anything to him at all.

Well, Everard thought tiredly, he'd trusted him thus far.

D'Arcy rolled over, squashing the pillow beneath his chin. "I didn't hit my head," he said genially. "It was bashed in."

There was a glug of liquid, a clink of glass, and like magic, Thom proffered two glasses of brandy. D'Arcy brightened instantly.

"*Good* lad," he repeated, sitting up. "I don't know how you do it, Ever. I have two, two-fifty men"—he took a sip—"not a one as loyal as this."

Everard ignored this plain untruth.

"I don't think we have much time. Or am I mistaken, and you killed that watchman for nothing?" He caught Thom's startled jerk from the corner of his eye, and added, "Not Marley. Another. None of ours."

D'Arcy sighed. "To be sure, I hadn't planned on murder for a nightcap. Unfortunately for the man, I recognised him. He's the same foreigner who replaced one of my own night watch, night before last. The same night they brought in…" He trailed off, waving, and scoffed into his glass. "As though I wouldn't notice!"

"But why—"

D'Arcy finished his drink. "I don't know. It's not coincidental, for damn sure. But he was just an obstacle, not why I came tonight."

He leveled a gaze on Thom, who was listening rapt and trying to look as though he wasn't.

"Too late for that," Everard said resignedly. "Too late when you handed him your ring."

D'Arcy grunted. His gaze didn't waver. "And when he didn't swim to Kingston to pawn it."

Expressionless, Thom calmly plucked the glass out of D'Arcy's hand, refilled it, and replaced it.

D'Arcy said, "Hmmm," shrugged, and faced Everard, elbows on knees.

"Come morning, Everard Rubén, the Marines will arrest

you for conspiracy against the Crown." He sipped at his brandy, pillow across his middle, and waited for a reaction.

Everard had none. His heart had dropped out of his chest. Beneath, there was nothing but awful freefall. He cleared his throat in an attempt to forestall the drop, and swallowed, but it did nothing.

D'Arcy went on cheerfully: "So, that obviously cannot be allowed to pass."

*Arrested?* Him?

"But—I've declared myself witness! They can't detain me 'fore the trial; it's not done!"

"It's not *legal*," D'Arcy corrected. "As to whether it's done, well, they're going to do it; so, what's the difference? They'll have you detained and your pirate hanged well before you can pen an appeal to the Secretary. For that matter, Johnson's already sent out the letter recommending your name be added to the Black List. I watched him draft and seal it."

"He's done *what?*" Everard took a deep breath. To be black-booked meant no commission, no position, no half-pay, no legacy, nothing. "That's to be done upon conviction only! How dare they."

He paced. "Why do they wait for morning?"

"Why does anyone put off anything?" D'Arcy said. "Why not wait, in their eyes? Where would you go?"

"Where, indeed." Everard didn't know the answer himself. But anywhere was preferable to being held uselessly captive while Vitaliy repeated the experience of court-martial, with no one to defend him.

If it were just him and his fate, Everard would not run and hide. He would withstand the ignominy of a trial like any other unfairly accused, innocent man, and that would be the end of it.

But it wasn't just him. Vitaliy sat dehydrated in *Brigitte's* prison hold. D'Arcy had killed a man, cold and calculated.

And now there was the boy, too, currently flitting around, packing Everard's trunk as though they were merely going back to Bess's Boarding-House on extended shore leave.

"Ja—Thom. Stop," Everard said. "You're a good, steady lad. But I cannot in good conscience—"

Thom pulled himself out of the linens, indignant. "Sir!"

"—a year and you'll make midshipman, three more you'll be nineteen and sit your exams—"

"Sir—"

"—run and deny everything they ask you, make yourself scarce, you've heard nothing tonight, seen nothing—"

"Sir, I'm Boy, third-class," Thom said, bravely. He met Everard's eyes, spine straight, feet together. "Sure as they'll make me sit witness and gi' me back my articles, no matter what's said. You can't leave me!"

Everard looked to D'Arcy for support. The man only shrugged. "He's right. A thousand others wait to replace him, too."

"You gave him your ring," Everard retorted.

"Ah-ah, don't you blame me. The moment you gave your name and word towards a pirate, Ev, you put him at risk."

This was painfully true.

"But as it stands, he won't be *hanged*!" Everard hissed. He turned again to Thom. "Beyond tonight, I can't be sure that won't change. You must understand that."

Everard was only beginning to understand it himself.

Thom opened his mouth, closed it again.

"And furthermore," Everard went on, "His Majesty has paid your wages up to now. I can't afford to keep you in my employ on my own."

But at this, Thom scowled, turned away, and renewed the rolling of shirts. "If I cared about coin, I'd'a stole the ring."

"There you are," D'Arcy agreed. "He's worth more to you than you are to him, by far. Especially if we are heading into what I think we are… a loyal servant could be indispensable," he said practically. "And we *are* speaking of capital crimes against the Crown, yes? Those which we do not normally commit?" He grinned.

Everard put a hand to his head and paced more. "God. God. Yes, we must be. We are."

"What… sirs…" Thom seemed to be struggling with the new, untested boundaries of their relationship, and no wonder; it had vaulted from master-servant to co-conspirators in remarkably short order. "I want to go, don't mistake me. But… can I ask what we're doing?" He blinked solemnly. "In the interest of being fully informed."

"That accent!" D'Arcy laughed. "A boy chameleon." He held up a fist. "Near as I can tell, Jack, we're going to flee the rightful pursuit of the law…" He ticked one finger. "… break a pirate out of the hold of a very large ship…" Another finger. "… because said pirate is the former lover to your dear captain, who has a heart the size of the Atlantic…"

Everard made a strangled noise.

D'Arcy's eyes were warm and laughing as he ticked another finger. "… your dear captain," he repeated, "whom I've always loved, madly and unequivocally."

Everard stared. Was he serious? Surely not. How hard had his head been bashed?

D'Arcy held out his hand, palm up. "… for whom, it seems, I would do absolutely anything."

There in D'Arcy's spread palm was a small iron key. Everard's gaze was torn between D'Arcy's handsome face and the ordinary-extraordinary object he'd presented.

"That— You…"

"So, shall we?" D'Arcy finished on a whisper.

"You cannot just… That wasn't even a proper list!" Everard croaked at last. He carefully took the key. "Thank you, Preston."

D'Arcy smiled wide for a moment longer. Then, sober-faced, he turned to the boy.

"And if, dear Jack," he said warningly, "you find anything objectionable in all of that, I must inform you that you'll be shut up in *this* here cabin until we accomplish our crimes. You understand."

"Errr—no. Of course not." Thom shook his head vehemently, eyes wide. "I mean yes. I agree with all o' that." The youth flushed hot-red. "I mean—mebbe not *all*—"

D'Arcy laughed and laughed. Everard covered his eyes with a hand.

The boy blew out a breath, and tried again. "It's very romantic! Especially… especially the bit about him being a pirate." His eyes lit up in the way only a fifteen-year-old's eyes can at the prospect of excitement, of adventure, of unknown.

And then: "Are there pirate *girls*?"

D'Arcy had recovered enough to say tearily, between fading chuckles:

"God, yes. Absolutely. What kind of sailor are you, haven't heard of Anne Bonny?"

It was only as Everard went abovedeck for the second time in the early hours of la madrugada that he felt it: freedom. True liberty.

Not like the Yanks called it, liberty and property, or some-such. This was liberty of the mind and spirit, knowing one was taking one's own destiny firmly in hand. It was a feeling of *finally*; por fin y postre. At last; at the end.

And to the end it might very well be; but God, was it exhilarating.

He felt it as the three of them filed up out of the hatch, and he walked quickly, his heels snapping on the deck. It was loud. He didn't care.

Is this how D'Arcy felt all of the time? Fearless, and flying for it?

In a blink they were beside the larboard jolly boat, and D'Arcy and Thom began relaying her down rapidly, rope falls whooshing in the blocks. Two could do it; thanks to the *Netley*'s size, its jolly was hardly larger than a canoe.

For they did need a boat. There were three of them, and were taking along all of Everard's worldly possessions in a small ironbound trunk besides. Everard could've swum the harbour as well as D'Arcy had, and Thom surprisingly assured them that he could swim, too, but in wake of the sudden cold, in the interest of conserving energy towards infiltrating the prison hold of a frigate-of-war, they decided on the risk of the boat.

As the jolly slid down, Everard stood observing: straight, unmoving, heart thumping wildly beneath his own hastily donned undress coat. As though everything in the world were normal, and he were still captain of this little ship, awaiting transport. At three in the morning.

His uniform was their temporary shield against enquiry, and then he'd cast it off—forever.

D'Arcy looked strange tonight, and it was not so much that he was working ropes like a common sailor as that he was without his blue superfine coat and breeches. Tonight he wore wide-leg cutoffs and tie-waist shirtsleeves; Everard's loaded pistol hung belted at his slim hip. His arms were taut muscle against linen clinging rather damp and close. As he let the boat down slowly, lit by the silver moon, he grinned over to Everard; chestnut hair shone silky and curling from lake-water.

Memory hit Everard with acute force, and he remembered —though he tried and tried not to—precisely why he'd let the man break through the shell of strict acquaintance and let him have his way with him, rank or no rank.

Had he been speaking seriously earlier? About love?

The jolly hit the water and steadied, and D'Arcy clambered over the rail and down, Everard's little trunk under a strong arm.

Everard was to go second. He swung himself over the rail, and looked to Thom standing waiting, ropes in hand.

Taking the boat meant desertion in no uncertain terms. Desertion, grand larceny, intent to conspire; and all of that only the beginning of their criminal acts.

"You're quite sure, lad?" he whispered. "Absolutely and totally?" The youth could still go back, say he'd been ordered under threat, say he'd been coerced—

Thom threw ropes to D'Arcy and nodded, once. "Yessir."

Everard climbed down. Well, he'd tried.

Meanwhile, D'Arcy had sat himself to larboard and was readying the oar in the row-lock. Everard scowled and muttered into his ear:

"Away with you. You swam the harbour, for God's sake. Thom and I will pull her."

D'Arcy gave him a long look, then stood and sat to stern. He put crossed ankles on Everard's trunk like it were a footrest and lounged with elbows back.

"Aye, cap'n," he mouthed, and saluted as easily and inso-lently as he had three years before. It made Everard smile.

He gestured Thom to the starboard oar, and sat himself, removing his hat and unhooking his captain's coat, laying it down folded. He removed his black glove with his teeth. As useful as the leather was aesthetically, he preferred the grip of flesh on wood when rowing. Other men got by perfectly well with assistive hooks; he had a whole thumb, two knucklebones, and a working wrist. It'd taken some time to get right—and he could only pull on the larboard side—but it worked.

D'Arcy inhaled sharp. His face was calm, and he was still lounged, but Everard knew precisely what had shocked him. He had forgotten: the man had not yet seen his hand as it was now.

D'Arcy, never a coward, met his eyes with wide, sympathetic ones. He said nothing, only bit his lip.

Everard looked down. In the foggy dark, the hand was stark and pale and odd-looking on the oar. Or so he imagined it was odd-looking to D'Arcy; to him it was just his hand. Sometimes, his missing fingers seemed to have complete sensation, the same as they had before York. Sometimes, it felt as though he'd never had fingers there at all. He wiggled the knuckles, and wondered what to say. Would D'Arcy think him incapable, insist on rowing himself?

D'Arcy smiled. "Not a thing," he echoed his earlier self softly. He flopped back, one hand behind his head, the other holding Everard's pistol across his lap. "Pull her, boys."

D'Arcy murmured into Everard's ear as he raised oars just within range of the *Brigitte*:

"Barring any mole watchmen… see you in a moment."

He saluted, handed back Everard's pistol, and, with Thom providing counterweight to starboard, slid himself agilely into the lake, feetfirst. Then he was no more than a wet sable head treading soundlessly forward, and they watched him climb up, up the quarter gallery. Like the *Netley*, *Brigitte* was a skeleton at harbour, with her men at liberty ashore; still, Everard's heart squeezed, watching him push up and over the quarterdeck rail.

D'Arcy had taken an incredible risk tonight. Had said *we* and *us* and *let's*. But he couldn't truly mean to give up rule of the *Brigitte*—could he?

Everard hadn't answered his letters, but he'd read them. He knew D'Arcy had been intended for bigger ships in the Caribbean—ships of the line, even—before he'd mysteriously requested the Lakes Service. God knew why he'd done that, except that despite his heroics in battle, his ruthless reputation, he'd never burned with ambition like Everard had.

Maybe that was reason enough.

In the starboardside quarter-gallery window, lamplight bloomed to a soft glow. Ready, go.

They rowed quickly to the docks, tied up the jolly. Everard entrusted his belted trunk and pistol to Thom.

"To Bess's," he said simply. "Await us there."

Thom nodded and jogged down the dockyard, out of sight.

Bess's Boarding-House was the winter establishment for officers and their manservants, tidily kept by an honest widow—to whom Everard paid a full year's rent, regardless of his occupancy. The boy was well known there. Everard could only hope he wouldn't be robbed on the way.

He stripped down to breeches, touched the key knotted safely round his neck. Took a deep breath, and dove.

It was time to rescue a pirate.

# SEVEN

Everard almost wept to see the Jacob's ladder hanging from the *Brigitte*'s elaborate gold-and-black quarter gallery. There was being patronising, and there was consideration—this was the latter. The deadrise on this lake-locked frigate was flatter than a sea-goer but still significant for a one-handed man to climb.

When he clambered over onto the quarterdeck and found it mostly deserted of the watch—the lone topman was faced deliberately away, bless D'Arcy—he let out a shaky, exhausted breath.

The frigate's entrance to the captain's quarters was, like the *Netley*, thankfully belowdecks; when Everard tried the latch, he found it unlocked.

Inside, D'Arcy wasn't pacing, smoking, or even drinking. He lounged in a plush red armchair in full undress, half-turned away from the window, his own hat and pistol in his lap, staring pensively at the cabin door with a finger over his lips. His hair was re-greased, though still damp, and his expression looked far away and troubled.

And so despite the ladder, despite the man's words, and

despite his actions, Everard felt a shock of fear trickle down his neck. His skin went goose-pimple, all over, and not from the chill of being dripping wet.

It was a trap; D'Arcy hadn't meant any of it; he would take Everard at gunpoint and arrest him, the Marines would walk in and take his half-naked, one-handed self down to the hold and—

He must have made some noise, for D'Arcy turned and gave Everard a familiar, wry smile.

"Sorry, Ev." He scrubbed his face with his hands. "I ought to be on the knife's edge of awareness." His gaze darted quickly over Everard, up-down. His eyes widened, and went elsewhere, everywhere else. He stood, and cleared his throat. "No time to be woolgathering. Did Thom get off the dock aright?"

Everard's face heated with shame. Of course D'Arcy hadn't betrayed him. Hadn't he only just given his pledge? "He did. Er—thank you for the ladder."

D'Arcy waved this off, still not meeting his eyes.

The problem was D'Arcy tended to say things he didn't mean, and sometimes those things were hard to distinguish. Three years out of touch—rhetorically and literally—and Everard's directional instincts regarding the man were no longer as unerring as they used to be.

Everard stood, straight and awkward, dripping blue-green Lake Ontario onto the rug.

D'Arcy pulled down the shutter of the lamplit window, latched it. He turned down the lamp, blew it out, and brushed off his palms. He turned round, a strange expression on his face, his glance somewhere around Everard's wet knees.

"You're never nervy about this?" Everard said, bewildered. "Or is it the damned hand?"

"What?" D'Arcy's glance flew up, finally, and he laugh-groaned, squeezing his eyes shut. "No. I'm sorry. I'm trying not to…" He groaned again, and spun and bent, reaching for something laid over the chair. "Put this on, for God's sake," he demanded, thrusting forth the blue wool—his old lieutenant's coat? "Before I disgrace myself utterly."

*Oh.* "Really?" Everard bit his lip and took the coat in his arm. "You should be used to seeing men of all sorts, shirtless and in wet breeches," he admonished. "Or no?"

D'Arcy muttered something and threw him a towel.

"Would you mind—a shirt?" Everard said innocently, toweling his hair.

Linen came flying, sheetlike and billowing. Everard caught it and tugged it over his head.

"This'll drown me," he remarked of the coat as he shrugged it on. "*Y mira.* I was right." He flapped his arms, demonstrating the slumping epaulettes. "Why haven't you sold the thing?"

He knew why. Independently wealthy, D'Arcy didn't have a need to sell his expensive uniforms to pay for the next iteration.

"Reasons of sentiment."

"Hmm. No hat, I suppose."

"No, sir. You'll have to make do."

There came a small groan from the berth—which, Everard belatedly realised, had its curtains tied firmly shut.

"What the devil?"

D'Arcy shrugged reluctantly, grimacing. "Johnson. Told you he had my cabin, didn't I?"

"Oh, dear God. The port admiral? Have you lost your mind?" Everard pulled the curtain tie, yanked them open; there was Admiral Johnson, hog-tied in rope and irons and gagged with a wooden bit. He looked to be semiconscious.

Everard put a hand to his stomach; all the air had gone out of his lungs. To think that he'd thought— Well.

"Were your senses *actually* bashed out of you? You're the son of an earl! You could have got out of this"—*this* being losing a prisoner under his watch—"with a shrug and a by-your-leave!"

"If I wanted, maybe. That, and a fair amount of coin," D'Arcy agreed. His expression darkened. "He called you Blackhand."

Everard shut the curtains, ignoring the squeezing in his chest.

"Sant Jesús. Let's go."

At the door to the pine-bound sickbay—temporarily doubling as a prison hold—there were two admiralty-supplied marines posted watch. Everard gave D'Arcy (and his pistol, and garrote, and God knew what other weapons he had on his person) an uneasy glance. The plan was to talk themselves out of this particular problem, not knock heads; Everard's borrowed uniform was to that end. But would D'Arcy follow it?

Three in the morning, a ridiculous request, and nothing more than their rank to carry them through it. But D'Arcy had already overtaken and held hostage an admiral—*and murdered a man,* a voice whispered—so what were two lowly marines?

"Hullo, privates," D'Arcy greeted. "How is the pirate this fair morning?"

The leftmost marine blinked in surprise as both saluted. He was the same sunburnt young man who had been gentle with Vitaliy's gag yesterday. Everard wondered if he had been posted to Vitaliy's guard for the duration, and if Vitaliy had somehow, in that short time, turned the man sympathetic.

If he had, Everard doubted it'd been intentional.

"Quiet tonight, sirs," the marine replied. He was exceptionally soft-spoken, like a kind priest. "'Tisn't morning already?" he asked, and eyed the moonlight shining into the hold around the mainmast.

*Shite.* This one wasn't having it.

D'Arcy surged forward. "Good to hear. Excuse me, boys." He made as though to open the sickbay door—

—only to be barred by two crossed bayonets.

"I say, let me through." D'Arcy gave a feigned, gentleman-weak struggle.

"Begging your pardon, cap'n," the right marine said. "We're told no visitors, no entrance. Special circumstance."

D'Arcy went still. "Special circumstance is why I'm here," he insisted calmly.

A distinctly protective gleam came into the left marine's eyes. "It's for his sake as well as yours, captain." He gripped his gun more firmly. The bayonet end looked well sharpened, though he must have known his range of motion would be challenged, there in the low hold.

D'Arcy backed up a step—not quite far enough for the bayonet's use. "Lord above, an honest marine," he muttered, intentionally loud. "All for a sodomite."

It had the desired effect. The left marine's stance went even stiffer, and he paled.

"Sirs, I am sorry." Soft, but firm. "But there will be no crimes done here tonight, no matter the prisoner's charges."

Brave lad. If Everard weren't so desperate to get Vitaliy free, he'd hug him.

Instead, he watched the right marine, whose blank expression had faltered into a frown. He apparently did not wholly agree with his contemporary.

Everard shifted his weight to his right foot, coughed.

D'Arcy nodded in response. He'd seen it too.

Change of plans.

D'Arcy lunged. His hands flew; he gripped the left marine's bayonet gun and thrust it—*chunk*—deep into the deck above their heads; he pushed the freckled redcoat back with one arm. The young man was sent stumbling, straight into Everard, who steadied him with a tight hold.

"Don't move, Private," he warned. He was obeyed.

Meanwhile, the right marine stood no chance. D'Arcy had drawn his pistol in the same moment he'd pushed the younger out of harm's way. Everard wondered, for a moment—

The marine fell to his knees, dropping the gun clattering onto pitch-and-plank, and his hands went up, far above his head.

"No, wait, wait. Do what you want, rape him bloody, I won't hear nothing." He spat on the floor. "I'd'a let ten of you through if it wasn't for Saint Cunt over h—"

*Crack.* Blood and brain and black tufts of feathered, high-top bicorne went flying; the man toppled, missing fully half his skull.

The marine in Everard's arms jerked and whimpered. Everard knew him no less brave for it. He had winced badly himself, and his ears rang, pulsing with imagined, repetitive reverb from the shot.

"God, Preston."

"Prick," D'Arcy said calmly. He leaned to pluck the keyring from the dead man's belt, tossed it to Everard. "Trade you."

"Er… indeed. He won't hurt you," Everard added to the marine. Though really it was useless reassurance, because who could say? He'd just point-blank *shot* a man of their own, a Royal Marine, for no cause—well, hardly any cause— at all.

He nudged the stunned man forward. D'Arcy put a hand on the man's shoulder and spoke to him, hopefully repeating that he would not, in fact, shoot him in turn.

It rang through his head like the gunshot's echo: *Is this the true Preston D'Arcy, released from all consequence?*

Everard worked the key in the door quickly; they had very

little time now. Whatever Marines were still upon the *Brigitte* would soon come running.

"God damn it." His hands were shaking. He shoved the door open with a kick, he was so desperate with nerves.

*Who have I released upon the world?*

The moonlight came through the darkness of the sickbay to reveal Vitaliy crouched against the curve of the hull, arms shackled to two thick frames, ankles wrapped together with fetters. No hood, no gag, but—

*Who will I release upon the world?*

Vitaliy raised his head. He offered no greeting, only a cool, blue, heavy-lidded gaze that was harsh and judging, disapproving and… damning.

Everard swallowed. He was never, ever sick aboard a ship.

"Er… we should… I'll… um." He yanked the little key and its lanyard out of his shirt and over his head, and bent to unlock the fetters. Those first, so he wouldn't have to look Vitaliy in the face again just yet.

Vitaliy didn't move as he was freed. Didn't speak. There was only the heavy *clink* of shackles falling away, and D'Arcy's murmuring from beyond the door, underlaying the unmistakable sound of retching. The young marine, no doubt.

The right wrist shackle was proving stubborn; Everard thought he would have to bash it with something to get it to separate. And again Vitaliy didn't so much as flinch as his arm was manipulated, puppetlike, as Everard slammed the cuff again and again against the frames of the hull—not until he slashed the skin between the two knuckles of his own left hand in the process.

"Shite-fucking-Christ!"

Then Vitaliy, expressionless, tensed his arm and did it himself, dealing the shackle's killing blow with a powerful *thwack*.

Everard sucked at the cut to draw a bit of blood, and hopefully the chance of lockjaw, out of him. He spat, and looked up to find Vitaliy staring, his stern brow slightly furrowed.

"York," Everard said, "shortly after we met."

Vitaliy opened his mouth—

D'Arcy stuck his head into the sickbay. "Best go, Ev."

Beyond the dead man was the mainmast hatch, rope handholds and stair rises unfortunately splattered in gore. But it was the closest exit. Everard ran up, lips pressed tight, trusting Vitaliy to follow; he did.

It wasn't until they reached the starboard side quarter railing and Everard had hauled himself half over that he realised: the freckled marine was still with them, and D'Arcy had paused, bent forehead-to-forehead with the redhead redcoat, whispering frantic and quick and pleading.

"Uh." Everard had only a moment for a stunned pause. Belowdecks, there came heavy, running boots from the direction of the forecastle. Everard turned to ask Vitaliy could he swim—

—just as the man launched from the rail in an impressive dive.

Everard followed. When he surfaced, he heard two heavy splashes to his left, along with the soft, shocked gasp-coughs of a man who really *didn't* know how to swim, and who was being hauled forward despite it. He hoped to hell D'Arcy knew what he was about.

The marines lined up along the quarterdeck, guns straight and at attention; the sergeant-at-arms began the high yip of firing cadence.

*"Make—aim! Set—"*

They swam.

# EIGHT

The Widow Bess—of the eponymous boarding-house in
Kingston—was, in Everard's estimation, a saint of a
landlady. She was tiny, unassuming, discreet in all senses of the
word, with a winding knot of curly silver hair and a spine of
Sheffield steel; no person alive would dare cheat her rent. Her
rooms were rat-free, and her savory scones were light and
served with butter and her own chicken-and-leek stew. Everard
paid her a whole year's worth for the four months the *Netley*
was laid up in winter dock, and considered it a bargain
investment.

But even a saint of the Widow Bess's calibre would balk at
receiving four large, wet, injured, and exhausted ex-officers
into her parlour at quarter-five in the morning.

Everard stood on his wobbly land legs and stared up at the
backside of the neat two-story brick building, thinking even
one wet, bedraggled ex-officer might be too much. Could he
really bear another casualty? Drag another down weighted into
the deep beside him?

"No," he panted. "It will have to be Maud's, I think."

He glanced over to Vitaliy, who leaned barefoot against the

brick alleyway, shoulders bowed and arms crossed, impassive. His fine-silk hair was already drying, as he'd lost the tie for it somewhere in the water, and white-blond wisps swept across the sharp bones of his face.

For him, Everard had thrown away his uniform, his reputation, his career, the *Netley*, and the respect of a hundred crewmen. All in a blink, and he'd do it again.

But the loss of Bess's seemed worse than all of the rest combined. No surprise, really, as it meant warmth and food and home away from home, and Everard was both tired from swimming and exhausted from his sudden conversion of personal values. Surely, if he'd had a true home, he didn't deserve to go back there.

And Vitaliy wouldn't even—hadn't yet, anyway—said so much as a thank-you. Everard was afraid if he confronted the man, he'd get the same as he had before: a short rebuff. *You've done enough.*

And then, God forbid, Vitaliy would simply walk away.

D'Arcy held his coat out over the cobblestone with one hand; the other he had upon the shoulder of his sunburnt, ginger-hackled tagalong, who was apparently named Bellingham.

"C'mon, Ev. The coat's wool, you've ceased dripping, and you've somehow retained your boots. No one is going to notice you're wet."

Everard was momentarily offended.

"It's not that. I mean, it is. Of course people shall *notice*. But…"

It wasn't that he cared about his own appearance precisely, but rather what his hatless, damp, wrong-rank appearance of five in the morning would do for the Widow Bess. Or rather, what it would *not* do. Hers was an officers' boarding-house. To approach it, and be seen like this by the wrong person, could bring its reputation—and, correspondingly, Bess's—lower than he could bear. And a woman's reputation, he wanted to say, was more tenuous than wet paper cloth.

But he found himself too tired to explain. Why didn't D'Arcy—a full-blood gentry—simply understand this?

"No," he said at last. "I'll write for Thom in the morning, and he can meet us as he chooses. If he chooses."

"Oi!" came a bellow; they all jumped.

"Shite-on-a-*stick*." D'Arcy laugh-groaned. "The watch."

Another bellow. "Oi, there!" A shrill whistle.

"Gad, I haven't done this in decades," D'Arcy said. "Run!" Laughing like a loon, he tugged on Bellingham's hand, shoved at Everard. "Run, run!"

Everard ran. He didn't look to see if Vitaliy followed.

Maud's was notorious. It was also immaculate, well-lit, and—miracle of miracles—smelled of chicken pie and baked goods. Being tavern and boarding-house, it was larger than Bess's at nearly three storeys; its south, red-brick side was thickly enlaced with summer ivy.

Maud herself turned out to be Matilda Liliana Inocente de Guzmán-Delaney, who was already up at such an ungodly hour due to some mysterious inner workings of the tavern kitchen. When D'Arcy knocked at the alley-side door, she peered a dark eye through a viewfinder before yelping.

She embraced D'Arcy, damp and all, and they were then all four of them pulled before the massive cook hearth, being beaten by towel and apron alike. In rapid Spanish she berated them for their carelessness against la gripa, el tós, que les iban a poner muy mal y ni ella ni Dios sabía de que más—

Within the space of the two apologetic sentences in Spanish that Everard offered in return, she'd sussed out Everard's faint Català—which no one had done since he was twelve. She continued her reprimands in the said-same language, and Everard, dumbfounded and with skills shamefully rusted, enquired in his mother's tongue that he was much gratified to know her anew, but did she not have dispensable to them a room—for sleeping?

In the end, she had two rooms, and miraculously so because it was not a short-term hotel that she ran, it was to be very clear, but D'Arcy was family, although he did not keep yearly accommodation; and since the war had only just ended, there were still many sailors and their agents coming and going in Kingston, so she was nearly full up; lucky they had come when they had. Desayuno was at seven and supper a la misma hora, but of the night, and lunch was to be on their own terms, but there were bollos available at any hour for the asking.

"Yes, ma'am," Everard said to this trilingual barrage, knowing there was no other possible response. "Very many thanks. I—we are indebted to you."

D'Arcy was grinning, but of course his sailor's Spanish was passable for comprehension. Bellingham looked as though he had not the slightest idea what had just gone on, and didn't care; in shirtsleeves with hands clasped before him, the vicaresque impression remained. Vitaliy was stoic at the door, arms crossed, his skin still pink all over from the rough drying.

Everard enquired after the bollos—to be sure it was in fact the sugar-encrusted bread and not a euphemism for genitalia towards which he had no affinity—and Maud put a quantity of them in a cloth and tied it. She led them up the stair to the second floor, before a six-panel door likely older than herself.

This opened onto a curtained four-poster bed flanked by two windows, an armoire, and a sitting table and chair beside the red-brick fireplace. The second room was identical, she explained, connected through the left-side door, as the pair of rooms were meant for husband-and-wife apartments. She dimpled knowingly. Everard wondered precisely how discreet D'Arcy was—or wasn't—there.

Probably not very. He was beyond caring.

With a warning against crumbs in the bedsheets, Maud left them.

Bellingham St. Clare sat on the edge of the first four-poster, spine straight. A moment later, he gasped and scrambled up—because he was undoubtedly still damp.

D'Arcy laughed. "That's your side, Bellingham." He untied the sack of bollos, pulled three forth onto the table napkin. "Ever? You want to...?" He jerked his head left, to the connecting apartment, and made significant eyes towards Vitaliy, who was peering out the curtain to the dawn-lit street below.

Everard was too tired to even pointedly ignore him. He merely clutched fingers around D'Arcy's wrist and pulled him towards the connecting door.

"Oh? Hey, you don't need to—ow! All right, I'm claimed, I'm claimed—"

There was no way in hell he was leaving D'Arcy with the traumatised tagalong before he could properly question the man about his intentions. D'Arcy, not the marine.

On Vitaliy's behalf he worried not at all.

The second room was as promised: identical except with blue bedcurtains instead of maroon, and three windows instead of two. He nearly slammed the door shut behind them, like a child in temper—but the thought of Maud's kind dimples stopped him.

"Sit," he demanded.

D'Arcy sat at the duplicate spindle-leg table. He'd kept the napkin of bollos; now he bit into one. "Going to miss these," he said thickly. "You don' wan' any?"

Everard sighed. "No."

"What d'you want, then?"

*Primarily, sleep.* But first: "May I undress?"

"Wha—" D'Arcy coughed on sugar. "By all means," he croaked, waving the bread. He hummed. "Preferably a slow means."

Everard tugged off the shirt and, after a moment of indecision, laid it over the fireplace screen. The utterly ruined boots came next. He stood these in the breeze of the open window.

D'Arcy watched, rapt, chewing.

The breeches were fawn leather, and their wet abrasiveness while running had made his legs feel as though they had been lightly scrubbed all over. A wonder he still had hair there. He unbuttoned, peeled them down, inside out.

"Why are you on given name terms with a private-marine?" Everard asked.

D'Arcy swallowed the last bit of bollo and twitched his fingers delicately free of sugar. "That's none of your concern."

Though he'd unbuttoned the knees, the breeches had taken the stockings with. Ah, well—the things had holes anyway. On to drawers.

"You shot a man point-blank for name-calling. If not for the Ontario, I'd still wear his blood."

"I don't see any now," D'Arcy agreed with a wolfish grin.

Everard pushed open all four blue bedcurtains—a four-poster was brilliant in an Upper Canadian winter but stifling in summer—then turned down the sheets, and climbed in.

"It was murder, Preston."

"Because we neither of us has ever done *that*, while in the service."

He had a point.

D'Arcy stood. "It was a horrific name. And he was a prick. Do you mind if I also…?"

Everard raised up on elbows to see over the footboard. He intended nothing. That didn't mean he couldn't watch. "Not at all. Do you?"

D'Arcy gestured southward. "Obviously not." He did not take slow means; the waistcoat fell fast despite a dozen buttons. Then the pantaloons—linen, lakewater-stained. No drawers, and D'Arcy plainly did not mind being watched.

Not that Everard didn't already know that.

"You haven't changed at all."

The shirt went in one easy pull.

"I'll agree with you there," D'Arcy said. He raised an arm and sniffed. "Ugh. Excepting I smell like rank seaweed. Apologies in advance."

He moved round to his side, pulled down the sheet, and climbed in. He rolled onto his stomach, which, all things considered, couldn't have been totally comfortable.

"Never think of it," Everard replied, sliding farther over. He'd forgotten how very much space the man took up.

"Think of it too often," D'Arcy mumbled.

Everard slid down to his own pillow. "Preston."

"Wmph."

"Did you pay that marine to keep him safe?"

One hazel eye opened, blinked. "No."

"No?"

"Nuh-uh. That's Bellingham St. Clare for you."

"So, you did put him on as guard!" Everard said triumphantly. "And you said they weren't your mar— *Eemph.*"

D'Arcy had put a hand over his mouth. And he did indeed smell like seaweed—seaweed and sugar.

"Lower your voice, for fuck's sake," he whispered. "Yes, I put him on your pirate's guard. Last night, before supper." The hand slid free. D'Arcy sighed. "Look, it's not for me to say. Not my place. But you think there's *anything* that happened on my ship that I wasn't aware of?"

*Saint Cunt.*

"You mean…"

"Mm. He was a deserving prick."

Everard was silent for a long moment. "Jesus."

"Mm-hmm." D'Arcy snaked his arm over Everard's waist. He left it there, heavy and warm. "Nobody raids Maud's. We're safe here. Go t'sleep."

Sometime later, Everard woke. He pulled on the creased-but-now-dry knee breeches, took two bites of leftover bollo, and opened the door to a domestic scene. There was D'Arcy in the corner armchair, an unfolded *Niagara Independent* in his hands. Bellingham St. Clare lay upon the neatly made four-poster, reading a pocket-sized King James Authorised Version. Vitaliy sat on the little spindle-chair in the corner: knees wide, chin back. He was being shaved by—Everard blinked—the steady Thom.

"Morning, sir," Thom murmured. "Met your pirate." The razor—Everard's razor—made a soft shushing *scrape-scrape-scrape* over the hollow of Vitaliy's cheek.

"My...? Er... morning, Thom." Everard cleared his throat. "It *is* still morning?"

Thom nodded. *Scrape-scrape-scrape.* "Yessir. A hot one, though, surely." He swished the razor in steaming water; the noise made Everard's skin erupt in goose-pimple chills.

From behind his paper, D'Arcy snorted. Vitaliy, however, didn't even blink—his blue eyes continued staring straight up to the ceiling. He barely seemed to breathe.

Did the man never twitch? Was he never nervous? He was positively Newtonian.

"You got out of Bess's all right, then?" Everard asked. "No trouble?"

"No, sir. No trouble." Thom indicated the table with a nod:

there was Everard's little dome-top trunk, atop it one of his own clean linen shirts, a summer-weight waistcoat.

"Thank God." Everard shoved the remaining bollo into his mouth—hours old and with sugar gone sticky, it was nonetheless delicious—and threw on the shirt.

"Wasted as a ship's boy, that one," D'Arcy remarked. "Shaves like a valet."

Everard grunted agreement. He knew that, although his own face barely required biweekly attention. Had Vitaliy asked to be shaved? Had Thom offered? D'Arcy still had last night's sable stubble, so clearly he hadn't intervened on his own behalf.

Thom drew the razor away from Vitaliy—who was still perfectly unmoving—and smiled. "Thank you, sir. My ma 'n pa are both in service in Montreal, so I know my way about shaving. Though… the French are not so hairy, I think. Like you, cap'n." He bent, focus renewed.

*Now* Vitaliy looked at Everard, sidelong. There was a slight crease denting the end of one blond eyebrow, a tiny furrow of query above the other.

Was he remembering? Impossible to say.

"Unless they're Breton," D'Arcy added, oblivious; he turned a page. "Look out then. They've pelts."

Vitaliy's glance slid back to the ceiling. Thom scraped carefully round the soft, curly sideburns, *scritch-scritch-scritch*.

Watching the man be shaved felt intimate. Commonplace, and astounding. Vitaliy hadn't been hanged; he lived. Surely, he couldn't be a true criminal, a pirate after all, sitting there so handsome and quotidian and ordinary.

Everard stared, knowing it was awkward behavior. He wanted to be looked at again. Looked upon and maybe even thanked. Instead, he was ignored and—

*Thwack.* Paper cloth hit him in the chest. He clutched at it and glared at the culprit. D'Arcy raised insolent, sleek eyebrows.

"They were looking for you," he drawled.

"What, at Bess's?" Everard's heart sank. "Already?" Had they been rough with their demands? Did she know of his charges? Had he kept the good widow from anything at all?

"At the docks," came a soft, deep voice from the bed: Bellingham St. Clare. "Marine patrol. They were dawn seize orders."

"Yes, I'm aware," Everard said. "I was told it was to be dawn, but that was aboard a ship in harbour. I didn't think they'd put out a goddamned redcoat patrol for a witness!"

Just what in hell had Vitaliy done in his pirating? Had the admiralty ever been so dogged in their pursuit of one, save Blackbeard? Special-order marines, a covert court-martial…

The marines. He paused, suddenly realising. "You're who told Preston about my impending arrest. Aren't you, Private?" The address slipped out of long habit. He really mustn't do that anymore—as it was no longer his right.

D'Arcy stood from the armchair. "Everard…"

The young man went so pink that his freckles nigh on disappeared, but he nodded. "Yessir."

"Then thank you indeed, Mr. St. Clare, for informing him," Everard said, turning to face the bed. If Vitaliy could not recognise his own sacrifice, he could bloody well recognise the poor marine's. "Though I very much regret you had to be further dragged into this, and hope you don't come to feel the same."

They were the right words with the wrong tone, that sounded insincere even to his own ears. Mr. St. Clare ducked his head to his miniature scripture, his flush deepened to crimson.

"No, sir."

Everard pulled on his day waistcoat with especial vigor—to hell with doing up buttons. "No, no—if everyone would please cease calling me sir!"

Vitaliy's glance snapped back to him; this time, his brow was unmistakably furrowed, but Thom was finishing the last scrapes over his skin.

Thom withdrew, stropping the razor with wide eyes. Vitaliy sat up, put hands on his knees—

Nothing. Still nothing. He was a statue, bloodless except for an inevitable nick by his jawbone that let a tiny drop of red.

D'Arcy took him by the left arm, spoke into his ear. "What the hell's wrong with you?" He pulled. "Stop glaring. Come on —breakfast. You need it."

"And then what?" Everard spat. He tried to shake free, but D'Arcy held his elbow fast. "After breakfast, what? And what about the patrol?"

That was the question, wasn't it?

What now? *What now?*

"After breakfast," D'Arcy said, unperturbed, "lunch. Then a nap? I haven't had an undisturbed nap in years, seems like." He made to open the door. "Or we could fuck; haven't done that in as long—"

He hissed, and let go Everard's arm. Vitaliy was there beside him; he had plucked D'Arcy's hand free and dropped it, like moving a kitten. It seemed to have taken as much effort. Then, ignoring D'Arcy's grunt of protest, he stepped forward, and—slowly, watching for Everard's flinch—reached and smoothed down the lapels of Everard's waistcoat.

"What are you doing?" Everard asked stiffly.

"Dressing you. Might I?" Vitaliy asked.

"I—er—all right?" This close, he could feel the heat of Vitaliy, the life of him. He still had translucent lines of lather on his cheeks. He smelled like olive-oil soap curing in the sun.

One by one, Vitaliy began to do up the little brass buttons of the waistcoat. Everard didn't move; neither did anyone else.

Vitaliy said, "I will tell you what after, if you wish to listen.

You're due at least that. Regardless of the circumstance, I owe you my life."

There it was. And Everard didn't know what to feel after all.

"I'm not due a thing," he insisted. "I wanted—"

"I owe you my life." Vitaliy finished the last button, trailed a knuckle back up the neat line. He met Everard's eyes and stepped back. "I can maybe give you a different one?"

Everard stared. "Never say you're *actually* a pirate? A real one? You said you were *Russian*."

The room was silent. Everyone, even Thom, looked at him. D'Arcy sighed, and flopped back into the armchair. "Only you, Ev," he muttered from behind an arm.

"You didn't know?" Vitaliy asked. That brow furrowed again.

"Your charges, you mean? I didn't hear them. Well, I hear them, but don't listen," Everard explained. "Else they get… affixed. Stuck." He gestured inanely to his head. "Words read aloud are too close to seeing words on a page."

Deeper furrows. "Ah? But—"

"Yes," Everard affirmed. "I know it makes no sense at all."

Vitaliy shrugged. "Charges aside, my flotilla steals weapons from those who shouldn't have, gives them to those who should. For this they call me pirate."

Everard goggled. "Your *flotilla*?"

Vitaliy hesitated, drew a hand through his as-yet-unbound hair. In three years it had only got longer and more subtly white-gold, not quite yet turning silver: unbraided, it reached the ties of his shirt and beyond, ends curling to mid-chest.

"I've missed something here," Everard said slowly. "A flotilla. *Weapons.* I thought… freshwater. Furs, tea, that sort of Lakes pirate. Not…" He was at a loss. "Who the devil *are* you?"

"You know my name."

*Vitaliy Gray.* Everard's heart beat faster. "Yes. Yes, I'd thought so."

"You do," Vitaliy insisted.

"Oh, for God's sake," D'Arcy interrupted from across the room. "He's Vee. He's always *been* Vee."

Vee. *Vee.* It didn't sound right, didn't look right… until Everard remembered, from his time off the Atlantic coast years past, one particular wanted advertisement. The centre focus of which had been—instead of the tiny, ugly caricature—an elaborate majuscule *V.*

*ONE THOUSAND AMERICAN DOLLARS REWARD. Pirate Leader V. Varfolomey of the Pirate Ship SÉVÈRE, Menace of the Coast Atlantic, Gulf of Spain and Caribbean. ONE HUNDRED for INFORMATION, REST upon DELIVERY of ABOVE MENTIONED.*

Everard remembered thinking it must have been meant as a copy of the pirate's signature, thinking what a self-important pirate captain he must have been. Not much else.

"V. *Varfolomey?*" Little wonder they'd black-booked him, tried to arrest him; he'd only perjured himself for the single most famous pirate on the Atlantic. "But—but the print is nothing like you," he protested. "Nothing like you at all!"

For one thing, they'd left out the beautiful mouth. Whoever had made that print clearly did not realise its value—in identification or aesthetics.

Vitaliy grimaced, lips flattening. "It is not as though I've sat for portraits."

"You ought do," Everard replied unthinking. "Er," he revised, "were circumstances… different."

Vitaliy blinked, and then smiled; a slight, boyish curve of corners that seemed to completely contrast with Everard's idea of an infamous pirate, of who Vitaliy said he was.

V. Varfolomey: the man about whom no one could say for sure what the initial had originally stood for—*vicious*, or *victorious*, or *violent*—because Varfolomey was known to be all of those things.

Everard looked at that smile and thought: what if *V* was just Vitaliy? Vitya?

He put palms over his eyes, clenched his teeth against the threat of a high, desperate-feeling laugh. No wonder he could no longer read even D'Arcy. It seemed Everard had well and truly lost his bearings when it came to other men… if he'd ever had any at all.

He groaned. "Weapons. And how many ships in your flotilla?"

He hadn't expected an answer, but Vitaliy politely said, "That I cannot say."

Of course not. "How long have you been a pirate?"

"Lord God above," D'Arcy muttered. "Oh, sorry, Bell."

"Some years," Vitaliy replied neutrally. "It depends whom you ask."

"Or which government?" Everard pulled his hands away and began to pace from the connecting door to the exterior one. His own Atlantic service had ended abruptly in 1812 with the destruction of the *Wanderer*, and he'd surely seen the wanted notice repeated in the *Gazette* before.

"But if you are *so* famous, why would they hang you as Navy, under an assumed name? The Crown doesn't need to court-martial a mere pirate!"

It was one question too many, or maybe *mere* had been the wrong choice to apply to a man with control over an entire flotilla. Vitaliy drew back, raising his chin. His lips set into smooth marble, the corners flat as his dark eyes.

But it was a reaction, and Everard relished it, stood still in the wake of it.

*The man does feel his pride, after all.*

"I owe you my life," Vitaliy said. "And some kind of recompense for the implosion of your own. But though having fucked me seems to have motivated you to speak up for me, a *mere* pirate, it doesn't entitle you to judge me."

Vitaliy spoke like a king, a tired one who was unexpectedly virtuous and used to constant assumptions to the contrary. A high-handed one, too. Everard felt his color rising. Recompense.

Did Vitaliy think he wanted… money? He'd disdain saving his life for having shared his bed but would offer him *money?*

"Answers are all I want from you. Fucking's got absolutely nothing doing. Is that all it was to you? Truly?" He pointed to D'Arcy, pale in his chair. "All that Preston's done?"

"Oh, no," D'Arcy said at this. He stood. "Don't you involve me in this mutual-guilt crusade. Bell, another breakfast is in order, d'you think?" He gestured to Thom. "You too. Out, out."

Thom protested, "But—" even as St. Clare dragged him across the doorway.

D'Arcy muttered in Everard's ear as he left. "Don't kill each other."

Everard barely heard this, or the door's latch *snick*ing shut behind him.

Vitaliy opened his mouth, but Everard wasn't done.

"I'm sorry it offends you I wasn't able to leave you to hang. And furthermore, did it for less motivation than you apparently deem sufficient. I suppose a pirate such as V. Varfolomey has a wealth of avenues for escape; you didn't need a once-upon, forgotten lover to hoist himself upon a pike for you. But it is what it is. It's done."

Vitaliy shut his mouth.

"Or d'you think I should have done it for somewhat else? For Varfolomey's greatness?" Everard mused aloud. "Perhaps for the money I imagined you would offer me in recompense? Is that what should have motivated me instead?"

Vitaliy stared. He looked as though someone had slapped him with a satin glove and demanded answer, and no one had ever dared before.

"Is it what you want?" he whispered.

Everard believed it that no one had.

"God. No. Sant Jesús. Look, at risk of confirming everything terrible that you seem to assume of me: I truly don't care that you're a pirate—that you're… him. Varfolomey. It has no bearing."

No bearing, except that three years earlier, Vitaliy hadn't said he was Varfolomey, hadn't told him the whole truth. Absolutely no bearing.

He laughed. "Obviously it didn't, because I hadn't realised. But you could have been any Jack Tar, the guiltiest man on deck, and I'd still have said what I did because it was *you*, Vitya. I don't understand in the least why you think sharing what we shared shouldn't have influenced me in that way. It did. It has. It will forever."

Vitaliy's eyes were very, very wide.

"So, no. I don't want money. Nor recompense. Nothing at all, except to know you're not dead. But…" He sighed. "I do believe I am entitled to a few questions? Answers? Perhaps?"

"You—answers. The truth."

"Yes."

"That is it? All you want?"

"Yes."

Vitaliy nodded. "You can have it. Ask me whatever." He went back to the basin and rinsed his face, then dried each hemisphere with the towel Thom had left.

Of course then Everard couldn't think *what* to ask.

"This—what I've done," he began, after a moment, "it doesn't tie us together irrevocably, regardless of motivation.

You can of course go your own way, as you have done. You don't owe me a thing, going forward."

Vitaliy lowered the towel.

Everard thought: maybe it hadn't been to evoke an angry response in Vitaliy that had thrilled him, but instead the simple fascination of watching the man think, watching emotion ripple across his face in degrees.

What settled there now looked like understanding—and resolve. Decision.

*What decision?* Everard wondered.

"Do you say what you mean?" Vitaliy murmured. He felt at his newly clean face with fingertips. "Because I also prefer truths. And I think what you *mean* is that you don't wish to be left behind."

Everard blinked, taken aback. It was a little too close of a hit. "Good God." His face felt shot-hot again. "One doesn't just declare what one feels!"

Vitaliy smiled, a mischievous curl. "But why not say what you want? It's not a problem, wanting. And…" There, that resolute look again: wide-eyed and sincere. "You haven't yet heard my proposal."

"Proposal? Oh, 'what after'?"

"Mm," Vitaliy confirmed. "Are you hungry? The lieutenant had his breakfast already, but you have not."

"He's not my…" Everard waved. "Yes, I am."

"There is a safe, and good, coffeehouse… unadvertised…"

"Safe for a pirate? Or safe, like…" Everard gestured between them.

"Safe, like that." Vitaliy's smile spread, broad and soft. "This time, we neither of us have hats."

# Nine

The coffeehouse looked nothing like a traditional club. The door opened to the parlour of what appeared to be a modest private residence. It even had a kind of butler, who stood immediately when Everard walked in, his eyes flashing warning. He looked Everard up and down and stepped forward, hands casual at his hips—the casualness that betrayed the presence of some kind of weapon.

Definitely not a traditional club.

"That door's not the one I think you were wanting, sir."

He was big, white, and, from his accent, Welsh. And when he met the man's black eyes, something in Everard threw up signal flags. *Same?*

The man seemed to return that strange recognition without a lick of surprise; he jerked his head in an acknowledging nod. *Same.*

Nonetheless, when Everard refused to turn round and leave, the man spread his hands and said, "We're invitation-only, friend, not a penny club. I'm sorry, but I don't know ya. Owner won't allow walk-ins."

"Er…" Everard began, about to explain that he did have

an invitation of sorts, or he thought he had—where was Vitaliy?

He appeared at last, shutting the door behind. He slid his hand on the small of Everard's back, making him jump, and coughed politely. "Hello, Aedd."

The Welshman's entire manner changed. He exclaimed "Vee!" and pulled Vitaliy into a fierce, slapping hug. "'Twas said you were for the hulks!"

Vitaliy nodded. "Hanging, too."

Aedd laughed. "Should've known they wouldn't get ya. Coffee!" he declared. "That's what you need." He turned away, beckoning them down a hall, at the end of which stood a door. "Who's the waistcoat?" he threw over his shoulder.

"'s'James," Vitaliy said. The stark affection in his voice startled Everard more than the falsehood.

Aedd chuckled. "Ought to be more careful. James here almost saw the end of my knife."

There was a pause.

Vitaliy said, "James can handle himself."

The doorman turned and grinned toothily through a black beard. "Only jesting. C'mon."

Everard snuck glances over to Vitaliy as they walked—he found himself somehow looking down, which was absurd, because he remembered quite well how their respective bodies lined up, and Vitaliy was definitely the taller. But Vitaliy was hunching somehow, and had combed his hair back severely against his scalp, had queued it into a tight knot at the nape.

In short, he looked different, yet again. What connected the pirate Varfolomey, of Caribbean and Gulf of Mexico fame, to little Kingston, Upper Canada?

The Welshman pushed open the door to reveal a narrow single-file stair, and the familiar noisy clamor and clink of a coffeehouse came down like a wave.

"Good to see you, Vee. Have fun, boys."

The door shut behind, and they climbed. At the top of the stair, Vitaliy held out his hand. Everard understood; doorman or no doorman, there would be eyes on them as they entered—eyes looking for mirror images, for *same*. He took the hand with his gloved one.

The staircase opened to an ordinary-extraordinary first-floor coffeehouse, sweltering in the June morning.

Ordinary: a handful of two- and four-top tables on pedestals, some of them occupied, were situated around a centre serve-station. This was manned by a white woman in a peach-colored dress and bonnet. To the left of the tables were four intimate wood-panelled booths with hat hooks; on the far wall, three twelve-pane windows overlooked the street and beyond, to the water.

Extraordinary: he and Vitaliy passed muster with no more than a few glances, and then they were ignored. Everard let out his breath.

Vitaliy let go his hand, and Everard went on to the farthest booth: unoccupied but for a bright stream of morning sunshine coming through the window. Vitaliy veered to the serve-station bar in search of a coffeepot. Hopefully a large one.

Through the panes Everard could see the masts and drawn-up sheets of *Netley*, naturally still in harbour. She probably already had a new captain read to her decks. It felt strange to see her unchanged when so much for Everard had.

Everard reflexively reached for his hat to put on the hook—found no hat—and sat sheepishly on the bench seat that faced the windows. He had the feeling Vitaliy was the sort to like to watch the door, "safe" or no.

"I didn't know Kingston was a large-enough settlement for such an establishment," Everard said when the man had returned, cups and coffeepot and newsprint-wrapped pasties in hand.

"And you a Navy man." Vitaliy sat, glanced round at the sparse occupation. He poured unerringly into both cups. "It was louder during the war, I'll grant you. Sugar?"

"No, thank you."

Vitaliy's eyes crinkled as he lounged back against the panelling, cup in his palm. "Didn't think so."

Everard watched the steam rise from his own cup and be lit into opacity by the sunshine. He sniffed appreciatively.

"Oh, good day," he said, pleased. "That isn't twice-boiled."

"No." Vitaliy sipped, heedless of temperature. "Amélie would have the server's head."

Everard marvelled to think that Vitaliy had been in Kingston at some point in the past three years. Long enough a time to know the manager of an invitation-only coffeehouse, one with a custom of men like them. He'd been so close… if Everard had been even a fraction less reserved...

*Let's not fool ourselves,* a voice whispered. *Uptight, not reserved.*

He wondered if D'Arcy knew of the place. If they served alcohol, almost definitely he did.

Vitaliy did like to watch the door. Everard couldn't blame him. V. Varfolomey, a thousand American dollars on his head; in his shoes, Everard would do the same. In fact, perhaps it was a practice he too ought to take up, now there were officially redcoat patrols out for him.

The problem was that if he let such a paranoia sink in, it would never let him go. Where Vitaliy kept discreet watch with heavy-lidded glances, Everard would sit like someone possessed, fingers under his thighs, staring wide-eyed at the door.

Indeed, best not. He curled his hand around the cup and sipped cautiously.

And then sipped some more. Just-off-a-boil hot, the coffee was certainly not the watery stuff doled out by ship's mess. It was not even the tea-like replacement served in larger cities. It was true coffee, the rich stuff of his boyhood a stone's throw from Arabia. He groaned.

Vitaliy asked, "What do you think?"

"I may curse," Everard admitted. "It's very good." He looked up. Vitaliy was smiling.

"Surely, this can't be the local preference," Everard marvelled.

"If custom doesn't like it as-is, they water it."

Everard bet that they frequently did. As for himself, he was going to be very awake, very soon. "Is this Brazilian? Cuban?" he said, half to himself. He sipped again. "Not Indonesian, thank God."

Vitaliy leaned forward. He looked intrigued. "Why not Indonesian?"

Everard held up a finger. Well, a gloved thumb. "For one, acidity isn't right." He licked his lips. "And I do believe my lips are about to go numb from the stimulant effect."

Vitaliy's gaze dropped for a moment, slid back up. He prompted, "For two?"

"For two," Everard said, "Dutch East India are some ungodly, unprincipled bastards. They'd have a monopoly over *coffea arabica* given half a chance, and work the enslaved Javanese fingerless doing so. I'm glad this isn't theirs." He sipped again. "Well, probably isn't."

"It is not." Vitaliy smiled again, close-lipped. "The Navy man cares for the provenance of coffee?" he challenged.

"I know a bit about trades, commodities, the like—I've read Locke as everyone else." Everard coughed. "Anyway, my father is—was—in business. A tradesman. I told you I was of common stock," he said, somewhat defensively.

Vitaliy's eyebrows rose. "Locke, as everyone else." He took a long drink of coffee. "And the Portuguese, the French, they are exempted their cash crops?"

"Of course not," Everard huffed. "Look, you—you cannot

bring me to a coffeehouse, pour me the stuff, and then reprimand my drinking it. I don't see you abstaining."

Vitaliy chuckled. "No." He pushed the pasties closer to
Everard. "Do all Navy men still carry a grudge against the
Dutch? I thought that war was before our time."

Everard unwrapped one and sniffed it: lamb and onion.
"Thank you. I'm glad to hear you recognise that fact. In 1780,
I was still in skirts. Nothing doing with merchantmen."

Vitaliy smiled, softer this time. "As was I."

"I suppose you weren't always a pirate. No, my grudge
against Dutch East India is that they're slaver bastards."

Vitaliy raised his cup in mock salud. "So says the moral
Englishman."

Stung, Everard merely said, "One tries." He lifted the pasty
in return salud, took a large bite, and ate in silence. He wasn't
English, not really, but it was hardly worth disseminating the
nuances of his complicated citizenship to a pirate.

Then it occurred to him: "Aren't you, though? English?
You were lieutenant-marine…"

"An Englishman?" Vitaliy shook his head. "No. American.
Pressed."

Everard sat back. "American." He laughed. "Of course you
are. You're the reason we went to war, you know, you lost
American boys." As Everard, too, had been lost—except from
Spain.

Vitaliy shrugged. He himself was not partaking in pasty,
but tapping his fingers on the tabletop in some kind of chanty
rhythm, glancing towards the door at intervals. His cup sat
empty. He had not poured himself another.

A suspicion formed, perhaps spurred by the drug or the
steadying food. Everard lowered his voice and asked:

"It's not only weapons you cargo to and fro, then?"

Really, no ship ever carried a single commodity, not if they
could help it. But what he wanted to know was simple: was

Vitaliy a slaver, like so many pirates were since the laws had gone through?

"No," Vitaliy replied. "Not only weapons."

Everard's stomach twisted.

"You wish to know if I'm a slaver bastard," Vitaliy said carefully. "Yes?"

Everard nodded.

Slowly, Vitaliy reached for the coffeepot and refilled Everard's cup.

"You really don't know who Varfolomey is," he said.

"I don't," Everard admitted. "The Lakes Service is fairly isolated, not much in the way of word of mouth."

"So, why not ask?"

"This again." Everard laughed faintly. "Who the devil *asks* such a thing? What manner of pirate are you, now that I've realised you are one? What sort of criminal have I released unto the world?" He sat back. "To be honest, I haven't contemplated the total reach of it yet."

Vitaliy nodded. "You should have. But I'm not a slaver. I have never made a coin from the sale of another human, nor owned one."

Everard was so relieved, he almost dropped the cup.

Vitaliy went on: "But when I can buy it, coffee is a commodity I transport." He tapped the coffeepot. "This is Haitian, delivered not a month past."

"Haïti, of the massacre?"

"Haïti, the revolutionary nation." He frowned. "War is war. One doesn't say *America, of the massacres.*"

"Doesn't one? But I take your point. I'll be honest—I don't know much about American history, save that we lost. Twice." He sipped. "Did you say when you can *buy* the coffee?"

"When," Vitaliy emphasised. "It requires taking a loss."

Everard, surprised into rudeness, almost swore. "Oh, come on."

Vitaliy said nothing.

"America has drunk coffee since its inception," Everard went on. God save him, the stuff made him talk. "It's as patriotic as Yankee Doodle. I cannot think of a thing less likely to stand for freedom than slave-grown coffee, but there you have it; it isn't tea. With Madison's bloody restrictions and tariffs, you an American, and what you can't throw a stone in Boston without hitting a coffeehouse… you can't see a profit? Even when buying it?"

*Not stealing it?* he left unsaid.

Vitaliy raised his eyebrows. "You are worried I am a slaving pirate, but have some objection to my taking a loss on what is usually a slave-grown crop?"

"No," Everard said emphatically. "Quite the opposite. But—"

"Are you a man to care for profit, Everard?"

Everard paused.

"I— No. I mean, I'm a—I *was* captain of the Royal Navy, entitled to shares of my prizes above and beyond the salary, which is fairly significant… why *else* should I have joined the service, pray? Renown? The incredible rate of officer death? Or maybe was it the impossible odds of promotion? Authority?"

Vitaliy leaned forward, palms flat on the table, his expression intense. "Yes, why else? Why *are* you a twenty-year Navy man, Everard?"

*Why, indeed.* "Well, primarily," he snapped, "abject violence and criminality doesn't particularly seem to affect me. There is that."

Vitaliy laughed. "You mentioned. It is certainly a prerequisite. But a greedy man—a man concerned of the loss of all those things—renown, authority, salary"—he ticked off fingers —"would not have done what you did yesterday. Do not you agree?"

Everard harrumphed. "That was impulse, and I believed you relatively innocent. And how the devil do I find myself explaining economic motivation to a pirate, anyway?" he said, incredulous. "You aren't known for taking losses, you realise."

Contrary to popular belief, ships were not really profitable things of themselves, but giant, floating, wooden estates that threw money and labor and materials and men to the sea at a fairly predictable rate of loss. And pirating was a business like any other.

"So, why would y…Vee? For that matter, how could he do so, and stay afloat? What about tobacco? Sugar? If one objects to profit from one cash crop with questionable sourcing, why not all?" he demanded.

Vitaliy sat back. He looked as though he were trying not to smile. "Why not all?" he said.

Everard put his head in his hands and groaned. "You cannot be an actual pirate. I refuse to believe it. You must see it's all very incongruous to expectation. Every part of this. Of you."

"Oh, I do see." Vitaliy hummed. "Every part?"

Everard flushed as Vitaliy laughed.

"Let us forget not the testimonial of a night shared in bed," he said. "Or did that too not meet expectation somehow?"

Holy good God, he hadn't even lowered his voice.

"Two nights!" Everard corrected, his face hot. "And I had expectation of neither of them." Then a chill came over him as something occurred, a motivation, perhaps, for Vitaliy to be so angry at him. "I have no expectation of more, mind you," he said hastily. "I didn't—I don't want anything from you. That wasn't at all why I…" He trailed off.

Vitaliy gave him a long look.

"You told me why," he said. "But we will see. You already know what it looks like to the outside." Vitaliy made the two-finger salute known to all marines, as he had when they had first met. Blond hair on his hand and wrist shone curly and light-tipped in the sun.

*We'll see?*

Everard cleared his throat. "What it looks like to the admiralty, you mean. They, too, think you bought me?"

Vitaliy nodded. "The admiralty *and everyone else* will think I bought you." He frowned. "And I am not a man known for such things. Bribery."

"You're— He's— You're not?"

"In any incarnation, including that one," he confirmed.

Everard was silent a moment. "But, Var…er, is his reputation not…"

"A slaughterer?" Vitaliy lounged back against the bench, arms spread, chest broadening. Out of the dust-mote line of sun, but still close.

Everard swallowed.

He was a *liar.*

He didn't have expectations, but he did want.

Vitaliy watched him from under heavy eyelids. Patient. Waiting.

Everard took a long drink of coffee, not that he needed more.

He said, "Yes. What is bribery in the face of that? But I think you… you, the flesh-and-blood man in front of me, not the pirate… are not a slaughterer. Not really."

"Do you." Vitaliy blinked, slow. "The flesh-and-blood man and the pirate are the same."

"It behooves a pirate to be known as vicious. You've only just got done telling me."

"I won't lie to you, if you ask."

"No need," Everard insisted, though saying it aloud did make him feel a little like he'd lost his mind. As though it weren't absurd to justify a man's moral character to his face. "You apparently aren't concerned to make a profit with the most profitable commodity on Earth besides sugar. And one cannot forget that just last night, you judged me harshly for murder. Which, mind you, I was only party to, which happened for the sake of your own survival. I almost wanted to turn straight around at your expression."

"I almost wanted you to," Vitaliy agreed. "But I know that blame is with the lieutenant."

Everard slapped the table, ignoring the swoop his stomach had done at that.

"There!" he said triumphantly. "A man can't change so much in three years. Don't you agree?"

Vitaliy pursed his lips. "I don't. It is dependent on the years themselves, and which ones in the line they happen to be."

"Well, of course—"

"What's more," Vitaliy leaned forward again, "you can't expect the decisions of the future to produce the same results as the past."

Everard scoffed. "This is personal conjecture based upon observations of the near and immediate past. Some hours, not a decade. And if you could only see the horror that is my unceasing memory, you'd find even those of three years ago to be extraordinarily accurate."

"Observations." Vitaliy's satisfied look made his eyes glint. "Then it *is* belief. Not conjecture."

"It is still conjecture, because obviously I have not observed you at every possible moment—" Everard narrowed his eyes. Another suspicion was rapidly forming. "Did Thom give you leave to borrow aught beyond my razor?"

Surely, that was absurd. Even if the man had, for some reason, plucked *A Treatise of Human Nature* out of Everard's trunk, he probably wouldn't have had the time to read it in the interim hours, much less form complicated opinions around the thing.

Astoundingly, it was Vitaliy who flushed then: pink

splotches on flat cheekbones, rouge sparingly applied. Everard remembered that feature too well—remembered that it only appeared at the utmost.

"I've offended you at last," Everard said quickly. Why did he so relish prodding the man into strong emotion? "I'm sorry; I don't mind if you had. It was only a handful of books and letters, I don't own much in the way of physical capital"—and didn't really need to, with his memory—"but you were welcome to it, as Thom was doubtless aware."

Vitaliy blinked. Opened his mouth. Closed it. Leaned even closer, and put a big hand over Everard's left one.

Everard startled but then remembered their surroundings. He nonetheless felt very visible, exposed.

"Why don't you but ask me," Vitaliy murmured, "what kind of pirate I am?"

"Stubbornness?" Everard offered, weakly.

Vitaliy shook his head. His hand slid off Everard's, and he stretched, arms high over his head. He yawned hugely. The blush had remained.

Everard did not, absolutely did not stare. There was that quotidian beauty again, fascinating him.

"You'll find out soon enough," Vitaliy said at last.

"Oh, shall I?"

Vitaliy hummed. "If you wish it."

Everard kept quiet. If Vitaliy was going to tease him with whatever proposition he hadn't yet put forth…

*Why not but ask?*

He sighed, and gave in. "Have we finally come to 'what after'?"

"Nearly. I am enjoying this too much." Vitaliy drew his fingers over his smoothed hair. "You did not know who I am, so maybe you don't understand. It has taken me years to get Vee's reputation as it is. And now to the world it seems certain he has bribed a captain of the British Navy."

"This is… *worse*… than general piracy? Slaughter and destruction?"

"Morally, no. Practically…" Vitaliy sighed. "…Yes, it is worse. I cannot have men—Englishmen—expecting bribery from Vee. I can't afford it."

"Literally cannot?" Everard laughed. "Is there a going rate of ruinous extortion? Surely, there are only the two options, bribery or violence. As a rule of piracy."

"As a rule of humanity," Vitaliy agreed, "it is one or the other. And…" He smiled. "…Not literally incapable, no. I am sorry to say he is a successful pirate."

Everard took a moment to think why this statement had so lacked braggadocio, framed with the typical polite modesty as it had been. Maybe it was the third-person distancing. Or perhaps just Everard's own radical views on capital tinging the matter.

"He's wealthy, you mean."

"Yes. You might see for yourself soon," Vitaliy said lightly. "Still, we must find some alternative than that he has compensated you financially for your loyalty. Varfolomey's influence is almost all in hearsay. A pirate's reputation is everything he is."

The man was very reyish, after all; he only lacked a rubied crown. Everard let it slide, because it was true. What he'd done had felt rather like loyalty.

"You would rather men—other pirates—turn tail than engage him. As I understand, that's been the point of insignia for millennia. But, you'll pardon me for asking, how does escaping His Majesty's noose make him any lesser in the Caribbean?"

"There are governments there, recognised and unrecognised—"

"Haïti?" Everard interjected; Vitaliy nodded.

"—that depend on others' reception of my trade. Governments that I depend on receiving *my* trade," Vitaliy emphasised. "It's all connected, sticky, like web. None of them must think I am connected in any way to the Crown, or they will reject me and my ships and my people out of fear of their own betrayal, or worse."

"But if you are American, is that not just as bad?"

Vitaliy paused. "It would be," he admitted. "But while you know my true name and heritage, there are few who do. Very few."

That gave Everard a happy thrill. *The truth.*

"And so Varfolomey…" he prompted.

"Is my grandfather's name. Also was Russian."

"I gathered," Everard said dryly. "And so has everyone else —I suppose that's the idea? Russians are goddamned vicious sailors, I'll give you that."

Vitaliy smiled. "And there are almost none of them in America."

"But *we* have—the English, I mean—the Royal Navy—I trained a company or two of Russians. They've been allies once or twice. Is that not also too close an association?"

"Mm," Vitaliy agreed. "Yes, you are seeing my predicament. And now"—he pointed to Everard—"three *Englishmen* have saved me. The Navy let me run. How does it look? It looks like I am now the Crown's."

"Let you?" Everard gestured round the coffeehouse. "You haven't even run yet!"

Vitaliy ignored this. "But you see that they will not attribute it to my especial skill in escaping fetters."

"They'll credit me, the supposed bribee."

"The supposed bribee, who is following lead from the admiralty, maybe."

"That is bloody absurd." Everard laughed bitterly. "The admiralty were going to arrest me! Is this the whole problem, my being English? Is that why you were so angry at me, pulling you from that hold? I saved your life, maybe, but also wrecked your legacy? Well, I'm sorry I am who I am, but there's nothing I can do about having been in the service. I may forge evidence, create it out of almost nothing, but it doesn't go the other way. I can't erase myself and my record from existence."

Vitaliy leaned in close, so that the stream of sunlight fell over him in profile. His eyes were lit into turquoise ocean, his hair ignited into gold.

"Do not *never* be sorry for who you are," he said fiercely. "I am not angry at you for being Navy. To be upset at that thing would make me... a hypocrite. Especially since you gave that thing away for me, my life."

Everard was stunned. "All right," he agreed. "I shan't, then."

Satisfied again, Vitaliy sat back. "You forged evidence, too?" he asked, after a moment.

Vitaliy really hadn't gone through his trunk. If he had, he'd have seen C's letters.

"I did," Everard said. "That was my plan when I thought you were innocent—not a pirate. Before it all went to shit and murder. I'd kept a few letters from an old acquaintance whose hand I know quite well... it was a matter of hours to forge more."

Vitaliy looked even more resolved. Towards what, Everard was becoming increasingly curious.

"Look here," Vitaliy said. "Your being Navy is only a... complication. A fact. But it still may ruin my reputation... *if* we do not make it popular that your motivation for saving me was something else than money, or king and country."

"Oh, well, good," Everard said, sarcastically. He crossed his arms. "I hope you've remembered that I am not at all moti-vated by such things as sentiment, nor nights shared."

Vitaliy laughed. "No, no—you've guessed it! That *is* my solution. If you will agree to it." He grinned, and three years were gone, disappeared.

"Er… what? What do you mean?"

"It is perfect," Vitaliy said. "It suits both our needs. You do not want to be left behind, and I cannot be known as in bed with the English."

In the corner of Everard's vision, Vitaliy's right hand reappeared from beneath the table, came close to his own. He tapped something solid-sounding onto the table.

"Unless actually in bed. With one Englishman."

"I'm not really…" Everard looked down. Between his thumb and forefinger, Vitaliy held—

"*What?*" Everard exclaimed.

—a wide golden band of a ring.

"Yes," Vitaliy said seriously. "Everard, marry me."

# TEN

He was going to say yes.

Of course he would.

He shouldn't.

The hot morning had turned into sweltering, oppressive afternoon, with another of those strange fog hazes so frequent this year. On the return walk to Maud's tavern, he walked side-by-each with Vitaliy, discreetly spinning the gold band on his right hand. It fit well enough but also displaced his second and fourth fingers in a way that felt heavy. Odd. From the weight and thickness of the gold, it was a significant piece, which made him uneasy, as he was sure that he'd never taken something so expensive into his possession before.

Vitaliy had asked Everard to be his matelot, his inheritor in case of death. His business partner. His everything partner. His husband—in name.

There was just one thing that gave Everard true pause.

It seemed Varfolomey *was* a wealthy pirate. So, if he said yes, barring the signing of proper papers, that was what Everard would become. Wealthy.

Everard didn't like owning things. Showing wealth. *Having*

wealth. Despite having been an officer for a decade and more, with wars against several nations and a fair few prize ships under his belt, by choice he was of little circumstance. With his own room and board and meals taken care of aboard his ships, Everard had lived cash-poor, with few possessions: nothing that couldn't fit in his sea chest. It'd always been more than enough. What monies he'd received surplus of this he'd sent over time to Catalonia in care of his madre; the rest went to voluntary associations. His mother had enough now to buy coal and swine and mountain-calves unto the end of her days, and not be beholden to Anderson Calicoes for a single peseta more.

He'd simply assumed the Navy would keep him on in perpetuity, at half-pay at least, with pension afterward. It wasn't even an outlandish assumption. It was what was done, once one made post. It was commonplace.

Unless, of course, one had given one's name as witness to a weapons-smuggler pirate and had nearly been arrested for it.

Everard's memory might have been spectacular, but his ability to plan for a future that didn't include service to the Crown had, he realised now, been a bit lacking.

He looked down at the ring again. He shouldn't have put it on. He should go and do what he should've six months past, as the admiralty wanted—except now, unlike before, he had no pension awaiting. Not that he cared about that for his own sake. No; he ought to go back to Catalonia, beg his brothers' forgiveness and reconciliation and ask for a spot as a manager. Or a clerk. Anything gainful. They likely wouldn't care who or what he'd been for the British, even with his having been on the wrong side since the beginnings of the First Coalition.

Twenty-four years, though. They wouldn't even recognise him. He wouldn't recognise them.

And Vitaliy had been exactly correct. He did not want to be left behind. More so now he knew who—what—Vitaliy truly was.

Wealth notwithstanding, why not tie himself irrevocably to a large, blond, and very attractive pirate who paraphrased David Hume? He was fatally curious to see firsthand what sort of pirate Vitaliy Gray had made himself into.

"How did they detain you?" Everard asked now. "A thousand dollars on your head, and you don't have an idea who was motivated to betray you?"

"I have several ideas," Vitaliy said. "It doesn't matter who was it. Thanks to you, they did not succeed."

"It doesn't *matter*?" Everard laughed. "A surfeit of options for betrayers, I suppose that's being a true pirate."

Vitaliy shrugged. "Anyone may arrest me, and call it fortune. You, even, this minute. Why should I count opportunists?"

*You, even, this minute.*

Everard couldn't even feel indignant at the jest. Vitaliy had plainly said it only because he believed it untrue. Believed it, had for the moment taken it into himself as a true thing that Everard would not betray him, that Everard wasn't an opportunist, that Everard would support him.

Everard squinted down at his worse-for-lakewater boots as they stepped over the cobblestone pavement. Between Vitaliy's belief in him and *thanks to you,* he felt much the same as he did watching sunlight reflect in jewellike bits off a calm sea: content and at peace. The feeling that things, for the moment, seemed all right.

Perhaps it was the coffee.

"Well, I want to know who if you don't."

Vitaliy ducked his head. He smiled. "Please, always say what you want."

Everard returned the smile. "Let's assume it wasn't an opportunist," he said, "since you are humouring me. What were you doing when arrested?"

"I was in Philadelphia," Vitaliy said easily. "Acquiring a press."

"A… press?" Everard shook his head. He had imagined heists on a massive scale; a sea battle worthy of addition to *A General History of the Pyrates*; a duel set for ambush; a midnight assignation gone terribly wrong. "I wasn't expecting that."

"Nor I," Vitaliy said with a laugh.

"What happened? You couldn't find a bent print shop? In Philadelphia, the city of liberty? Last I was there, one could not turn the corner without getting a face full of paste and broadsheet."

"Oh, no. The printer was an honest one, or I thought him so." Vitaliy slung his hands in pockets. "But while I knew hardly anybody was successful getting a press to the Americas, I did not realise the Spanish were willing to do violence to anyone to prevent it." He frowned, and despite their being in plain air and on the street and hatless, stopped and rucked up his shirt high, and twisted enough for Everard to see a pink-black, ridged scar on his lower back, quite near where one would aim for the liver.

"Déu meu," Everard cursed.

"Yes. And it was almost my mother in my place—she knew the printer." He let the shirt drop, not bothering to re-tuck. "A dangerous thing, ink on paper."

"Absolutely," Everard agreed. "All this and you don't care to find out who betrayed you?"

"No. It had nothing to do with Varfolomey."

"Hmm." Everard wasn't convinced.

"It was the first time I've used personal connections for pirating. It will be the last."

They walked on.

Everard asked, "But where did the Navy come in, arresting you?"

"They came in on the Delaware."

"Funny." Everard smiled despite himself.

Vitaliy shrugged. "A ship pulled me out; they were Navy."

"And someone just happened to recognise you?"

"It does happen, time to time," Vitaliy said. "You see? No conspiracy. No plot."

But what if someone had somehow connected the two anyway? Clearly, Vitaliy had taken pains to keep his identities separate; but what if?

"It surely looks that way. Or was meant to look that way. But who recognised you? What ship pulled you up?"

Vitaliy grunted. "That none of it matters."

"Hmm." Everard couldn't tell which: if Vitaliy honestly didn't care or if he was merely keeping things close to the chest. He let it drop for now. "Who in the Gulf wants presses?"

"Everyone," Vitaliy said frankly. "But especially México. New Granada. Haïti. Those previously controlled by the Inquisition, mostly. They seek uncontrolled presses to publish something beyond scripture."

"What kind of press were you for? The new Stanhope? Columbia? A standard Gutenberg? And London-manufactured or American?"

Vitaliy cocked his head. "It was a press. It was expensive. It came in many crates. More than that…ehh?" He made an unknowing, dismissive noise, very Slavic. "You were in printing?"

"I was. Haven't been, for many years." Everard paused. "The past three in particular."

"Ah," Vitaliy said, thoughtful. "Left-handed."

A heated flush of memory: Everard's left hand round both their pricks, slick and hot against the snow-damp, Canadian spring air. Groans and gasps and bitten lips.

"Er… yes," Everard said wryly. "I get on all right with the other now. Though there was some accommodation involved."

The look that Vitaliy shot him said he hadn't missed his

meaning—or the memory. "I'm sure. What did you produce? Books? Pamphlets? Handbills?"

Everard hesitated. If there had been any one thing, besides fucking other men, and before rescuing a criminal, that would've got him court-martialed and cashiered, it was his political plates and writings. His alter ego as an anti-monarchy, anti-capitalist writer and satirist wasn't something he'd admitted to anyone except D'Arcy. It did contrast rather strongly with twelve years' officer's service to the Crown, after all.

But if he said yes, they were pledged matelots. If Vitaliy was fucked, then so was he; he imagined the reverse was true as well. And a pirate wasn't likely to be threatened by a handful of borderline legal scratchings, was he?

"Some books. Children's, a frontispiece or two; I'm no William Blake. I did the simplest sort of block print. Newsprint, broadsheet, cartoon."

"Cartoons." Vitaliy frowned. "You were a propagandist?"

"No," Everard said quickly. "A satirist. Quite different."

But Vitaliy had withdrawn: physically, and in his enthusiasm, too. He put his hands behind his back. "Quite the same," he insisted softly. He sounded disappointed.

Everard stopped dead on the pavement, turned to face him, though they were within sighting distance of Maud's already. "Difficult to please, aren't you? What do you know of it, sir 'comes in many crates'? It isn't the same, not at all. Have you seen proper satire?"

For the second time that day, Everard noted that when Vitaliy was challenged, his eyes became large, observant, and unblinking. "What I have seen of cartoon generalises cultures, whole races, whole peoples, into caricature and farce."

Everard harrumphed, turned away, and walked on, agitated. Vitaliy followed, more calmly.

"You're not wrong," Everard said to his boots. "But then you've only seen it badly done, stuff made to sell. The lowest denominator of satire stoops to such things. Satire's meant to do the very opposite: to contradict, criticise the general societal viewpoint, which, yes, I think it not wrong to say, does include a deal of racialism." Then it all came out, like confession. There was nothing more to hide. "I admit mine weren't popular; if you've seen one in circulation, I'll be surprised. I wrote them mostly against the war—both of them—but as I wasn't much interested in poking fun at 'old Boney'"—the sailor's name for Napoleon— "they weren't favorites. I made them anti-capitalist, but I couldn't sell anything too radical, too guillotine-y. Obviously. So, I made some centered around mad John B—His Majesty. Those did sell: to Yankee presses. A few secessionist Canadians, too."

Vitaliy, still with hands behind his back, had relaxed slightly. More than that, he had matched his steps with Everard's, walked so close their shoulders nearly brushed.

"Anyway," Everard went on, "it was only a hobby, so I wasn't beholden to take commissions I didn't agree with."

Vitaliy nodded once, and said mildly, "How fortunate."

Everard had the distinct impression he was still being Judged, and so shut his mouth, coffee's effects upon him be damned. They were both silent for the remainder of the walk, until soon they came to Maud's ivy brick, and Vitaliy murmured, "A moment?"

Assuming the coffee was affecting the man in a different way, Everard paused and turned away, sheltered from the sun in the alleyway adjoining Maud's. Here, a pleasing coolness reflected from the greenery, and a warm breeze off Lake Ontario swooped round the building's corner, whisking away the smell of city street.

But instead of relieving himself, Vitaliy walked across the dirt and mud and stone and begged something from a sassafras tea vendor on the corner. He exchanged a ha'penny for what-ever it was; Everard hoped not sassafras tea.

Vitaliy returned, his right hand cupped protectively against the wind around something, which he then put to his mouth. A cigarillo, tobacco-brown: its end glowing red-orange, its smoke sweet-smelling. Not tobacco inside, then, but hemp, cannabis. It'd been a lit coal that he'd requested from the tea vendor.

With smoke trailing from perfect lips, Vitaliy asked, "Do you mind it? I don't want to smoke in the room."

"Not at all," Everard said quickly, realising he was staring. He cleared his throat. "The wind's clearing it, in any case. Where on earth did you…" *Smuggler. Pirate.* "… Never mind. Really, you'd think you were straight off a Frenchie." Napoleon's troops were famous for their enjoyment of hashish.

Vitaliy chuckled, eyelids lowering. "Did you make that into caricature, too?" He politely held out the tied cigarillo.

Everard declined with a wave. He'd had enough plant-based stimulation for the day. "I did not. Is cannabis another commodity of yours?" he returned lightly.

"No," Vitaliy replied, equally lightly. He offered nothing further.

They stood there companionably as he smoked. Both of them were ignored by the few passersby—likely since they had no hats. And a thousand dollars on Vitaliy's head or no, Everard was glad of the excuse to linger. He crossed his arms and, in the hollow of his elbow, spun the gold band with his thumb, over and over and over. How strange it was. To be offered such a thing, and for it to signify apparently almost nothing, except perhaps that Vitaliy didn't mind the thought of Everard being his ever-present company. He certainly didn't seem to mind it now.

At last, Vitaliy inhaled deep, and pushed the lit end out on a brick. He looked up, pupils wider, black and compelling in the midday sun, and Everard startled.

"Well," he laughed. "I'm glad you asked me what you did before you became intoxicated."

Vitaliy smiled, a little more lazily than before. "Ah, no. It would not have changed anything. This is mild stuff."

"Everyone has their vice, I suppose."

Vitaliy made the noncommittal noise again. "Eh, as a vice it would not be worth it—it makes the sea glare murder, on a fair day."

Everard nodded like he knew.

"It isn't the opium, at least," he said reasonably. "Or tobacco."

"No." Vitaliy regarded the last bit of cigarillo between his fingers, and flicked it into the street. There it would be smashed beneath a carriage wheel or four, with all the other leaves and detritus, and be returned to the earth. "Never those."

Everard expected the man to turn round to Maud's parlour entryway, but Vitaliy kept steady eyes on him.

"I have an idea," he said, after several heartbeats but very few blinks. Everard felt watched closely, as though the enlarged pupils helped Vitaliy in this, like a cat's eyes in the dark. "Dependent on how you respond to my offer. And… how well you do get on with the other hand."

"Er… an idea?"

"Do you still draw satires?"

# Eleven

W ith nobody left behind, the five of them paid their way to Boston. There, they acquired another press, more carefully this time, with D'Arcy and Bellingham St. Clare sharp at pistols outside the printshop as the transaction was made, as a cart was hired to carry the many crates to the harbour. There was a sense of urgency to Vitaliy, though he said he had only just crossed the end threshold of time he'd promised his pirate crew that it would take to acquire the thing and return. Three months, he said he'd told them, at the most. It'd been four.

Everard understood. Piracy was a business in hearsay and reputation but also goods and services. V. Varfolomey's legacy would go on everlasting with or without him, but though the physical logistics themselves had continued in spite of his rumored capture, it was only because they'd already been meant to.

And because Varfolomey apparently had an extremely competent second-in-command.

"Milly is capable enough for two captains," Vitaliy insisted.

"Ten, even. And the crew will realise I haven't deserted them, once it's known I'm not dead."

Which it would be, soon; already reports had been printed about Varfolomey's escape. It would grow like flame up and down the North Atlantic coast, singeing his reputation at edges —saved by an Englishman!—at least until Everard's satires ran in this week's printings, and they changed the shape of it.

Conveniently anchored there in Boston harbour, loyally awaiting Varfolomey's word in spite of its absence, was the *Enemistad.* She was a two-masted brig with eighteen guns, a complement of sixty-odd, and a regular, thrice-a-year path between Boston and the Gulf.

Her American papers were so legitimate-looking, even Everard's forger's eyes couldn't have told anyone differently.

"But who *are* you?" he exclaimed, turning them over and back within the safety of the brig's greatcabin.

Vitaliy looked amused. D'Arcy beside him was skeptical and arms crossed, still resentful—he hadn't yet forgiven Everard for the matelotage. The captain of the *Enemistad,* a Mr. Allen Forsythe, who was quite an ordinary, bookish-looking man, for being the first pirate captain to whom Everard had politely introduced himself (aside from Vitaliy), insisted angrily:

"They are legitimate! From Madison's own hand—not even his secretary!"

Everard had suspected this himself, though it seemed impossible. But there it was in his hands, a president's signature endorsing a pirate's ship.

"Right," he said. "Well." He rolled them back into their case, still marvelling. Small wonder V. Varfolomey was infamous, with that kind of internal reach. He began to see why the Navy had wanted his execution kept quiet, under wraps in rural Upper Canada. Anything to avoid a martyr—especially one with influence upon the United States President.

"Onward," he jested weakly.

The voyage lasted eight days. And several times along *Enemistad*'s trajectory south, rolling over in his little, singlewide merchantman's bunk, D'Arcy snoring above him, Everard caught himself wondering Why, and especially Why with So Many Persons. But there was no help for it. D'Arcy had clenched his teeth and said Wherever you Go, Ever, I Go, and had always gone with the wind in any case, so Why Not; Thom was manservant steadfast, instantly coveted. Bellingham, donning vicar's accoutrements, which Everard was unclear if were a disguise or not, clung to D'Arcy like a waifish, deep-voiced duckling.

Vitaliy didn't seem to mind his tagalongs, but Everard, matelotage agreement or not, felt the responsibility of them all very keenly. He consoled himself by remembering that they were sailors all, and what was a sailor if not quite used to being sent to all the obscure corners of the seas?

And the corner that V. Varfolomey occupied was obscure indeed.

"Your flagship," Everard asked at breakfast, because V. Varfolomey was of course important enough to have his own flagship, like a bloody admiral, "is called *Sévère?*"

Vitaliy nodded, thumb between his teeth, slurping off melted butter and American honey—Everard had tried hard not to notice any of this—and said, "She's in Matagorda Bay."

Matagorda Bay, Nueva España, a tiny, dangerously unin-habited bay on the western curve of the Gulf of México.

"Do you expect… problems… in retaking her as captain?"

The thumb came free, sank to break apart another bit of saturated bread, and back in it went, 'til it was sucked clean and shiny wet. "No," he said thickly.

Vitaliy would not eat sugar, in his coffee or otherwise, but yet clearly had a voracious fondness for sweets.

He swallowed, and shrugged. "I may have to fight for her. Some of the crew insist on… older ways and means."

As though it were nothing.

"Fight? D'you mean dueling? Or…"

D'Arcy snorted. "Nothing so civilised for pirates." He sipped at coffee—heavily doctored with rum—and was reclined in a chair. His shiny-booted ankles were crossed over Everard's knee.

Everard had allowed this intimacy at first only out of sheer curiosity towards Vitaliy's reaction. When there was none, he let it continue with conflicted, slightly shameful pleasure, for D'Arcy had been short and distant with him since he'd returned to Maud's that day in Kingston. Nigh-delirious with fatigue and caffeine, Everard had felt the agreement he'd made with Vitaliy stick suddenly in his throat as D'Arcy's expression slid into disbelief and hurt.

Now D'Arcy's—frankly territorial—message was plain.

Vitaliy received it without a blink.

But then, he had been carefully explicit as they signed the legalities. Their agreement didn't preclude Everard from relations with others, and he himself cared not at all. It felt pointed, especially with D'Arcy sitting glumly as witness, Bellingham St. Clare at his side.

"Matelotage," Vitaliy had explained, "is not a marriage as most understand. Not anymore. It is mostly inheritance, convenience. No pirate on the *Sévère* will care if you are found outside my bed. And," he'd said thoughtfully, "the existing relationship explains the lieutenant's presence, even if we leave him out of the papers." He signed his elaborate majuscule V with a flourish; Everard signed his own meager initialed scrawl; and that was that. It was done.

Naturally, he'd said nothing about relations with his own person.

"I mean a fight to the death," Vitaliy clarified now. "Which is not by any means excluded from civilisation," he said pointedly.

D'Arcy rolled his eyes.

"But aren't pirates supposedly democratic?" Everard asked.

"Yes," Vitaliy said firmly. "But as I was never turned out nor campaigned against, but only presumed dead, I may challenge my elected replacement, if there is one, and defend my own prior election. And they also may choose a fight to defend the crew's most recent election." He pushed the last of the honeyed bread into his mouth, though seemed now to savor it less as he chewed. "It may be pistol proof, but more likely fists."

"Why not have another election?"

"Expediency," D'Arcy quipped.

"Bloodsport," Vitaliy said. "We don't yet live in an age where violence isn't valued at utmost, and crew want a leader who will defend them to the last, and prove they did not desert them willingly."

Hither to last week, Everard never had and never would've deserted a posting of his own, but Vitaliy spoke of captaincy like a privilege instead of duty or right. He spoke of captaincy and leadership as though it wasn't often like herding bouncing seals, hanging on to authority's slippery fur for dear life, only one's read-in admiralty papers and the occasional reluctant striping backing him. Perhaps piracy was different in that way also.

"'Government: the greatest of all reflections on human nature,'" Everard quoted. "They want a man after their own hearts."

Vitaliy smiled. "Yes. But I'm not worried. If they've chosen anyone, it will be Milly, and she is too fond of her own command of the *Birch*. And does not want me dead, last I asked."

*She, her. Command.*

"She? Milly—your fleet master—is a *woman*?" Everard said, aghast. Sailors sometimes had feminised sobriquets, so he hadn't thought anything of the name—Milly, how ridiculous—

upon first mention. But the pronouns plunked down like stones, undeniable.

"Mmm," Vitaliy confirmed; he sucked his thumb clean of the last swipes of honey from his tin plate. "Mind, I hope she hasn't tried to take the *Sévère* after all. She claimed her own captaincy via election, whereupon the previous captain was only two days gone ashore. He returned, claimed his prior election, enraged… Milly defended the *Birch*'s crew faster than I've seen prior or since."

D'Arcy removed his feet from Everard's knee and leaned forward, fascinated. "Pistols, surely? Was the other captain a drunk?"

Vitaliy chuckled. "No." He didn't offer further.

"And the crew?" Everard asked, though now it seemed a given. "They accepted her henceforth?"

Vitaliy stood, brushed off his trousers, and took the stack of tin mess plates into his arms. "They elected her. They loved her." He smiled slightly, admiration and pride clear on his face. "And then she replaced them. One by one."

Everard frowned. "With whom? Other… electors?"

"A select crew," Vitaliy said cryptically, walking away. "You'll see. And they love her even more."

# TWELVE

July 1816
Matagorda Bay
Pirate flagship *Sévère*

Vitaliy's flagship, the *Sévère*, was of course nothing less than an ex-Spanish meregildo. She was a massive 112-gun beauty, a *Santa Ana*–class ship of the line built in the late 1790s that Vitaliy had overtaken outside Havana and had refused to give up as prize to his president Madison. Everard liked him just for that. Her sails were square and plentiful, well kept, full-rigged; twin mermaids curled over the three-tier quarter gallery. She was so grand, this floating castle, that Everard wondered how Vitaliy had ever voluntarily left her, even for the sake of a free and unrestricted press.

Tonight in the greatcabin, as the light faded into magenta sunset, Everard's new pirate husband sat casually dwarfing a plush, red armchair. Vitaliy was peaceful, head bowed, his big hands counting away at stitches: a pair of socks, worked first thing upon arrival, like that was the thing he had most looked forward to, having been away.

Everard was no one to judge. He had coffee beside him, strong as he could bear, kept hot in its cup by a small flame beneath. It was lightly raining, but nobody was yelling about any leaks, and not even the large gallery windows let in a drop. He had before him on the desk a long list of ship's miscellany, delightful minutiae he'd thought he'd never have the privilege of overseeing again in his life.

Even if it was pirate and, strictly speaking, illegal.

The companionway door slammed, and D'Arcy burst in, dripping wet, startling Everard so that he nearly dropped his quill.

"Here's another," D'Arcy proclaimed, and tossed something down onto the desk before Everard.

Everard exclaimed, hastily rescuing his coffee as the smell of ink and damp paper cloth hit his nose: the *Louisiana Star and Chronicle.*

*COVERT SODOMITE, CAP'N 'BLACKHAND', SACRIFICES SELF FOR PIRATE-MATE, "V. VARFOLOMEY".*

"Huh," Everard said curiously. He set down the mug and splayed the paper flat. "They haven't censored this one?"

"I think," D'Arcy said, "we can definitively say that your deuced plan worked."

"We knew it had," Vitaliy murmured from the corner armchair. "Since I was received without challenge." Everard glanced over, but the man kept his kohl-darkened lashes lowered to his knitting, his expression neutral. Everard wasn't sure he'd even flinched.

Three weeks out from Kingston, the two still did not get along.

Everard had avoided the subject entirely. Sequestered within this sunny, pale-blue-painted greatcabin, Everard had thrown himself into understanding what he could of V. Varfolomey's vast network of trade routes and partners, ignoring D'Arcy's cold standoffishness—and frankly everyone else, too.

Vitaliy had had only one proviso to Everard's purview of the *Sévère* at anchor o'er the past week: that he observe only, and not try and assert authority in any way. Everard didn't need reminding of this, knowing what the average sailor's feelings towards Navy officers had always been, how thinly even his own crewmen had tarred over their dislike of him and his position. It wouldn't take much overstepping on his part to remind pirates of his previous occupation, matelot shield or no. He was no V. Varfolomey, belovèd; he'd kept his head down.

Mindful of this, now he said, "You shouldn't be seen coming in here, Preston. You know that." He paused. "Especially drunk as you are."

There was a tense moment of quiet, of enraged breathing; beneath the rain he could hear D'Arcy's teeth grind from across the cabin.

"In fact, the lieutenant is welcome," Vitaliy corrected. He hadn't paused his knitting. "As is everyone."

"He—what? But this is your greatcab—"

"Allowed, not allowed," D'Arcy spat, "it doesn't matter. It's been made plain I am not wanted. Don't worry, I won't stay—I only wished t'give you that and say: I can't believe you've agreed to this, Everard Rubén." He didn't quite manage the *R*. "Your reputation, your name, dragged through and spat on"—he glared at Vitaliy, who remained unperturbed—"have you even read what's being said?"

Everard hadn't gathered the courage yet, no. What would be the point? "Yes. Some of it I wrote."

D'Arcy scoffed. "*If* you were actually fucking him, I might understand. As it stands… well, nothing's standing, is it?" he said meanly.

Everard's face flamed hot. "Preston! It's done, anyway. Leave be. And while you are at it, sleep it off."

D'Arcy raised his hands and left, heels snapping unevenly, rain cloak fluttering.

Vitaliy did not even look up. It was a sort of relief.

In the end there had been no fight for his captaincy. Romilly René—the infamous Milly—had exclaimed at the approach of their gig, though she had been informed by her Jack slightly in advance of its arrival into Matagorda Bay.

Hand-in-hand, like the coffeehouse, Vitaliy had dragged Everard up onto the *Sévère*'s massive quarterdeck first thing. He'd introduced him to René—Everard could not abide "Milly" for someone so obviously authoritative—and then later announced him to an anticipatory all-hands, all-fleet crowd as what he was now: V. Varfolomey's matelot, his inheritor, his partner, who had saved his life and their pirate livelihood along with.

Everard was therefore—with a fierce, showy, and prior-agreed-upon kiss—easily read aboard. Not as captain, not as master, not as anything of authority, but as a mate. Matelot. Partner.

No one had blinked except Everard; Everard, whose jaw had dropped as four hundred hands cheered en masse below them, hats pitched high in response to their kiss like a wedding. Vitaliy, far from having to worry about being supplanted or turned out, was apparently extremely well liked.

He'd chuckled at Everard's shock, said, "Council approved," and pulled him into a second, not-prior-agreed-on-but-still-welcome kiss. Everard had responded fiercer than he'd meant.

But then Vitaliy had… abruptly left, seven long days, his motivations or destination unknown. *Take care of her; I'll be back soon.* René herself said it was nothing unusual for him, especially on the western Gulf coast, so close to his economic rival Jean Lafitte. Him, Everard had heard of.

Everard wondered if Vitaliy had a shore wife, in New Orleans or perhaps nearby Galveztown. He had no idea if he regarded women in that light. Some men didn't mention wives, even after all manner of intimacies; Vitaliy didn't seem the type.

Well, all 112 guns of the *Sévère* were still of a piece. No one had mutinied; there was not the slightest talk of an election, not since Vitaliy had miraculously survived his ordeal and had brought back thousands of pounds of goods to sell from America on the *Enemistad* besides; no one had attacked. Even the Gulf rain had held out until now, the sun setting pink and rising to blue skies, again and again.

Everard sighed and pulled the newspaper closer.

D'Arcy was right. Their plan *had* worked. No one was talking about V. Varfolomey bribing the Navy, no, sir.

The original satire—for this was a copy, done by an in-house satirist—hadn't been Everard's best work, but not his worst, either. Vitaliy hadn't wanted the block print of the trial to resemble him in any significant way, but Everard thought including the waist-to-shoulder ratio of his shirtless figure was harmless enough—and very well represented indeed. Certainly it was a distinctive-enough feature to have been copied by several satirists employed by presses up and down the Atlantic coast. The version in the *New York Journal* in particular had seemed sympathetic; they'd made both cartoon depictions roguishly handsome, and had inked twin rings on their hands, as though he and Vitaliy were protagonists of a dramatic serial and not a maritime scandal worthy of His Majesty's censure.

(Canadian gazettes, they'd heard, were now forbidden to run any but the most redacted of stories. Sodomy, it was feared, was catching.)

Here, the *Louisiana Star and Chronicle* had used Everard's full surname—their motivations for doing so painfully obvious. *De Anglada* sounded plenty foreign.

"What says the uncensored *Star and Chronicle?*" Vitaliy asked.

"Oh!" Everard started. "My apologies. D'you wish to see —?" He began to gather the newsprint, but Vitaliy shook his head.

"Er—they haven't changed the verbiage, to effect," Everard said, laying it back down. He cleared his throat. "The caption is new, though. *'John Bull's Turn-Coat Shame.'*"

Vitaliy hummed. In this version, his caricature looked almost angry to have been spoken for, rearing back from Everard's outstretched arm.

*Turn-coat shame.*

Everard said, "They have laid it on a bit thick, haven't they? Very American."

Vitaliy said nothing; he glanced up quick, and down again, needles clicking away.

*Angry* wasn't too far off the mark, come to think. Vitaliy had seemed upset to be rescued. In fact, Everard still wasn't sure Vitaliy felt at all grateful for his interventions. Obligated to him, surely, in his debt—the gold on Everard's right ring finger said that well enough.

Even if the agreement had meant nothing else in practice.

And—D'Arcy was ruthlessly correct on this point—he did mean *nothing* else. Not on the voyage of the *Enemistad*, not ashore, and not here. For all that Vitaliy's eyes had shone wide with anticipation, that day in Kingston, as he proposed they join hands and fates in matelotage, thus far he had been altogether ambivalent towards the more… traditional benefits of the agreement.

But it was for the best. While Vitaliy was already indebted to him for what he'd done, Everard couldn't broach the subject. Wouldn't. It would be putting expectations, *obligation*, on Vitaliy that he didn't have and, frankly, didn't want.

*I saved your life because we'd fucked once; now let's again as a thank-you?* No, Everard thought queasily. He thought not.

But… *had* Vitaliy offered it as part and parcel of the matelotage? Freely and openly? Did he want that? Had Everard agreed to it, unrealising?

*… unless actually in bed, with one Englishman.*

Everard might partake, if offered, perhaps—no, he'd be lying to himself if he thought he was capable of refusing. If Vitaliy had proposed they take it up again, out of interest only, perhaps as a happy clause within the agreement, purely convenient—

No. But he hadn't. Not a word. And to ask after the consummation of a barely legal pirate marriage done for the sake of public reputation? Absurd. Everard would never.

He was restless, though. Restless and wanting.

Vitaliy had hardly been present to put forward such a thing in either case. Today was the first day that he had spent longer than an hour aboard the pirate flagship. Tonight would be Vitya's first night spent aboard. Their first night, sharing this greatcabin as sworn mates.

Everard was absolutely not nervous.

He picked up the quill, dipped it, and made one tick more upon the lengthy list before him. First nights were new to Everard; administration of ships was not. His mind didn't need written lists, but it liked them, and a captain's requirement of documentation was drilled into him. Vitaliy didn't mind him making them as long as he burned them after.

Three-quarters of the way down, Everard made another tick with some trepidation, clearing his throat. This, unfortunately, he had to bring to Vitaliy's attention.

"René sent her Jack to us at breakfast. Galveztown port authority let out a corsario en route to Florida last night, with two dozen Black and one dozen Indigenous slaves aboard. Unpapered. Of course, she carries a Mexican marque."

Vitaliy's lips pressed thin.

A marque was a privateering ship's official papers, allowing her to act under authority of the issuing country—sometimes in violence. That a ship carried a marque from any rebelling Spanish colony, as Everard understood it, meant that even with the anti-slave trade laws being what they were, neither American nor British ships would seize her due to neutrality agreements; nor could they pay other privateers to do so.

It was taken advantage of by many, Varfolomey's contemporaries most of all. Jean Lafitte in particular.

"She is sure it was to Florida?" Vitaliy said.

Everard reached for the stack of papers adjacent to his left elbow. "The letter reads—"

Vitaliy waved off his ignorance with a flop of knitting. "The states are selling 'stolen' slaves back to their rescuers, at half-price, with good title. They're en route to New Orleans," he said firmly. "Afterwards they will go to Spanish Florida, slaves and fresh titles in hand."

*Profit yet to be made.* Everard frowned. The tick mark he'd scratched beside *R. René's Letter* stood out brutishly, ink slowly darkening as he stared at it.

"That's horrid."

"That is capitalism."

They shared a grim look.

"Will you try to catch her?"

Vitaliy shook his head. "I don't take slavers outright. It is too dangerous for the souls aboard. But… what was her name again, the corsair?"

Everard double-checked, mostly for show; he had the feeling Vitaliy thought his memory was mere conceit, instead of the fatiguing burden it was. "*Anemone.*"

Vitaliy stood and stretched, arms high. "Forget the rest of

the list," he said, "it will wait, and Milly will meet us at Haïti. Are you hungry?" he asked abruptly.

Everard replied he was not, gracias.

"You've eaten? No one saw you at dinner mess."

Keeping watch on him in his absence, was he?

"Earlier," Everard said. "At lunch bells, I believe."

Vitaliy looked taken aback. "It's…" He groped for a pocket watch, and Everard had a small thrill, recognising the gilt thing. "Half-nine?"

"Yes." Everard frowned. He wiped the quill, set it down, and self-consciously stacked the list onto the pile of papers to be burned. The watch bells rang every half hour, and yet Vitaliy had lost track of them? "I'm sorry," he said stiffly. "If I had known you were staying aboard tonight, then I would have requested something be brought up."

Vitaliy's expression flattened; he seemed irritated. But when he replaced the pocket watch with a one-armed shrug, the expression melted away.

"No, don't bother Rob," he said, meaning the ship's cook. He walked to the sleeping alcove. "Do you sleep to right or left?"

Everard slept in the centre like any single, average-sized man would. Was Vitaliy taking the subject where he thought he was? He looked over.

The hanging cot which Everard had been occupying the past week, alone—Vitaliy's cot, at his insistence—was not average-sized. It seemed to be a custom model, wide enough to accommodate the man's size. Wide enough for two.

Now Everard noticed that thoughtful Thom had acquired another pillow; it sat neatly beside. He felt his face turn crimson.

"I… don't," he said uncertainly.

Vitaliy gave him a sidelong look beneath his lashes. "You do not sleep either?" He began to pull his shirt from his breeches. "To which side does the lieutenant shove you, when in he sneaks?"

His true accent, slipping through; Vitaliy was more tired than he let on.

"He— I— To neither side," Everard said indignantly. He looked politely away, down to the desk, and found his hand clutching the edge of it, like his straight, tensed arm alone kept him back, kept him seated there. "D'Arcy does nothing of the sort. Sneaking."

Vitaliy hummed. "Fine, too. Though I do not think it will fit three." He paused. "It may. I've never tried."

*Three….?* Face still hot, Everard peeked over once more.

Vitaliy was down to drawers now, and not much else. Socks, too, the madman.

"I don't wake for much," Vitaliy said, "but I do object to… hummm, elbows meet ribs." He pushed aside the mosquito netting and clambered in, fell onto his back; the cot swayed, silent, with the force of it. He threw an arm over his head, large and bare and blond-fuzzed. His hair spread across the pillow like a fan.

Everard stared, suspended, bewildered.

Ought he join him? Sleep in the armchair? Find a hammock belowdecks? That last was not very mate-like, at least to crew eyes.

"And cold feet," Vitaliy breathed, already half-asleep. "I object those."

"Er," Everard began, "d'you wish that I… sleep… um…?"

"Oh, no. You can sleep where you like." Vitaliy roused slightly, and squished himself, broad shoulders and all, further into the side of the cot closest to the wall. It swung more with the movement but didn't creak. "Only, please you will keep in mind?" he murmured.

Everard supposed he had his answer. One of them, anyway.

"Cold feet," he replied, and cleared his throat. "No, of course not."

Vitaliy smiled, and fell immediately to sleep.

Everard woke first. It was still raining, a light tapping on the deck four feet above his left ear. The sun wasn't yet up, not that it mattered; once awoken, he would stay that way.

Beside him, Vitaliy seemed as though he would stay asleep. The slow sway of the cot had pushed them together in the night, and his warm naked back was practically stuck to Everard's front, both of them sheened with sweat. Last night's air had been the muggiest Everard had experienced yet in the Gulf. He hoped it would only improve. He missed the crisp snap of early Canadian fall.

And snow. He missed snow, after all. The first occasion that he and Vitaliy had slept beside one another, in the fur trader's cabin three years past, sharing warmth had been a necessity, a delight. Not a consequence.

Best not think of those memories now, pressed up against so much of the man as he was.

Everard slowly unglued himself, groaning, and rolled onto his back. He bent his right leg to keep Vitaliy from falling into him; for other reasons, too. A hank of olive-oil-soap–smelling blond stuck to his cheek. He hooked it gently free.

*I don't wake for much,* Vitaliy had said. That had been the truth.

Above them, the rain spattered louder against the deck: one of those rolling rains that sometimes preceded a hard gale. It meant Everard really ought to get up. Morning storms at sea were the most dangerous, as no one could see what manner of clouds had come towards them in the dark. But as a floating base, practically a village unto itself, the *Sévère* was already hove to, far enough from shore and sheets backed to let her go whatever unsteered way she would in the Gulf.

He should still get up, but Vitaliy was breathing deep next to him, the cot swayed comfortingly with the roll of the ship, and he didn't even have a particular need for the head; so he was unusually tempted to fall back to sleep.

Everard compromised. He put an arm behind the pillow, took a minute to think.

He didn't know why he was there.

He knew his own motivation towards saying yes to such a ludicrous arrangement—extreme curiosity, loneliness, novelty, sheer lack of option—and knew Vitaliy's given one: his reputation. But he didn't have an idea why Vitaliy had not only given Everard charge of a three-deck *Santa Ana*–class but had also signed the necessary papers to make Everard his legal inheritor to her. Nor why he had shrugged away the potential appearance of another lover, then made room like Everard belonged beside him regardless.

On the one hand, it seemed monumental; on the other, it seemed like nothing. It was either a lot of baseless trust or very little care. Everard wanted to entertain neither option.

The wind was in fact picking up, and crests were buffeting the ship irregularly now, so high that Everard could hear them slapping even there within the stern. The cot swayed more and more on its ropes. The whole ship heaved, bow up, and the desk chair scraped across the floor an inch or two: a telltale sound that would have woken Everard in a moment had he not already been alert and listening.

Vitaliy, however, was dead to the world.

Everard raised up on elbows, mindful of the low mosquito net, and looked over. Vitaliy's sleeping profile, barely visible in the dark, was as beautiful as ever.

He whispered, "Vee?" and raised a hand to nudge—

Sitting up had been a mistake. A sudden lurch turned gravity sideways, and sent Vitaliy's bulk flopping back as the cot swung, sent Everard bodily into him. "Oof."

Vitaliy began to grumble and stir, hands reaching, groping—

"Sorry," Everard said, "hang on—we've heeled a bit, it'll come round—"

An arm came round his waist, clutched him close. Held him there, strong as an iron band. Everard froze.

"Vitya?"

"Mmm." Vitaliy shifted restlessly, still holding Everard close. His other arm wrapped around, almost in a hug—and all at once he used the sway-roll momentum of the ship heeling back to larboard to shimmy his body further beneath Everard's. He fit Everard's hips neatly over his own, and made a deeply pleased noise, low in his throat.

Everard had already been in a bit of a precarious situation, prick-wise; the pleased noise certainly didn't help. Then gravity resembled its normal self, and brought Everard's weight down. Vitaliy was as hard and hot beneath his drawers as Everard; he couldn't help but gasp.

Vitaliy splayed his legs accommodatingly, slotting Everard between broad firm thighs; he rutted up, a roll of hips. He mumbled, "Mmm?"

*Holy Good God,* Everard thought. Vitaliy wanted him after all.

He really hadn't had expectations, but...

"Wait," he groaned, "wait, Vitya. We can't—that is, we shouldn't, not now."

Vitaliy's arm held fast around his waist; his other hand gripped onto Everard's arse and clutched him insistently closer.

Everard resisted, held his hips as still as he could bear—they seemed to want to press and grind of their own accord—and tried to prop up more of his weight on his knees. What he wanted was to do precisely the opposite, to put hands to either side of Vitaliy's waist, let his weight fully down, kiss him, everywhere. But Vitaliy's strangeness held him back.

He remembered a lazy, sleepy midnight conjugation, once upon a time; Vitya had been quiet, but intensely responsive all the same.

*A man can't change so much in three years.*

"Vee?" Everard rested his forehead on the other man's. "Are you awake?" he whispered. "You don't seem quite yourself."

Vitaliy grunted, "Mhm."

It sounded affirmative enough. And the rutting continued against him, slow and molten. Everard kissed the soft mouth carefully with closed lips—as perhaps he could coax the man to his normal responsiveness that way—and received a dark, needy whimper that sank straight into his gut. Hadn't he heard that sound in his dreams ever since?

Still he held back.

"Vitya," he said regretfully; every bit of him trembled with restraint. "It's still raining—there's a storm."

"Evra'd," Vitaliy mumbled, and then was silent. Everard, really alarmed now, raised higher to look at him properly.

What seaman didn't react to the word *storm*?

Vitaliy's eyes were closed, and a tiny furrow creased between his eyebrows; his lips were red and parted, unsmiling, his breath increasing. His hips moved up, up, up, and his hands roamed, all over, up Everard's back and down again, clutching.

Everard bit his lower lip, hard. The exquisite drag of linen between their pricks seemed suddenly very, very wrong.

For Vitaliy wasn't awake. Not at all.

"Vitaliy," he said urgently now, one hand pushing down on the man's warm hip to put more space between them, the other pushing himself up, not wanting to break his grip too harshly. "Wake up. Vitya."

Nothing, except increasingly aggressive rutting, murmurs of what sounded like encouragement in slippery, lilting Russian. Vitaliy's legs wrapped round Everard's own, pulling them closer, closer.

Everard said, "Vee," loudly. "Vitya," he said, directly into an ear.

Sant Jesús, the man was completely insensible.

"For God's sake," he said, even louder. "Vee, wake up!"

Vitaliy inhaled like someone surfacing. The rutting stopped abruptly, and Everard felt the man's awakening jar into his bones. Muscle and limbs stiffened, and hands jerked away from Everard's arse. Blue eyes opened in bleary horror.

Thus freed, Everard quickly pushed himself up, backing onto his knees. Vitaliy sat up, too, shoving back into the corner of the cot, breathing hard. Prick still hard, too, Everard noted dimly, though he knew that meant nothing at all. Not compared to the thin-lipped look of disgust on Vitaliy's face.

Everard's stomach dropped. Dear God, he'd assaulted an unconscious man. One who, in the daylight, hadn't encouraged him at all.

"Oh, God. I'm sorry." He scrambled out of the cot so fast, he sent it swinging anew and almost fell. He caught himself luckily with his left hand against the rug, and picked himself up, so ashamed he felt his skin would dry to a crisp around his bones. "I'm so—"

"Don't," Vitaliy said thickly, harshly. A wakening voice, truly this time. His fist gripped the cot's corner rope tight, his arm wrapped round, like an unsure child did on a swing. "Wait. Please."

Everard waited, not that he knew what for, or where he would go in drawers and nothing else.

Above their heads, the rain came again, a sheet of it falling down, and then another, in unmistakable rhythm. Vitaliy looked up, eyes wide. "A storm?" His expression twisted, and fell into flat, bitter understanding. "Tell me. What have I done?"

Everard stared. "What *you've* done?" he said, incredulous. "Nothing. It was me, my fault. I'm truly sorry. I didn't realise at first that you weren't aw—"

"Nothing?" Vitaliy said. He looked down to his still hard, linen-concealed stand, as if he didn't recognise it, his expression strange. "I did nothing?"

"Well, there was…" Everard was torn between the truth and reassurance. Because it was definitely not nothing, what had happened, but, in Everard's eyes, it was also nothing serious, what Vitaliy had done. What *he* had, though…

"You were… er… I was… I believe you wanted me to…"

"Oh," Vitaliy said, relaxing slightly, "like that?" His shoulder dropped as his hand groped low, beneath him, exploring.

"No!" Everard's face burned. "Jesús," he cursed. "I wouldn't have— I didn't— Nothing happened."

Vitaliy exhaled. "Nothing." His eyes narrowed. "Why not?"

"Er." Everard blinked. "Because you were…" Too insistent? Not insistent enough—in the proper way? "… asleep?"

Vitaliy's knuckles on the rope were white knots of tension as he pulled himself out of the cot and swung gracefully down. Half-naked, still hard and unconcerned for it, he walked to the night-black windows. The rain whipped the six-panes with pitter-patter drops and shining rivulets.

"I should apologise," Vitaliy said slowly. "Not you. I should've… warned you. It doesn't happen often, only when storms are imminent, or I am extremely tired." He grimaced. "When I have not been with someone for a long time, too. I don't ever remember the act, so it is easy to forget it happens at all." He crossed his arms around himself, big shoulders slumping. "I did not think it through. I'm sorry."

Everard didn't know what to say. He was—and this was putting it mildly—horrified. And not on his own behalf.

Vitaliy looked over his shoulder from within a curtain of hair. He pushed it behind one ear and peered at him anxiously. "I did not do anything you did not like? Or…" He swallowed, "… Did not want?"

"No!" Everard said hastily. "I liked all of it, up to the point I realised you were completamen—completely—insensate. That was the only part that was… objectionable."

Vitaliy nodded again. He seemed relieved. "In past episodes, I have usually been the receptive party."

*Episodes.* Everard felt sick. It had happened before, and Vitaliy didn't *remember* it? Remember men taking advantage of him? Rolling him over, pushing up his legs, making him whimper and accommodate them?

"No one's ever woken you? Never?"

Vitaliy turned halfway. "One other, once. No one else much minded I was asleep, no. Not enough to tell me they did. I do eventually wake," he added, with an uneasy smile. "And it hasn't happened in… years. A decade. Longer."

Everard did a quick calculation. A decade, more: from what he'd said three years past, ten years before had been Vitaliy in the Marines, Vitaliy pressed into the Navy.

"God. I'd like to give them all what-for—"

There was a hasty knock, and the greatcabin door swung open. Thom stuck his head in.

"Storm, sirs" was all he said before popping back out.

"Shite," Everard cursed.

The rain was in fact hitting the deck harder, and voices and footsteps of the hands abovedeck had grown tenser, louder with alarm. A hard gale, at the least.

Everard went to his trunk and pulled out knee breeches and a waistcoat. One leg in, he was obliged to crouch and clutch at the trunk, as another sharp heel of the ship to starboard almost sent him sprawling.

"Gah. It's a storm, all right."

Against the roll, Vitaliy had only leaned, thighs tensed, arms raised to take hold of the rafters above. He, better than Everard, knew the heel and heave of his ship, felt every push of water and wind in his centre. He offered his hand as the ship righted; Everard took it.

"I'd run her, won't you?" Everard asked, pulling his waistcoat shut. "We're out far enough."

Not that any sailor with half a brain would dare put a *Santa Ana*–class between a lee shore and the northeasterly trades, and have her at risk of running aground. They had more than plenty of room to open the sails and flee the storm, using its own gale.

"Yes," Vitaliy said softly. "Put her out before the wind. She can take it."

At 2,100 tons and a draught height of almost seven-and-a-half meters, stuffed to ribs with cargo and enough rations to last two hundred men the winter, Everard damned well hoped the meregildo could take it. Unless the storm was a hurricane —then they were probably fucked, no matter what size ship they tied themselves to.

"All right." He eyed Vitaliy's still-bare chest. "Are you not coming above?"

"Go tell León to fly her, as far as she'll go," Vitaliy said. "It's time for the *Sévère* to come out of hiding." He about-faced and stepped close. "Thank you for waking me," he said. Carefully, slowly, smoothly, he leaned in, and, seeing no resistance, kissed a stunned Everard on the mouth.

There was nothing of revulsion in the way Vitaliy's closed lips pressed sweetly against Everard's, the way his hands bracketed Everard's face, the way his fingers curled into Everard's hair.

The ship began to roll again. Vitaliy pulled back. "I'll come up in a moment. Don't forget to tie yourself down."

Twelve-ish hours later, they'd made it through. The storm hadn't been a hurricane, thank God; it had come in from the west, a land storm that'd strengthened over the warm water of the coast before it reached them; but it had been fierce, hard enough to push the *Sévère* to the edge of a loop current. Now she had been put hove to, with most of her sheets tied up, made into a floating village once more; almost every watch took a well-deserved meal and rest.

At sunset, fresh off his own turn at a short but badly needed nap below, Everard climbed the hatch and gratefully took in the scent of a light wind coming off a calm Gulf sea. And then, with almost more gratitude, he took in the sight of Vitaliy Gray.

The man was perched in the starboard-side foremast shroud, a dark silhouette against a purple-orange dusk. He was alone, coatless, unusually shirtless—he almost never bared his skin to the daylight—in belt, breeches, and boots. His left knee bent at a right angle to the one beside it, and his arms were slung behind his back, elbows hooked over lines. A classic sailor's pose, for a rare moment of rest, of observing a beautiful post-storm sunset.

Everard almost didn't want to disturb him. But while Vitaliy clung high enough to take in a decent view—six or seven lines up from the rail—he was also still within spoken earshot. Accessible.

And sure enough, he heard Everard coming. He turned his head in profile, greeted him before Everard tried to say anything.

"Matelot." Though Vitaliy's voice was roughened from hours of yelling, retching, inhaling salt spray from the storm, the word sounded lovelier in his fur trader's French than it did in others' workaday Jackspeak. *Ma-te-lou.*

"Vee," Everard replied with a smile, though he wished he could call Vitaliy by his name and not the moniker. He touched his hat out of habit, remembering too late that Vitaliy didn't care for deference.

Vitaliy looked tired and strangely wary. Everard felt his smile falter. He didn't like feeling that Vitaliy was reluctant to see him, though it was certainly understandable if he was.

But he pressed on. A man wanting to be left totally alone would've climbed higher, out of reach.

"Calm at last."

Vitaliy nodded once. Then, quietly, he said, "Yes."

Everard, heartened by this small effort, said, "Will you not take a rest shift?"

Vitaliy looked over in surprise. "Now?"

"I hope I haven't kept you from it."

Vitaliy stared down, still and intense, saying nothing.

"I wanted to make you aware there's no hesitation on my part," Everard said, "in sharing your bed. To sleep," he clarified hastily. "I would wake you whenever... whenever is needed. That is, if you would trust me to do so. If not, I can easily find other—"

"It's not that," Vitaliy rasped. "You can sleep where you like, with me, with whomever. Or not sleep. But look: the water is too blue."

A crystal-blue sea. Deep, deep water; it meant they were well into the Gulf.

"Smack on ninety degrees west," Everard agreed.

Their latitude, too, was concerning. The storm had pushed them into the deeper waters southeast of Louisiana—the most dangerous area of the Gulf, and not only because it was August and nearly hurricane season. They were directly placed along Jean Lafitte's well-known routes.

"It is farther east than I've been in some time," Vitaliy said.

"Kingston was seventy-six degrees west," Everard pointed out.

Vitaliy slid him a patient look. "Farther east than I've brought the *Sévère* in some time," he corrected. "I cannot rest. I must keep watch."

Earlier, when the storm had ceased and the wind had died to almost nothing, the sun was pulled to the horizon in the sextant, and they found she'd run much farther than they'd thought.

Vitaliy had clicked shut the hack watch—his gilt pocket watch, temporarily put into service keeping Greenwich Mean —and cursed. "You were right." A natural navigator, his mind worked maths and maps the way Everard's did the written word, and easily time, distance, and speed came together to confirm their charting. "Ninety degrees west, forty-one north."

Everard yawned. "Halfway to Florida. Should we have kept her hove to instead?"

"No, no. I agreed to run her." Vitaliy gestured to León, the bo'sun, straight-backed at his side. "Heave to, but keep a full watch after the first rest," he ordered. "Everyone is to keep a sharp eye. The sharpest," he emphasised.

"Señor." León nodded, and Everard could tell he approved. *Time to come out of hiding.*

Not just well liked, Everard realised then. A true captain, Varfolomey hardly ever had to say any order twice.

Now Vitaliy looked up to the topsail. "Hoist the Spanish, while we're at it?"

The Spanish flag; an almost impenetrable alias, given that the meregildo was Spanish-built.

"It may be advisable, so close to Florida," Everard said. "Unless she is too well known for subterfuge?"

Vitaliy shook his head. "Eh, no. Not if we don't raise the black. There are six of her, identical. One with the British, too, I believe? I will nail the disguise myself."

The disguise in question was a thin, curved, and cleverly painted piece of hull, meant to attach to the quarter gallery and rename the *Sévère* as her sister-meregildo doppelganger, the *Reina Luisa*.

"Yourself?" Everard said. "Have the carpenters do it, for God's sake; they weren't abovedecks all night, in the spray. You're so tired, you'll kick through a window, like as not." He thought of Vitaliy with lead and glass shards stuck in his ankle, his calf, his thigh, slicing through the femoral—they'd got through the storm intact and now this—

Vitaliy's eyebrows rose a fraction, increasing the depths of the hollows around his dark, dusk-lit eyes. "Am I?" he said mildly.

"Well, I was about that tired myself, anyway."

Vitaliy shrugged.

"Look," Everard said, "I'll leave you the cot, if that's the issue. I can bunk with Preston, wherever he is. But you should re—"

"Sail!" came a cry.

Vitaliy swung himself down to the deck. No longer than a second with a glass to his eye—produced from apparently nowhere—and he had relaxed.

"It is Milly, and the *Birch*."

Everard startled. The *Birch* was meant to have come from Belize; to already intercept the *Sévère* when she had been thrown by the storm was an impressive feat. "So soon, and with the storm?"

"The *Birch* makes six knots," Vitaliy said, climbing the ladder to the quarterdeck two steps at a time. "We're back on trajectory, and there's nobody better at a dead reckon than Romilly. Especially the *Sévère*'s." Everard followed, trying not to stare. Vitaliy's shoulders gleamed moon-white in the slanting sunlight. There was not a single scar upon his back—the tell of having been beneath a good former captain, or perhaps only that Vitaliy had kept a low profile during his time with the Marines—but he did have a spread of densely packed freckles, twin wings across the shoulder blades. Fascinating.

"She must know the ship quite well."

"Very," Vitaliy said bluntly. He called to León with cupped hands. "Signal her to fall back—to come alongside at dawn!"

"Oh, indeed?" Everard said.

Vitaliy nodded. "We took her together. She named her."

*And then you made me your matelot, and gave half of her to me?*

Romilly René was a close and faithful second; that much was clear. She'd kept the flotilla afloat and intact and crewed the entirety of Vitaliy's absence, no small thing. But to what precise *degree* of close and faithful, Everard was afraid to ask, for fear of what he'd find. Had she been expecting what he had given to Everard? Partnership? Inheritance?

*Women are more than lovers or wives,* he reminded himself. *They're ruthless, too.* This one was second-in-command to a pirate fleet.

"But in the end she preferred the *Birch*. All-women crew, you see," Vitaliy added.

"The *Birch?*" Everard startled. *A select crew.* "I didn't know. How odd."

"Is it?" Vitaliy murmured. He put the glass back to his eye and cursed. "Ah, damn. She has Louis-Michel with her."

Louis-Michel. Very informal, that.

"Oh, Alarie?" Louis-Michel Alarie: the incumbent governor of Galveztown, appointed under authority of revolutionary México. From what little Vitaliy had said of him, the man fancied himself a nation-state maker of the likes of Washington. "What has his own navy?"

Despite how disdainfully Vitaliy, the man, had spoken of

Alarie, Everard got the impression that Varfolomey, the pirate, was wary of him—or at the least, held him in careful consideration.

"Aye." Vitaliy handed him the glass. "He's been a privateer, too, in his own right. But call him governor to his face. He has a temper."

The *Birch* was quick, even in the post-storm calm, for she was a galley frigate, with sail, oars, and a full rowing crew—of women, apparently, who knew—at her disposal. She was close enough that Everard could in fact see Romilly René standing at the bow, her tall column of dark curly hair, and a man close at her side: shorter, but standing slim and proud and regal in what looked like impeccable emerald satin.

"They're making good time." Everard raised an eyebrow. "You didn't mention Alarie was a dandy."

*And handsome, too,* he didn't say.

"He's French," Vitaliy said shortly, as though this explained away it all. "And he can wait until the morrow." He jogged down the quarterdeck ladder, disappearing below.

*Hmm.* Left with the glass, Everard raised it once more. Louis-Michel Alarie: temperamental filibuster, dandy, privateer, commodore of the Galveztown navy.

More judgment than that, Everard would reserve.

# Thirteen

I t became immediately too dark to risk the *Birch* coming alongside safely, but her captain seemed content with the signal of wait-for-dawn. She pulled back to a comfortable distance, her own raised Spanish melting into the orange sunset.

But her looming presence nonetheless caused Vitaliy's vigilance to wane slightly. He declared it a holiday of leisure due the storm, and had rum and port wine and gin pulled up from the stores, to great enthusiasm. Petty gambling in card games was temporarily allowed—which Everard thought was unwise but refrained from saying so—and drums and music made enclaves of merriment wherever one went throughout the three-decked ship.

Subtlety was not required of the *Sévère*, even in enemy territory. Most captains, even pirate ones, would pause at attacking a galley frigate and her meregildo escort.

Despite all this, Vitaliy himself still insisted on standing watch in the ratlines, in the tops. Everard attempted initially to keep him company, but León the bo'sun, high on victory against the sea, pulled him beneath his arm and dragged him into a round of chanties on the weather deck before he could insist otherwise. And one round turned into several, and fingers of liquor, hands of cards…

They gathered their breath in the dining parlour: León in search of more rum, Everard in search of where the hell D'Arcy could've got to. A whole port wine cask brought up a half hour since, and Everard hadn't had eyes on him since the return of the seas to tranquilidad—

"Oye, ten." León handed him a tin tumbler. Everard clutched it to his chest, then handed it abruptly back.

"No, mejor no."

León was the *Sévère*'s impressively bearded, brown-complexioned bo'sun of two years: by his own definition, half Indigenous Mexica, half Spanish Criollo. The language of the *Sévère* was broadly French, but with him, Everard found himself slipping into Spanish that was less and less a sailor's neutral Castilian and more his own childhood, rural patois. León apparently found the lack of distinction between Everard's *s*'s and *c*'s endlessly amusing; and for some reason after the revelation of el seseo, he'd that night stopped calling Everard Spaniard, which Everard appreciated profoundly.

He felt still too recently arrived and, if not detached from, then still *other* to the crew; to be accused of not only *Navy man* but *Spaniard*…

The problem was Everard felt more unsure of his place there than he'd ever been aboard a ship, undefined as his role was as Varfolomey's matelot—and he'd never possessed an easy camaraderie with anyone in the first place.

Well, excepting D'Arcy, but Preston had given them no option but to be intimate, like it was and had been forever inevitable between them.

… perhaps a thought for a soberer Everard. But—where *was* he?

León stood at the bottom of the ladder, waiting patiently.

He really was very friendly, and very attractive, and very skilled at the upkeep and scheduling of a pirate meregildo.

"Thank God the *Birch* crew was held off 'til dawn," Everard mused to the man as they unsteadily surfaced to the weather deck.

"¿Y eso porqué?" León asked amusedly.

"Erm. Because on the *Birch* they're ladies. Lady pirates. Women." He belched. He had not been quite this affected by liquor in some years. "They should not… It will begin to get… It is already a bit brutish here. Really, no, thank you," he said, to the proffered rum.

León handed the mug to a grateful passersby. "Brutish?" His eyebrows rose. He chuckled. "I forget. You haven't met Romilly's women. I dunno if you have seen what rowing does to the physique…"

He made a suggestive noise, and gave Everard a warm, encouraging look over his mug, one that was clearly meant to be reciprocated. Or appreciated. Perhaps he wanted Everard to appreciate women's physiques?

Either way, León possessed an appealing, soul-deep sensuality that Everard was not at all used to being on the receiving end of. He certainly seemed easy to say yes to. And the fact that he was seeking yeses—at the very least Everard's encouragement—beneath Vitaliy's nose seemed quite bold.

Almost literally beneath Vitya's nose now.

Everard put his hand on the stanchion rail, looked up. Vitya was still there in the foretop, leaning on elbows, hair loose and blown back by Gulf breeze. Tireless.

"Ya veo como es." León sighed. "Vale. Best I go." He put a hand on Everard's elbow, drew him back away from the rail. "Don't climb the shrouds as you are, friend. You will not convince him to come down tonight, anyway."

"What is he vigilant for?" Everard muttered. "Men overboard? Jean Lafitte? It's two in the morning."

León laughed. "Sometimes he is just like this, man." He saluted. "Drink water. Sleep. Find your lieutenant, maybe. Vee will see you at the rendezvous."

He was probably correct. He'd had it from Vitya's own mouth.

*Sleep where you like.*

After some enquiring, leveraging social clout he didn't feel he possessed, and a little outright bribery, Everard eventually found D'Arcy: asleep in the old teniente's quarters two decks below. How the devil D'Arcy had acquired the use of an officer's apartment on a ship of two hundred pirates he didn't know but didn't care, so long as it didn't harbour fleas. Everard crawled in top and tail; D'Arcy murmured his name and curled a hand contently around his left knee; and that was that.

Until: the hand on his leg tightened, and fingers wiggled underneath, scritch-scritched in the soft hollow.

"Gah." Everard squirmed sideways. "D'you mind?"

D'Arcy laughed huskily. "You're drunk," he whispered. "How novel."

"You're not," Everard retorted. "How novel."

"Mmm." Less amused.

"Why not join in?"

"I've watch at eight bells. Also, didn't feel like it."

"You and Vee both."

"That surprises me not at all."

Everard frowned to the darkness. "You're still angry with me."

A pause. A long breath. "Yes, rather."

Everard made a hesitant noise, a squeaky, beginning-of-sentence noise.

"No," D'Arcy interrupted him. "Not right now, Ev. Sleep it off."

Everard was still for a moment. Then:

"Budge over?"

D'Arcy sighed. "We're not nineteen, Everard—this is a single-wi— *Oof.*"

Everard hummed happily. D'Arcy didn't wear drawers or a nightshirt to bed; he was sleekly fuzzy absolutely everywhere.

"I hate when you're tipsy," D'Arcy whispered, resigned. He put a hand up to Everard's head, left it gently there, curved over his skull.

"No, you don't."

Sometime in the night, D'Arcy had maneuvered them into opposite positions, so that Everard was to the outside, one arm hanging, and it was D'Arcy who was squished against the apartment panelling, draped halfway over him. Everard lay awake in the dark predawn, sober, sweating all over, with silken curls in his face and drool on his shirt.

"Preston," he whispered.

"Mmn."

"Preston, you're angry with me."

"Recently?" the man breathed, into Everard's left pectoral. "Yes. Right now? 'm asleep. So should you be. Some of us have responsibilities to get to in the morning."

Everard was silent. It was a fair point.

He… didn't, not really.

He'd worked as much as he could without stepping on anyone's toes; ships always needed something done, and after twenty-four years of sailing, there was nothing he didn't know how to do, even on a meregildo. But Vitaliy had said—at least implied—he keep his head down, and León hadn't given him anything on which to focus. He had no position. No outlined duties. Nothing.

The one contribution he'd made was shave a good thirty

seconds off the gun drill, and even then, it wasn't significant; 110 guns at a firing rate of a ball every two minutes was… obliteration, in no uncertain terms, to almost every other ship upon the sea. Not to mention there was no formal gunner nor gun crew; in keeping with Vitaliy's egalitarian policies and rotating schedules, his pirates were generally unspecialised. Rather anti–Adam Smith of him. Well, he thought, anti-Smith, except where it gave the pirates the potential to specialise themselves where they wanted, instead of being obliged to, say, haul lines for years on end…

In *either* case, most of them knew how to call a cadence and load powder and shot already; and anyway, they weren't truly a warship. Everard was, on a whole, unnecessary.

"All right, sorry." He wriggled free, ignoring D'Arcy's soft grunt, and slid over the side, lowered himself onto the floor. He grabbed his boots and his hat and his coat. "I will let you sleep."

As he closed the door behind him, he heard D'Arcy's low cursing, scrabbling as he rolled himself over the wooden side of the cot. "Oh, for fuck's… Everrr," he groaned. "Wait—"

Outside the apartment threshold, Everard bent to replace his boots. D'Arcy caught up with him, barefoot and bare-legged in a billowing shirt.

"I didn't mean take yourself off," he muttered, putting his forehead on the doorway. "I meant… Wait. I thought you'd something to say to me?"

"I don't. I did. I don't know."

"Of course." D'Arcy blinked sleepily, squinted one eye. "Sure you're sober?"

Everard sighed. "Yes. It was only… Yes."

D'Arcy waited.

"I'm sorry," Everard blurted. "I wanted to… I feel as though I must apologise."

D'Arcy lifted his head. His curls were spiky and wild from

shared humidity and using Everard as a pillow. He looked astonished. "For what? For waking me? Or…"

Everard blew out a breath. "For—everything, I suppose."

"Ooh." D'Arcy held up a palm, a boy about to receive a sweet, and then wiggled his fingers. "Which encompasses…?"

Everard crossed arms over himself and glared at the hand. "Not answering your letters. To start."

"Aha." D'Arcy reached out to Everard's elbow. "I like this. This is worth the getting up." He nudged Everard closer, pulled with a single rough finger. His eyes were very dark. "Go on, what else?"

Everard took one step forward. "Not trusting you."

D'Arcy began to back slowly into the apartment, one hand still curled beneath Everard's left elbow through the linen; his only beckon.

The only physical beckon. There was much to be said about the state of his eyes, the deep rough of his voice.

"Mmhm. There's a lot you don't know, true. But keep on."

Everard took two more steps. "I'm sorry for dragging you along here, to the *Sévère*. For the loss of the *Brigitte*." His career, like Everard's, gone in a single shot. "The *Wanderer*, too."

D'Arcy grunted. "Acceptable losses, and neither of them your fault, mind. Especially the *Wanderer*. That decision you made under orders, with myself and four others to consult."

By now they stood half-deep in the apartment, close together in near-total darkness. Everard's breathing had begun to stutter, take thought to regulate. D'Arcy's too.

Everard whispered, "Mostly, I'm sorry for being impulsive, with Vee. Perhaps not thinking the agreement—the matelotage quite through." What had it got them? Any of them?

D'Arcy reached over his shoulder, pushed the door shut. He didn't take his eyes off Everard, not once, even as the dark shuttered close around them.

"It's your decision, Ever, and it's done. Here we are now."

He stepped closer, breathed in Everard's air as quickly as he let it out. "I'll take standby. I'll take whatever you'll give. Just don't go on to apologise for forgetting me, hmm?"

"I couldn't do that. I tried. To no avail."

D'Arcy put his forehead on Everard's shoulder and groaned. "If I'm shit at lists, you're shit at apologies." He laughed, soft in Everard's ear. "An apology for that would be 'I'm sorry, Preston, for denying both of us... this...'" His hand found Everard's left wrist, pulled it close beneath the hem of his shirt, to his arse. "... for the past year and more."

"*That's* what you wished me to apologise for?" Everard said, disbelieving. "I'm sorry, then. For your poor, poor, neglected prick." His hand squeezed of its own accord. "Come on, now. I'm sure you had plenty of company to help you through such a trial."

"Maybe I did. Stubborn ass. Come here."

He kissed Everard. A fierce, biting kiss, harshly breathless, strangely goading. It was all D'Arcy: *You think I can't make you feel?*

Everard returned it in kind. *You think I don't feel?*

He pulled D'Arcy's nightshirt between his thumb and knuckles. Slid it against D'Arcy's upper thigh, the hollow of his hip, higher, pushed it up, up, up.

D'Arcy wrenched his mouth free, gasping; he shrugged, and the shirt was gone over his head, his curls skewed even wilder than before. "Please fuck me."

D'Arcy, fearless and direct and demanding as always. It worked extraordinarily well on Everard.

"Yes," he said.

He pulled D'Arcy's mouth back against his and rucked up his own shirt. Unbuttoned his breeches only so far as was necessary, and shuffled them backward. They bumped into what served as the apartment's little desk. It was narrow, not more than a foot wide, more a part of the wall than actual furniture. It would suffice.

"Find aught to hang on to," Everard muttered into D'Arcy's neck, and then spun him.

D'Arcy groaned. "Christ. God."

But he obeyed, raising his arms, clutching onto the shelving above them. His arms flexed, corded and taut. Everard watched the shoulders bunch in the darkness, and hoped the fixtures could take it.

He knew D'Arcy could.

Everard knelt.

"Oh, my God." D'Arcy looked down over his shoulder. "Really, the cot is right there—"

"Don't," Everard said roughly. He drew his hands up smoothly furred thighs and splayed them. Tugged on the hollows of D'Arcy's hips, the narrow, muscular arse, until D'Arcy reneged, cursing, and arched the small of his back.

Then, in his second-favorite manner, Everard applied himself to another man.

D'Arcy breathed hard. "You could have—some time ago— turned me over and…" He moaned; a hand came down onto Everard's head, wove through his hair, urging him and his tongue forward. "Ff… thaa-at. Done that."

D'Arcy, in his most intimate place, was as hot as sin, silky with sable curls, mild and salty: from seawater, or maybe half a night's sleep worth of clean sweat. Everard wondered what the clear green Lake Ontario would have tasted like, there and elsewhere on his skin—after a night swim, a rock-beach picnic, a breathtaking forest cliff dive—

D'Arcy had asked to be put on the Lakes Service for a reason. Was this the reason?

Maybe he should apologise for denying them a year's worth of assignations.

Too late now. And beyond time to stop thinking, besides.

After a little while, D'Arcy was cursing and trembling above him, very close to release, and thoroughly ready for fucking. Everard drew back, satisfied with his work, and bit gently onto the firm curve of arse, breathed deep through his nose to calm his own arousal a bit.

"Preston," he muttered. "You're lovely. Who've you been keeping yourself so neat for?"

D'Arcy detached his clenched fingers from Everard's hair, lifted his head from between taut, trembling shoulders. "Wha?"

"St. Clare?" Everard murmured. He brought his right hand round, to D'Arcy's front, and stroked the slick length of him, slow and careful.

D'Arcy laughed, breathless. He let his forehead fall to the partition wall. "Bell? No, I don't think this is… quite… what he likes."

"Mmm? No? Seguro?" *Are you sure?* He kissed and nipped, because he could. "Has he tried it?"

D'Arcy groaned and rocked, forth and back. "Not with me."

Everard, mildly surprised, let him fuck his hand for a few more thrusts, then pulled away.

"Who, then?"

D'Arcy grunted at the loss. "Oh, that was a serious question? Not just possessive banter?" He raised his head and gave Everard a damp-curls, darkened-brow glare over his shoulder. "Who for? Would you not be so utterly dense?"

"What?"

"Christ, Everard." D'Arcy had been pliable and loose in his hands; now he stiffened all over.

"Oh. Not for me?" Everard stared up. "No. Really?"

"Of course for you, sod it all." D'Arcy sighed and used his free hand to rub at his sweat-slick face. "Ugh," he muttered. "I'm going to lose my stand. And it was an impressive one. This was going so well." He straightened, and let go the shelving. "There, it went. I don't know why you must always look so disbelieving," he said, to the wall.

"Disbelieving?" Everard managed.

"Horrified, then." D'Arcy sidestepped away, out of reach. "And here I thought it was only that I was your lieutenant that put you off."

"Put me... Of course it was that!" Everard protested. "There was a clear imbalance— I was your superior—"

"And then you weren't. But no," D'Arcy went on, "it was your complete and utter distaste towards affection. Mine, my affection. Since you have accepted and disseminated your pirate's showy commitment just fine."

The Eton schoolboy had returned; a bad sign. Everard stood creakily, rubbing at his knees. "That isn't real."

"Horseshit it isn't." D'Arcy stooped to pick up his shirt. "If it weren't, he wouldn't have done it. And what is real?" he demanded. "Does your repetitive denial of my feelings negate them into nothing? Make this"—he gestured between them, a swooping shadow in the dark—"somehow illegitimate?"

Everard opened his mouth, but D'Arcy held up a hand. "Do not you dare say it's only real when reciprocated and that you do not. I'll take standby, Everard, but by God—not that."

Everard winced. "You're not... standby. Of course it is real. And...and reciprocated," he admitted. "You realise I wouldn't have been much use to you, just now, if it weren't. I am terribly fond of you. I always have been."

D'Arcy huffed. "You'll excuse me if I don't quite believe it."

Everard's chest squeezed. "I'm sorry you didn't realise."

D'Arcy crossed his arms over his own chest.

"Well, no," Everard revised hastily. "That wasn't it. I didn't let you realise it. I didn't make it known."

"In fact," D'Arcy said, "you made the opposite well known to me. Went out of your way, I'd say. Three *years*."

"That's fair." Everard swallowed. He had no excuses that weren't utterly caddish, selfish, cowardly. But maybe D'Arcy wanted them regardless. "It was a bit excessive. I realise that. But it wasn't intentional."

D'Arcy raised disbelieving eyebrows.

"Really," Everard insisted. "I hadn't meant to let it go so long. And they kept arriving. Each one made it more difficult to write back. Made the gap larger. Not that I didn't welcome them! I treasured them." He gestured to his head. "They're here, Preston. Forever. I don't need to carry them with me, and not only because my brain is the way it is."

"You kept C's letters," D'Arcy said, almost inaudible.

Everard gestured helplessly. "He died before I was in the habit of not keeping things. Personal property. Afterward, I couldn't rid of them, it'd be like to kill him twice. I don't… You weren't going to die," he said fiercely.

"But I *could* have."

Everard resolutely ignored this.

"And then you made post of your own, and that seemed right. It was vindication. I knew… I *thought* maybe I had held you back from promotion, those years. From your seeking it."

D'Arcy laughed, somewhat bitterly. "Promotion in the art of war. Against this. Against us. Absolutely, that's what I wanted."

"Well, wasn't it?" Everard demanded. "Why else accept the posting?"

D'Arcy spread his hands. "Admiralty demand? Money? Paternal order? Yes, why else accept a dead-end posting in the great wilderness of peacetimes Canada, I wonder."

"Oh, now, really."

"Probably I knew you'd wished I were your equal." D'Arcy raised his chin. "And then I was, and you still wanted nothing doing. What d'you think of that?"

Everard didn't have an idea what to think. "Don't tell me that *is* why," he rasped.

"Then I shan't tell you."

"I… One doesn't just uproot their whole life for another! Not for nothing!"

D'Arcy reared back.

"No. Not for nothing," he said coldly. He sidestepped around Everard with quick, stiff movements, wrenched open the door. "Only you are allowed that, matelot."

# Fourteen

"Lovebirds, hello!" came a loud call from below the rail: Romilly René.

She quick-stepped up the ladder and over, skirts and lace flaring.

Romilly René was a tall Frenchwoman of about Everard's age, with thick brown curls wrung into corkscrews, and from the look of it, a fondness for powder and rouge, shaped beauty marks, and quantities of lace. Like Vitaliy, she was slightly out of current mode; also like Vitaliy, the old fashion suited her well. Everard imagined she'd been born a half-century too late, and the world had simply refused to conform to her, instead of the other way round.

She strode onto the quarterdeck, imperial as a queen, and Everard tipped his hat. He didn't bother asking himself how a staggeringly beautiful woman in a bow-strewn waistcoat, sword belt, and panniers came to be elected pirate quartermaster of a seven-ship fleet, captain of an all-women rowing crew; his world-views had been turned quite upside down since a small village's worth of people had cheered at seeing him kiss another man. It merely was; the rest seemed irrelevant.

How she climbed the ratlines in Rocaille panniers, however…

Perhaps they were detachable, like a cape. He had less than zero knowledge of women's clothing beyond the visible superficie.

And in any case, she wore a proper hat, a functional-looking straw broad brim with ribbons and a feather.

"Fleet master René," he greeted.

"Matelot Everard! Good to see you once again," she said sincerely, in English.

She turned aside, and greeted Vitaliy with busses on each sharp cheek. She was tall enough that Vitaliy didn't have to bend much for her to reach him; a good thing, because Vitaliy had put on a pair of tight breeches and equally restrictive cornflower-blue waistcoat, neither of which Everard had seen upon his person before. His hair was neatly braided, tied with matching blue ribbon; Everard hadn't seen that before, either.

"I am sorry, mon cher," René murmured to Vitaliy, low and close. "I have brought one thing you wanted and one you did not." Vitaliy looked startled, exhausted blues darting quickly over to Alarie—who had just come upon the gangway presently—before his face settled into flat neutrality, and he nodded.

Of course, then Everard wanted to know what she meant and, furthermore, which was which; wanted and not—but he was distracted soon enough by Louis-Michel Alarie himself standing before him.

And good lord, as judgments—descriptors—went, *handsome* wasn't up to snuff. Not even *very*. *Dandy* was still accurate. But *handsome* had been Alarie's bearing… at a distance.

Up close, the man was downright head-turning. He had honest, liquid-brown eyes, as darkly lashed as D'Arcy's, but more perfectly spaced and set; also the straight nose and dusty-pale complexion of a Grecian bust. His lips were plush, pink and curving; his smoothly shaved jaw hadn't yet lost a bit of definition, because he couldn't have been more than five-and-twenty.

Everard's stomach did a hop-skip, jealousy and wariness and appreciation all in one. He saw now precisely why Vitaliy had put in the effort he had towards his appearance. *Might he have a history with him, too?* he wondered.

Although, he thought, their own history hadn't warranted any such effort.

Alarie came close and greeted Everard in the Continental way, the same as Romilly René had done, cheek to cheek. Everard didn't smell a whiff of hair grease, powder, or scent as he endured, just French soap and warm skin.

"You, then, are the infamous English matelot," Alarie said, in French.

For the umpteenth time, Everard was not English, he really wasn't— "Yes. Everard Anderson de Anglada, and pleased to make your acquaintance, Governor."

"De Anglada," Alarie murmured as he looked him over, up and down, distant and cool.

*Ah.* Head-turning, surely, pretty, definitely; but there was something… missing in that assessment, at least for a man Everard had assumed had a specific kind of history with Vitaliy. A certain recognition, unmistakable understanding; both were completely absent in the face of stone.

For while Vitaliy could also go as still and blank and impersonal as a statue, he resonated with awareness and recognition. This man *was* a statue—at least where other men were concerned.

"Glad to see you exist as more than rumor, matelot." Alarie patted Everard's shoulder. "A Navy man gone pirate… but it is peacetimes, yes? And piracy is what comes of the scraps the English give their career men. I cannot blame you at all."

As though Everard's move to piracy had been financially motivated, not personal, hadn't been done to save a man's life?

This, from a commissioner of a tiny thread of an island? A man not more than five-and-twenty?

"Surely," Everard agreed. It cost him nothing, really. At least Alarie hadn't said anything about the hand or called him Blackhand.

Alarie smiled, and turned to Vitaliy.

"Mon ami Vee, no assemblage for me?"

To Everard's surprise, Vitaliy was blushing, two ruddy spreads over the tan of his cheeks. "The storm was a hard one, Governor," he said crisply, and made a short bow. "The *Sévère* crew are still at leisure, and I saw no need to disturb them."

Flushed, maybe, dressed and brushed to the nines, also; but Vitaliy wasn't backing down.

Alarie looked surprised for a moment. "At leisure still, and it has been a whole half-day?" Then clicked his tongue, self-recriminating, as René inhaled behind him. A hell of a thing to imply laziness in the *Sévère* crew, in Vitaliy, and the man knew it; he backstepped quickly. "No, no, of course, mon frère, I am sorry. The *Birch* was beneath the squall. A surprisingly competent crew in a storm, and all of them les femmes!" he murmured conspiratorially. "But I must congratulate you in this, Vee. The best transport a man has had on a ship in time's memory, I daresay."

Vitaliy looked conflicted. Behind him, René rolled kohl-dark eyes. She swished over to the gangway to negotiate the belay of some kind of cargo.

Alarie pulled Vitaliy aside, pointedly away from Everard. "But have you received my letter latest? It is maybe not enough compensation now, given circumstances of your liaison récente. I confess not knowing the upkeep of a husband as compared to a wife, but…"

Vitaliy let himself be dragged down to the weather deck. He didn't look back.

Everard was left alone, feeling contemplative and oddly resentful, until:

"Ladies' man," D'Arcy sing-songed softly into Everard's ear.

He jumped. "Preston. Where the devil—?"

D'Arcy steadied him with a hand on his back. He was hatless, dressed in his de-epauletted captain's coat and tapered pantaloons; three pistols hung on his belt, no surprise. "Every bit of him. Don't even try."

"I rather gathered—"

"I know, I know. Emerald satin. Even so." D'Arcy smiled sidelong. He had excellent instincts towards sniffing out men like them; a skill sharpened by years of navigating public schools and tonnish ballrooms—whilst being very attractive.

"I don't know what that has to do with… Neither you nor I wear *emerald.*"

"And yet." D'Arcy grinned. He nodded to Vitaliy on the gundeck beneath them, who was totally leaned in to the dandy revolutionary's words, like he spoke gospel instead of straight insult. "But *he* doesn't know."

"I can see that," Everard said stiffly. "Thank you."

"Or perhaps doesn't care?" D'Arcy said. "Small wonder; with that face, it's a weapon. You think the war would've gone the same, if Ol' Boney looked like that?"

Everard didn't bother to answer seriously, only took D'Arcy's arm in his. "You are a menace."

They paced the quarterdeck like taking a promenade.

"Have you forgiven me, then?" Everard asked.

"Might have begun to do so, for the majority part." D'Arcy patted his arm. "Menace is that pretty-face Frenchman, make no mistake." He hummed. "Although I certainly wouldn't mind enthralling a pirate captain to my own gain, even were Varfolomey a woman. Five sloops, a galley frigate, and a meregildo for my navy? Absolutely."

Alarie wanted Vitaliy for his navy?

Of course he did. Who wouldn't?

"You deal perfectly well with women, Preston." In bed and out of it. It was another reason D'Arcy was so shrewd: he had no whispered reputation or specific social circles to signal others what he was; it was left to him to chance whomever he would.

D'Arcy dimpled. "True."

An awful thought occurred. His indifference to Everard aside, could Alarie be similarly minded to D'Arcy?

"You don't think they *have*…?"

"Fucked?" D'Arcy finished for him, and laughed. "Christ, no. Knowledge does not enthrallment make. That there is a man left curious."

"Oh." Everard harrumphed. "I suppose." Was that what Everard lacked? Novelty? New-polished shine? He'd been had, quite thoroughly, and more than once; perhaps Vitaliy had simply moved beyond the already known.

*A man can't change so much in three years.*

*I don't agree,* Vitaliy had said.

Were those the words of a man bored by prior acquaintance? Surely not. But then…

*You can't expect the decisions of the future to produce the same results as the past.*

Everard scowled.

D'Arcy laughed more. "What a fierce face you make." He leaned in, whispered, "You're more than pretty novelty, Ever. Only say you'd like me to demonstrate."

Everard gave him a look: half fondness, half exasperation. He knew D'Arcy knew he appreciated the sentiment from the way the man's eyes crinkled at the corners in response.

"How is it below?" Everard asked, after a comfortable silence. "Is piracy as you imagined it? Your French is up to par?"

"Oh, sod off, my French is and always has been magnifique. But yes, it is every belowdecks ever imagined." He pouted. "With significantly less roving and thieving than I'd hoped."

Everard laughed. "The *Sévère* is too big to go roving. She's more of a floating station, as I understand."

And she was. Piracy being a business, one that competed for men with profitable merchantmen and others, the crew were each contracted to Varfolomey's fleet in renewable terms of four or six months. Written into said contracts was a mandatory stay upon each of the seven ships—excepting the *Birch*, which didn't allow men and didn't share crew. For everyone else, sixty days each year were required upon the *Sévère* and no longer, to discourage coveting of her and also laziness. Not that sailing a meregildo allowed for layabouts. It was fair and equal to divide it such, Vitaliy insisted—kinglike again. And, Everard supposed, also practical: keeping an end date in mind for each man probably helped with mutinous feelings while at-anchor with no prizing.

"A pirate's summer home!" D'Arcy proclaimed, chuckling. "With a firmly established hierarchy, despite what your pirate spouse proclaims of equality."

"Hmm." Everard was curious what he meant, but didn't want to press for specifics, not up there in the open where anyone might hear. "You've retained your sapphire, anyway. And gained not one but two pistols, I see."

"But two are loaded," D'Arcy said, offhand. "You're not the only one with a reputation, you know."

"You alarm me," Everard said, truthfully. He hesitated. "I know you have. I heard what kind of captain you became." *What kind of legacy he'd given up.*

D'Arcy squeezed his arm. "Isn't that something?" he said lightly.

Below, Romilly René had interrupted Vitaliy's tête-à-tête with the French governor, and the two pirates' attention turned to the multitude of crates, hogsheads, and jute sacks being swung over the rail and stacked on *Sévère*'s deck. Vitaliy frowned as he looked up over the creak of block and rope.

So, this was the unwanted thing René brought, then: not a person but cargo. But what could it be? They were quite full up on provisions for the foreseeable future, so it could be nothing needed upon the *Sévère* herself. Was Alarie thrusting stolen goods upon Vitaliy to transport, with the fleet master as go-between? Weapons? Coffee, or sugar, or maguey? It could be anything, but whatever it was, its presence troubled Vitaliy.

Everard disengaged his arm from D'Arcy's, murmured a goodbye, and stepped down the ladder to meet René at the gangway rail.

Maybe Vitaliy would let himself be bullied by a pretty deceiver, but Everard had no such bias. Like it or not, the *Sévère* was now legally half his, and it gave him an advantage: he had a say in what she carried.

"As far as I am aware," he said to the fleet master, "we have plenty of provisions. What are we taking on?"

René laughed. "You do not know." She whistled and gestured, and a barrel was rolled their way. She caught it agilely, produced a mallet and wedge from her belt, and in very few thumps, had cracked open the head. A sweet, familiar, and extraordinarily rare smell rose.

"Vainilla!" Everard exclaimed. He looked up to the stacked barrels with the same marking as this one's and made a quick count. There were many. "Vanilla, by God. No wonder you made good time." Cargo like that, one wanted more than a swivel gun and a rowing crew to protect it.

René made an agreeing noise. "It meets your approval?"

She buried her hands in waxed linen and brought forth two bundles of brown-black beans, each as thick as a man's arm. The scent came in waves to Everard, dense and heady.

"Goodness. It's wonderful. Now put it back," he said hastily.

René snorted and replaced the vanilla. "Relax, matelot. It sat in a beach warehouse while our capitán was set to hang. It will bide a little more air."

Not sugar. Not tobacco. Not cannabis. This was how the smuggler V. Varfolomey made his money, how he came to do business with revolutionary México, how he could afford to take a loss on Haitian coffee, why he had business in New York and Kingston and Philadelphia. *Vanilla.*

But why would Vitaliy frown over such a bounty?

"All this in exchange for a printing press?" he asked. "The crew must be ecstatic."

"Non, this barrel alone is worth much…" She looked up. "Oh, now you are jesting." She grinned, showing sharp eyeteeth, well-kept, and Everard smiled back. It was a contagious grin.

"We took a prize with vanilla cargo once," he remembered. *The* Growler, *two guns, two masts, schooner.* "It was by accident that we came upon her, and the captain didn't flee, though she was tiny. Must have thought to bluff his way through the boarding."

"No stone unturned, you Navy." René tapped the barrel hoops back into their places.

"Yes." Everard couldn't tell if this was judgment or not. "It was only a pair of crates, unmarked; we found them at the utmost by smell alone. The captain cried."

The final hoop slotted into place with the ringing of iron. René's smile looked different now. Vicious. "At the end, they all cry."

Everard paused. He had, despite his best efforts, seen too many men dead to be able to contradict this.

"She wasn't one of yours, I presume?"

She laughed, replaced the mallet to her hip. "Non. One of ours would not be *accidentally* taken upon by a man-o'-war." She gestured to the boy Thom, who was going round distributing grog to the loaders.

It had been a brig, in fact; but Everard said nothing.

Handed his own mug, he sipped gratefully, though really he'd done no work at all.

René drank heartily. "And as you can see, there are more than a pair of crates," she remarked. "And are not stolen, besides."

"Oh, really?" Why did that surprise him… not at all? "What is its provenance? Obviously New Spain; but where?"

"A tribe in the mountains, once conquered by Aztecas for their crop," she replied. "The Totonac. I have never been, and cannot pronounce the ville." She grinned. "The silver with which to pay them, I do not regret to say, is stolen, and Spanish."

Everard laughed. "Naturally."

Romilly René studied him for a moment. She had a startling pair of grey eyes, wide and deep-set, and a smudge of kajal only made them more mesmerising, only reminded him more of Vitaliy as he'd first met him.

"Pretty, when you laugh," she said, abruptly. "Such a voice. And very black eyes. I see it now."

"Er…"

"At first, I wondered you would be so loud about your alliance. I thought you stupid, to put it in frontpage. I thought, there is a man who will get himself lucky to be tossed over."

Everard frowned. "Because… we are lovers?" *Presumably. Presumably lovers.*

"Non, not with the scary brows, mon amour. Not at all. Vee has never hid himself to anyone; what more means the world? It is because you are Navy officer."

Ah, yes; that problem. Only the reason entire he had done the cartoons at all.

"Was," Everard corrected. "No longer. You think it means I'll hinder Vit—Vee—in his endeavors?"

René blinked at the slip, and damn Everard for a fool. Did she, too, know Vitaliy's true name?

"It doesn't matter what I am thinking," she said.

"And yet you are telling me. I shan't. I've no reason to."

She patted the vanilla barrel. "And plenty of reason not, I hope."

Everard nodded once, let her keep her assumption. "Anyway, there's really no moral distinction between illegal and sovereign-sanctioned plunder. At least not for officers-in-charge."

"Oh, no?"

"Not in my experience. God knows no one forces a person to sit the lieutenant's exams. Now, a Navy crew…"

"They are not free."

"Precisely." He ducked his head. "Responsibility scales, you see."

René put her hands on frothy panniers. "You are a career man, and understand this?"

"Nobody paid my commission, ma'am." Not that it worked quite like that in the Navy.

"Hm. Best to leave moralistics to Vee; with these I am not so good. I do what the crew ask of me, nothing much more." She eyed him. "I do have a question for you in especific, matelot. A favor."

A favor? "Venga," he prompted, curious. *Go on, then.*

"How free you are with your self." René's eyes narrowed in

amusement; rouge-red lips stretched wide. "I will ask: how much of his ear do you have? Truly?"

Damn. How much pull did he have with Vitaliy, indeed. What could he say? If he said *hardly any*, his status as matelot was immediately in question. If he said he had his explicit trust in all things, he would be lying through his teeth, boasting dangerously to the one person who could refute the lie. If he said he didn't actually know... which was the truth...

"That's dependent on the favor," he said slowly. "Do not you also have his… ear?"

She laughed. "Non, I do not. You are so very Navy. I am not and cannot be his, and he cannot be mine. We are opposite, quartermaster and captain, as is meant to be. Democracy, yes?" She grinned. "The checks and the balances. Maybe you are not so familiar."

Everard blinked.

"Anyway," she said, "I thought you would wish me to owe you for this favor, but I see not. Only give your counsel, then?"

Everard bit his tongue and nodded, somewhat hesitantly.

"Now that Vee has a…" René paused. "… *kept* man, do you think he ought to once again take receipt of his rightful shares of reward?"

Kept man—?

Everard sipped at the half-decent grog, gave her a cool look. She thought he didn't know about Vitaliy's take? And thought he would care, upon learning this fresh unknown? He couldn't give less of a damn about how many shares Vitaliy kept or didn't. He hadn't even held on to his own captain's salary, save to pay for room and board.

But not even Vitaliy himself knew this. It was one thing to give up a Navy salary voluntarily, with promise of pension and future; another thing entirely to be penniless and desperate before the man who had offered him half a bloody ship.

"Or shall he continue on as he has? Refusing them?" she

asked, blackened eyelashes lowering. "He has not yet informed me, so I would ask you," René said. "And of course it is entirely my business, if new articles need to be signed."

Ex-lovers, Everard thought suddenly. Almost definitely.

He frowned, made it obvious. *Scary brows.* They were effective. "You needn't remind me who you are, ma'am. I am perfectly aware. He hasn't told you of a change," he said, "because nothing need be changed. His shares will continue to be distributed to the crew at large."

René apparently could go as flat and expressionless as Vitaliy; she did so now. But it was a tell of its own. He wondered who had learned it first. Who had approached whom, to be co-pirates. How long they had been lovers. If she knew his true name. If she knew of his sleeping issue.

Then Everard did begin to lie through his teeth.

"What is more, you're quite mistaken. I may be matelot, but I am not 'kept,' as you say. I was a Royal Navy captain for twelve years. A career man." He raised his hand in salud, smiled blandly. "How wealthy do you suppose that will make one?" He leaned in, and whispered, "Why do you think he wanted me?"

René recoiled, nostrils flaring.

He let victory show on his face, just a little, before finishing off his grog.

She slapped the mug out of his hand. His left hand.

The tin fell to the railing, bounced off with a loud *clang* and flying drops—Everard winced—and dropped into the water below, ker-*plunk*. Then Everard had a lot of woman and lace threateningly close to his person.

Holy good God, she was truly as tall as he was.

"You are a fool," she hissed, directly in his ear, "and a liar. You think Vitya's motivated by something as small as wealth? Or you'll just imply that? To *me?* Who holds his balls? To *anyone?* After so much paper farce?" She leaned, spat rougey phlegm directly on his boot, and came back up to the level of his nose. Everard saw nothing but grey eyes, fury, a vague dark halo of curly hair. "You should know better. It is this thing that separates Vee from le crétin Lafitte, Vee's ungreediness that holds him in higher esteem than Lafitte to Haïti and México, the reason why they will even give him time of day. And *you*, the man supposed to him closest, you will refute it?"

Everard hadn't known this. Hadn't realised it at all. "I—"

René leaned even closer, 'til he thought she might try to bite off his nose. "Lucky you said those liar's words to me, and me alone. If I catch you again spreading shit about Vee, undermining him to save only your pitiful pride, matelot… I don't care who you are or what kind of magic cunt you have. You will not live to kiss him goodnight. And Vee will not care, for his business is utmost. *You* are… convenient." She sneered.

Then she about-faced, bows fluttering, skirts heaving, and stomped across the cross-gangway to the *Birch*, out of sight.

Everard leaned heavily on the rail. Naturally, the commotion had caught everyone's attention; the stunned quiet that had fallen over the loader crew was already giving way to speculative murmurs.

Worst of all, Vitaliy stared over, Louis-Michel Alarie curious at his side. Vee's expression was as flat as René's had been, and he stood deadly still. Everard couldn't look away. Some mate he was.

At last, expressionless, Vitaliy turned back to Alarie. Arm-in-arm, they went into the companionway and then the great-cabin; the door shut firmly behind. Everard frowned.

Someone thrust a fresh, undented mug into his vision: two fingers of straight rum, unwatered. He took it gratefully and looked over. He expected D'Arcy, but it was León.

"Words of advice, matelot," he rumbled. He, too, said it *mat-low*. "You know no one fucks with Vee?" A broad brow waggled. "Excepting you."

Everard grunted. Thankfully, his face couldn't get much more enflamed.

"Pues hombre," León said, thumping him on the shoulder with a palm and a knowing look, "entiéndalo. Not even Vee fucks with Romilly René."

Everard wished he could believe that.

# Fifteen

By lunch mess, they'd sailed clear of both Jean Lafitte's territorial waters and the loop current, and were making three knots southeast past Havana. There were no storms nor sail on the horizon. D'Arcy was by now back to his usual self, but that might have been that the *Sévère*'s cook—Rob Appleby—had made good with the fresh rations, having taken the influx as an excuse to slaughter a quantity of the ship's cocks, "for space." The result was an exceptional spiced capón a la barbacoa with sauce, and fluffy rice and potatoes, fresh and unbored by bichos.

They'd taken on Louis-Michel Alarie and his pretty face in one of the teniente's cabins, since he shared their ultimate destination of Haïti. The *Birch*—which had a necessary Spanish marque—had left their convoy outside Havana, leaving the *Sévère* to give the slaver port a wide berth.

To Everard's dismay, Romilly René still did not join her but stayed on, apparently essential. Selfishly, Everard wished that she had gone, but no; there she sat beside Vitaliy, her long, ruthlessly clean nails digging into fowl flesh and pushing it daintily into a rouge-stained mouth. While Alarie ate in the greatcabin parlour, as befitted His Governorship, Vee never took his meals there, but seemingly at random hours with the crew mess. By chance, they'd all ended up together today, awkwardly ignoring each other from opposite ends of the table.

Messes upon the Sévère were organised thusly: everyone ate in shifts, either in the second-deck teniente's parlour, with its long table and row of windows, or in the regular mess, where the proximity to the galley was preferable for a hot meal —except, of course, at the height of Caribbean summer, when nowhere without a through-breeze was preferable.

It was nearly like being a midshipman again, except that the rations were vastly better. The company, too.

D'Arcy hadn't been telling the full truth when he talked of crew hierarchy. The crew sorted themselves into shift watches, messes, and ingroups as persons were wont to do; there was a gang of Welshmen all the others kept warily clear of, reminding Everard of Aedd from the coffeehouse. But quite like nearly every person aboard knowing their way around a cannon, jobs and responsibilities were unspecialised, and no one was held higher than another. Food rations were portioned as equally as could be managed.

Above all, Everard realised, the main difference was choice. No one had been wrangled from the docks with ropey sailors' arms and shoved into a dirty, sloshy underbelly hold. They'd chosen—even if it had been that choice, between the devil and the deep blue sea, or between the sea and slavery—and would get a fair share for at least four months' term.

Early on, he'd asked Vitaliy what portion of his crew was plucked from enemy prizes, and the offhand number had shocked him: almost no one had been forced over the years. Unofficially, of course, because forced men could be tried as reluctant criminals instead of wholehearted deserters. But although there were a bare handful they'd picked up from storm wrecks—and true, most preferred solid land after surviving a wreck—most of Varfolomey's pirates were hired in much the same way as on a merchantman, only with terms far more appealing, and that it came with a higher risk of death.

Of runaways and plunderers and exiles, Vee had first pick.

That, he thought, was probably enough for Jean Lafitte to hate his rival on its own.

Lacking old newsprint gossip as research, Everard asked D'Arcy what of the *Sévère's* reputation with prized crew. He chuckled, said, "Of those ships he's boarded? Probably few enough persons left in shape to force, if I'm being honest."

It meant no mercy. No survivors. V. Varfolomey didn't play games; he was deadly serious.

D'Arcy watched his expression, snorted, and said gently, "He's not a hunter, Ev. If anything short of a man-o'-war's stupid enough to take on a pirate meregildo with a fleet behind her, they deserve it."

Everard had some thoughts on that, most of them disagreeing.

He watched Vitaliy give a quiet half-smile to something Romilly René said. At the moment, his lips were more starkly outlined than usual, bloodred from the heat of the spice rub Everard could still feel on his own tongue.

Vitaliy looked up, first all around the dining room in a quick sweep, and then directly to Everard, like he'd known he'd been watched all along. He murmured to René and stood.

The moment, two moments it took to reach Everard were long ones. Everard looked down to his nearly empty plate. What would he say? What did Vitaliy want? Was everyone else in the mess watching his approach?

D'Arcy was tense beside him. And how many years had Everard, that he himself felt as unsure as a boy?

He looked up just as Vitaliy got near, as he placed a hand on Everard's shoulder. The tips of two long fingers nudged close to his nape and beating pulse respectively, a featherlight touch. Calculated, almost proprietary affection: he was aware of the audience, too.

Lucky, that in this heat, Everard wasn't wearing a shirt with more collar—then there were goosepimple chills cascading down his neck, and Vitaliy's half a smile had slowly become a full one. Everard couldn't help himself. He smiled right back.

Vitaliy removed his hand and leaned to murmur, "Have you finished? I have something to show you. Will you come?"

D'Arcy coughed obnoxiously. "Oh, bravo, well done."

Everard said quickly, "Yes, let's," and stood.

They exited to knowing mutters and chuckling. The first two-finger whistle that started off a true cacophony was unmistakably D'Arcy's.

Everard felt somewhat forgiven. Not enough.

Vitaliy shook his head, but he kept his smile.

"I'm assuming that was intentional," Everard said, when the noise had faded, and they had put some distance behind them, "but not intended for aught. Yes?"

For Vitaliy had led him not to the greatcabin for a sort-of assignation, as everyone undoubtedly had assumed, but down to the orlop to the carpenters' workshop.

Vitaliy stilled before the door. "Does it bother you, what they think?"

"No," he lied. But that he'd have preferred it *not* to have been farce was what bothered him at present. He wasn't going to say that. "What need do we have of Perran?"

Perran was ship's carpenter, a solid Cornishman of the best sort of seaman, with a salt-grey beard and arching black brows; he was gruffly friendly to Everard in spite of the deserter's brand the Navy had burnt into the flesh of his left cheek.

Vitaliy hesitated, hand on the latch. "Nothing of him. It is still in many crates," he said. "But it is a gift. For you."

"A gift?" Everard said, stunned. "Whatever for?"

No one had ever gifted him anything, not even a bottle of spirits. Not that he would've wanted them to, or that he would've kept any said gift in his possession beyond a week; still.

A soft pink flush had returned to Vitaliy's face. He rubbed the back of his neck, scratched his fingers into the nape of ribbon-bound hair. "I would have said yesterday, but there wasn't time. I wanted to have it built…" He trailed off. "But as it happens, I am not a patient man."

"Oh, no?" That wasn't the impression Everard had got. Not at all.

Vitaliy nodded solemnly. "The sea takes what little I have."

"That it will do," Everard said politely. He was eager to get back to the gift. "Er, what is it that's in many crates?"

Then something in his memory hitched, spun round to the proper place, and he realised—*it comes in many crates*—

"Oh, you didn't!" he exclaimed. "Not a bloody printing press?"

"I did," Vitaliy said, smiling now. He pushed open the door.

Neither Perran nor his apprentices were anywhere to be found—Vitaliy had timed their intrusion well—but taking up most the floorspace was, in fact, a grouping of timber crates.

Vitaliy cleared his throat as Everard goggled at the floor. "You could build it faster than I, anyway."

"Yes, probably," Everard said at once. "Well, not by my lonesome. But—good lord, it *is* a press, isn't it!"

What was wrong with him? He sounded *eager.* Delighted, even. Everard didn't want to own a printing press. They were huge, expensive, required regular maintenance, and he had no place to put it—

Vitaliy nodded. He looked pleased. "Yes, it is."

"How the devil did you manage this? I was there when you purchased the other! What kind did you…"

A press was a thing, a tangible, beastly piece-of-property *thing*. But a *useful* thing. It didn't merely sit and exist; it produced, produced information and knowledge—

"May I see it?" Everard asked at last.

Vitaliy pulled down the lantern. Flickering light bloomed. "Of course."

Everard yanked a crowbar from its tiedown on the bench and cracked open the crate most easily reached: which happened to be largest. Nails fell dully onto the floor as he shoved at the top; then Vitaliy came to his assistance, and they lifted it clear. Everard buried his fingers in straw that smelled sharp and metallic, as though someone had just bled all over it.

"Aha," he said, and laughed, a little maniacally. "It cannot be."

"Careful—rats," Vitaliy murmured. Everard barely heard him. He touched cold, greased cast iron, felt down the rough curve of an arc, squat and bell-shaped.

"It is a Stanhope!" Everard exclaimed. "But so few of these exist this side of the Atlantic…" His right hand traced over letters, revealed them: *STANHOPE, INVENIT*. And beneath that: *Nº 76*.

"*Aided by thee,*" Everard whispered, "*O Art sublime! Our race spurns the opposing bonds of time and space.*" He shoved straw to and fro, revealing more and more black iron. "*With Fame's swift flight to hold an equal course, and taste the stream from Reason's purest source…*" She was immaculate, not a speck of rust on her. "*Vice and her hydra sons, thy powers can bind, and cast in Virtue's mould the plastic mind.*"

"Hydra sons of vice." Vitaliy had a smile in his voice. "I have met one or two, maybe."

Everard looked up and grinned. "Printer's Grammar, 1808. There's a print of a Stanhope as frontispiece. The poem is McCreery—pray do not ask me to recite it in entirety; it's thirty-some pages."

"I won't." Vitaliy's eyes glowed in the lanternlight. "Though it reminds me of another… do you know it? 'On the Freedom of the Press'?"

Everard sat back on haunches, crowbar over his knee, and thought for a moment. "Offhand… I need a visual callback, an image, a page, a pamphlet… Who wrote it?"

"Franklin; the Almanack. No need," Vitaliy said quickly, as Everard opened his mouth in sudden recall, "I know it." And he recited:

> *The Press from her fecundous Womb*
> *Brought forth the Arts of Greece and Rome;*
> *Her Offspring, skill'd in Logic War,*
> *Truth's Banner wav'd in open Air;*
> *The Monster Superstition fled,*
> *And hid in Shades her Gorgon Head;*
> *And lawless Pow'r, the long kept Field,*
> *By Reason quell'd, was forc'd to yield."*

Everard knew he'd never, so long as he lived, forget this moment. While it wasn't exactly remarkable for him to remember a moment—especially words read or recited—he'd never seen anyone do it quite as eloquently or as… beautifully. Vitaliy had a deep, soft voice, and they weren't even in theatre, but a dusty, unexpectedly resonant woodshop in the heart of a pirate ship.

Everard cleared his throat. "That one is very like, now you mention. A bit less abstract. Ah—and a rather longer piece, for Franklin, isn't it?" He stood, put his hands on his hips, and stared down at the new press so that he wouldn't stare at Vitaliy, make the man feel awkward. "You're quite familiar, then?"

Vitaliy made a small, amused noise. The quiet subtlety of it emphasised just how close he stood, not that Everard wasn't very, very aware—

"Not as well as you, perhaps. Philadelphia was my boyhood home," Vitaliy said. "And my mother, political."

"Ah."

"Yes."

"And yet 'It comes in many crates'?"

Vitaliy shrugged. "You are pleased?"

"Of course," Everard said hastily. "It's wonderful. Thank you. It's just I've never owned such a thing before." *Or anything.* "And—where are we to put it?"

Vitaliy drew back. "Put it?"

"You said you'd wanted it built… Where had you in mind?" Inspiration struck. A floating castle… "Aboard the ship? Oh—the greatcabin? The parlour? Large enough, surely. Gad, but do you think it might need some sort of gimbal?"

There was a long pause before Vitaliy replied, slowly, "Built… at whichever destination you chose."

An equally long pause, as Everard's pleased, sea-sparkle feeling faded, in favor of confusion. "Destination?" he asked. "Is there one in mind?"

In his mind, he hadn't much thought beyond the load and unload in Haïti. If he had, he might have imagined a perpetual loop of the Indies, doing pirate things like hunting Spanish men-o'-war and Portuguese merchantmen, endless sun and sail.

Vitaliy, too, had two deep lines of confusion between his brows. He looked uncomfortable. "Wherever you like. We will meet with the *Vuelte*—she will go on to Philadelphia. *Enemistad* will call in Boston…"

He trailed off. Everard was silent.

"I have a house there," Vitaliy said abruptly. "Philadelphia. Which is now yours, legally. Two stories, brick-built, in town…

I don't have slaves—if you stay ashore, the Crown is unlikely to reach you—"

"I don't want..." Everard's reaction was visceral, gut-borne. Nausea. Not only did Everard generally not do well with long stretches on land, but... a *house*? *Property?*

"It would be simple to convert it to a printshop... hire help... You would be well needed," Vitaliy finished. "Necessary, in fact. You could be wealthy, not even including what I will send you."

At a loss, Everard stooped to retrieve the nails he'd scattered. He shouldn't have been so hasty, should have counted and bagged them. The carpenter would not thank him for leaving them.

*Needed. Necessary. Kept, kept, kept.*

With anger-fueled strength, he heaved the crate cover back over the Stanhope, one-handed, before Vitaliy could attempt assistance. Everard could not, however, accurately hold a nail with his left thumb and knuckles—nor switch hands and grip the hammer well enough to pound straight.

He stood there for a moment, with the nails in two useless palms.

"I don't want a house," Everard said. "Or a printshop. Or" —he made a face—"*wealth.* I've already a ship—half a ship..." He trailed off, as Vitaliy looked mildly horrified. "Yes? Or was I completely mistaken?"

"No," Vitaliy said quickly. "Yes, I mean... no. The *Sévère* is... I don't own her. We don't," he corrected. "The crew owns her, piecemeal. They decide her leadership. But I would have too much stake in it if I were her owner. No crew would agree to keep me as her captain if I did, not when half are joiners late off greedy merchantman. I thought you knew this. Would know this."

*You should know better.*

Everard truly didn't know anything at all, did he?

He placed the nails atop the crate, a neat little pile of iron. He faced Vitaliy, who was stoic but for a hint of wariness.

"Then I thank you. But this"—Everard swallowed down more anger—"*press* is not a gift. It's employment."

Vitaliy stepped forward. "It *is*—"

"Would you oblige me to print whatever I liked, or only certain truths? Advertisements? Cartoons?"

"I would not control—"

"And what else might be included in this shore arrangement?" Everard whispered harshly. "Hmm? Shall I be shoved over to one side of the bed upon every instance of your being at port? A shore wife?"

Vitaliy sucked his pink, spice-swollen lower lip beneath the other, let it go even redder. His eyes had narrowed. "That is not what I had in mind, but your disdain is showing quite clear."

"Oh, indeed? Perhaps you had need of one? It won't be me."

Now Vitaliy's eyes widened. "You demean women—"

"I'm not demeaning nothing, sir—"

"Your tone alone—"

"I am simply declining your offer. Because first and foremost, I am a sea man—"

"I know," Vitaliy growled.

"I was a captain—"

"*Please* let me speak!" Vitaliy's voice rose.

Everard winced. Resonant, indeed; and it was a small space. Chastened, he shut his mouth.

Vitaliy breathed, cursed viciously in Russian, pulled his hands through his hair, and said softer: "I'm sorry. I should not yell. But I cannot think whole thought with you biting from every word, and also you speak quickly, it is very difficult."

Everard counted two, three heartbeats before he responded.

"I'm sorry. Truly. I didn't realise. Don't apologise for

yelling; I'll have been yelled at plenty, you know. Navy man." He wasn't sure anyone had ever apologised for it before. "And with considerable less cause and… desperation." He paused again. "Perdóname. What were you to say?"

Vitaliy took a deep breath. "The press *is* a gift. It trails no strings. You can print what you like, where you like; here, on board ship; it is your machine. I thought you would like to become printer. I thought the house convenient, as it stands empty. I didn't mean to imply that sort of sexual arrangement without asking, not that it would be bad thing for either. And…" He looked up to the ceiling. "What else? Yes." He met Everard's eyes. "I did not think you would ever want be truly pirate, so I found solution for you. Or not solution; alternative, option. Options are good. But I see now I should've asked."

Everard sat on the crate, waited ten heartbeats this time, just to take all of it in properly.

"You do know your way around a lack of articles, you Russian."

Vitaliy blinked down. He hadn't refreshed the kohl pencil since the storm—Everard suspected he didn't know how heart-beat-inducing it made him look, or he'd have done it for Alarie —and his lashes were so blond as to be nonexistent. It was charming.

Then he laughed, and sat beside Everard on the crate, crossing his boots at ankles. "Only when not trying," Vitaliy admitted. "Between Russian father, Quaker mother, and trader French, it is a wonder I am understandable at all."

"Don't forget Jackspeak. Which was your first?" Everard felt he already knew.

"It was Russian. Seal-hunter's Russian. Mostly curses."

Everard laughed. "Curses are first to come. Ask any child."

"But I didn't speak until I was yea tall, on fishing boat with my father, so that is why." Vitaliy gestured, perhaps three feet high. "Otherwise, it would have been my mother's plain speech. Although English comes better than all the rest, so mayhap it still was."

Everard understood then. "Your mother was a shore wife?"

"Is," Vitaliy corrected, then frowned. "Isn't. She lives still. But she and my father never wed, and she certainly never waited ashore for his return."

Everard wondered if that also meant he hadn't returned at all. It wasn't the sort of thing one asked.

"I have the utmost respect for shore wives," he said, "wed or not. I do. I merely don't wish to resemble one."

Vitaliy's mouth quirked. "Nor have need of one?"

"God, no. Wish I could have had, some days, but no. Not built that way, I suppose." With his thumb, Everard began to arrange the nails beside him into formation.

After a moment, he said, "You thought I wouldn't want to stay upon *Sévère* as a pirate? After everything? I should think I have the qualifications. A suitable epithet, ready-made," he jested, waving the gloved hand. "A handful of capital offences. An infamous pirate of a spouse." He looked up. "Don't I?"

"Yes." Vitaliy sat as though to brace himself with both feet. "Of course, legally, you do."

*And otherwise than legally?* Everard thought greedily.

"Is more than a shore wife would have, come to think," Vitaliy mused, then looked suddenly worried. "Why are you unsure of this?"

"Er, well… can it be quite… legal?"

He watched as Vitaliy's realisation dawned.

"Oh," Vitaliy said. "Oh. No, that is different too." He peered at him, concerned. "I did say that, no? That fucking is not a requirement of the partnership?"

"Well—er—not precisely," Everard admitted. "No. You had said something of sharing a bed…?"

"And we are." Vitaliy looked scandalised. "I could not oblige sex from you too! Considering all you have already given up. And what of the lieutenant?" he asked shrewdly. "Are not you and him…?"

*Oblige sex from him!* It was almost laughable.

"No, Preston isn't… Well, there's no understanding—but that is a separate issue from you and I," Everard said firmly. "And I don't know that I would call it obliging you. For my part. In fact, I wouldn't call it that in the least."

Vitaliy leaned forward, elbows on knees, his expression keen. A physical, yearning representation of *Please always say what you want.*

Everard said quickly, "I might yet… want that. So long as you do. As long as you have done. Have wanted that."

Vitaliy nodded understandingly. "That. I think the answer is yes, I do and I have. But please say what? I prefer it direct."

Everard blinked.

Vitaliy smiled innocently. "As you perhaps remember."

Did he ever. "I… Yes." Everard cleared his throat. "I want to stay," he said. "I want the press. And I want to… want to share your bed. Again. Not only intermittently. Not just for sleeping; for fucking. While you're awake, I mean. I'd wake you whenever might be needed—"

"Direct enough," Vitaliy said, and pulled Everard close and kissed him.

It began fierce, then turned cautious at once, tentative and restrained, until Everard reached to the cursed-ribbon–bound hair and tugged firmly. He felt it best to remove any doubt. He was all-in, every piece.

Vitaliy understood. He groaned, plush lips opening; he tasted of spice and pepper and coffee. His skin was still soap-soft; he'd commandeered Thom's excellent shaving services early this morning.

Everard kissed along the sharp jaw to curly sideburns and back again, down, and delighted in this further shared thread of companionship, of connection. He kept on kissing 'til Vitya was cursing, trying to lean back and pull him onto his lap simultaneous, and the man had an arm locked tight around Everard's waist.

Everard drew back, breathing hard, and made a wondering glance down to the crate beneath them; looked up and saw Vitaliy considering the same. Their eyes met, and Vitya nodded.

"Eh, not quite a bed?" he said, and they both giggled.

There was some shuffling, tantalisingly brief contact of firm warmth beneath linen; a scattering *ping-plink-plink* of nails across the floor. Vitya lay back and shifted one large thigh to the side. Everard found his way between salt-streaked boots to sink his hips precisely where they belonged.

The ship creaked, block and tackle and decking and mast; beneath them was the more-immediate strain of the crate as it did its best against their grinding. Vitya had a one-handed grip of the plank edge nearest his head for leverage, and was pushing up. Everard had grip of Vitya himself, fingers clutching where neck met shoulder, pulling his too-clothed self forward and back, trying to press every bit he could against the taper of warm muscle beneath.

"Jesus sainted." Too much clothing; too little air. He felt desperate, a sailor upon first stumble into a brothel, sort of desperate, without due cause. He pushed up onto both hands. "Can't—not much more of that. Undo your blasted breeches?" he pleaded.

Vitaliy laughed softly and complied. Like D'Arcy, he didn't wear drawers. It was delightful.

Everard's mouth burned with spice; fellatio seemed sadly out of the question. He stared down, wishing it were otherwise. Then Vitaliy helped with the buttons of Everard's own fall, quick and unerring, and Everard decided this was an adequate solution, after all.

He reached down with his right hand. Vitaliy pushed up

and touched his forehead to his in… sympathy? Memory? Who knew, but Everard appreciated it—and then Everard pressed their pricks together and went to work.

Vitaliy was so present, clutching at him everywhere, kissing and biting and writhing beneath him, Everard wondered how or why anyone could've ever continued on when he was disturbingly asleep. Lackwits—idiots—worse, he called them. Meanwhile, Vitya was there, and his, and there, his head went back, and there, that flush—

Vitya pulled him in for a blazing-hot, all-consuming kiss. It disturbed the rhythm, though neither of them cared. Even so, Vitya soon seemed frantic; he broke free to simply moan. Everard levered up, pushed forward and down within the guide of his fingers, slowly and deliberately, and watched Vitya's shudder start in his thighs and tremble up, out of gasping lips. He was quiet, so quiet, one felt almost obliged to watch, so as to miss nothing. Not that it was a hardship.

As things got dire, Vitya shifted to put a boot down flat on the floor to brace them, and Everard made room in the tangle of thighs and hands to let him thrust, let him to abandon. He worried again for the crate beneath them, even as he wanted to test it further.

In the end it held fine, complaining only once under the onslaught of Vitaliy's slow, rocking tremors and great inhales. His head was thrown back again, his eyes shut tight, hair splayed loose everywhere in his drive towards crisis. Everard held them together, all coordination gone. He could only watch in awe.

"Sant Jesús," he muttered. "Vitya. You're beautiful."

Vitya's eyes flew open, shined and blue-black, just for a moment; they fluttered shut as he went suddenly rigid all over, trembling, teeth deep in his lip.

"God, yes, come," Everard said.

Vitya came with a groan Everard wished he'd been close

enough to swallow. He leant forward to try and catch the last of it—and Vitya's lips against his, the rush of spice and breathy heat on his tongue, the extravagant new slickness between them yanked him, tumbling, over the edge.

Eventually, he could breathe again.

"Jesus," he said. "And that just frigging?"

"Mm." Vitya smiled, looking half-stunned, half-asleep. He still had eyes closed, and his broad hands wrapped tight around Everard's knees. God, but they were both a mess.

Feeling mellow, quieto, satisfied regardless, Everard said, "At this point, I think you may have to maroon me."

"What?" Vitaliy murmured. "Who has threatened that?" He frowned. "No."

"To get me to go, I mean."

Vitya relaxed. "Oh." He snorted. "No," he repeated. "That is not an option."

# Sixteen

They built the Stanhope in the greatcabin parlour, in place of the little round dining table that Louis-Michel Alarie had been occupying for his meals.

The reasons were quite practical: the parlour sat in the centre of the ship, where the walls were straight and the ceilings highest. Neat, efficient little thing that the press was—its bell-shaped frame stood only as tall as Everard's breastbone, its base slightly longer, so it could be operated by one person alone—one still needed room to maneuver round the thick, T-shaped base, to roll the ink, to pull the handle.

And it gave Everard a strange, petty pleasure to see the governor displaced from his supper table that night. Alarie had come in expecting a set table, and found them both hard at work. Though of course the man bore it with perfect, composed grace—especially when Vitaliy promised him a prominent place in the officers' dining cabin thereafter.

That was a strange offer. But Everard, exhausted, presently in shirtsleeves and a heavy leather apron borrowed from Perran, was too elbow-deep in black grease and cast iron to pause for more than a moment to wonder why egalitarian Vitaliy was being so deferential to a mere governor. Deferential to anyone at all.

He did not, however, anymore think mere infatuation was driving it. For one, Vitaliy had stripped to buckskin breeches, and above those wore no more than the sheen of sweat he'd acquired from lifting and placing cast iron. Only a man as solidly a ladies' man as Alarie could be so indifferent to such a presentation.

And Vitaliy was observant. He'd have noticed Alarie's indifference. Surely he had.

Currently, Louis-Michel Alarie looked more covetous of the press than of Vitya.

"Everyone will be devoured with envy," he crowed from his unhelpful lean against the window. "A floating press! No one will be able to seize it! They will not know from whence the sedition is coming! I wish I'd thought of it myself."

"I as well," Vitaliy murmured, and caught Everard's eye meaningfully.

Everard hoped his flush looked like exertion. "Bolted to the deck now," he said. "So I'm afraid you can't have her for yourself, Governor."

Bolted she was, thrice over for security; and her assembly was nearly, nearly done. Two-handed, Everard slotted the handle bar into the spindle, grunting slightly, and secured it behind with its nut. Then it was time. He push-pulled the handle once, slow and experimental, watching the spindle turn clockwise and the attached lever swing and pull at the main, longer lever. Metal moved on metal, smooth as silk. The massive screw in the heart of the Stanhope turned, and down came the wide, flat platen, onto the padded carriage beneath. And even with the ship making three knots, she came down straight.

Success.

"Oh, no, I know," Alarie said easily. "I do not have a ship so enormous as to fit such a beast, in any case." He patted a crate, apparently unaware that it held the lead type. (Baskerville; Vee had good taste.)

"We may negotiate terms if you like," Vitaliy said shrewdly. "Nonexclusive, of course."

Alarie blew out a breath. "Pirates," he muttered. "Concerned for a profit always. Of course, nonexclusive."

Concerned for *profit?* Alarie didn't know Vitya very well at all.

"Mina may be tempted by it too," Alarie went on. "You ought ask him."

"Mina will have brought pamphlets of his own, yes?" Vitaliy asked. "Ahead of the matter."

Martín Francisco Xavier Mina; a Spanish Army ex-officer who was attempting to gather American, British, and Haitian support for a campaign against the Spanish Crown in México. He was set to meet them in a few days in port Haïti.

Alarie brushed this off. "I do not know. Can indios even read a civilised tongue?" he mused.

*Déu meu.* Under cover of shirtsleeve, Everard rolled his eyes. As Alarie seemed to speak French and only French, he found this more than a bit rich. He swiped sweat from his forehead and peeked over to Vitaliy. He was stony-faced, lips pressed tight.

"All men deserve access to the written word, Governor," Vitaliy said. "All persons," he revised.

No—there seemed no possible way the man who had denounced colorist satires would be interested in donkeyish Alarie, romantically or otherwise.

So, why did Vitaliy tolerate him? Oblige him?

Everard push-pulled the handle. This time, the "kiss" of pressure from the platen upon the carriage looked a tad excessive, but that was easily fixed. He reached up and adjusted the main lever's length a hair, a twist of the screw end, and push-pulled again. Better. Though he suspected with the movement of the ship working at her, he'd have to be adjusting that screw near-constantly. It was a small price to pay.

"The Spanish is probably our best bet, for pamphleteering," Everard said. "Followed by French. Tribes will have translators, missionaries, churchmen. Though are you sure, Governor, that you want to disseminate war and revolution to tribes who may neither know nor care? I understood it was criollos whom La Corona was executing." Criollos were white persons born in the Spanish colonies; a slight tick down the casta ladder, behind Spain-born españoles.

"Again," Alarie said, in French, "I do not know Mina's *precise* plans. Thus far, he wants only naval escort from me, and soldiers from Haïti. But a body's a body in war, my friend. You, career man, Englishman, should understand this."

Everard grimaced. "In fact, I tried my damnedest not to. As would anyone with a functional soul." He wiped grease from his knuckles and thumb, removed his apron, and looked up.

Vitya had been watching him. His eyes were half-lidded, and his bottom lip had been sucked beneath the other. He glanced to the greatcabin door, back again, and raised a thick blond eyebrow in question.

Everard was absolutely exhausted—but yes, absolutely, yes. Whatever that invitation had been, yes.

First, however, there was Louis-Michel Alarie to be dealt with.

"Fancy a nightcap, Governor?" Everard said, making a quarter-turn. "I do feel for you, having your supper accommodations displaced." He nodded to the greatcabin, forced a smile. "But there is the desk to sit around. It's quite a large desk, in fact." He raised his eyebrows. "Large enough for three."

Louis-Michel Alarie stood suddenly from his lean, his pretty eyes downcast. "Oh, you are very kind," he said quickly. "You English, always kind. Non, I must not—I need to rest for our rendez-vous at the junta."

Behind him, Vitaliy smiled wide. He brushed a palm over his mouth, turning quickly stoic just in time for Alarie's about-face and curt bow.

"Goodnight, Governor," Vitaliy murmured, and bowed.

Everard didn't bother. Alarie's eyes hadn't moved from the floor.

Alarie backed through the parlour door, shutting it firmly behind. They listened to his steps fade into the depths of the ship.

"Well," Everard said. "That confirms it utterly."

He caught Vitaliy's eye, and they shared a muffled laugh.

Everard sighed. "I shouldn't have done that, perhaps."

Vitaliy remained in the doorway, leaning with arms crossed, outwardly quite relaxed. His eyelids were lowered, his perfect, heart-shaped lips set in a peaceful quirk. They matched the tawny pink of his cheeks.

"It was… blatant," he admitted.

"It was, wasn't it? And slightly mean."

Vitaliy shrugged. "Nothing he doesn't know. Or… encourage, time to time."

That said a whole hell of a lot. "Had you known?"

"It took me longer than it should have."

"Deception a-purpose, I'd bet. With a face like that?"

"Maybe."

"He tried to exploit it?"

"And succeeded," Vitaliy said. "Mostly. I suppose I am easily led."

"Oh, come on." Everard laughed. "Easily led? You? Have a

look at me, Vitya. Do I strike you as very urbane? Debonair?" He rubbed hands over his filthy, sweat-damp breeches in illustration. "As though I've led you anywhere."

"You could," Vitaliy said. "If you wanted."

Everard had his doubts. He was still wondering what had happened to the dark intent behind Vitaliy's sidelong glance.

"He's the donkey, not you," Everard declared. "And I don't like him."

Vitaliy's face remained calm, unmoved. He nodded, as though taking this into serious consideration. He jerked his chin towards the Stanhope. "Is it as you expected?"

"Oh, yes. Every screw accounted for, and not a bit of rust. Thank you. She'll do beautifully."

"Good."

Sometimes, Everard thought, there was such a thing as too much patience.

But then, perhaps it was intentional. *You could. If you wanted.*

And if that was what Vitya wanted…? To be led?

"I'm too tired to set type tonight and test it properly, though." Everard stretched. His shoulders ached from turning the wrench in wide arcs, over and over. That wasn't why he stretched. "Tomorrow."

Vitaliy was faultlessly observant. "Shame," he murmured. "I could watch you pull that thing all night."

"Oh?" Everard stepped a bit closer—not close enough to touch. "As it happens, I like to be watched."

Vitaliy said nothing. His lips twitched, and he raised his chin.

Invitation.

Everard reached down to the fall of his breeches. He drew his prick free from drawers and let it bob. "This is what you meant?"

Vitaliy's gaze slid south, back up again. Surely it was.

Everard undressed. Shoes, socks, drawers. Clothing duly banished, he took himself in hand.

Vitaliy shifted once to readjust—a very necessary maneuver—but otherwise remained still as Everard stood before him, stroking himself, up and down.

Facing Vitaliy like this was like facing the sun as it hung low on the horizon: warm and golden, throwing everything it touched into sharp relief and saturated colors. Just bright enough that when one turned away, it glinted at edge of one's vision. One wanted to stare, but knew one mustn't.

Everard did anyway.

"Next time," Vitaliy said, voice low and rough, "the apron and nothing else."

Everard hastily paused. "God." He groaned. "You want this to end, then, as soon as may be. What happened to all night?"

Vitaliy lifted an eyebrow. "It wouldn't be a bad thing."

"Says the man with nothing urgent in his hand."

"I want to look." Vitaliy blinked, slow. "Looking is fine?"

"Mmm." It was, Everard thought, quite obviously more than fine. "Yes." But…

*You could.*

"If I have further plans for you, Vitya?"

Vitya inhaled. Leaned there, staring and wanting.

"Fine, too," he whispered, at last.

*Lead on.*

Everard backed until his bare thighs knocked against the iron ribs of the Stanhope. Vitaliy pushed off the doorway and followed him, step for step. The carriage touched Everard's back like a shock; he groped blindly behind him, and pulled. The wheel spun, and the carriage slid forward with a loud, firm *thunk*—precisely where Everard needed it to be.

He hauled himself up, weight on his palms, and settled his arse down upon the flat—holy God, *cold*—surface. He thanked brand-new bearings, three-quarter-inch bolts, cast iron brackets wider than his arm. Also that his bollocks were still high and close from taut, unresolved arousal; the rest of him could absolutely bide.

He watched Vitaliy's expression morph through realisation, disbelief, and then steady contemplation.

"Well, Vitya?" he demanded. He resumed his stroking, up and down. "Will you fuck me?"

Vitya swallowed. He crowded in closer, until he and his ropes-climber body stood near enough to warm him.

"These plans of yours sound like blasphemy," he murmured.

Everard laughed. "So sayeth the ex-Quaker, atheist pirate."

Vitaliy bent closer, put his hands on Everard's chest, trailed fingers down, and clutched tight round his waist. He smelled like iron, sweat, honey-on-toast sweetness. "You want to screw on an *altar*," he whispered.

Everard shivered. "Yes."

"You want me inside you. Seventeen hundred pounds of cast iron beneath you?" Vitya splayed his hands over Everard's thighs, stroked down, lifting and spreading as they went.

"Yes."

Vitaliy still had breeches on. He nudged him wider. "A very expensive fuck if it fails." He pushed Everard lightly on the chest.

Everard lay back as if liquid, as if compelled. He put both hands up behind him, gripped hard to the shoulders of the press. Thanked God he was tall, and put up his feet. The height was nearly perfect; Vitya had only to bend his knees a little—Sant Jesús, cast iron was cold on his back.

"We built her," he gasped. "She won't fail."

Vitya let go one leg. He unbuttoned and, in a flash, pulled out his already-wet cock. He laid it down in heavy promise, a perfect, blazing-hot fit in the crease of Everard's thigh and hip, just beside Everard's cock. Then he leaned and put hands to either side of Everard's waist, and gripped the flat iron carriage. He pulled forward, pushed back, testing; skin slid and stuttered on skin.

"It yet rolls," he said, revelatory.

Everard was breathing very hard. "That was the idea."

Vitaliy smiled down. "You have good ideas."

"Thank you."

"But you remember the trestle table?"

"In York? How not?" In the cabin—the second night—Vitya had splayed himself over the little table, a display of broad chest, tapering waist, tawny, inviting fur, a bright and erect cock. Everard had fucked him so hard, the trestle support beneath them had cracked and split, forcing an abrupt, giggling redirect to the hearth-warmed plank floor.

"You will have your recompense for it?" Everard asked.

The sliding movement seemed to enrapture Vitya; he stared down. "No. Only that it will have to be gentler than that, I think."

"By all means," Everard said, panting now. "As long as there *are* means."

"Mmm," Vitya said, promisingly. "One moment." He twisted round, one way, then the other, searching. His eyes lit upon the tin of beeswax, with which they'd greased the iron.

"Absolutely not." Everard laughed, nudged him away with a foot. "Look among the crates."

Vitaliy gave him a curious glance but went; Everard was treated to the glorious sight of his arse in buckskin as he bent and rummaged.

"Further plans," Vitya said, amused, finding his quarry. He returned in a moment, the bottle of sweet almond oil in hand. "When did you— No. I will not ask."

Slick, so slick between their pricks now; Vitya slid him on

creaking wheels until they groaned, and Everard was arching up, his fingers painful on the iron.

"Now, Vitya. Now."

Vitya was all black-eyed, focused intent. With one hand he held the carriage still. The other helped with his insistent breach.

"Only just," Everard began— "*God.*"

The man's prick, God help him, was as thick as the rest of him.

Vitya halted, his breaths coming harsh through his nose, his lips pressed tight. They bloomed red as he let them go and exhaled, slow. He stretched to kiss Everard's grimace, a question as careful as his fingertips were, tentative over Everard's thigh, his bollocks, his prick, stroking him softly.

"Good?"

Everard breathed. "Yes." He hooked one leg round Vitya's hip. Pushed off the press's shoulder with his palms. With a steady, insistent slide forward and one rather loud groan, he brought Vitya further into him—all the way.

Vitya jerked against him, his eyes wide.

"You," he gasped. "I meant to…"

"I know what you meant," Everard said. "You meant it slow and decent." He laughed. "This enough lead for you?"

Vitya pulled Everard up, cradling his shoulders in spread palms, wrapping him close; this time, his kiss was more like himself, startling and sweet. Devouring.

A contented quiet settled in: shuddering breaths, soft noises. Everard accustomed himself to the intrusion of hot, pulsing warmth, and pulled close every bit of Vitya he could touch. His muscles slowly became liquid again. Vitya sensed it, and let him go; gooseflesh pricked up all over Everard's skin in the absence of proximity, at the renewed touch of cold iron on the small of his back, on his hands.

Then Vitya gripped the carriage again, wrists tucked in tight to Everard's waist.

"It will have to be gentler," he repeated, almost apologetic. "But I will do what you want."

"I want you however, Vitya."

Vitya began to move, sliding Everard forth and back in tiny increments upon his prick. Beneath him, the wheels squeaked and groaned. It was both erotic and unnerving; Vitya's rapt vigilance betrayed his own fascination. His pace quickened, slides lengthening; Everard felt increasingly less like he was being fucked, being entered, and more as though he were an object: one of Vitya's self-infliction, of Vitya's pleasure.

He liked it. Perhaps a little too much.

"Déu meu," he gasped. "Wait, I'm too close, I'll—"

Vitya stopped, buried halfway. He hardly seemed to breathe. Everard breathed for him, and then some.

Slowly, Vitya resumed, hips twitching the barest amount. The carriage moved by inches.

It had an effect opposite to what Everard expected.

"Oh, Jesus, God," he groaned.

The height of the press; the angle of approach; the persistent thick presence of Vitya's prick, or perhaps its curve; whatever combination of circumstance this made sent shocks of pleasure driving into Everard with every small thrust.

Vitya didn't stop. Neither buried himself, nor withdrew.

It was maddening.

It was driving Everard to climax with surprising speed.

"Why are you— Vitya, fuck me—else I'll not be able to hold back—"

Vitya looked intent. He smiled a tiny smile. He did not let up.

So much for leading.

"For god's sake, *thrust*, else I will…"

Vitya wrapped fingers round the head of Everard's cock, and stroked: gently, lightly, not nearly enough.

Or so he thought. "Oh, no." Everard cursed as his thighs shook, and climax came upon him. "Oh, god."

That was him with his head thrown back; him panting, pleading, writhing. Through it all, Vitya kept up his subtle thrusts, kept Everard close and restrained as he trembled, kept him atop the carriage as he arched.

"What—in—hell," Everard panted, at last. He looked down, and saw no spend but a slick wetness. He was still hard beneath Vitya's fingers. "*How* in hell—"

Vitya put his thumb to his mouth, looking pleased with himself. He withdrew carefully, hauled Everard up, brought him close, kissed him again.

Head spinning, Everard attempted to snatch back flailing lines, to seize control into his grasp once more.

"Take me to bed," he said against perfect lips.

Vitya hummed, wrapped Everard's legs and arms around himself, and lifted. Carried him with heavy, thudding steps into the greatcabin, dropped him down into the cot. Undressed totally, and then laid himself over Everard, dense and warm, and kissed him and kissed him until Everard's legs spread and his cock ached.

"Vitya," he begged. "Please."

"Now," Vitya whispered, "I will do what I want."

"What… ever," Everard muttered, mad with lust. The rag-stuffed mattress was bliss beneath them. "However you want it."

Vitya shifted, set down Everard's legs that swayed like reeds, and straddled his waist.

Everard's focus wavered, addled with desperation, confused by lust. He stared down.

"Dear God. Like this?"

"Yes," Vitya confirmed, nonetheless a question.

"However you like," Everard replied dazedly. He reached down, fumbling to assist, pushed himself upright. He was wet all over from the strange, pseudo-release. It would more than do. "I should warn you, I'm not sure that— It might not—"

"Fuck," Vitya said softly, and sank down.

"Might not take much," Everard finished, wheezing. Yes; despite his misgivings, he was absolutely going to be capable of further release. Currently, it was held back through force of will alone.

Vitya kissed him. Even his breaths were quiet.

But he had his recompense. Everard held on for dear life.

# SEVENTEEN

Days later, long before first light, Everard sought answers simply, in the way Vitaliy seemed to always encourage from him: by asking.

They lay rocking in the massive cot, beneath the A-frame ripple of mosquito net: side-by-side, sticking, and sated. Vitaliy had mentioned in his direct way that he did like to be awoken, impromptu, for sex—as long as it was assured he *was* truly wakeful before proceeding. Everard had done this gladly, with enthusiasm, and there'd been a lot of proceeding, with gloriously no interruption at all.

Then he worked up his nerve and asked about Alarie.

Vitaliy said, "Louis-Michel wants me because he had me last year in Cartagena."

"Oh?"

Vitaliy shifted onto his side and brushed his socked foot against Everard's. Everard found Vitya's preference for socks in the Caribbean heat mildly strange but also endearing. The wool tickled; the sheet woven betwixt their bare legs felt floaty and cool.

"Not like that," Vitaliy said. "In his flotilla. He was commodore, at the siege. Do you know of it?"

He did. News of that conflict had reached Upper Canada, and he remembered it well. Spanish Royalists, intent on reconquest, had sieged Cartagena de Indias for months on end; reports were that a quarter, maybe even a third, of New Granada's population had starved.

"The *Sévère* carried Cartagena's marque at his request," Vitya said.

"At his plead?" Everard jested.

Vitaliy laughed softly, without humor. "No."

"Wasn't it horridly brutal?" Everard asked. "Four, five months long?"

"One hundred six days. Eventually, we took as many as we could to Les Cayes, but… many died."

"Damn the Spanish," Everard said fervently. He paused for a brief, silent prayer for the dead. Vitaliy withdrew a foot and pushed the cot into a slow rock once more. The ship was forever in motion, but Vitaliy minded being still even more than Everard.

"Weren't you privateer for Madison, you said?" Everard asked.

Vitaliy inhaled like he'd been drifting off. "Early on, yes. Not beyond 1815. Madison tore up every commission as soon as he could, to appease the treaty and your Crown."

"Not my Crown," Everard said unthinking, surprising himself.

Hadn't he thought it many times without being able to say it? Why now?

"No?" Vitaliy's surprise floated up, a query mark of curiosity. But he said nothing further.

Everard imagined his thoughts. Not his Crown? He, the twenty-year career man? *That* Crown wasn't his?

Backtracking, regretting, Everard spoke hastily into the quiet anticipation.

"How many prizes did you take for Madison?"

"Twenty-two, not including the *Sévère.*"

Everard whistled. Prizes were sometimes valued at one hundred thousand American dollars. "Your riches aren't just vanilla."

"No." The query mark was still there, faintly. "Do you mind?"

"That I've tied myself to a king's ransom, you mean?" Everard turned his head and kissed him, slid his tongue over the soft, welcoming fullness. "It's an unfortunate complication, but I'm accustoming myself." He reached, found Vitaliy already half-hard from the brief kiss. "You could spill on my chest—make it more worthwhile."

Vitaliy laughed, warmly this time. "I like that you mind it," he said, low. "I like that my wealth gave you pause. I won't keep it forever."

"I know that." Vitya would keep it only as long as he must, to accomplish what he needed to, in order to succeed. "You needn't justify it to me, of all."

"But I do," Vitya insisted. "Because you care for it." He levered himself up and over, straddling. "And I want you to like me. The man. Not the pirate."

"Er… no question of that, I hope," Everard said dazedly. He stroked a thick thigh, flexed his fingers over fuzzed warmth. "Surely by now my alignment has been made clear?" The gold ring glinted in the moonlight. "I said yes. I want to stay. You gave me a *printing press.* I like everything about you, Vitya. I'm honored you want me by your side."

Vitya gave a happy hum. Then, slowly, deliberately, he stroked himself. Everard was pinned, laid flat, stunned speechless not by the weight or even the beauty of Vitya's body over him, but by the solemn, deep earnestness in his expression, the burning affection in dark eyes.

Everard had for once said the right thing. It seemed Vitya, the man—the strictly egalitarian, majority-elected, reluctant captain—did in fact like to be worshipped. Adored.

Everard thought, *Worship I shall.* And so he put out his tongue, and his fingers, and pulled the man closer.

"C'm'ere," he said. "I'll show you how much care I have."

Afterward, Vitya bent, breathless, and licked errant drops from Everard's skin.

"D'you think we might've met on the Atlantic?" Everard mused, gasping.

"Mm." Vitaliy kissed up to Everard's collarbone, soft and sucking. "Maybe." He veered down, and Everard seized with ticklishness. "No, I think not. I would've hoped not. I know of your record."

"Do you? Have you been speaking to Preston? He inflates these things out of proportion, you know."

"Hmm," Vitya said. "No."

"No?"

Vitaliy glanced up, then pointedly down. "He does not."

Everard blinked. Laughed, a little disbelievingly.

Vitya slid further south, with purpose, and Everard wanted that—desperately—but his prick could wait. Probably should wait, in all honesty. He pulled at shoulders instead and said:

"No, I still do… No, hang on a moment; I do want to talk of Alarie."

Vitya halted. "Now? You haven't—"

"Yes, now, in earnest. Else it'll never happen, and I let you do that. I can't exactly bring it up abovedeck, can I?"

Vitaliy sighed but drew back.

Everard said, "Alarie went from being commodore of Cartagena… to governor of unknown Galveztown. Not a lateral move."

"Mm." Vitaliy flopped onto his side.

"You won't help him take it? Galveztown?"

Vitaliy snorted. "I don't need to. It is no more than a sandbar." He paused. "He did ask, but I refused."

Everard's ears pricked up at this, crackling with focus. *I refused.*

That was, in his eyes, plenty reason for a man like Louis-Michel Alarie to hold a grudge. Plenty motive to want a man dead. In a true navy, such a thing would have got a man executed for dereliction of duty. And the refusal of Alarie's authority, even an authority granted by a failed nation-state, would have stung.

But V. Varfolomey was a pirate-privateer, an outlaw, untethered to any jurisdiction at all. Surely, Alarie had gone into the relationship realising that.

If he still to this day wanted Vitaliy and his ships for his navy, why would he have had him captured, court-martialed, and hanged?

"You, Vitaliy, refused him, or did Varfolomey?"

Vitaliy hesitated longer than was usual. "It was… personal," he said at last. "We had a falling-out. But Alarie's sheltered slavers before. Varfolomey has excuse enough."

"You fell out badly enough to leave his navy, refuse him aid?"

Vitaliy grunted. "Yes. Besides that, he wants muscle for his own gain and glory. Not as aid for México. He's a filibuster; a power-seeker; a user. Something I didn't realise upon first acquaintance with him in Cartagena."

Gain and glory. This flew close enough to Everard's own career heart that he felt defensive. "Well, gain and glory, achieving a greater good… they can go hand-in-hand. Yes?"

Vitaliy nodded. "Sometimes, they can," he agreed. "But intention matters."

Everard raised up on an elbow. "But how can one judge that of another?"

"I have seen what motivates him."

"How can one know a man's heart by observation?" Everard challenged. "There must be a reason Alarie defected from France, from his profession, from his family, and became a filibuster. Has he told you why? Has he a manifesto? Would you believe it if he had?"

Vitaliy was silent.

"Take yourself. Who knows what drives you but you? Or take Varfolomey, even. Surely, no one *truly* thinks he is motivated by altruism alone. It would be… unnatural. For any man, if not especially for a pirate."

Vitaliy looked displeased. "Unnatural," he said.

"Saintly is what I meant," Everard said hastily. "Martyrlike. Unachievable legend. Heracles. Atlas."

"That isn't better than unnatural," Vitaliy said slowly, and gave him a pointed look. "It is still *other*. But I see what you mean. To be a pirate is to be a legend; a story; judged on surface." He settled onto his back, put his head into the cradle of his left elbow, and wiggled wool-sheathed toes. "That was intentional, and truthfully I don't think they are comparable situations. Varfolomey is necessarily exaggerated. No one expects a man with flaws and desires behind him."

*Not until you told the world you wanted me,* Everard thought.

With the space of Vitaliy's body open, welcoming him again, Everard shifted closer and crowded in, so that their noses nearly touched. "And a very good raised black he presents," he whispered. "But you said the pirate and the flesh-and-blood man are the same." He tapped Vitaliy lightly on the chest. "So, what's changed to impede that altruist, judgmental heart of yours? Why do you need Alarie?"

"I don't." Vitaliy turned his eyes downcast, swept them back up over Everard's face, wide and earnest. "Varfolomey does." He lowered his voice. "He wouldn't oblige him more than outwardly but for Jean Lafitte."

Everard drew back. "Lafitte is such a threat to you? Preston said he has only a few schooners, war hero or no." He sneered. To think that such a man was dubbed a hero of anything.

"It'd be unwise to consider him not a threat. But lately, neither he nor his brother has been seen at Barataria or New Orleans. Not once o'er the past months, before even I was detained in Canada."

"Mayhap he's dead," Everard said. "Caiman-eaten. Barataria's a swamp, isn't it?"

Vitaliy smiled. "No, I doubt he's dead. I think he is too restless since his American pardon."

He sat up, drew his hands through tangled hair, pushed it behind his ears. "I think that he is planning. Sitting on a corsair in the Gulf with his secretary, writing letters."

"A secretary. He sounds quite dangerous," Everard teased.

Vitaliy nodded. "He is," he said, matter-of-fact, either ignoring Everard's tone entirely or not hearing it. "His loyalty is as unfixed as his citizenship. He's American now, but before that, he was spying for the British, and before them the French."

"What a coincidental pattern," Everard said dryly. "Who do you suppose is next?"

Vitaliy's gaze turned suddenly serious, fixed on Everard. "Spain."

The query mark was back, loud as a bell.

Everard swallowed. "Of course. Galveztown. He'd want it for Spain, then. And Varfolomey, in contrast, has declared his support for revolutionary México?"

"No," Vitaliy replied. Still serious.

Vitaliy wouldn't… suspect Everard? After all that, for an offhand, accidental remark? For a surname, a language? Vitaliy had been more forthcoming, more honest than anyone he'd ever met. Trade routes, ship manifests, crew numbers, gun counts—he'd kept nothing back.

Vitaliy nudged closer, 'til his knees were touching Everard's hip. He began to pull at the sheet entangling Everard's ankles.

"No?" Everard watched warily. "Not even México? I thought…"

"Varfolomey declares for no one now. I learned this lesson with Alarie, and Cartagena. But Spain is his enemy. And the enemy to most of the *Sévère*'s ports of call."

"Slaver bastards," Everard agreed.

He resisted the urge to defend himself against those cool dark-blues. Could Vitaliy really think him a spy? With their history? It made no sense.

What in hell would the Spanish crown have wanted in York, Upper Canada, anyway?

But one couldn't just say *Yes, I am Spanish, not actually English, you have me there; but not a spy, I swear it.*

In the silence, Vitaliy bent to Everard's left ankle, sheet in hand, and wrapped one tail around. He glanced up as he tied a knot that Everard didn't recognise—Russians had their own system of knots—but it had a slip loop. When he had finished, he sat back, and waited to see what Everard would say.

Which was a mystified "Er" but definitely not a "No", which was what he suspected Vitaliy was looking out for.

He didn't want to give it. He wanted to see what came next.

"Are we done with talking?" Vitya said. Watching him, he wrapped Everard's other ankle with long fingers and pulled it closer, across the width of the cot. Then Everard's legs were spread obscenely, toes almost meeting each corner, one thigh resting across Vitaliy's lap.

"Yes, fine, if you wish." Done talking, but Everard's prick had a lot to say about this situation. "Are you really tying up a man with six fingers?"

"Yes," Vitaliy said, and then did the same to the right ankle —again inserting a slip loop, drawing the sheet taut between Everard's spread ankles. Everard groaned.

"The stones on you. Mayhap I should revise— Are you really tying up a Navy man? With *slip loops?*"

"Yes," Vitaliy said, this time with a smile.

"How insulting," Everard said. "I thought pirates only tortured those less than forthcoming."

Vitaliy slid out from under Everard's leg. The look on his face was strange. For a moment, Everard thought he'd changed his mind, that he would undo the knots himself.

"That was a jest," Everard said quickly. "I didn't mean it."

"If I want to know something I don't," Vitaliy said, slowly, "I will ask."

Everard's heart thumped. He raised up on elbows, careful not to move. Even done in linen, the knots would fall apart at a sharp movement.

"All right. But what is it you think you know?"

Vitaliy straddled over to kneel in the wide space between Everard's knees, and sat back on socked heels. The mosquito gauze framed him like a caped cloak, shimmering in the horizontal dawn light.

"I know you trust me," he said.

He didn't wait for confirmation. He put a single finger on the tip of Everard's prick and drew it straight and upright, until Everard shivered.

"I know you want to be here. With me."

Vitaliy dragged his finger down, back up again.

"I know you speak like an Englishman…"

He grasped firmly, broad callused palm and long fingers cool and practiced, and stroked once.

Everard gasped. "S-so do you," he said, "when you wish it. Lieutenant-Marine."

"But you are not one." Vitaliy's gaze was dark blue, flame

where it was hottest. "I have known that since I first put my mouth on you."

"*Christ.*" They hadn't done that yet—not in three years—not since York. Everard wanted it more than air, and couldn't think why he hadn't asked for it from get-go. "Really? You did?"

Vitaliy nodded, and stroked slowly, up and down. "And I know your heart."

"Oh, God." Everard writhed. "Yes, you do. And I'll tell you whatever, you know," Everard rambled. "I'm Spanish Catalan—pressed from the docks of Barcelona at twelve—forged my citizenship papers to make officer—I've never known anything but the British Na—"

Vitaliy leaned in quick, and kissed him, hard, on the mouth.

"I said I will *ask*," he said, forehead against Everard's, lips still touching. "Do you wish me to suck you or not?"

Everard gulped. "Please."

"Good," Vitaliy said. He nudged Everard's thighs carefully wider, slid down onto his stomach. Settled in and hooked his elbows to either side of Everard's hips, watching him the while, as if to promise, *This isn't going to end soon, oh, no.*

Then he took him in, all the way down.

"Ohh, Sant Jesús. Vitya."

Even after last night, Everard wouldn't outlast the fading-orange dawn. He was damn well going to try. He put a hand up to push back the bed-mussed, fine-silk hair, to gather it—

*Crack-boom.*

Vitaliy flinched badly, gagged, and, as Everard exclaimed and reached for him, levered himself upright. "*What?*" he gasped. His red-lipped expression was pure disbelief and shock.

Everard sat up. "God, are you all right? Was that *our*

cannon?" he asked, idiotically, because obviously it had been. "We weren't heading *into* Havana port, by chance?"

Vitaliy launched off the cot like a north-woods panther, just as silent as one; Everard shook his head to clear it, and scrabbled at his ankles, cursing the world. Thankfully, Vitaliy's mysterious slipknots worked as intended. Vitaliy thundered out of the greatcabin in no more than a shirt, leaving the door ajar and Everard hopping into drawers.

Abovedecks, the cannon shot had already scrambled a fair few others from their beds and onto the weather deck: Louis-Michel Alarie, D'Arcy, León the bo'sun. Thom stumbled up out of the hatch, ahead of Stephan the surgeon, quickly followed by Romilly René.

"Who dares?" Vitaliy demanded. "Which cannon was shot? Milly?"

Romilly René answered quickly: "Ángel." Every one of the *Sévère*'s cannon were stamped and named. "Second deck, larboard bow."

"The powder room?" Everard inquired.

"Secure," León said. "Unbroached."

Mystifying, but… "Thank God."

"Sail, to larboard!" called out Louis-Michel Alarie. They all hurried to the rail.

There, D'Arcy handed him a glass, along with a raised eyebrow.

"You look…"

"Yes, rather, thank you," Everard finished for him. He raised the glass. "Oh, *damnation*. Well, there's wherefore the shot."

There was a ship on the dawn horizon, its bow pointing in the *Sévère*'s direction. A ship-of-the-line, riding the trades to Cuba, colours undetermined. A ship to whom the *Sévère* had just made a warning shot, as though she were really a Spanish warship, wanting their colours. And at the moment—Everard twisted to confirm—the *Sévère* was still flying the red-yellow-white.

"Pure provocation," D'Arcy said cheekily. "And a good morn to you, too, Ev."

As they watched, the *boom* of reply shot came, its smoke puff trailing up. But still no colours came.

Shite. They either recognised her as an enemy or didn't trust she wasn't.

"She's Armada. Who the fuck was watch on deck?" Vitaliy growled.

León opened his mouth, but Vitaliy didn't wait for a response. He hauled up onto the rail and into the mainmast ratlines. Everard put down the glass and watched him go, blinking. Vitya really hadn't put on anything but a shirt—

He disappeared. Then something large and dark tumbled over the edge of the topmain platform where he had entered. The falling, rolling thing narrowly missed the mainsail yard; and before anyone could yell, there was an incredible, meaty *splat-thunk* onto the deck before them. It was the sprawled body of a white man, someone Everard didn't recognise, covered in blood and bowels, very dead.

"Good lord!" Everard exclaimed.

"Madre mía." León crossed himself rapidly.

Stephan the surgeon crouched over the broken body, needing no more than a moment. He shook his head. "Dead an hour, at least."

"Putain," Alarie cursed. "We have been infiltrated a-purpose."

Everard looked up to D'Arcy. His eyes were wide. *Another false watchman? Here? In the middle of the Gulf?*

There was a sharp whistle, and Vitaliy appeared again over the platform.

"Marcus is dead," he called down, loud but weary. "I need a chair."

Thom ran to retrieve it.

Vitaliy gave Everard a long look, one that said: *You know what to do.* Then he disappeared back onto the platform.

And Everard did know.

"León," he ordered, "an immediate all-hands, please. Fleet master René, take ten crew and search the ship, bow to stern. We've traitors aboard."

If anyone minded the abrupt shift of authority, it didn't show. León's whistle blew, and the bell was rung. Romilly René disappeared; Everard heard her bellowing orders below.

León ran to the foremast. Everard feared what he'd find.

D'Arcy crouched beside Stephan. "Marcus put up a fight," he murmured. "This one bled out?"

Stephan nodded. The ship's surgeon was a slight, soft-spoken Black man with whom Everard, chronically healthy on the water, hadn't had much conversation with one-on-one, but knew from the post-supper singing and music that the whole ship indulged in. He had a Philadelphian accent in a beautiful low baritone that—more often than not—smoothed over Vee's hesitant, staccato fiddle-playing, and steady doctor's hands that corrected Vee on his fingering.

Everard hadn't missed his subtle survey of Everard's defi-nitely-not-syphilitic forearm upon first meeting. The protective-ness for his friend and captain had endeared him to Everard instantly.

"Here." Stephan pointed to a red-soaked rent of trouser. "Or here." A lower right-side puncture, equally soaked. Marcus had fought hard and fierce; his murderer hadn't outlived him long.

"The poor brave sod," Everard said.

Thom returned, chair slung over his shoulder.

D'Arcy stood. "I'll help with the chair." He handed Everard one of his pistols, and then up into the ratlines he too went. It would take two to maneuver a dead man into the sling chair and carefully belay him down.

Louis-Michel Alarie stood behind his own gilt spyglass, eyeing the ship on the horizon.

"What do you think, Governor?" Everard asked. "Is it Armada?"

"I believe yes," Alarie said crisply, after a moment. "Her make is very new: anti-revolutionary, as they have used against us in Amérique du Sud. I will say… seventy guns? But quicker than you would think. And she's windward, of course—on the trades."

"Right," Everard replied. He blew out a breath. The *Sévère* was anything but fast: most especially when sailing against the wind as they were. "Well, shite. What's the chance of Vee tacking and fleeing her?"

Alarie's eyes flicked over, as if wondering why Everard didn't know the answer to that. Everard wondered too.

"With men murdered on his deck?" Alarie tapped his lips. "Very small, I think. Especially now we have shot at her." He grimaced. "We have a rendezvous."

# Eighteen

Three hours by Vitaliy's hack watch, 'til the warship would be close enough to engage; a forenoon confrontation.

Not much time at all.

Abovedecks, they'd found every man of the fourth bell watch had been murdered sometime in the predawn. León had found the foretopman as dead as Marcus, similarly garroted. They had a hasty funeral, and René turned up three more infiltrator unknowns from her sweep, three more infiltrators that someone had let aboard.

Two and one-half hours.

All three gun decks had been cleared for action. The crew hammocks had been rolled, lashed, and stacked into the rail stanchions as a canvas parapet against musket sight. Even the guns in Vitaliy's greatcabin had been run out and pointed.

Vitaliy had the infiltrating Spaniards gagged and tied to the mainmast while he held council on what to do with them. It wasn't a long discussion; mostly, the question was whether they had the time to coerce information from them, and what use it would be. It was only at René's anticipatory gleam at the suggestion of torture that Everard fully understood the strange, conflicted look that had come over Vitaliy earlier, because it came down over his brows like a shadow again.

Everard thought of León's comment. *Not even Vee crosses her.*

In the end, the verdict was almost unanimous: given the little time, and since the fourth bell watch had all been garroted, the pirates kept to their infamous code of reciprocity. They hauled the infiltrators up in tight nooses, the loose end of each threaded through a block and winch that was cranked much too slowly for mercy. They were hung from the bowsprit, better to be seen by the advancing enemy.

Everard had seen worse in the name of what the Crown called justice. He tried to keep this in mind, observing Vitaliy as the sentence was meted out: his straight back, flattened lips, and slight, troubled frown.

But reciprocal violence was written into his articles, the pirate code of law. His hands were tied.

*How are you truly a pirate, Vitya?* he wondered. *How is this the man Vitaliy Gray became?*


Two hours.

The Spanish ship—named by the three dead instigators as *San Telmo*—crept closer, sending up signal flag after signal flag, until finally they raised the inevitable: surrender or face death.

To this, the *Sévère* raised the massive black, with Varfolomey's signature calligraphic V upon it in stark white; beneath it, the deadly red. No quarter made in battle.

No point not to. The *Sévère* could not flee if they wanted to keep course, and the crew wouldn't want her to even if she could. They wanted recompense. Justification for losing five men, for the backbreaking trouble of sailing a massive, slow meregildo. They wanted battle, the thrill of another Spanish warship prize.


One and one-half hours.

"They are holding back. I don't think they will try and destroy her outright," Vitaliy said. "Though five years ago, Spain would have scuttled her."

He was seated high up in the foremast ratlines again, fully dressed in a plain but effective uniform of navy blue breeches, white linen, brown herringbone waistcoat and leather bandolier. His hair was plastered back in the tight queue it had been the day of the coffeeshop, when Aedd the butler had received them with unexpected violence.

"They may also want *you*," Everard said quietly.

He received a deep scoff. "I am not so important." Vitya squeezed Everard's hand.

He'd learned this about Vitaliy: before a battle, he wanted little talk, and almost no contact but touch. Today he'd settled for Everard's hand loosely in his as they sat up high, alternating the spyglass and mugs of cold Haitian coffee between them, watching the Spaniards crawl over their lines in preparation for battle.

It was hard to be still, but Everard had realised over many previous battles that pacing the decks only agitated everyone else, and didn't help his own state of mind that much anyway.

"What about Alarie?" he asked.

Vitaliy hesitated. The way the morning light glanced off the flat, golden planes of his face, curved over his parted lips was devastating. "Maybe they want him, yes."

"Will he keep to his cabin?"

"Louis-Michel?" Vitaliy's eyebrows rose. "No. He may act above us all, but he is a sailor. A fighter. Bolívar appointed him commodore not for nothing." He slid over a glance. "Don't underestimate him."

One hour.

Everard's arse was numb and cold from leaning on tarred hemp line, his face hot and dry from the beating sun. The southeast wind had picked up drastically two points forward to starboard, inhibitory to the *Sévère*'s tack but advantageous to the enemy. The mood on the *Sévère* was muted vibration, anticipatory held breath.

Beneath them, a glint of impeccably kept pistol caught Everard's eye, and he glanced down.

D'Arcy had come jogging up the hatch. Bright sable curls blew wild in the wind as he stood on the main deck and looked unerringly up to where Everard stood in the ratlines.

Then he put hands in pockets, set his shoulders, and strode determinedly in their direction.

Everard inhaled. "Oh, God."

He knew that look. That beeline. That intent.

Vitaliy lowered the glass. "Hmm?" He followed Everard's attention, and made a low, amused noise. "Ah."

"He wants..." Everard trailed off, cleared his throat.

Vitaliy found his hand and squeezed it. "I know what he wants." Heart-shaped lips quirked. "Do you want the same?"

Everard flushed all the way to his first waistcoat button, despite the sun.

"He's accustomed to... We may have—er... before a conflict. On occasion. So, I can see where he might think—"

"Not what I ask," Vitya murmured. "Do you?"

It *sounded* like a trap, a trick question, gammoning. But it didn't feel like that. He still had not the least idea what to say. "I..."

D'Arcy came beneath the shroud. "Ever?" he called up.

It was all he said. All he had to say. Fearless, fearless D'Arcy.

"Oh, lord." Everard's breath felt netted, caught somewhere beneath his stomach. "All right, yes, I do. But… I don't understand."

Vitaliy squeezed his hand once more, then pulled free, retrieved his pocket watch. "He left it late, but you've a little time." He nodded to the *San Telmo*. "Too much wind yet to engage. Not without risking us raking her through."

That was true.

"But you truly don't mind?" Vitya's indifference towards D'Arcy had been one thing when he and Everard hadn't been sleeping together regularly. Now, though…

But Vitaliy shook his head. "No, matelot. Not significantly." He smiled. "Options are always good."

"Right," Everard said, baffled. "I don't know if…" *Options.* Was that what D'Arcy was? "Well. I'll… take you at your word, then." He detached himself from the lines and about-faced to climb down. He acknowledged D'Arcy, who nodded and bounced on his heels once, straight-faced.

Was he an option? Or was he inevitable?

Everard made one last look over. Vitaliy's attention was vigilant and workmanlike again, already back on the glass.

Everard stepped sideways, straddling, invading space. "Vitya."

Vitaliy pulled aside the glass with a grunt of surprise, caught Everard by the waist as he leaned in, and let the lines take their weight. Everard kissed him, full on the mouth.

After a moment, Vitya broke off, biting gently. He mumbled, "Go."

Everard went before he lost his nerve entirely.

On deck, D'Arcy looked up at him from under tumultuous curls. "Braggart. Peacock. Bull. What a display."

Everard smoothed his waistcoat. He was already breathing as though he'd climbed four sets of ratlines, up and down.

"You are the very devil, Preston. I cannot believe you."

D'Arcy grinned like a fool. "Yes, you can. You've done this before."

Oh, he had. "Come on."

He led the way.


Three-quarter hours.

In the Navy, nobody had much read into their disappearing on the cusp of battle. Even if Everard looked out of his wits with anticipation, D'Arcy had a dissembler's effortless nonchalance, an ease that usefully deflected attention.

Too, he was very good at remaining quiet under duress.

D'Arcy followed him, calm and hands-in-pockets. But as they swung round aft to the teniente's quarters, surrounded by pirates and cannon and all the preparations of battle, D'Arcy pulled him against the partition wall and kissed him, leant the whole of himself against the whole of Everard, chest and hips and knees.

Everard gulped as his stomach swooped in shuddering leaps. He glanced round—

"Ever." D'Arcy drew his attention gently back, and the look on his face—no dissembling today, no, sir—Everard's mouth went dry. D'Arcy's eyes were dark, long-lashed, mischievous beneath arched brows, almost villainous in their knowledge: *You know what's to come, and you can't stop it.*

No. Not if it killed him.

D'Arcy pushed his hips in close once more—making Everard gasp louder than he meant—and reached for the latch of the apartment door.

"You'll have to be gentle," D'Arcy murmured against his

lips as their steps tangled, as Everard was pulled across the threshold. "Careful. Quiet."

"Right." Everard stamped down disappointment, ashamed at himself. It didn't matter. "Of course." Then he paused. "Really?"

D'Arcy laughed. He kicked the door shut; it creaked and then banged. Resolute.

"Hell, no. Absolutely not." He'd at some point undone all Everard's buttons, and now spread clothing aside for exquisite access. He leaned in to nip at Everard's ear. "Like the first time, hmm? But loud."

Everard groaned.

"Yes, precisely that loud," D'Arcy said approvingly, and kissed him.

*The first time.* Too long past. Everard had known that First Lieutenant Preston D'Arcy wanted him. Despite Everard's best efforts, D'Arcy had known he was wanted in return.

And so, with a Frenchie bearing down on them, mere minutes away, D'Arcy had given him one significant look as he handed over an impeccable diagram of the ship's maneuver. A rueful smile.

"Now, Everard," he'd said softly. "If you want it—now, or not ever again."

A hell of a thing to say, especially as the first time he'd used Everard's given name. Not particularly nice, either, to give him an ultimatum under the influence of the strain of battle.

Of course, Everard had then found himself pushing D'Arcy against the perforated companionway door—the only standing room in the place; it wasn't a large greatcabin—and before Everard really understood what was happening, emotionally, had had D'Arcy with arms splayed, back arched, holding the worked-filigree door shut. D'Arcy kept watch and held his body taut as Everard screwed into him like he had never before done to a man, hard and fast, dizzying with the effort not to breathe. He hadn't even once got himself fully inside; it should've been unsatisfying. But D'Arcy had left a bite mark the size of a doubloon through his lieutenant's uniform sleeve, and Everard had remembered nothing of the battle afterward, just that it'd got them promoted.

And the guilt. He'd remembered the guilt, too.

Now D'Arcy spun round against the door, shoved down pantaloons. *Like the first time.*

Everard had made a choice then. He'd made a choice today, on deck, with Vitya's urging him on. *Now, or not ever again.*

Maybe not an ultimatum. Perhaps a warning.

*But I could have died.*

Why was he so—goddamn—fearless?

D'Arcy jerked. "Fuck, oh, fuck." His fingers on the wood spasmed.

It wasn't like the first time. Perhaps a little bit, in the lack of space. In D'Arcy's taut, locked muscles. In the positioning, in the shape of Everard's hands grasping his hips.

Otherwise…

Everard sheathed himself fully, nudged them forward. D'Arcy put his weight on his forearms, banged a fist on the door, took hiccupping breaths. Everard began anew.

"Shit, oh, Jesus *Christ*, ohhh, Ever. Keep talking. D-don't stop."

Was Everard speaking? To him, the loudest thing was his breathing; it kept coming back to him reflected from D'Arcy's skin, hot and damp.

When did they get so close? There was no space between them. D'Arcy's fingertips now only grazed the door in faint, just-in-case support. Everard had gathered the rest of him in, and he was no longer taut, no fight left in him, no resistance, no demand.

Everard's face felt wet alongside D'Arcy's, and he didn't know what from, sweat or tears or both—or whose.

"Bed?" he gasped.

"Bed," D'Arcy agreed.


ONE QUARTER-HOUR.

"If that was the last time—if I die today—top marks," D'Arcy slurred.

"You won't d—but you are ridiculous." Everard pulled on his stockings. "You said that in York." He nudged an oil-shiny arse cheek with a finger. "And on the *Wanderer*. And—"

"Did I?" D'Arcy huffed. "You and your memory. I don't remember what I said after. I *do* remember that prick." He rolled, stretched, and yawned; when he opened his eyes, their hazel was bright and alert. "Now I can fight."

Buttoning his waistcoat, Everard shook his head. He leaned down, squinted presumptuously, and kissed him on the forehead. "Was I sufficiently loud?"

"Mm-hmm." D'Arcy ran his hands through curls. "I'll say." Stark naked, he launched up like a man ten years younger. "This is a delightful tradition. Let's keep it."

"You know," Everard said with a laugh, "I rather think we have."

# Nineteen

"Larboard-aft battery, run out guns!" Everard bellowed.

The second-deck guns were hauled forward to their ports. Everard crouched to run behind the line of cannon, making an ungainly almost-crawl across the deck as he craned his head to take their sights. It wasn't what an officer usually risked doing, and it wasted time, but he had to be sure he still had a high angle before smoke overcame them.

Vitaliy was abovedecks, calling for the *Sévère* to tack into the wind, the madman, and the mizzen was backed and straining to brink. The effect was she heeled sharply to larboard, making a high cannon-shot trajectory a tall ask.

Through the port Everard watched the horizon rise, the *San Telmo* and her gun ports upon it. Now, now, now—

"Fire!" He slid clear of the last gun.

Two dozen wicklights came down; the second gundeck went bright with sparks; sleds creaked and rumbled with kickback.

Everard picked himself up and breathed deep. He hadn't been this close to burning sulfur in years.

"Sponge!" he called, in cadence just the same as he'd said a hundred times in battle, but never here. "Shot your guns! Fast as you can go, boys; again!"

Miracle of miracles, they listened. The *Sévère* had no gunner, nor formal gun crew. She was no longer a warship, but a pirate, half-merchant. She had almost nothing left in the way of orderly procedures of warfare.

What she did have was the bones to support the machine of war: 110 named cannon, shot, powder, and plenty of skilled crew.

Everard, too.

"Run 'em out!"

*Suppressing fire*, Vitaliy had ordered—told—him. *Keep them outrange. Aim as high as you can.*

Everard sighted just one gun this time. High, all right. "Fire!"

Sparks lit the deck into firework orange and smoke and shadows, and another volley was let free.

He didn't know why Vitaliy wanted high suppressing fire when he had initially refused to tack and flee; nor why he was tacking and fleeing now, and risking being overtaken with raking fire from the *San Telmo* if they were unable to complete the turn.

But he wasn't captain. It wasn't his place.

"Sponge! Shot!"

He did wonder how much of the cargo Vitaliy was interested in keeping dry and intact. A man concerned for his profit —and his crew—would have fled long since.

Above them, the mizzen and main yards creaked as they were braced to larboard; feet stomped and ropes sang in their blocks. The *Sévère* began to heel less and less, levelling; they were almost directly in the wind now and would soon lose their broadside.

"Run out, run out!"

In guns, the *Sévère* had the advantage of numbers over the

*San Telmo*, 110 to seventy-four; but as it had stood with the wind and the heeling, her third-deck ports had been nearly in the water, making their numbers skirt equal. Now, however… there was an opportunity.

"Fire!"

As the smoke streamed, Everard barely waited for the kick-back to settle before he threw himself down the hatch.

"Third-deck larboard-aft battery, run out your guns!" he bellowed; there was a flurry of activity as the order was repeated. He thought he could time the cadence so that there was hardly a pause between the second and third decks' firing. He hadn't controlled a three-deck gun crew before, much less a three-deck not-gun-crew, without subordinates; but he was damned well going to try.

Beneath his feet he could feel her begin to heel starboard, which meant she was really tacking. It was excellent news, but it also meant now or never, if he wanted to utilise the third deck broadside—

"Fire!"

She was really turning now. He stomped back up the ladder.

"Second battery, secure larboard guns and run out to starboard! Third battery, sponge and ready once more!"

Everard stomped back down. He needed a subordinate. Three. But third deck's guns were pointed; good.

"Fi—"

"Belay that!" came a snarl just in time. Vitaliy came down the ladder, eyes wild. "For fuck's sake! I said aim high, top decks only, matelot!"

Everard's built-and-tested cadence died to a whimper, beats of a failing heart. He had never seen Vitaliy quite so angry.

Nevertheless, he snapped, "You certainly hadn't!" incensed to be interrupted, overruled. "You said suppressive fire! Which is effective only so long it is sustained!"

The crew halted, watched them uneasily. Shite. The start of battle, and him undermining Vee's authority—

Vitaliy clutched his arm, pulled him close. "You will blow us all to heaven," he muttered in his ear. "No," he said, as Everard stiffened, "don't be insulted; it is nothing to do with skill. I will show you why." He ordered up to the second deck, "Repeat larboard fire 'til we've tacked about!"

They did, guns ablaze; and just like that, Everard was made redundant again.

"I'll blow us to kingdom come, will I? But a crew with no cadence, firing at their leisure won't?"

Vitaliy ignored this and released him. "Come down with me. They can spare you."

"Of course they can," he said bitterly. He thought now he must've looked quite the fool, running up and down, trying to rope a pirate crew into a Navy rhythm.

"They can spare me, too," Vitaliy said. "Milly has the helm."

Curiosity was winning over anger. Slightly.

"Down… to the hold?" he asked.

"Yes."

"You'll abandon your post? Now? As they surely overtake and board us?"

Vitaliy frowned. "There's no one else for this," he said. He slung himself down the ladder, into the deep, dark hold.

Everard followed. What did that mean? Something Vitaliy couldn't trust to another soul.

Vitaliy jumped down from the last rung and brushed off his palms. He picked his way across the keel, unerringly pushed through straw bales and hanging stores to the stacks of hogsheads.

Everard, not knowing what he searched for, paused to scratch his comedown-trembling fingers against the velvet skull and flicking ears of a white ship's cat lounging in its hammock.

It blinked sleepily at him, too full on rats to be more than nonchalant at the scrape and boom of guns directly above.

Vitaliy disappeared aft and didn't ask him to follow.

Everard felt absurd to be idle.

"White can't be an advantage to you, down here in the dark," he murmured to the cat. "Brave little thing."

The cat splayed claws and kneaded the miniature hammock, and then leapt down to the keel and trotted off, tail high, in the direction Vitaliy had gone.

There was an abrupt lull in the guns, seawater slapping against the hull; they'd completed the tack.

Vitaliy emerged—sidestepping the cat—with a trunk over his shoulder, not much larger than Everard's own little sea chest.

"Funny the cats haven't scattered, what with the guns," Everard said.

Vitaliy glanced back. "That cat is white."

"And so?"

"White cats are frequently deaf."

"Huh." Not such a disadvantage, after all. "What's in the trunk?"

"I will show you—in the greatcabin." Vitaliy dug in his pocket, held out the magazine key on a lanyard. "We'll need a twelve-pound keg."

"A *keg?* You're jesting."

Vitaliy stared at him. He wasn't jesting.

"I don't fit in the magazine. Is that all right?" He hesitated. "Would it… disturb you? Being near to powder?"

Everard laughed. "I won't fit much better. And that question is a little bit belated, Vitya, when I've been breathing sulfur for the past hour at least."

Vitaliy looked even more concerned; his hand pulled back.

"But no, it doesn't. I was too close, and never felt the magazine blow." Everard waved his left hand. "This was a crushing injury: my wrist got pinned, and the fingers swelled. I came to beneath a column of brickwork"—*and bodies*—"as Preston was pulling me out."

"Oh." Vitaliy's eyes went wide. "York? The magazine in York?"

"Mm-hm," Everard confirmed. "About a week after we… er… met, in fact."

Friendly fire. Deadly self-sabotage. Whatever one called it, the major-general of York had ordered the magazine set to blow, and it had: heedless of any and all soldiers within the periphery, including him. Everard, completely unaware of his retreating superior's plans, or indeed that he was retreating at all, had pushed together a small line of trembling-knee militia on the road against the approaching Yankee stars-and-stripes, had called something resembling a firing cadence, and—

Powder had gone off, but it hadn't been the militia guns.

"But in all seriousness," Everard said, "you want me to carry a twelve-pound keg through three decks of guns and *live fuses*? What in hell's name is in that trunk?"

Vitaliy wiped a hand over his mouth, blew out a short breath. "I trust you not to trail a path. Do you trust me?"

Everard slid his shoes off so he stood in stocking feet—for the magazine—and sighed. "You know I do. Give me that."

Vitaliy handed the key over on an outstretched finger.

Everard grimaced. "The *Sévère* has need of a powder monkey, do you know?"

"We are not usually a warship." Vitaliy peered down. "Those stockings have holes in," he murmured.

"Yes, they do."

"Wind?" Vitaliy demanded as they crossed into sunshine and salt air.

"Sur'east-by-east," León promptly replied.

Vitaliy nodded. "Pray it doesn't change." He looked up to the foremast, the sails there all filled now that they'd tacked around, and checked his hack watch. "And clew up the foresail and mainsail again."

Everard pursed his lips. Two courses drawn up? That didn't make sense. Didn't Vitaliy want good headway? Were they not fleeing? Had Everard not been scurrying forth and back, maintaining suppressive fire to prevent the *San Telmo* from overtaking them?

"I want her moving lateral to leeward," Vitaliy said, unnecessarily—as lateral movement could be the only result of such a bizarre directive. "Slack the starboard braces," he ordered, and squinted up, "twenty-five degrees."

A twenty-five-degree swing would put both yards almost abeam, parallel to the wind, slowing them quite a lot.

Everard said, "Hmmm."

"Keep me advised of our speed," Vitaliy said to León. "I want it taken every five minutes." He glanced over. "Input, matelot?"

"Not at all," Everard said politely, though the question, really, was *why* Vitaliy wanted the *Sévère* to do these things. "Where d'you want the bloody cask of explosives?"

"In a moment. Come behind the staysail, so they don't spy us by chance." There, he stepped in a circle, peering around sentry-like. "Where is the lieutenant? From you, he is never very…"

D'Arcy appeared: shirtsleeves, frilled; sailor's trousers, plain; mysteriously no gun bandolier. He'd been amidships, hauling lines. "Why the devil've we put up the frigging course… Holy gad, is that a powder keg?" His hand jerked forward, as though given the chance, he would snatch the keg and throw it over the side. Everard sympathised. His whole person crawled with unease.

"Lieutenant," Vitaliy said, not unironically. D'Arcy swiveled his attention and bowed. "Are you as good a shot as you say, or is it boasting?"

Everard said, "He's actually quite deadly—"

"One-inch grouping at twenty-five yards, unrifled." D'Arcy narrowed his eyes. "Why?"

"And with a shotgun?"

He dimpled. "Disallowed shooting in six shires, outside of competition. Ev"—he twitched his fingers for the keg—"give that here."

"I am perfectly fine, thank you," Everard said coolly.

Vitaliy was intent. "What about a harpoon gun?"

"Oooh," D'Arcy said, light in his eyes. "Never that. Are you offering? What's the calibre of such a thing?"

"Four-bore. Can you shoot it from the larboard gallery?"

D'Arcy bounced on his heels and whistled. "Four-bore. Can I? Absolutely. Spring-loaded or powder?" His glance flicked to the keg. "Silly question?"

The *San Telmo* issued another, not-so-distant warning shot. Vitaliy frowned and gestured them into the greatcabin.

They filed through, Everard leading, D'Arcy following, Vitaliy bolting the door behind—which he'd never done before, even at intimate moments. Inside, it was semi-dark; there were no lanterns and no candles lit. Only six-pane-divided sun rays slanted in at midday vertical. On the white rafters above, the reflection off the sea shimmered and wove. The doublewide cot was hauled up tight to the ceiling, out of the way of the run-out guns.

Everard set the keg down beside the desk, feeling suddenly rather queer. It took him a moment to pin down the sentiments, floating end-over-end like a handkerchief in the wind: regret, nostalgia, worry, fear.

Vitya bent his head to his hack watch once more, nodded to himself.

Everard hoped he knew what he was doing. That whatever it was would succeed. Because at some point in the past month, this ship, this cabin, had become home. Now he imagined it splintered, shot through, glass and lead blown out and the spray let in; his throat closed up in tight knots, pushing against his breathing, strangling it. He wanted to stomp like a child and scream and demand why weren't they to flee with the wind, when there was so *much* at stake—

"Oh, look at *him*," D'Arcy murmured.

Propped against the panelling of the larboard gallery, between two open windows, was indeed a massive shotgun with a harpoon spear sticking out of the barrel, gleaming steel. The harpoon trailed a lead, the end of which was connected to a—

Everard inhaled. "Floating torpedoes. Dear God."

Vitaliy's retrieved chest held several more harpoons, all with loops at the end. A tidy stack of torpedo shells lay open-face beneath, ready to be filled.

Everard was at a loss. "You said aim high…"

D'Arcy peered through the open window, unaffected by violence as usual, only intrigued. "How many did you put already?"

"Three," Vitaliy said, and jerked his chin towards a deskbound map. Everard leaned over carefully; he felt stiff and weak at the same time.

There on the grid were three neatly penciled x-coordinates, exactly along the spiked line of the *Sévère*'s recent, perfect tack.

She *had* to move laterally or else cross her own line of traps —traps her own captain had set.

Everard cursed. "You had these—these torpedoes—in here with us the whole time." *With us, as we slept, as we lay awake, as we fucked.*

Vitaliy glanced up quick, then down, and nodded, eyes on his task. Black powder hissed as it fell from the keg; he was already filling the war weapons, setting some kind of clockwork mechanism within, placing careful wicks, sealing them tight. There was precisely enough powder in the keg for all, which must have been intentional. Everard was for once glad of Gulf humidity.

He shook his head. "This is madness. You could sink us as easily as any other, Vitya, if the wind so much as…"

"Mathematically—if I have calculated it correctly—we should not ever get close." *If the wind holds,* Vitaliy didn't say. *If our movement stays on trajectory.* "They're on timers, all. If the *San Telmo* chases us at the speed she was, and follows our dead reckon, the floating leads will drag her hull and stick there. A little while after…"

"They'll blow holes to either side of her hull."

"Mm."

"Genius," D'Arcy said. He had loaded the harpoon gun monstrosity and was lifting it, settling it against his shoulder, sighting it. "Wind is southeast-by-east… how many points into it, Vee?"

"Two, for compensation," Vitaliy responded. "East by south."

D'Arcy adjusted his broad stance. Everard's heart clutched. *I wish Vitaliy had picked anyone else for this,* he thought. *Anyone else.*

Absurd. He'd seen Preston D'Arcy covered head-to-toe in blood, grease, mud, sick, seawater; a mix of all of these. Had seen him injured, grinning, battle-mad, thrilled even as they'd failed and been defeated and the ship around them flared with sinking flame. Had seen his face, calm and pale as he twisted his belt round Everard's left wrist, held the smashed hand there in his lap.

Everard set his jaw. "Vitya. You don't know there aren't captives on that ship."

"No." Vitaliy stood, strode to the companionway, wrenched open the greatcabin door. "I don't know. Starboard-aft, return two shots to leeward!" he bellowed. It was repeated—Romilly René—and the scrape of two gunsleds was heard, very close.

Covering fire—just as Everard's suppressing cadence had been. Distraction from the true task. He felt sick.

Carefully, Vitya tied one torpedo to the harpoon's lead and, leaning out the window, let it hang from his hand, over the water. With the other hand he retrieved his pocket watch.

"I want them in our windward wake, lieutenant."

"Right-ho."

Vitaliy studied the watch. D'Arcy waited, stock to shoulder, curls ruffling in the breeze. On deck, the cannons went off.

"Fire," Vitaliy rasped.

The flint came down. Vitaliy let go the torpedo barely in time. The shot seemed as loud as the cannons; the recoil made D'Arcy almost stagger on his feet, and Vitaliy put up a steadying hand to his back.

The harpoon sang, the torpedo catapulted. Both splashed down and became invisible amid the foam. Everard wondered how Vitaliy had managed the others alone.

"Damn!" D'Arcy rested the stock on his thigh and circled his arm around. He whistled again. "Four-bore, I'll say, I think my shoulder's paste. Are there many more?" he asked ruefully.

"Five," Vitaliy said. "We'll switch off, you and I. The interval is seven and one-half minutes."

A waiting constellation of unseen death, destruction. Everard palmed his face in despair.

"Vitya…"

Vitaliy picked up another torpedo. He said fiercely, "You're right. I don't know there aren't lives held there against their will. I can't know that. But as best as I can tell, she's an anti-revolutionary, a man-o'-war, built to purpose. Not a merchantman, not a slaver. Most likely, she's full of soldiers. Fighting men. Mercenaries."

"Even so—"

"And they will chase us. They will broadside us. They will board us. They will steal Haïti's weaponry, the supplies for Montserrat, our cannon, our gunpowder, our shot. They will sink us to every man. No survivors, because they can. And then —*then*," Vitaliy stressed, "the few who may survive, they will sell at auction in Havana—papers or no fucking papers—if they so happen to have skin any darker than you and I." He glanced down to his watch, up again. "And I will use *every* resource available to me to ensure that does not pass. Including violence."

"Including war crimes!"

"I am a criminal."

Everard ran his hand through his hair, tugged at it in desperation. He wondered at which point he'd lost his hat.

"I know. But you're not only that. I know what's done, Vitya. I've done it, for God's sake. I admit to having been the less-moral between us; you know whose crown I was obliged to. I only hoped you'd be different. A man who flees rather than fights. Who does the most good with the least harm inflicted. Who *survives.*"

Vitaliy's expression wiped clean with hurt and surprise; then it twisted. "I don't know what you were expecting from me. I am a weapons smuggler. A thief of justice. No matter in whose hands they end up, no matter what cause, justified or no: I deliver death and violence."

"I know that. But must *you*—"

"Must I enact it? By my own hand?" Vitaliy said. "It is effectually same to pull the trigger as to hand it over loaded. There are no alternatives here, now, in this moment. This isn't the Navy; there is no gentlemen's agreement. It has never been just our own physical selves we have risked. You knew this." He checked his watch again, a swoop of pale lashes, then raised his chin, his jaw set in defiance. *You chose me.*

"Yes," Everard said. He showed the ring. "But I chose a man of morals—or so I thought."

"Everard," Vitaliy said wearily, "you chose a pirate."

There were several heartbeats' worth of silence.

D'Arcy cleared his throat. "Don't strain yourselves on my account." He grinned weakly. "I haven't really a proper functioning conscience to crack in the first place. So"—he saluted —"one fewer worry for both of you. May I shoot another harpoon, please?"

Everard sighed. Calming, but regretful, weary, he gestured to the pocket watch in Vitaliy's hand. "What's the interval? Seven and one-half? I'll keep the time."

# TWENTY

As the gun's last recoil rocked a bruised D'Arcy back onto his heels, Vitaliy gave orders across the companionway to drop the courses, swing the yards back, and fly. Then it was cat-and-mouse—with the mouse's impossible flight pulling the cat by imaginary leading strings into the traps.

Vitaliy had calculated not only the speed of the *San Telmo* and its dead reckon towards them, but the wind's effect on the harpoon's flight, the push of Gulf current on the floaters, the time it would take the snagged warship to almost reach the *Sévère*. He had apparently done this in his head, all while seated at Everard's side in the shrouds; he hadn't seen him write a thing down. Genius indeed.

Out of nine torpedo mines, five threw up miniature frothing waterspouts, harmless in the broad middle of the Gulf; another failed to detonate entirely.

Three clung like burrs to the *San Telmo* and struck target.

They triggered all against her larboard hull, just as she came within cannon range; but Everard didn't need to order a single volley. By the time the Spanish warship managed to come close, she was thoroughly holed, and had heeled so sharply to larboard that she needed most of her men to plug the leaks, and had no energy or portholes available for gunning. She began slowly to wear to her starboard, away from the *Sévère*.

Still she raised nothing white.

To Everard, this seemed nonetheless a victory, a retreat, if only Vitaliy would take advantage and flee.

But the crew's energy was restless, muttering, anticipation wasted, and Vitaliy said nothing.

Then the *San Telmo* raised her final signal: the black.

Vitaliy didn't appear at all surprised.

"Bring her alongside," he said calmly. "We will board her."

To this, there was crew cheering.

In the greatcabin, Vitaliy pulled sword and pistol and axe from their mounts on the wall and strapped them on, one by one. Around his arm he'd tied a band of sailcloth dyed with bright indigo, the same as the crew. Over his chest he buckled a bandolier that held a massive, arm-sized knife. He drew it forth and back again in its sheath as a test: it was a rectangular, hook-pointed, finely serrated fishing knife.

All Everard could see was that knife snatched and used against Vitaliy himself. This didn't detract from his fury. It made him all the angrier, the futility and unnecessity of it.

He shut the door behind him, pressed his back against it like a guard. "You knew she was pirate," he accused, low. "This whole time."

"And whose she is," Vitaliy admitted, unblinking, without guilt.

"Jean Lafitte."

Vitaliy nodded.

"If you'd only said—"

"It changes nothing." He cinched his belt. "Many will still die."

Everard threw up his hands. "Not if we'd fled! You *lied* to me."

"No." Vitaliy's eyes had gone wide and warning. "It *is* a Spanish anti-revolutionary. Lafitte is allied with the Spanish, as I said. He will do everything they would, and more."

"Deception by omission, then, if we are to debate semantic nuance. Por Dios."

"One man doesn't make the difference," Vitaliy snapped.

"Now, look—now you *are* lying outright. I'd bet he's the reason entire you've done every bit of this! Is *he* who betrayed you, Vitya? This is your revenge?"

"Ah, fuck," Vitaliy cursed, apparently quite beyond. "No, I do not have time for this. For this, with you." He brushed past Everard, a glancing sidestep, and put his hand on the door. "Are you boarding her or staying behind?"

"Am I—" Everard drew in a breath through his teeth, also quite beyond. He grabbed at Vitaliy's shoulder. "What?" he demanded. He waited, with sick anticipation, for Vitaliy's glance to drop meaningfully to his hand. "Why in hell would you ask that?"

The dark gaze didn't waver from Everard's own. "I don't ask it of you. If you—"

"No, no. I'm sorry, I've said it wrong: why would you *wonder* that? Is it a heavy question in your mind, whether or not I am a coward? Incapable?"

Vitaliy went still beneath his palm. The anger wisped out of him, dissipated like cooling steam.

"Ah. No, Everard," he said. He put a hand to Everard's face, the juncture of jaw and neck, softly clutching. "I question nothing. What you did for me in Kingston proved you to be one of the bravest, most capable persons I have ever met. I don't need battle to confirm what I already believe."

"Oh," Everard said. *Proof. Belief.*

Vitaliy wouldn't say those words lightly.

Vitaliy said, "If you object to fighting, it won't make me think differently of you. *I* object to fighting," he admitted bitterly, "but I haven't the choice of it, because of Varfolomey. The creature I've made him—myself—into. So, I am asking you. Asking, not assuming, because you still do have a choice, if you want it."

Everard dropped his hand; Vitya caught it in his other.

"You are my matelot. My partner in all things. If you do choose, and we are to cross the rail together, it will be back-to-back, protecting the other. I pledged that, too. I would make you aware that I will fulfill it to the death. Either way, I will never let Lafitte give you to La Corona."

"Oh," Everard said. "No, you… needn't worry over that." If the Spanish weren't hunting Varfolomey—supposedly—they absolutely weren't hunting him, a complete unknown. "They shan't get you, either. Not if I've say in the matter."

Vitaliy didn't blink. His steady gaze said simply: *I know. I believe you.*

"Well, then!" Everard said. "I'll need sword and axe."

Back-to-back, shoulder-to-shoulder, Vitya kept his word.

Under cover of musket fire, they were up and over the gunwale in three heartbeats, a froth of screaming, jangling metal, creaking rope. The *San Telmo* was heeling so hard, they landed on a weather deck made into an uphill battle; worse, its new-built planking had been slicked with oil and water. They and six others plonked straight onto their arses first thing, which flattened them against the Spaniards' receptive fire but nearly slid them into a miniature cheval-de-frise of sharp pikes beneath the rail. When in hell, Everard wondered, had they had time to build that?

Vitya swore, *thunk*ed his axe into the deck for purchase just in time, knuckles white, his grip painful beneath Everard's left shoulder as he pressed him bodily down, but it halted their slide. He bellowed, "Sand bags!"

These flew, hitting dully around them and bursting; one grazed Everard like a punch, and he kicked it, coughing, spreading the sand.

A bit ahead of schedule, but they would've needed them for the blood, anyway.

Then a pirate—an *enemy*—with Quixote-era mustachios swung down to them from the high quarterdeck. The spike of his axe loomed towards Everard's head. Everard raised his cutlass—*crack*—and the arc of the man's axe jerked and collapsed into loose strings and floppy limbs, a marionette abruptly freed. Nothing Everard had done: a musket ball had spun its way through his ochre bandanna, exiting over the ear.

*D'Arcy*, he thought dimly, but couldn't look back. He touched his filled glove to his lips and away in a kiss, tasting iron, and pushed the man and his brains off his lap. First blood.

Louis-Michel Alarie ran past, boots flinging sand, flanked by several of the *Sévère's* pirates, screaming war. As if spurred, Vitya hauled Everard up; they went on.

Above them, the jolly roger threw a wavering noonday shadow. But Jean Lafitte was nowhere to be seen.

Vitaliy's intuition had at least been correct about the *San Telmo* pirates; they were not slaves, but majority white men, Spaniards supplemented with mercenaries, from the sound of them, German, Irish, and American, sailors and infantry alike. There weren't as many as expected—another advantage.

Everard had forgotten how to breathe, it seemed, but not how to fight. With every step, every swing of sabre, worry and hunger and shuddering nausea shoved down to a tiny corner of himself, forgotten. But as they crossed the chaos of the deck,

something peculiar happened, over and over: Everard's oppo-
nents spotted him and hitched, took a breath, paused.

Close quarters meant no one had much choice in their
combatants, and in fact if one could easily tell friend from foe
in the writhing chaos and the smoke, it was a lucky thing, even
with the indigo armbands. But men went the way of least resistance, and in battle Everard had never been avoided so much
as pushed aside, assumed to be neither a challenge nor an easy
target.

Today, however…

Another Spaniard fell before him, kneecap shattered from
Everard's sabre hilt, and in the frenzy's brief pause, Everard
looked askance.

Yes, that would do it. Vitya—tall, broad, copper-haired
from blood, teeth gritted and breathing hard—was certainly
not the way of least resistance. Brutality surrounded him like
an indestructible soap bubble, glimmering rainbow and poison
swirl.

To Everard's eyes he was half-unrecognisable.

"Back me," Vitaliy gasped then, as though it needed
repeating, "to amidships." He hefted the axehead closer into
his palm, looking oddly frustrated. "Change of plan. Something's wrong."

Everard nodded. He was amazed at Vitya's clarity of
thought; he himself felt encircled, cushioned from reason by
gun smoke and blood-spray fog. He shook himself.

*This is what they respect him for,* he thought. *This mask he wears.*
What a damned waste. Violence was common. Expected. Not
particularly difficult.

They made their way, ducking, shoving, sabres outflung, to
the midships rail, where Vitya applied his axe blade in wide,
powerful swoops into the cheval-de-frise beneath, dismantling
it to crumbles and splinters. His goal seemed to be the *San
Telmo*'s yardarm braces.

Vitya swung at the larboard braces, rapid and accurate; rope after thick rope was cut. Like felling trap-set saplings, the braces sprang free from tension and flew high. The mast groaned as the wind took the yards round and got hold of the freed sails, setting them flapping.

Everard discouraged a sharp-toothed, junk-beribboned pirate—no indigo—away and down to the deck with a thrust of blade to the shoulder. He looked up. He yelled, "Vee, you'll dismast her!"

Vitaliy withdrew his knife from the bandolier with his left hand and stepped over the pirate still bleeding at Everard's feet.

"Yes." He bent, quick and unceremonious, and slit the pirate's throat.

It was then that Everard realised: he meant to disable the *San Telmo* irreparably.

"You know," Everard said, "I don't think he would've got up?"

Vitaliy grimaced as he straightened. The look in his eyes was frightening: as flat as the night sea.

But then, they'd flown the red. No mercy; no quarter.

Then, quick as a flash, he raised his pistol from his belt and shot it over Everard's shoulder; there was a *thud* as someone hit the deck behind him, their weapon clattering away.

"New plan," Vitaliy growled. "I was wrong." He brushed sticky blond from his forehead.

Everard spun, clutching his ear, to goggle backward. Vitaliy's aim wasn't terrible, either—ball straight through the neck—though Everard could've done to keep his eardrum intact. "So, *kill everyone* is your recompense for it?"

Vitaliy shook his head. He backed against the rail and began to reload his pistol with Marine efficiency. Everard covered him, back to his front, sabre ready, though the battle had already begun to stale, fizzle in their favor. One after another, the pirates of the *San Telmo* were realising their fate and running.

"It's Lafitte's ship," Vitaliy said. Everard heard him spit cartridge paper, heard the hiss of powder. "Lafitte's flag. Lafitte's men, Spaniards, mercenaries. But he is not aboard. This is a captainless ship."

"What?" Everard said, shoving off a man who'd decided to make a last stand, bashing him in the head with the sabre hilt. "A captainless warship?" The man collapsed. Everard rationalised: drowning while unconscious was better than bleeding out. Surely. "Is that even bloody possible? And if that is the case, then—do pardon my French—what in blasted hellfire are we *doing?*"

Vitaliy grimaced again, pulled back on the hammer. He shoved the gun into his belt. "Someone wants this ship. We must ensure she does not return to Cuba—with or without her new leadership."

Vitaliy crossed the deck to the starboard mizzen-yard braces, and cut those, too, swift *thunks* of his axe. No one tried to stop them; the battle was nearly over.

*New leadership*, Everard thought. A slot-in captain for the Spanish *San Telmo*. Someone waiting in the wings of the *Sévère* with her crew. Someone who had been sailing with them, waiting for their chance, their rendezvous. Someone who worked for Lafitte, or La Corona, or both.

Someone who knew Vitaliy, who had maybe expected a ship from him, who would use a meregildo to defeat a man-o'-war. Someone who had stayed on with them beyond Havana instead of leading the *Birch*.

*Romilly René*, bells rang in his head. *Romilly René. It must be.*

Louis-Michel Alarie appeared from the smoke, covered in sand and viscera, and launched himself up onto the quarter-deck. He leaned out far over the rail, swinging an enemy hat like a flag.

"Indigo pirates of the *Sévère!*" he bellowed, to an answering cacophony, up and down the deck. "We have our victory! Take what prizes you may carry… et retournez dans le navire!"

The second cheer was deafening.

# Twenty-One

After Vitaliy had briefly gone back to the *Sévère* and returned, down the hatch of the *San Telmo* they went, into the smoky dim of her second deck. The *Sévère* crew had already swept through there, fierce with victory and intent on plunder, and enemy bodies were sprawled to every corner, sliding down to larboard, where the deck was lowest. Several hammocks still hung from their hooks: an extreme dereliction of procedure in Everard's eyes. Neither were there signs that the guns had been cast loose, or even attempted.

Everard said, "They didn't clear it for battle?"

Vitaliy surveyed the deck with narrowed eyes. "I'd thought they wanted to take her intact. But this…"

For a warship to not clear the gundecks for battle… but instead spend the time to build a cheval-de-frise of pikes on deck and slick it… it made no sense.

"Why not surrender, straight off?" Everard said. "Why risk you broadsiding and sinking her, and no defence?"

Vitaliy frowned. He looked troubled. "Someone who thinks they know me well in a fight would have made that gamble."

"That you wouldn't sink her unless direly provoked?" Then Everard caught on. "Oh, *you*, you mean, not Varfolomey."

Vitaliy nodded again, carefully sidestepping a wrong-way limb. "Me. Someone who knows the man behind the mask."

*The one who counts the souls imprinted upon his own.*

"Out of curiosity, how many such someones are there?"

Vitaliy didn't answer.

"Right," Everard said. "Well, let's take her sword before she sinks, shall we?"

In the *San Telmo*'s greatcabin, there was nobody sitting in wait, but no sword, either. A handful of hammocks hung from the cabin rafters—further confirmation of a leaderless crew, and little to no preparation for battle—although the captain's built-in cot to starboard looked rumpled and slept-in, too. Maybe they'd drawn straws.

There on the desk the planned trajectory of the *Sévère* was plotted on a Gulf map.

"This is absolute madness," Everard revelled, looking it over. He paged through the scattered, chicken-scratch captain's log. It revealed nothing in Spanish or English.

To plant false watchmen, pay four score mercenaries to sail a warship, and yet not utilise her properly…

"I simply can't believe they've managed this," he mumbled. "To rendezvous two warships of the same bloody Navy fleet would be feat enough."

Vitaliy said, "It is just hunting. With enough foreknowledge, easy enough."

"It seems they had a lot of that," Everard said. "But nobody knew of your torpedoes?" he asked, half-hopefully, because it would certainly help narrow the potentials. Not that he wasn't pretty damn sure who had done this. *There's nobody better at a dead reckon, especially the* Sévère*'s.*

"Not a soul."

"Damn. But then why fight anyway, once she was holed?"

"They need the ship. They couldn't have her run."

"Yes, but to provoke boarding… Varfolomey honors a surrender, doesn't he?"

Everard didn't have to ask. He'd heard the crew stories, told to him many times over and sung of at least once, how the *Sévère* herself had been taken: nary a drop of blood fell as the massive meregildo changed hands, the Spanish captain's own shirt off his back making the final flying white. The defeated crew and captain had been left alive in tenders just outside Spanish Florida, to flounder and make their way north. To maybe even find their own fortunes in America, if they would.

Vitaliy looked over. "Always. If I had a guess…" He jerked his chin back to the second deck, the bodies and blood and viscera sliding down. "These were mercenaries," he said, low. "Paid to engage, to hunt. Nothing unusual for Lafitte. But I was thinking it felt like we'd outnumbered them by a larger margin than we should have."

Everard cursed. "You think it was slaughter a-purpose?"

A slot-in captain and a replaced crew. Why trouble with mutiny, he supposed, when you could sail off with one's own man-o'-war and half the loyal crew who had just prized her?

Vitya swallowed, nodded. "And I called for no quarter."

"But—salted earth," Everard marvelled. "Who would do such a thing?"

So much callous death, and behind it the would-be captain, taking the *San Telmo*'s helm at incredible cost. Everard looked back to the hatch, where dust and smoke swirled in the light, falling peacefully in the deadly calm.

"The *Sévère*—is she in danger? We're not worried of her being cut free and run, now we've been"—he swallowed—"victorious here?"

"No." Vitaliy shook his head. "No. Milly has her; she's secure."

Everard's heart thumped. How could he broach it, that

awful suspicion? That awful knowledge? "I'm not sure… Would not René…? I don't wish to imply—"

"I know you and Milly do not get along, but that doesn't mean—"

"Do not get along? She spat on my boot!"

"She's allowed to dislike you, matelot." Vitaliy ran a palm over his mouth. "The lieutenant is there," he added. "If that reassures you more."

That was true. Everard had wondered what Vitya'd said to D'Arcy to convince him to stay back from the boarding party. But he knew over D'Arcy's dead body would he let René or anyone take the *Sévère* and leave Everard behind.

"Does it reassure *you*?" he asked. "Preston's being there?"

Vitaliy gave him a serious look that told him his hunch was correct. "I use advantages as I see them, yes."

Everard bristled. "He isn't an *advantage*. Or a tool, or an… an option." *Or a standby.* "He's my— He's a *person*—"

"A capable person, who advantageously agreed to do what I asked."

*He thinks D'Arcy capable?* Everard thought. Well, and rightly so.

"Excuse me—" Vitaliy swayed suddenly, lurching right.

"Whoa." Everard groped for an elbow. "What the devil?"

Vitaliy pushed him away and stumbled outside the cabin, into the hold; finding a douse bucket, he knelt, and promptly vomited.

"Er." Everard ventured out. "Were you hit beneath the belt?" he asked softly, as though this weren't the reaction of most soldiers, coming down from a fight.

He merely hadn't expected it from Vitaliy—for some reason—especially not so soon.

Vitaliy spat. "No." He gagged once, shuddered, picked himself up from hands and knees, and stood with a groan. "I am fine. That has been coming awhile. I am well."

Everard wasn't convinced. Vitya stepped back into the *San Telmo*'s greatcabin and slumped into a chair, his strength seeming somehow lesser. He shook all over.

That was bad. Everard shut the door and bolted it, set down the ship's log. "Vitya. Now I'll ask you to tell me seriously: does the battle shock affect you so acutely as a usual circumstance?"

Vitaliy laughed harshly into his palms.

"All right." Everard crouched and put a hand on his shoulder. "Now I'm really quite worried. We should go back to the ship—"

Vitaliy hunched away. "Do not—please don't touch…" He shuddered. "No," he gasped, as Everard drew hastily back. "Wait. In fact do touch. But… more."

"Er." Everard blinked. "Surely. What might I do?" Despite his concern, he smiled. "I'm going to need it direct."

Vitya breathed out slow, but his lips twitched in faint amusement. "Lie upon me," he said at last. "With all of your weight. Please," he added.

"Gladly," Everard agreed. "Let us only return—"

"No! Here." Vitaliy stood and unbuckled his bandolier, let it slump to the floor. "Now." He began on the blood-spotted gun belt, hands frantic.

"All right," Everard said again. "Hang on. Let me. We can take a moment, I'm sure. She won't sink yet—I can still hear prizing going on."

"Perran's mates have come over," Vitya mumbled. "For the holes."

"Good."

He removed Vitaliy's belt, the herringbone waistcoat, pulled the shirt free from breeches, and, at Vitya's nod, tugged it off. The breeches themselves, unfortunately, had to stay. He maneuvered Vitya backward, until he was knees-back against the built-in, and threw the patchwork quilt across the mattress, praying for no fleas. Everard laid his pirate down, boots and all.

Prostrate, Vitya shuddered silently, fists tight at his side.

"Just a moment." Everard went to double-check he'd bolted the door. He even put a chair at angles beneath the brass knob handle. If the *San Telmo* would sink suddenly, he'd break a window.

Then he did as he was asked. He stripped his own filthy outer layers, nudged between trembling thighs, and spread himself along Vitya's length.

"You're not injured anywhere?" he asked, rather belatedly, and felt Vitya shake his head beside him on the pillow.

They lay there, just breathing. Vitya's breaths were deep and long, the big body rising and falling with an imprecise rhythm not his usual. Sometimes, the breaths hitched and held. On one of these, Vitya's hands came up to Everard's shoulders, his back, splaying wide, and pulled, as though he could've got any closer.

"I'm not the heaviest option," Everard said apologetically.

Vitya let out the breath, trembly and unsure. "It doesn't matter."

"I smell pretty horrific, too."

Vitya shook his head again. His own scent was sharp and metallic—not from blood but from sweat dried amongst fear and terrible strain. He clutched harder at Everard for a moment, and then with a sigh his arms came fully round Everard's waist and loosened.

After a quarter hour, his breaths settled, though his body remained tense.

Everard, whose own reaction to battle was a few hours off at least, and who was neither anywhere close to sleep, had in the meantime put one ear alert to the crew's footsteps up and down the weather deck. Things were progressing normally, in that someone had pulled up from the *San Telmo*'s stores of liquor, and singing had begun alongside the goodwill repairs Perran was ordering.

The other ear he'd put to listening to Vitya's closing throat and halting lungs, as the man attempted to broach speech, again and again, giving it up each time.

Eventually he succeeded: softer than a whisper.

"I called for no quarter."

Everard remained still. He didn't know what to say. It was true. Vitya had done that. Had followed through with it. Put his own knife and gun to it.

"We flew the red, as Varfolomey is known to do," Vitya pressed. "For those who seek a fight, no quarter. It is meant to make others resistant to meeting with the *Sévère* at all. It *has* made others careful with her. But…" He stopped.

"Then a man-o'-war with ulterior motives raised the black and wasn't," Everard reasoned. "They engaged us. Hunted us. What were you to do otherwise?"

"Listened to you. We might have fled."

Everard had thought so, had obviously thought he'd been in the right at the time, but now, hours later, faced with circumstances and consequence, he knew better.

"And risk a mutiny? Wreck Varfolomey's reputation? Risk further challenge against him, future loss, because of it? No, Vitya." He pulled a bloodied-knuckle hand up and kissed it. "You had it right, and I was wrong. I think too much like a Navy man with the reputation of the whole Crown behind him. I would've fled in your position—but you could not."

Vitaliy growled; it ended in a choking sob. "And then someone u-used *me* and *my ship* as *weapons.*"

Everard nodded, scraping his cheek against fuzzy, damp blond, nuzzling. If he lifted up, he'd have to peel himself free. "It would seem so."

"S-someone who knew exactly how to manipulate my

approach, our approaches, both of us. Vee and Varfolomey *both*."

"Or perhaps," Everard said, "someone shot off provocatory guns, put you into a corner, and faced you with an impossible choice, all for the possibility of meager gain." He raised his head, met Vitaliy's eyes. "What do you think of that?"

Vitaliy shook with laughter and tears; these ran streaming into the silvering hair at his temples, until he dashed them away with ringed fingers.

"I think sounds familiar."

"Damn, but it does!" Everard said lightly. "It sounds quite like anything I've ever done. Or any sailor or soldier." He put his forehead on Vitya's beautiful high one, just for a moment, and then settled back. "You understand. You were pressed. As I was."

Vitaliy nodded. "Fished out of the Delaware."

He didn't have to say more.

"A Barcelona dockyard, for me. How many years?"

"Fourteen."

"You're much more a Vitya than a Henry."

Vitya snorted. "I am both. But firstly, Vitaliy Gray, American, born to unmarried Russian and Quaker in a brick-built house on Water Street, Philadelphia."

"We've one of those in Kingston." Everard blinked solemnly down. "It is still called King Street."

Vitaliy's shaking was a better percentage laughter then, so Everard went on.

"Everard Rubén Anderson de Anglada," he introduced himself archly, "a su servicio. Fifth son of an English bastard of a textile-mill owner and a Catalan farmer's daughter."

"A textile mill," Vitaliy whispered raspily. "Cotton?"

"Yes."

"American cotton?"

"It is undoubtedly so now. My father—well, it would be Lucas, my eldest brother, who has charge of it, since the bastard's dead—takes it from raw to printed lienzos and then trades it straight back to the states. I know that much from letters; I haven't been back since I was pressed. If we ever…" Everard cleared his throat. "… If you and I ever make it to Philadelphia, I could still point you out Anderson calico at ten yards."

"You have not returned in twenty years? Some history there."

"Twenty-four years," Everard said. "The history is my madre had always the latest calicos: in layers sufficient to conceal that my father kept her half-starved."

Vitaliy inhaled. "I'm sorry."

"Mind you, it wasn't a question of monies."

"Mmm. And still you do not make a habit of eating dinner," Vitaliy said, sad and revelatory.

"A habit long-standing. Either I was fed from the profits bled from slavery, or I took meat from her mouth." He licked his lips. "Fairly literal, some days. Five boys, you understand."

Vitaliy's arms came back around him, squeezed him closer.

"A boy of—twelve, you said?—should not have to worry over such things," he said, quietly into Everard's hair. "Nor would most begin to think of them. But you forged yourself papers to be legally English… without a need?" he questioned.

"Well, I didn't wish to claim his particular paternity, you see, and since I was pressed… I'm not acquainted with a sole relation of his in London, anyway; probably they disavowed him, too, or he came from nothing. Later on, D'Arcy got me into the necessary officers' clubs and made my tradesman pedigree mysterious enough no one dared ask."

Vitaliy nodded.

"And d'you know how many Andersons there are in the Navy?" Everard said dryly. "Forgery was the easier option."

This time, the laughter was unmistakable.

"You," Vitaliy gasped. "I'm sorry. You are telling me awful things…"

"Oh, but I do understand," Everard replied immediately. "I feel quite the same." He paused, considering. "Though the reflection of it is likely less pleasing—far too many brackets, lines."

"Mmm. No." Vitaliy shifted. "It is a serious face, and no wonder," he said. "Until you lift that judging eyebrow, and the light shines in…"

"Er."

"You are doing it now." Vitaliy pressed his fingers in hard where they rested on Everard's back. "Especially the judging. No, it's the right brow," he said, as Everard rubbed his left one self-consciously. Vitaliy pulled his hand gently away, wove his fingers through Everard's. "And whomever told you it was an unpleasant face is a liar. Or jealous," he added, uncharacteristically undiplomatic. "Too much comparison to your pretty lieutenant, maybe."

"Oh?"

Vitya thought D'Arcy was *pretty*?

"But the two of you are like sunset and night."

"Inseparable?" Everard said, jesting—and was startled when Vitaliy nodded.

"Also… incomparable. Impossible to compare," he clarified.

Flustered, Everard said, "Sounds like a man-o'-war." He cleared his throat. "You're speechifying. You must feel better?"

Vitaliy grunted, a deliberate show of quiet. He shifted once more—a roll of hips, with definite intent—

Everard laughed. He'd been aware of this… development, but that Vitya would bring attention to it now surprised him. "Madman. I couldn't possibly. In another's bed?"

"I could," Vitaliy said frankly, and tightened his grip on Everard's back, as though preparing to flip them.

"No, sir," Everard said, pushing the big hands away and down. "No, you have consigned yourself to lying in the unknown of this mattress, whilst I have not—you are my island—see how I am not touching?"

Vitaliy's gaze turned dark and intent, dusk-blue sea sparkle.

"Do not you dare," Everard warned.

"Vermin jumps, anyway. You are already contaminated."

"You shan't—you won't—*no* te creas—"

They grappled half-heartedly, laughing; Vitaliy unwilling to press the advantage of his weight, Everard unwilling to give up his own superior position of limbs-on-limbs—at the same time earnestly trying not to touch any part of the quilt beneath them.

Three loud *bangs* of a fist upon the door came, rattling the window glass. Everard swiveled round to see wavering stacks of brown curls, a feathered hat. *Romilly René.*

He was immediately sobered, alert, as he raised up on elbows; Vitaliy ceded the fight, suppressing giggles.

"Lovebird layabouts!" came, singsong. "I am sorry to interrupt your victory fuck, but I have been here waiting for the distribution going on one-half hour."

"Milly," Vitaliy huffed, exasperated but relaxed.

Everard levered off, handed Vitya his shirt, and went to remove the chair from the doorknob—

Vitya held him back by the wrist. "Thank you," he said, low. "For your care."

Everard could only smile over his shoulder as he unbolted the door.

Romilly René *tsk*ed in disapproval. In her hands she held a massive ledger, pen and ink.

"That cot, over that beautiful grand thing? Disgraceful." She nodded to the desk—which *was* rather large, come to think—and looked them both over: their hastily undressed state, obviously having been intimate.

"Milly," Vitaliy said again.

She said nothing, but her glance lingered briefly on Vitaliy, a flash of appraising concern so fast, Everard almost missed it.

He did not miss Vitaliy's reassuring nod, the twitch of his smile.

René worried for Vitaliy? For the aftershock, which surely she must know about already? Or merely that he had disappeared alone with Everard into the depths of an enemy ship? Everard, who knew precisely what she was?

René said, "We had best hurry. Matelot, your Fitzwilliam is half the way to three sheets flying already."

"My… who?" Everard said, bewildered and caught off-guard by the address.

Vitaliy cleared his throat. "The lieutenant."

"Oh, Preston. Yes, that would be his usual." Everard slept like the dead the night and the whole morning after conflict; Vitaliy apparently was sick, and shook; D'Arcy… drank. "Though I will say his name is not Fitzwilliam." He paused, as Romilly René smirked.

"But it is… D'Arcy?" she said, in the English way, drawing the *a* long.

"Oh!" Everard laughed despite himself. "The fashionable novel, you are referring to. I… had been meaning to pick up the second edition, when next in London."

Which, now he thought of it, might well be never.

"Is he so drunk as to be incapable?" Vitaliy asked René, ignoring all this.

"Half of the way, I said," René responded. "The matelot reads the English novels? Hmm."

"The thing sold its entire first printing," Everard said. "Of course I've read it."

René nodded to herself, darkened eyebrows pushed high. "Very black eyes and now this, et alors."

# Twenty-Two

Perran the carpenter estimated the *San Telmo*'s repairs would bite two days from their journey, no more. Meanwhile, the *Sévère* would have to stay close and be tied alongside for ease of transport.

Everard had watched Romilly René's face carefully as news of this decision was made to her, but nothing showed there—not impatience, not frustration, not anger. Only mild acceptance and slight concern, as one would expect from the goods and wages distributor for a fleet of pirate ships, who now had to consider the resource sinkhole of another massive man-o'-war—even one with few surviving crew.

Because she'd assured there were vastly fewer mouths to feed, hadn't she?

Everard, on deck repairing braces he'd helped dismantle, now watched the last keg of the five-eighths-divided rum roll across the amidships gangway to the *Sévère* and be received into Bellingham St. Clare's waiting arms. The young man waved, and Everard waved back half-heartedly, swallowing down his jangling nerves.

Where was D'Arcy? If he was *too* drunk…

Having two ships-of-the-line tied alongside was one of few situations that continued to grate on Everard. It was in a similar way that his *Wanderer* been lost, in '12: her mast had been toppled with shot, her bow spun round as a result, and then she had entangled so thoroughly with the Americans, unable to flee and unable to be repaired, that she'd been obliged to surrender. Then she'd been fired, sunk to the bottom of the sea.

It was the only sword Everard had ever given up as captain, so of course it was the one he had been court-martialed and made known for.

So, Everard made a few necessary suggestions. He made sure they offset all six masts apart from one another, in case of listing and collision; long gangways were pushed between the hulls so they wouldn't scrape. It would be only two days of cooperation, after all, and there was not a cloud in the sky to threaten a storm.

But now sundown was approaching. Battle fatigue was setting in, and with it, as always, reality and regret. Soon, Everard's body would make the decision for him, and he'd sleep whether he had something soft beneath—or a somebody beside—him or not.

He turned to Vitaliy: still there aboard the weather deck of the *San Telmo,* sat down with pen and paper and the nigh-impossible decision of which crew to allocate to their betrayer's new ship.

"She had better take Perran's first mate, just to be sure," Vitya said, "though he won't thank me." He stretched, arms splaying wide, and groaned. "Has her cook not been spared? Her doctor?"

René shook her head, and Vitaliy was silent.

Of course not—*no quarter.* But every one of the others saw it as a victory, a prize, nothing more. They hadn't seen Vitaliy shake and tremble below.

"She had no doctor," Stephan put in, standing from his crouch before the line of injured survivors upon the weather-deck—the frightfully small one. He wiped his pale palms clean with a cloth. "From what I saw. Mess of a surgery, let me tell you."

"Mmm." Vitaliy tapped fingers on his thigh. "No captain, no doctor, no master. And she was meant to have come from Spain?"

"Did she come from Florida, perhaps?" Everard suggested.

Vitaliy nodded. "Florida… or Louisiana. She could have taken the Loop and doubled back."

"But no gens de couleur among them." Stephan gestured to his patients. "White men all."

This, too, seemed an entirely intentional doing, and lent to Everard's theory that the person who had orchestrated this knew Vitaliy all too well.

It was partly why Vitaliy had spent so long in the shrouds, silent and observant against the *San Telmo:* to confirm she had no slaves, no coerced men of color fighting for Lafitte for him to defeat, to kill.

For that was how Vitaliy viewed what they had done in battle that day: murder.

Everard privately agreed. But then he had never attempted to place justice or righteousness onto such a thing. He had only seen it for what it was, which was death; for him, the presence of means or motivation made no difference upon the scales. It was still, strictly, killing.

Murder aside, it had been a necessary distinction for the *Sévère* to make in all her engagements. Any slave labor, any hint of human transport seen through Varfolomey's glass, pirate or no, and the *Sévère*, Vitaliy had explained, would turn away from her prey, from confrontation. Slavers would rather force souls overboard than be overcome and taken in by hunters. The time between hailing a ship and raising the black was too vast, and the window for rescue towards a drowning person too small—that is, if they were offered the chance of the water at all.

Heard of third-hand, at the distance of Upper Canada, this practice had horrified Everard. Had been horrified by the lengths of depravity that profit would drive humanity to. The lengths of cruelty. He'd wondered how any slavers were apprehended at all.

As a result of these horrors—which Vitaliy resolutely would not say whether he'd experienced firsthand—the *Sévère's* ripples were political and financial instead of literal, her violence second-hand rather than direct, her aid channeled and veiled in secrecy. It was a tightrope line.

And someone—someone there, on this weather deck, beside them—had exploited that fact, exploited Vitaliy's care to their own gain. Had brought the conflict to him; had pushed him forward and not held out a hand.

René fiddled with the pen, glanced Everard's way. "That is all officers accounted for, Vee. Who shall be leading her to Haïti?" she asked. "After all, we swim in capitaines." She grinned and winked. "Too bad they are Navy."

Everard looked away, too exhausted to even pretend to appreciate her false, friendly manner. There to his right, Louis-Michel Alarie leaned against the larboard braces, pulling a swig from a bottle of brandy. Damn him, too, for being a distracting, conspicuous donkey. He had got himself a sabre slash across the face—exactly parallel to the wide jaw—which although beginning to swell and pinken along the edges, turned his features appealingly rakish. It would make a handsome scar.

"Swimming in Navy," Alarie agreed, with a touch of irony and an unselfconscious nod to Everard. His firm lips curved around the bottle's rim, and Everard considered asking for a pull himself, even if drink would hasten his trajectory towards a pillow. "But that makes us lucky, see. Bolívar, too, is asking after paid English, Irish, German, for his cause in Amérique du Sud. And they are only mercenaries, infantry such as these crétins." He toed at the body of a dead, towheaded man who awaited only to be sewn up in a hammock. Then, noting Everard's glare, he drew back his boot, sheepish. "Not, hmm, experienced sailors."

Everard shifted to face the *Sévère*, as Alarie was suddenly unbearable too. D'Arcy was still nowhere to be seen on the deck.

*Where is he?*

"I will take her," Vitaliy said softly.

Everard turned round as Alarie rocked forward and exclaimed, "Pardon?"

René, too, squawked with indignation. There was no anger there, however: only surprise, disbelief.

"Do not be ridiculous, mon frère," Alarie began, "she has barely a skeleton crew——"

"Port-au-Prince may not even receive her," René said.

"I will write ahead to Pétion," Vitaliy said calmly, meaning the president of Haïti.

Alarie tried again. "I *had* thought ourselves of an agreement, Vee!"

*What agreement?* Everard wondered. Vitaliy waved sharply, cutting at the air.

"The *Sévère* is untouched. Nothing has changed."

Alarie scowled, straight brows contorting. "You cannot leave her again. Your men will be adrift. They expect you to lead so? You are their king!"

René cleared her throat. "We are taking the *San Telmo* into the fleet, Vee?" She bit her lip. "I am unsure for the resources…"

Of course she wasn't sure. It had never been her intention

to stay with the fleet, but to break out with her own command—

"For a little while," Vitaliy confirmed. "After the junta, I will take her on the Gulf Stream and put out to sell her somewhere in the States. Charleston. New Bern. New York. We will not need too much."

Silence. No reaction from either party, or Stephan, who had busied himself in sewing one of his dead patients into their hammock.

"Then who will take the *Sévère* in your stead, Vee?" René asked, twirling the feather pen once more. *The matelot?* she left thankfully unsaid.

Dark-blue eyes moved from where they'd been watching the weather deck to Everard's own. Vitaliy's face was otherwise impassive, but his chin rose slightly.

Everard blinked in surprise. He knew that look. That look had begun the whole thing.

*Take it. Take what I've offered.*

Everard raised a brow. *Really?*

Vitaliy's expression was somber and steady. He nodded once. *Another gift. A ship this time—truly.*

Everard's heart leapt as he considered it—as he seriously considered it.

He knew Vitaliy wanted someone he could trust to lead his beautiful flagship, someone he knew without a doubt hadn't tried to orchestrate this very end. Everard fit those requirements. And traditionally, it *was* what was done between matelots who prized together.

More ironclad than tradition: the rights of the matelot were written already into their articles, their word of law; if Vitaliy was absent, Everard could stand in his place for a time. None of the crew would question his appointment, ex-Navy or no.

They could spur an election, of course, but it probably wouldn't come to that in such a short timeframe. Everard's leadership had never sparked mutiny before. And it wasn't as though he hadn't fought for the pirates with his own hands; he'd received many an indigo-banded shove and handshake after the battle. He was well on his way to earning as much of the crew's respect as he'd ever had as a Navy captain, if not more.

Blackhand could become something more than a taunt. Something more than a comma-bracketed designation attached to V. Varfolomey. *Anderson de Anglada* could become more than a struck-through name in a black book.

It was possible. It would work. It was a sensible, natural decision.

But…

Taking the *Sévère* would mean putting a pause—if not a potential total end, if things went sideways—to what had just begun again between them. Everard quite liked what had begun again. Furthermore, he wanted whatever it was to be more than just property and trade and sex and battle.

He wanted… partnership. Companionship. Trust. Maybe something else, too. Rainy nights in the doublewide cot. Sunsets in the shrouds. To see the colorwork appear on the pair of socks Vitaliy had just cast on, for he suspected they might be meant for him. What use was ambition, compared to that?

And in the end, one Spanish man-o'-war, a captaincy, was quite alike another. He'd had captaincies. There was only one Vitaliy Gray.

Everard brushed bits of rope flax from his hands and stood. "Yes, who shall take her? I haven't been to the States in some years." He paused, mostly to give everyone, particularly Alarie, time to politely conceal any disbelief. "And never port Charleston. I've heard it is beautiful there."

The line of Vitaliy's shoulders relaxed. His chin dipped, and his heavy-lidded eyes softened around the edges. And that look—sheer, settled-in fondness—that look was new, and delightful.

"Besides," Everard added, with a good-natured grimace, "built-in though it may be, we know already the captain's cot doesn't harbour fleas."

Stephan snorted. Romilly René laughed. Alarie raised a perfect eyebrow.

Vitaliy had two bright spots of flush on his cheeks—flush that crinkled and rose as he smiled.

It faded too quickly.

There was a sudden agitation on the *Sévère*'s weather deck. A small, tightly knotted crowd had gathered, men's voices alternating angry and hushing each other. Everard craned to look: the epicenter was the weather-deck hatch, through which one Bellingham St. Clare came pushing through, bellowing they let him pass.

Everard's throat closed painfully, his heart beating in hard pulses. Vitaliy stood and yelled, and the crowd let up marginally; St. Clare was able to haul up and dash across the gangway.

He was visibly distressed, panting hard as he crossed the rail.

"St. Clare?" Everard said. He put out a hand. His question of earlier became urgent, a mantra, but he couldn't seem to voice it aloud.

*Where is D'Arcy?*

St. Clare skidded straight past him, coming to a stop before Vitaliy. He whispered.

Vitaliy listened. He looked up, stricken, to Everard, quickly over to the surgeon—oh, God, that meant something bad had gone on, something violent—and back to Everard. His expression was more cautious the second time around. Wary.

Everard knew then. It was heavy in his gut. He shook his

head, disbelieving, and managed nothing more than a gasping croak of enquiry:

"No?"

*Not Preston.*

Louis-Michel Alarie stood. "What's happened? Mon ami Vee? There was a fight? An attack?"

Vitaliy nodded reluctantly. He said, "The lieutenant."

# TWENTY-THREE

They'd left D'Arcy in the forecastle quarters.

He was laid across a pair of upright barrels that supported his trunk only. The rest of him hung down loosely. All four limbs outstretched to the floor, fingers curled, toes pointed down and trailing. His head slumped, chin pointed to rafters, his bare neck boneless except for a prominent, vulnerable Adam's apple. His face——

His *face.*

D'Arcy looked as though a demon had pulled him up by the chest to a great height and bent him and slashed him and then tossed him down broken.

He didn't look alive.

Everard made a noise, unknown, and halted, frozen; Vitaliy pushed gently past and blocked his vision with his breadth as Stephan rushed forward——

"Alive," the surgeon murmured straight away, as though marvelling. Everard sank down, his right hand groping for purchase. He dimly registered that he couldn't, couldn't faint—— he'd break his wrist——

Bellingham St. Clare appeared and supported him silently,

mercifully to the decking, and Everard crumpled like a fawn. St. Clare said something back over his shoulder to Vitaliy, and was replied; then the redhead put his hand to Everard's cheek briefly—a shocking intimacy—and stood beside him, rock-steady; though it seemed he, too, was holding his breath.

Vitaliy asked a question of Stephan, then abruptly pivoted. Withdrawing his axe, he viciously applied it to the decking beneath his feet. With four mighty overhead swings he cleaved one plank into a neat length the approximate size of a man. It was well-maintained, old-growth wood, speckled with fresh blood. Vitaliy made short work of it.

Behind him, Stephan's big dark hands hovered near D'Arcy's ears, close but not touching.

"He's alive, matelot," the surgeon repeated. "He's alive. Hi, man, you're alive," he said softly down to D'Arcy.

But Everard didn't dare believe it. He looked away, back again, tiny glimpses; he barely restrained himself from putting his hands over his face, though the one hand was the only thing holding him up, anyway, that and St. Clare's leg.

León's voice came from the doorway, soft and warning in Spanish.

Vitaliy didn't pause. He replied in the same language, "Me vale,"—*I don't give a*—and kept hacking. He wedged in the axeblade, levered the handle with two hands and a wide arc, and then the whole plank came cracking free. León made a sound like a defeated sigh, but he took the other end. They carried it over to the barrels and slid it beneath the surgeon's gently lifting hands, beneath D'Arcy's body, straightening him inch by inch. It was horrid.

St. Clare shuddered and squeezed his hand tight on Everard's left shoulder. Everard reached up blindly; the man's fingers were rough and slender, ginger-furred, short-nailed beneath his palm.

He cast his gaze about so as to look anywhere else than at

the listless D'Arcy, and noticed D'Arcy's pistols had been tossed far in the corner, into the dust beneath a trundle cot. They'd just left them there, useless; no one had even bothered to take them.

Everard was sick. He could imagine it too well: D'Arcy's being overtaken, being disarmed, being tossed down and beaten. The fight had been personal, targeted, planned. Not just a disagreement gone terribly rogue. Something else.

He saw—from the outside of his vision—that D'Arcy was laid totally flat now. He couldn't tell if this was better or worse. There was a groan that might have been his own or could've possibly been D'Arcy's, except that he looked so very dead.

Vitaliy held the plank at D'Arcy's head, shoulders bunching from the tight, narrow grip. León took the other end, and Stephan hovered to one side, rearranging limbs, putting back rent pieces of clothing. Despite this, one of D'Arcy's arms slid and fell, swaying.

"The greatcabin—straight across," Vitaliy murmured. His backward steps were careful and slow.

Everard scrambled farther out of the way, crablike, and watched them go.

Then they were gone, and he sat there on the floor, still and afraid, staring at the hole Vitaliy had left in the decking. He didn't get too close; alarmed crew had gathered beneath the missing plank. He heard their voices calling up questions. He imagined their craning necks, their wild eyeballs—Everard didn't want their eyes on him.

St. Clare was still there, though. First he retrieved D'Arcy's guns from the corner—checking their flints and primer carefully as he did so—and then he sat, settling them in his lap. He murmured scripture Everard knew was meant to be soothing.

At last Vitaliy came jogging back. He crouched before Everard's wavering, edge-curled vision.

"Come—he's alive," Everard heard him whisper, "awake. Come and see."

"Awake?" he croaked, lifting his head. "But… dying?"

Vitaliy hesitated. He put his hand on Everard's knee. "Most likely not, Stephan says."

"Mentida." *Lies.*

"De debò," Vitaliy responded. *Truly.*

Everard put out a trembling hand. "What… That isn't Russian?"

"No." Vitaliy pulled him up.

"Català," Everard declared triumphantly.

He let himself be led. St. Clare followed, pistols at his hip. As the three of them passed, Everard heard distant mutterings from the crew.

Vitaliy ignored all of it until they were beyond León's crossed arms and gleaming, cocked pistol and within the great-cabin. Then he bolted the door and let out a short, relieved breath.

Everard understood. The robin's-egg walls, white rafters, and six-pane gallery windows seemed practically like sanctuary. The great guns were tied up once more. The torpedoes were long gone. The cot had been lowered, its linens straightened.

Within it lay D'Arcy, decking and all, stripped bare for the surgeon's examinations still going on.

Everard staggered over.

"*Preston.*"

And then he wept.

# Twenty-Four

It was plain D'Arcy's convalescence would be a long and involved one, though the surgeon declared what he'd suffered as a bad beating and nothing more.

*Nothing more*, Everard seethed.

But D'Arcy himself concurred: for all that it had looked—and had meant to look, Everard rather thought—frightening as all hell, he wasn't permanently maimed.

"Could've been worse," D'Arcy whispered, on the second night, as he succumbed to groaning beneath Everard's ministrations of salve and bandaging. "Fists and boots only. A belt or two." He sucked in an inhale. "Careful, like. Hardly any malice."

"That's bloody well plenty," Everard hissed down, removing his hands. "Plenty to kill a man, no malice necessary. If you could see the extent of the bruising—"

"I feel 'em; *that's* plenty."

Everard was quiet.

D'Arcy had purple-wine streaks—veritable swaths—across his ribs, the splay of his back. Had yellowish grip marks on his shoulders and the inside of his elbows, as he had fought against restraint. Had a ring of swelling round his throat, where some-one's arm had yoked him. There were black-blue half-moons beneath both eyes from someone's hell of a right hook. Several hooks: there was a split along his cheek, and his whole nose bridge had swelled to twice its usual.

"I'm not dead, Ever." D'Arcy tried a wincing grin. "Nor yet close. I'm not missing teeth or limbs or eyes or essential appendages or even"—he paused, rolled over, and coughed—"fingers. All things considered, the pirates were nice about it."

"Jesus sainted."

Vitaliy, absurdly, seemed to agree. Arms crossed, standing quietly subdued at D'Arcy's feet, he nodded. "It says much that he lived."

"Much! Beyond a skull like a rock, it doesn't say at all enough—"

Vitaliy shrugged. "Harder to leave a man alive than to kill him by accident," he said softly.

"I know that!" Everard spat. "First and foremost that's missing is *why?* Why would anyone have such issue with him to do this—much less several someones?"

D'Arcy shook his head with a grimace, rolling it on the pillow. He squeezed Everard's hand lightly.

"Let it go, Ev," he breathed. "I need a bit of sleep, is all. I'll be upright within the week. Look after Bell in the meantime, won't you?"

"Preston—"

Vitaliy put a hand on Everard's arm. *Let him be,* his eyes warned. Everard gently let go D'Arcy's hand, setting it down deliberately careful, and turned away with an angry jerk.

Vitaliy said nothing. Over the course of the past two days, guilt had built upon him like a soft snow, chilling his presence to near-constant silence. Everard understood, he did, but he also wished to pitch and yell. He wanted to call an all-hands and declare there to be an interrogation; put up a reward; issue threats. He tried to think of what he would do if D'Arcy were still his subordinate aboard a Navy ship, and came up with nothing that translated here. Powerless, without influence, without station, he had no inkling how to deal with such a trespass against someone he loved.

Too, Vitaliy—who did possess these things—had done nothing.

"You *will* do something?" Everard demanded later, as D'Arcy slept fitfully in a half-drugged state beside him. "Surely, you cannot let this stand."

Vitaliy was knitting again, frowning, silent. Then: "No."

Everard truly wished to scream. "No, it mustn't stand," he gritted out, "or no, you will do nothing?"

"No, I can do nothing. Not more than I have already."

Only D'Arcy's presence kept Everard's voice low, and even with that, it was a mighty struggle. "Then what, pray tell, is the point of you?"

If a man could hide behind needles and sockweight spun yarn, Vitaliy was doing so then. He flinched but didn't pause. "Somewhat of what you are looking for Milly might fulfill. If you ask nicely."

"I can't do that!"

"But why not? She is crew advocate."

"He's not crew."

Vitaliy raised his eyebrows. The clicking of needles went on steadily. "Sorry? We are all of us crew. He signed the articles, did he not?"

"That's not what I mean. He isn't… he's not *crew!* He's… mine!" Everard's voice broke abruptly.

Vitaliy gave up on the knitting, setting it aside.

There was a long silence, wherein Everard wrung out the washcloth in the basin, and re-laid it upon D'Arcy's forehead. He'd reject it in a moment as he turned onto the swollen planes of his face, and jerked away onto the other; and then the cycle would begin again. But Everard could do this for him, so he would.

"I understand," Vitaliy said at last. "You want blood, and want me to order it using authority you feel I possess. I won't do that. I cannot. I am a figurehead, not an autocrat. Much less a despot."

"I'm not asking for that. I mean, I might want blood," Everard admitted. "Only look at him. I want the world to burn, and whoever did this to him, also. But you needn't reach all the way to despotism."

"Not for the world to burn?" Vitaliy challenged. "Or you wish me to put to pyre a handful of my own crew?"

"N-no," Everard stammered. "But, Vee—they—someone did this to get to you. Through me. Through Preston. Don't you see?"

"No. What you want," Vitaliy said, infuriatingly calm, "what you are ultimately asking me for, is rank. Preference. Elevation. You and he are maybe accustomed to this, but *this is not the Navy,*" he emphasised. "No pirate—none—has the status of untouchable. Nor should anyone. The crew elected me to provide them a service. A private vendetta—because this is private, it has nothing to do with me—is not that service."

"The hell it isn't! Fighting is supposedly disallowed! You're a pirate with a code of bloody *reciprocal violence*! If it were anyone else lying here—León—Stephan—René—"

*Me?* Everard thought, despairingly. "—would you do the same?"

Vitaliy shook his head. "You are still all ideal, no practice, Everard."

"Well—yes!" Everard exclaimed. Beside him, D'Arcy stirred, and he lowered his voice to a hiss. "I am! To be frank, I don't think I will ever *not* be, if this is what's required of practice—"

"I'm sorry, but I cannot help you," Vitaliy said coolly. "It is

Milly's place if he will seek compensation for the damage. I cannot undermine her."

"I will never—but she's the one who's done this! All of this! Don't you see that?"

Vitaliy closed his eyes, rubbed at the bridge of his nose. "Don't."

Absolutely beyond, Everard stood and threw the rag. It landed on the rug with a damp *splat.*

"On this you *will* heed me," he seethed. "There's no one else. She despises me, wants me gone, wants you supplanted. What better way than to send an irrefutable message that you cannot protect your own?"

Vitaliy placed both hands flat on the arms of his chair.

"Milly *is* my own," he said quietly. "You dislike her because you have had few enough interactions with women in your life-time that you see baseless fault in one who doesn't fit within your narrow view of how one should be. Or," Vitaliy added, "you are jealous. Either is ridiculous. I trust her, the crew trusts her, and that is all you need to know."

"Oh, dear God." Everard threw up his hands. "Now you will admit authority! In the name of blind trust! Trust her because you do! Well, I cannot. Not in this nor anything else. Certainly not to negotiate the justice of aught she made with her own bloodied hands. No."

Vitaliy stood: slowly; nonthreatening; weary.

"I'll leave you."

"Vee—"

"I would tell you to bring these insults to her face," Vitaliy said, "but I think Milly would kill you as a matter of honor. She had no hand in this. And if you will not accept my judg-ment on it—if you do not trust me—I can do nothing else to convince you."

He strode over to the door, opened it with careful, stiff movements.

"But," he said hesitantly, "I can… I *will* ask her what she plans to do in regards to what the lieutenant suffered today. It won't be blood, or justice; but she can make it known it isn't conducive to the goals of the fleet. I believe she will agree to this."

Thus deflated, Everard sank down onto the cot. He was careful not to disturb D'Arcy more than he had already.

*If you don't trust me…*

How could he, when Vitaliy was choosing her? Choosing another?

*And so have I,* he thought, pushing damp curls from D'Arcy's forehead. *Look how neither of us is choosing the other.*

No. There was no trust there.

"All right," he managed, just so Vitaliy would go. "I understand. Thank you."

Vitaliy nodded—and then he did go.

# TWENTY-FIVE

"I feel as though I'm sitting in on a honeymoon," D'Arcy complained to Everard on the third day, on occasion when Vitaliy was gone afuera. "Of a marriage of obligation and dowry," he added, the rasp of his endangered voice not enough to conceal his acute sarcasm. "And… knitting. For God's sake, Everard, don't hold back the fight on my account."

But Everard had to hold back; there was no alternative. If Everard confronted the true reach of his fury at Vitaliy's absurd stance, at his inaction, he might burst at all seams with no regard to casualties.

It was a good thing Vitaliy would be gone to shore for the junta.

That was all.

On the fourth day, the *Sévère* sat anchored in the bay of hot, palm-strewn Port-au-Prince. With some careful maneuvering, the *San Telmo* had ridden in convoy, Romilly René at her command. It made Everard nervous, giving the woman what she'd wanted after all; but the alternative was to split either from Vitaliy or from D'Arcy, neither of which was bearable at present. And she hadn't cut and run—yet.

Haïti was possessed of a beautiful port: above the palms and beach and town centre rose three verdant mountains. Atop the southernmost and tallest, three sea-facing walls of a star fortification stood halfway constructed in white stone, already studded with cannon. The message was clear: Haïti would hold its own against those wanting to take advantage of its new, probate statehood. But thanks to Vitaliy's missive ahead of them to President Pétion, they'd been recognised and hailed upon arrival, and neither ship had been shot through.

"Are you sore to be missing General Mina? Simon Bolívar?" D'Arcy asked that hot afternoon, rather obvious in his intent; Everard had been pacing the cabin for the past quarter hour at least. Vitaliy had managed to make the junta appointment, and was there now, sitting in a palace with unnumbered state-makers and influentials—to most of whom he'd sold crucial weaponry.

And he considered himself not a king?

Everard ran his hands through his hair. "No," he said. "Not precisely. I've no taste towards filibustering, and no doubt someone would only want to recruit me for the job. If not Mina or Bolívar, then another."

D'Arcy hummed. "Surely." He groped for his teacup and saucer, sipped tranquilly, and then: "But perhaps you flatter yourself?"

Everard stopped pacing. "I beg your pardon. Experience aside, my command of Spanish alone—" He sighed. There was no need to be defensive towards D'Arcy, of all persons. "But you are grumpy. Is it you that's sore to be missing the junta?"

It was an insincere retort; D'Arcy confirmed it with a snort.

"You know I've no interest in rebellion, revolution. Dem-oh-cracy," he said, crisp and sardonic. He replaced the saucer, pulled shut the mosquito-net, and pushed himself higher on the pillow, groaning softly. "You see where equality and fairness has got me?"

*So says the ton-born, third son of an earl.*

Everard grit his teeth. "I will have your recompense, Preston. No matter what Vee says. I swear it you."

D'Arcy lay back with a hum. When he closed his eyes, the asymmetrical swelling of his nose and his blacked left eye seemed rather pronounced.

Everard felt the sting of remorse. "I am exhausting you."

After a moment, D'Arcy gave a sharp nod. "In the worst way, I'm afraid." He cracked open one eye. "Read to me from that head of yours? I've read everything to be had in this godforsaken cabin."

Everard pulled his chair close, penitent. "Of course."

On the seventh day, Vitaliy made an unplanned visit back from shore, brief and without ceremony. Everard was within the printing parlour, sweating his bollocks off beneath the heavy apron, but working, useful at last; word had travelled quickly that there was a floating press arrived, with no commitments or restrictions and, most importantly, fresh ink and paper.

In accepting the jobs, Everard had been judicious in estimating how much time he would have to hand for printing, with D'Arcy laid up and him with nothing else to do. Unfortunately, he'd been less judicious in estimating how much two hundred impressions an hour would take out of him physically.

Thom had taken a shift or two, but his heart wasn't in it, and Everard felt guilty of wasting the boy's time. Felt Thom was maybe obliging him for the sake of his prior servitude. And since Everard was equally as incapable of paying him now as he had been when they'd slipped over the side of the *Netley*, he'd insisted Thom leave him to it.

Everard was rolling back the carriage on a wet page as Vitaliy crept into the parlour. He had obviously just come from Government Palace: he wore a fanciful blue waistcoat—the one that seemed as pasted upon his body as wall-paper—and a curly, out-of-date wig. His stance was anxious, with hands held behind his back, and he wore no weapons. He had never looked less like a storybook pirate. He was beautiful none-theless.

Everard waited, panting slightly, swiping at his forehead with his shirt.

"Yes?"

"Good evening," Vitaliy said, hesitantly. "How is she faring?"

"The ship?" Everard raised his eyebrows. "Or the press?"

Vitaliy's gaze dropped. "The press. I can see the ship is—"

"She's not rusted yet," Everard said, rudely. He peeled the page from the carriage and slotted it into the drying rack.

There was an awkward silence.

"Preston's back on his feet," Everard said, his back turned. *Not that you've asked.*

Another pause. Vitaliy said, "I passed him on deck. He looks well."

It was unmistakably a gentle reprimand, and well deserved on Everard's part. He turned round.

"I'm sorry—I don't have much daylight left to hand, and two hundred pages yet to impress..." The Stanhope was a dream of efficiency, but Everard was tired.

Vitaliy took one sideways step. "No. I am sorry. Only..." And then one forward step. His hands came out from behind his back, holding something: a wooden, leather-covered, conspicuously triangular box. A blush bloomed pink on his cheeks as he balanced the box—a hatbox?—upon a pair of stacked crates.

It *was* a hatbox. Everard blinked, his heart suddenly caught on his sternum.

"I know you do not like… things," Vitaliy said, still not looking up. "But you had brought only the one hat, and you seemed to… care for it." He made a quick, compulsive fist with his left hand, and then splayed it, held out a flat palm and pushed it towards the hatbox. *For you,* the gesture unmistakably said.

God, Everard was an ass. Maybe he was still angry, but that didn't mean he was excused to act like this.

"I do like hats," Everard said. "I like hats quite a lot." And he was sure that he'd never told Vitaliy how much, but he had obviously divined it anyway. "Is… that a hat for me?"

Vitaliy glanced up. The cautious, hopeful glimmer upon his face was nearly enough to bring Everard to his knees from shame. "Yes. It's meant to be. I hope it is recent enough in style… I was not confident about lace." He pulled the wig from his head and gave a tiny smile. "I'm not the best judge of such things. Perhaps obvious."

"No," Everard said, and Vitaliy's smile fell away. "I mean to say, you're wrong. It's not obvious at all. You look very nice. Beautiful," Everard said hastily. "And I'm sure the hat is beautiful too. But, er, the ink…" He gestured over himself, his apron that was covered in ink and bits of paper fluff. "I wouldn't want to…"

"No, I understand." Vitaliy plunked the wig unevenly back upon his skull. If Everard hadn't had ink hands, he would've centered it for him, pushed those fine blond hairs back into place.

"I should not have…" Vitaliy trailed off with a grunt. "I will let you to it. I must get back myself."

"Vee," Everard said, "wait—you could—show…"

But Vitaliy was gone—before Everard could even utter the smallest of thank-yous.

On the ninth day, the ship *Vuelte* of Vitaliy's fleet came into Port-au-Prince, all the way from port New York; D'Arcy was well enough by then to lean upon the quarterdeck rail and make a stream of quips at her loading and unloading.

"So—let me make this straight," D'Arcy said. "They are taking the vanilla, that has been paid for, from us, onto the *Vuelte*, to Philadelphia. It goes then to Europe. There's Haitian coffee—that has *also* been paid for—which also goes to Philadelphia."

"And Halifax," Everard added. There was coffee; there was sugar; there was tobacco and indigo. Incoming on the *Vuelte* were beans, oats, corn, peas, lumber; all of these could not get to or from Haïti by traditional means, since she wasn't recognised for legal trade by England or America.

He didn't mention Vitaliy's taking a net loss on the coffee. It was such an odd thing for a pirate to do, it was almost suspicious. And both of them were all too aware of the thousands of American small arms being loaded into the depths of the *Sévère*: paid for with pirated Spanish silver and Vitaliy's slowly eroding sensibilities towards ways and means.

*Intention matters.*

"And Halifax! There's no Navy there at all," D'Arcy said sarcastically.

"Vee isn't going to Halifax any longer. He'll stay with me on the *Sévère*."

D'Arcy sighed, slumping onto the rail. He winced as his elbows hit. "I ought have joined a merchantman."

Everard eyed him. They both knew profit shares weren't why D'Arcy had signed Vee's articles.

*Motivation matters.*

"That path would quickly land *you* in Halifax," Everard said, "in a hulk."

"Not likely," D'Arcy came back with. "Me, they'd send to Portsmouth, the better for my father to watch me swing."

Everard couldn't bear the thought. "The earl would pay your way, surely?"

"Yes—if only to avoid the scandal. Though if I'd a say, he wouldn't."

"Preston," Everard said, alarmed. "Say that isn't true. You wouldn't let them hang you, at any cost. Would you?"

D'Arcy gave him a strange look. "Whyever not, Mr. Morality? I am guilty of all of it. More."

"And whose fault is that, pray? Mine. Fuck the morals," Everard said fiercely. "They don't apply. There's no amount I would not pay to slip you free of a noose, had I the option. Do you understand me? I don't care if it's unfair or unjust. The thought of you…" He swallowed. "I have already had to comprehend it, you see, and it's—it's incomprehensible."

D'Arcy's expression was mingled consternation, shock, and affection. His lips parted, and he straightened so as to meet Everard's eyes. "I thought the point was that one's morals applied in *all* situations," he murmured, hair falling over his eyes. He needed a cut badly. "But, noted." He leaned in, like he would pull Everard close and kiss him, right there on the deck, in full view of the bay and the loader crew—he must be feeling much better indeed—

Everard stared, but all D'Arcy did was smirk and tilt his bruised chin. Then his attention was suddenly elsewhere: he nodded behind Everard's shoulder to the water's edge. "Though maybe don't mention that to our pirate egalitarian, aye?" he said, low.

It was rather too late for that, Everard thought as he turned, almost clocking D'Arcy with his nose in the process. "Vee's returned?"

He had. There was no mistaking the taper of broad back, the white-blond hair tied in a queue. He himself rowed the little tender steadily towards the *Sévère;* Louis-Michel Alarie and Romilly René sat at the bow, René's skirts marking a whole cargo of their own. She waved, then saluted cheekily. Alarie made no greeting, intent in conversation with Vitaliy; today's satin was a royal purple.

"Why the devil's the Frenchie still with them?" D'Arcy muttered. He returned the wave. "Wasn't he to move along to Galveztown with his new navy?"

"God knows." Everard wasn't much pleased either.

Pirates didn't pipe each other aboard, so Vitaliy's ascent went relatively unremarked. Everard, though, felt his matelot's steps upon the deck in his bones and blood; they jarred rhythm into his heart.

God help him, as angry as he was with the man, he'd still missed him. Had still felt the absence of his quiet presence like flesh torn out of him. Had put on the new hat this morning, because it was too fine to not, because it meant Vitya had thought of him.

Halfway across the deck, Vitaliy looked up to where they stood at the quarterdeck rail. His steps faltered, a hitch so small it was barely noticeable. Everard's heart stuttered with him.

But without a word, without a greeting, Vitaliy turned his face away—and ducked into the companionway beneath. Alarie followed, short on his heels.

"Ooh," D'Arcy said quietly. "Well, damn." He pushed his curls further down over his forehead. Vaguely, Everard was glad he was well enough to raise his hands past his shoulders without pain. "What'll you say to that, Ev?"

Everard took a deep breath. "I—"

There was a thudding crash from beneath, as though something heavy had been thrown; they both jumped. Vitaliy's low, angry voice shot, unintelligibly muffled, through the deck.

"What in hell—?" Everard started for the ladder.

He hadn't made it two steps before Louis-Michel Alarie came dancing out of the companionway. He shut the door gracefully behind himself, looking utterly unbothered at Vitaliy's uncharacteristic outburst of temper.

"Ah!" he said, finding Everard slack-jawed and staring at him from above. "The man precisely I must speak with!" He leapt up the ladder. "Do not you worry about Vee; his mood is rare only from being ashore—there is such heat!"

"Er…" Everard, not believing this for a second, glanced to D'Arcy with pleading eyes. "Quite."

D'Arcy—having miraculously understood—nodded and slipped behind him on the ladder, past the approaching Alarie. Limping slightly, he ducked into the companionway. Everard hoped he was well enough to deal with whatever he would find there.

But there were no further thrown things, calls of alarm, or angry voices; and so, Everard was slightly more capable of meeting Alarie's charming, smiling face.

He bowed. "How might I be of assistance, Governor?"

"I am going to be quite quick, very direct," Alarie began, "due to sheer lack of future opportunity. Please do forgive me. I wanted to have more ceremony than this—over a drink, or a meal—but circumstances…"

"Governor…?" Everard prompted.

"Yes, quite. The bare fact of it is, de Anglada, you were missed at the junta yesterday."

Everard blinked. "Indeed?"

"Yes. And it occurred to me, and several others also, you must understand, that you are a man of especial experience."

Everard said nothing.

"And you must know I do not have a man exactly like you at my disposal; which makes you such a unique opportunity. The British are unparalleled in skill—and your record is spotless—"

That wasn't right at all. D'Arcy's record as an officer was—had been—spotless; Everard's had been distinctly tarnished.

"Er…"

Alarie waved. "Spotless enough for a wobbly-legged new nation desperately in need of guidance. You do see?" He flashed white teeth.

"I believe so," Everard said stiffly. He believed he hadn't been more effectively offended throughout all his career. To say nothing of México.

Alarie nodded. "Good. Then I shall obviously make you vice-admiral—we do not do the red or the blue or the distinctions, there is only the one rank—you would answer directly to me, and none higher."

"Would I?" Everard murmured.

"Well, yes! It is settled, then. Mina has brought some seven, eight ships—a thousand 'maricones,' he said—"

Everard coughed in disbelief. "Marineros," he corrected firmly.

"That is what I said. A thousand sailors."

"No," Everard said. "No—"

Alarie peered at him. "Non? I could have sworn—but it was in the Spanish, perhaps I have not reproduced it—"

"Non," Everard confirmed. "I mean to say, it isn't settled. Not at all. I cannot be your admiral."

Alarie stared up.

"But—*no?* You would go from this"—he waved again—"from nothing, to be a kept man, a mate, to be an admiral! A hero! A revolutionary! Fighting against the enemy very same, the Spanish! My good friend—"

If Vitaliy had already lost his temper with the man to the

point of throwing things—little wonder—Everard didn't think he could make the situation much worse. He allowed himself to show the full depth of his feeling, which turned out to be pure rudeness:

"No. No, thank you. Never. I will not be your admiral, Governor. Absolutely not?" He tried this last in English, knowing the man understood it perfectly well. He raised his eyebrows expectantly.

Alarie shut his mouth with a snap, pushed out his lips into a boyish pout. "Hmm. Non, I will let you time to think upon it. A week. Yes? That is how long we will be in Port-au-Prince before we are departing. You will give me your answer then."

"No. No is my answer, Governor."

Alarie bowed. "I will not take offense at your bluntness, since I have had to be so unfortunately frank myself. But you will change your mind, I know. I am staying at the palace, naturally—" He did a little half-turn as he stepped down the ladder. "You might call on me there."

He fled, off the *Sévère* and agilely back into the tender, rowing quick as though he'd left torpedo bombs aboard and had to get outrange.

"Sant Jesús." Everard rubbed his hands over his face briskly. "Admiral." He let out a high laugh. "What in hell?"

He removed the hands to find he had an audience: Romilly René. She lounged in the mizzenmast shroud above him, smoking a cigarillo.

Disappointment rang clear through him. Did her being there mean Vitaliy was soon for the *San Telmo?*

But he finally had his answer. The broad panniers hadn't hindered her climb, nor had she accommodated them—she sat on the ratlines just as Vitaliy did, but with more concealment via lace.

"Alarie takes a tonic of coca leaf, from Amerique du Sud," she said solemnly. "I would recommend not to partake, if given chance." She flicked ash from the cigarillo into the water, blew a perfect smoke ring, and gave him a sharklike smile. "Trop bien, mon amour. Vee will be enchanted."

Everard stared.

She waved, smile widening. "Go on. Collect your reward, matelot."

# Twenty-Six

Everard flew down the ladder with the sure tread of a conquering hero, with his heart in his throat and his breath short. The swiftness of his decision shocked him, but like a few other decisions he'd had to make on the spur of the moment lately, it felt right. And not just because Alarie was an overstimulated, insulting ass—no, he could have wooed and wined Everard to limpness with smiles and promises of glory, and he would've had the same answer.

Why would the man think he would refuse the glorious *Sévère*, only to take the position of admiral? It made no sense.

Inside the greatcabin, Vitaliy and D'Arcy had reversed the strict positions they'd kept the whole week long. Vitaliy had partially reclaimed the cot and was seated on the edge of it, pushing himself back and forth with socked toes. His shoulders were hunched, his head was bowed, his hair loose around his face. He didn't at all look like a man in temper; he looked either desolate or very drunk. D'Arcy sat in the opposite corner, slumped in the plush armchair, totally sober, knees splayed and head back.

Everard didn't deceive himself that he didn't know what

the two of them had been discussing. No matter. He could set them straight.

But neither would look at him, and that seemed a bit of a prerequisite. He cleared his throat, a difficult task when he was breathing so.

"Alarie's offered—"

Vitaliy stood, and in three steps that utterly ruled out any potential inebriation, was in front of Everard, reaching—

Everard put out his own hand, upraised in welcome—

—but Vitaliy outstretched a sideways palm.

Everard stared like he'd never before seen a handshake greeting. He took the hand instinctually, felt the dry sailor's rough of Vitaliy's palm, and looked up to see Vitaliy's expression flat and tired and unfeeling. He frowned.

"Louis-Michel is more fortunate than he knows," Vitaliy said. His lips moved, but the rest of it was lifeless. "The position will suit you and the *San Telmo* well."

"What—the *San Telmo?* No." Everard tugged his hand free. "It— You think so?" he demanded.

"He has been looking for you a long while."

"Not *me*, surely—"

"Someone like him: looking for gain and glory. Someone like you."

Everard shook his head. "No—"

But Vitaliy went on, ruthless, as though it were all of it foregone. "He asked me find an admiral for his navy, since I would not be that for him."

Everard took a step back. "He asked you? And what did you promise him?"

"Nothing. But naturally I thought of you—that you might have it all back, everything you had lost. A ship. A position."

*A different life.* "You mean to say he'd asked you before… before all of it."

Vitaliy nodded, once.

"Before the court-martial? In Cartagena?"

Another nod.

"And the—the matelotage?" Everard said weakly.

"It would be considered ironclad assurance for Louis-Michel."

"Tied to you, I could assuredly be kept in line? A good little pirate admiral." Everard sneered.

Vitaliy shrugged. "That is how he thinks, if it isn't the truth. And it wouldn't be a bad thing. He won't manipulate you with Varfolomey backing you. Easy enough to go along with, yes?"

*Easy enough.* The words cut knives through Everard.

"I'm sorry, 'go along with'?"

Could their matelotage *still* be false for Vitaliy? A convenience? A… tool?

"You've… used me to placate him. That pretty French bastard. That's what I am to you? A political tool? Some kind of alliance?" He staggered back—Vitaliy reached out, stopped himself quick with a press of flattened lips, as if afraid—and Everard stumbled, shoulders back into the closed door to the parlour, meaning to flee.

But—the parlour, where the Stanhope press sat. The parlour, with dangerous paper and ink and even more dangerous words.

The press had been a gift. An option. An alternative. Vitaliy had, in fact, encouraged him *off* and away from the *Sévère.*

Alarie's motivations weren't Vitaliy's. They couldn't have been. Vitya wouldn't have manipulated him for the sake of Alarie. Because at no point had it seemed like Vitaliy wanted to utilise Everard for anything—so much so, in fact, that Everard had felt quite useless. *Kept.*

It had been by design. Not making Everard feel useless—that was Everard's own insecurities clamoring—but Vitaliy had carefully not obliged from him anything. Not a single thing. He'd wanted piracy to be Everard's choice. Had given him options.

That didn't mean he didn't *want* him to stay.

Everard glanced beyond Vitaliy to where D'Arcy sat lounged, totally unselfconscious to be eavesdropping. The very fact he wasn't up in arms at Everard's side, in defence of him, said almost everything.

Then D'Arcy looked up and smiled. Winked.

*If it weren't real, he wouldn't have done it.*

Almost everything.

"I don't believe you," Everard said quietly. "I think you are lying to me, Vitya."

Vitaliy's eyes widened. His skin was flushed in reverse, the pale chest blooming red beneath the laces of his shirt, his tanned face blanched grey as bone.

"That's what Alarie wants, maybe. But that wasn't what *you* wanted, when you asked me to be your matelot." Everard stepped closer and put hands up to either side of Vitaliy's face, threaded his six fingers through soft hair as gently and insistently as the first day they'd met—*Come here, come here, come close.*

Vitaliy, who had wept to be used as a weapon. Vitaliy, who had been pressed and made into a king's soldier and spy and people's pirate and revolutionary's filibuster and—while he slept, most vulnerable of all—other men's lover.

Vitya wanted him. Had wanted him. Wanted so badly now, he shook with devastation.

Everard said, "You wanted *me*."

Vitaliy let out a trembling, uneven breath. "I did," he confessed. "Yes. Yes. You are brave, and considerate, and very intelligent, and selfless and loyal, and I think war does not… the Navy did not deserve you," he said fiercely. "Neither do I. You should have the *San Telmo*, your own fleet, and gain and glory. But I want you here anyway. I want you because of it."

Everard said, "Vitya…"

"That's truth. The rest of it was a lie. I'm sorry. But here you are wasted, and everyone knows it. I thought you maybe wanted—if I could make it easier, make it justified for you to go…"

"Listen." Everard put his forehead on Vitaliy's, felt the man bring his hands over Everard's wrists—maybe to break his grip, or maybe just to touch him.

Everard said, "My answer to Alarie was no. I told him absolutely not. No. Never. I don't want to be his admiral. I wouldn't be his bloody king if he asked. I have what I want," he said firmly, and clutched tighter, moved the tips of his fingers across the sensitive nape. Vitaliy shuddered; his eyes closed. "I have it here. It isn't the *San Telmo,* or an admiralty, or a fleet, or glory. It's here. With you. That's all."

He leaned in—Vitaliy's hands over his wrists spasmed, and his breath came in hot, sweet puffs from that quiet, perfect mouth—

Distantly Everard heard the creak of upholstery, high-heeled boots stepping as quietly as they could manage with the halting limp; his haze broke apart in waves as he turned slightly.

D'Arcy put a hand on Everard's shoulder as he slipped past. He murmured the familiar, wry "Finally. Don't kill each other."

"No," Vitaliy said loudly.

D'Arcy froze, his hand on the latch.

"No?" Everard said, startled.

"Lieutenant," Vitaliy said, softer. His eyes were open, blue-black, pupils wide. His thumbs stroked at Everard's wrists, over and over, as he drew back slightly. "Lieutenant, he means you as well."

Had he?

"What?" D'Arcy's eyes flew up to Everard's, wide and

shocked, still layered with yellow-purple bruising; they flitted over to Vitaliy and back. His mouth opened, shut. "I don't... think so," he croaked. "Ever...?"

Yes. Of course he had.

Everard smiled waveringly, for now it was he who shook: with suppressed laughter, with delighted terror, shivering up from his gut, his groin. His heart couldn't take it.

"Yes," he whispered. "He has it right."

D'Arcy's eyes were narrowed, all-black, disbelieving. He swallowed.

Vitaliy's hands dropped away from Everard's wrists; they shared a look. Vitya nodded.

Everard slid his left hand free from the warm nape and beckoned.

"You're here, too, Preston. Or do I not have you?"

D'Arcy reeled.

"Don't be... dense," he whispered. "You've had me since you first put eyes on me, no question. But—Vee?"

Vitaliy smiled. "Yes, lieutenant. If you are well enough."

D'Arcy inhaled sharp. "You— Oh, sod off. Am I *well* enough?" He made an airless, rueful laugh. "Neither of you has the least idea."

He stepped forward, halted—then circled round them, once, twice, as though working out the approach most ideal. His limp disappeared, and the rest of his injuries seemed to have dropped away; he was as tense as a stalking predator. One of the sleek, sable-red, sharp-toothed ones.

"Think I've been at a stand for days, watching you two circle. Christ. Am I well enough. I'd have to be dead."

Vitaliy's pulse was wild beneath Everard's hand at his clavicle. His own heart was in much the same state, running so free and unrestrained, he was sure it showed in the buttons of his waistcoat.

D'Arcy stopped behind Vitaliy, close enough that his breath moved the fine-silk hair, warmed Everard's fingers.

And then he pounced.

He put his hands to either side of Vitaliy's hips and pulled —not quite far enough to break Everard apart from him—and nuzzled close where Vitaliy's shoulder met his neck. Vitya sucked in a breath and clutched tight at Everard's elbows; his head fell back and his eyes closed. D'Arcy slid his hands up, up, up across Vitya's chest. He met Everard's eyes.

"*Mine*," Everard mouthed. D'Arcy nodded.

Everard pulled his hand forward, slid it over Vitya's bared throat, entrapping him gently against D'Arcy's body. He felt his pirate swallow and gasp as he was made pliant by D'Arcy's slow grind behind him.

Vitya's hands dropped to help with endless ties, his tucked shirtsleeves; soon he was peeled down to breeches, white-blond curls, pale pink nipples, the taper of shoulder to waist that drove Everard to madness when he had it beneath him. Or above him. Anywhere at all in his vicinity.

D'Arcy's hands explored and pulled and splayed; his hips ground. Everard drew back and stared, biting his lip with restraint. Was this truly what D'Arcy wanted? What Vitya wanted?

Everard wanted it.

D'Arcy grinned as he watched him, sweat already on his brow, eyes dark. "Firstly, Captain," he gasped, open-mouthed against Vitya's pale, fuzzed nape, the shell of his ear, "kiss your husband. It's been a very long week." He pushed with his hips and hands, a sinuous wave, and Vitaliy straightened, pulled Everard close, and obeyed.

The kiss was soft and questioning. Everard didn't mind, for as long as those lips were on him, he was pleased to lean in and deepen it; but D'Arcy, never a patient lovemaker, seemed to become frustrated with this. He ground forward, gently shoving, pulling back, demanding response. Vitaliy grunted over Everard's mouth in irritation but, when a push-pull of D'Arcy's put their pricks at last into hot, still-clothed contact, gasped and even bit once.

Content with this, D'Arcy had moved back; to watch, perhaps, or—no, he was behind Everard now, and his hands were wrapping round, tugging at the buttons of Everard's fall, fast and deft. Vitaliy helped, now kissing Everard so thoroughly and full-on, it was a good thing Everard wasn't focusing on undressing himself.

Quite strange, to have four hands upon Everard at once, ministrating, disrobing, everything but his shirt. D'Arcy's fingers trailed his thigh, his calf, his ankle as each leg was bared; the odd kiss made a sparking path.

D'Arcy wrapped one hand round Everard's prick, positioning it tenderly. He pushed, moving the three of them in tandem, hands, arse, pricks. Everard broke Vitya's kiss to moan into his neck.

He didn't see why he and Vitya had an opposite state of undress until D'Arcy reached round and tapped significantly on Vitya's shoulders.

Vitya sank to his knees with a knowing smile.

Everard said, "Oh, *God.*" D'Arcy hissed his approval, hooked his chin over Everard's left shoulder, then drew up what he could of Everard's shirt tight in one hand.

Vitya took the head of him in swiftly, eagerly, wetly. Everard cursed.

"I thought so," D'Arcy purred. "Hell. Look at those lips. That prick."

Vitaliy gave them a dark-blue look, glare and—affection?— and consternation, and then redoubled his efforts; Everard, between flashes of starlike bliss, made another realisation: Vitya *liked* this, liked the focus on his lips, liked how D'Arcy had made them both into something almost object-like, framed for display—

He whimpered. "Ah—Jesus. Ah."

Vitya had revenge in the clutching of Everard's arse, hands hard to either side, spreading; Everard groaned. D'Arcy's fingers, missing nothing, insinuated themselves in the cleft there, pressing, stroking.

It was too much, all at once. "I don't think— Vitya— God — *Oh.*" He groped backward with his hand not wrapped in Vitya's hair. "Preston!"

"Quite right," D'Arcy breathed. "Good lord. I'd better stop, then." He caught the hand in his and squeezed. "Hang on, love."

"Hang *on?* I can't possibly— I'd like to see you here—" Everard made a desperate noise.

Vitya let go Everard's arse, pulled off his prick barely in time. Breathing hard, lips red, he shot D'Arcy a triumphant look of challenge that almost sent Everard over in spite of the effort of the abrupt stop.

Everard heaved in careful breaths. "I shan't survive," he gasped. "You'll have me wrecked between you."

D'Arcy laughed. "Not yet."

Vitaliy stood and kissed Everard, undoing buttons, not touching nearly enough skin as he removed Everard's shirt.

Everard made up for it by breaking free and revealing all of Vitaliy in a single rough shove of breeches. He was hard, already leaking. Everard stroked him with a tight fist, almost angrily; when Vitya drew back, it was with wide eyes and flaring nostrils. He looked up to D'Arcy and said roughly, "You, too."

D'Arcy laughed more as he stripped, which seemed to exasperate and endear Vitaliy to equal measure; he watched with gleaming, blue-black eyes. And as the last of D'Arcy's clothes had been toed away, Vitaliy's hips bumped against Everard's. He put a hasty, restraining hand on Everard's wrist.

Everard raised an eyebrow. "You did call him pretty." He looked back over his shoulder, and raised the other brow. "Turnabout?" he suggested to D'Arcy.

"Hells, yes."

D'Arcy was on his knees in a flash. After a confirming pause—Vitya nodded—D'Arcy took him in, all the way down.

Vitya's eyes went wide; he gasped in surprise. He looked up to Everard with a wry, shocked expression: *I didn't expect this*.

It was Everard's turn to giggle, sounding half-mad.

Vitaliy put his unoccupied hand on the panelling to brace himself, tensed his broad thighs. The hand he'd put in D'Arcy's curls clutched and seized, roving through.

Everard's laughter faded abruptly at the sight. "Oh, Dios," he said. "That looks…" He kept his hands palms-flat on his thighs so that he wouldn't work himself to spending in a second, was how it looked. He could watch it forever. "Good *lord*, Preston."

D'Arcy made a pleased-sounding hum, then truly went to task.

Vitya didn't whimper in his throes; he gulped, increasingly faster. But though the perfect lips had dropped open, turnabout didn't seem to be forthcoming—he wasn't reaching true desperation. There was no colour on his cheeks, and in fact maybe even the beginnings of concern between his brows. His fingers were too careful, too hesitant in D'Arcy's hair.

Everard touched D'Arcy's shoulder. He drew back, panting.

Vitaliy relaxed, relief apparent in the line of his shoulders and the instant drop of his hands. He shot Everard a grateful look.

"Right. Not your trigger," D'Arcy said, matter-of-fact, as he fell back to his heels.

Vitaliy shook his head. "Not especially," he whispered.

D'Arcy didn't move. "Hmm." His eyes narrowed again, polecat-like. "It's Everard's, though," he said, equally unconcerned. "Watching."

Vitaliy's gaze flew up to Everard, questioning. "Yes?"

Everard nodded, only somewhat reluctantly. It was true.

"Mm-hm," D'Arcy confirmed. "Look at him—he doesn't dare touch himself just now. Adores watching me swallow a man down. You'll believe it?"

Vitya grunted. And then—then colour began on his cheeks. His prick leaped anew. "Yes," he whispered.

"Good; you ought. And I think," D'Arcy said, "I think you also ought give him what he wants. What d'you say?"

Everard was incapable of words, excepting a strangled "Preston…"

Vitaliy was as still as stone. His eyes were very wide, bright, focused on Everard alone.

"I think," D'Arcy said, "you owe him quite a lot."

Everard held his breath, biting his lip hard. Suddenly, he wasn't sure this would go the way D'Arcy meant it to—Vitaliy had been so concerned about Everard obliging him—

—but his concern had been *Everard* being obliged to him, he realised. He'd been worried Everard would've had no other choice.

Not the other way round.

"Don't you?" D'Arcy said, murderously soft, sensing his kill at hand. "You began this. You want to do this for him. He deserves it. Don't you think so?"

The other way round… where Vitaliy was the one indebted —the one, perhaps, *obliging*—

Vitaliy shuddered all over. He looked as though he were on a precipice, disbelief and desire, begrudging admiration, too. His breath came in gulps again, and this time, no one was touching him; his prick leapt and bounced, leaking. Both his hands were spread against the pale blue panelling behind him, all ten fingertips white and strained as they held him up. His gaze fixed on Everard, agonised, black with want.

"I— I— *Yes,*" he gasped. "Fuck! You are a bastard. Yes." His hand shot out and pushed down his stand to the proper angle, the angle of unmistakable demand. *"Yes."*

D'Arcy wasted no time; Vitya's prick disappeared into his throat amid three simultaneous groans. Then it was turnabout after all; Vitaliy was cursing in half-syllables, his hands deep in curls, hips shuddering in restraint, socked feet flexing. His gaze never dropped from Everard.

"Thrust, Vitya," Everard encouraged. "Go on. He can take it."

Vitaliy gasped, in, out, louder than Everard had ever heard him. His eyes were wild, pale-lashed, a thing of beauty. "But…"

D'Arcy made an urgent, affirmative noise. Still Vitya held himself back.

"Preston's right," Everard said. "I don't dare touch myself. Not for a second. Thrust," he demanded.

"I cannot," Vitya gasped. "No—"

D'Arcy's wet back-and-forth halted; Everard put his thumb to his nape in reassurance.

"That's all right," he said soothingly. "Really. Dear God, look at you. Do you like me watching, Vitya?"

He didn't need an answer, and Vitaliy knew it; his head fell to the wall, eyes staring up to the rafters, chest heaving; he was rapidly losing the battle against stoicism.

"Yes," he hissed anyway.

D'Arcy chuckled and resumed. He let up astutely where he needed to let up, to let all of them breathe, stave off release, share incredulous, dazed looks. Then he went again. He really was very good.

Everard hadn't ever let D'Arcy suck him, because he

suspected it was a page, once read aloud, that he could never blot out, never turn back, never shut away. And someday, God willing, he would find out if spilling himself down D'Arcy's throat was in fact incurably addictive as it looked. Someday, but not today.

Today he wanted—needed—more than just watching.

He went to retrieve oil. Vitaliy watched him go, watched him return, prize in hand. His breathing increased, somehow, and he nodded.

Softly, Everard came beside them both. He nudged, and pulled, and made space. Then he was fully behind Vitya, tracing down the slope of pale back, pushing apart broad thighs with his knee. He splayed his hands across Vitya's bare stomach, because he could, sank fingertips into the warm, velvet juncture of thigh and groin, the firm muscle beside. He push-pulled him close, aligned his body with his own. Vitya still wasn't thrusting.

"Shall I help you?" He kissed him on the sensitive bit of his neck, the one D'Arcy had sniffed out immediately, and was rewarded with a deep groan.

"Please," Vitya whispered.

D'Arcy put a hand up to Everard's hip and squeezed hard. His eyes fluttered open, hazel, teary, yellow-purple beneath with bruising; Everard mouthed, *Mine.* D'Arcy's eyes squeezed shut.

No, it wasn't going to take much time at all.

The rocking of Everard's hips became Vitya's, and Vitya's prick slid forth and back across D'Arcy's tongue, pushed into his throat; they all groaned. D'Arcy's fingers clutched deep in the flesh of Everard's hip, the first barometer for which Everard was grateful; the second being D'Arcy's other hand, far below, deliberately stroking a very pink prick.

Everard had watched before, watched D'Arcy have a man with his mouth, stroke himself too. It'd never been like this, never so close; Everard had never touched in the moment. Never loved them both. Now he wanted to be everywhere at once. Instead, he put his left hand atop Vitya's, tangled it deeper into sable curls.

When he breached Vitya—Vitya preferring a cock directly, being very against fingers in the beginning—it was careful, excruciatingly slow, and accompanied by a litany of hard breathing, cursing and shuddering, goose-pimple flesh going pliant. D'Arcy drew back, murmuring praise and admiration until he could resume.

They shortly found themselves on borrowed time. Everard went as slowly as he could bear, partly because of the torture of already being on the knife's edge and partly because though he'd said D'Arcy could take it and he knew it to be true, he still worried—for all of them. Vitaliy would never forgive them if they made him inflict so much as a bruise, even practically thirdhand.

But slow worked well. Everard rocked and rocked until he was fully seated, D'Arcy's pulls bringing him forward, Vitya's full, sweet arse pushing insistently back.

Eventually, D'Arcy slid free with a cough, impatient, and took matters into his own hands: he put them on Vitya's hips and worked him backward, onto Everard's length and forward again.

Vitaliy gasped, slapped a hand over Everard's on his stomach, squeezed hard.

Everard looked at their interlaced hands, D'Arcy's beneath, taking control, Vitya's wet, slicked prick between; spotty black, fraying streaks of white overlaid it all.

"God." He was much too close—

Then D'Arcy growled, "Give him your arse, Vee. As though you mean to."

Vitya's reaction was extraordinary. Russian curses fell snarled from his lips; he clawed at the panelling behind them, clutched at Everard's hip; he shook, and groaned like Everard had never heard.

And then he moved. He gave Everard his arse, utterly and totally.

Everard held him up, held still, held back his own release by a bare, splintering thread. "Holy—Jesus—*God. Vitya.*" He wasn't going to last. "Preston," he said, urgently, "come up here, I want—I need— *Ah*— Mmph!"

Salty-sweet, breathless, ruthless, D'Arcy's lips on his sucked nearly every bit of consciousness Everard had left.

D'Arcy pushed Vitaliy fully against him, demanding they both still; unyielding as a standing stone, he pressed them against the wall. Everard thought: the whole ship could have rocked then, could've listed hard, and they would've gone nowhere. He felt the ridges of panelling behind him, slick with his own sweat, felt Vitaliy around him, hot and clenching. His vision swam as climax receded marginally.

In contrast, between them Vitya was incoherent, trembling, deep within the dark, heady place where one seeks release and nothing else. His head on Everard's shoulder rolled.

"Fuck—you—bastard," he mumbled.

That was meant for D'Arcy, who gave a soft, almost-cruel chuckle. "I have you, Vee."

Slowly, not letting Vitya gain forward ground whatsoever, D'Arcy began to rut. Everard thought he must have had a hand on Vitya now, perhaps was frigging them together, but he couldn't tell. He had eyes closed, was focused desperately on not spending: every one of D'Arcy's movements shuddered through to his core.

Vitya writhed, tried to move: he jerked forward, then back onto Everard, his thighs trembling, slick all over with sweat. His moans and desperate short pants were loud in Everard's ear, not helping matters in the least.

D'Arcy, ever observant and sometimes merciful, increased

his pace. When he reached up and grasped Everard by the shoulder for leverage, Everard opened his eyes to find D'Arcy's own glazed, fixed hotly upon him, feverish with love and awe and clear, heartbreaking relief.

"Mine," Everard rasped. "Mine, mine. Both of you."

Vitya shook between them. His breath turned shallow and almost nonexistent; he clutched at both of them in frantic, sliding grasps, pleading—and gasped and tensed and quietly came, wet heat everywhere. His arse clenched around Everard, and that was it, Everard was right there, coming with a searing lurch like tripping and falling in a dream, releasing deep, deep, deep—

D'Arcy laughed triumphantly and followed fast with a low, satisfied moan, his fingertips sunk in Everard's shoulder, his teeth in Vitya's.

When the spinning ceased somewhat, Everard was pleased and surprised to find he was both detached from the others and still standing, if leaning fairly heavily upon the panelling. Vitaliy was slumped over D'Arcy's shoulder, half-asleep already; D'Arcy murmured to him sweetly, affectionately as they stumbled over to the cot.

Everard shook his head, to see if the vision would waver away, like a sex-induced mirage, but it didn't. It continued, all the way to the point where D'Arcy laid Vitya down and rearranged his limbs for comfort.

Vitya murmured something enquiring, too muffled by bedding for Everard to hear clearly.

D'Arcy's response down was firm, dismissive, gentle: "Nearly."

*Nearly what?* Everard wondered foggily.

Vitaliy seemed placated by it; his breathing settled into his usual instantaneous sleep.

D'Arcy glanced up to Everard, assessing, knowing. "All right to walk?"

"In a moment," Everard said, thinking it truthful; but then he slid to the floor. "No—perhaps later."

D'Arcy laughed and came over. His head hit the panelling with a *thunk* as he sat, elbows on his knees. Everard looked him over: the silky, red-brown hair, the thick dark lashes, the all-over flush on his dear, handsome face. The yellow, the blue-green, the odd dense purple center of his bruises. In spite of everything—*because* of everything—they had to be painful.

"All right?"

D'Arcy slid sideways onto the scrubbed deck. He shifted to lie on his back; soft curls splayed as the heavy, warm head lay upon Everard's still-twitching thigh.

Everard put a hand on D'Arcy's chest. "Preston?"

D'Arcy picked it up, kissed it, and kept it. "Better than."

# TWENTY-SEVEN

*N*early *what?*

Days later, it kept Everard up at night, nearly what.

The *Sévère* floated hove-to just outside Port-au-Prince. Five bells and the moonlight on the face of the clock on the desk told Everard it was half-three in the morning. Vitaliy slept beside him in the tiered trundle—for the cot did not, in fact, fit three—oblivious, trusting, contentedly fucked out.

On Everard's other side, limbs entwined with his like a sucking nautilus, D'Arcy was rather less oblivious to his wakefulness.

"Got more sleep doing night watches," D'Arcy murmured in his ear. He patted Everard on the hip sleepily, and pulled him in even closer, spoonlike. "Tense in all the wrong places. What t'devil's wrong?"

"Would I could tell you."

D'Arcy harrumphed into his hair, sounding amused. "As though you've secrets."

He didn't. *But you do,* Everard thought. *You do.*

"I couldn't tell you," Everard said crisply, "because I haven't an idea why."

"You're… too happy?" D'Arcy taunted. "Too wealthy? Too well fucked?" He shifted suggestively and kissed his nape. "Can't remedy that last. Sorry."

Everard stiffened. D'Arcy harrumphed again, less amused this time, and retreated onto his back. The cots *click*ed together softly, canvas-on-canvas. Vitaliy didn't stir. He woke for nothing less than guns or vigorous shaking, sometimes both.

D'Arcy sighed. "What are you worried for?"

"Everything," Everard said honestly.

Another sigh. "… In order of severity, then? Surely, you've nothing but lists in that brain."

Everard didn't deny it, though they were more concurrent tallies of time and space, spinning lists going round an infinite axis like a star—

"Ascending or descending?"

"Descending, of course. Ass."

"Fine! La Corona," Everard said promptly. *Nearly what.* "Mutiny. A hurricane." *Nearly what.* "The *Vuelte* sinking in the Gulf Stream, and the crew's shares for the year with her. Two thousand small arms we're to deliver to México. Jean Lafitte intercepting us." *Nearly what.* "Every time you're out of my sight, that the next time I see you you'll be—"

D'Arcy nipped his shoulder. "I told you not to worry."

Everard scoffed. "Then I shall worry for St. Clare. Thom. Anyone who has associated themselves with me—"

Another nip.

"—ouch! Stop that, you—you—pup."

D'Arcy smothered his laughter with Everard's chest and a hand. "Not quite. Look, Thom's very well liked, nonthreatening, and a boy, besides. Even pirates have scruples," he said, not unironically.

"And St. Clare?"

D'Arcy sobered, notched his chin into the hollow of Everard's shoulder. "I'm not *not* worried for Bell," he said carefully.

"But," he said hastily, as Everard inhaled, "it isn't for that, or other reasons you might assume."

Everard didn't know what to assume, except that he knew D'Arcy didn't spend every night in the greatcabin.

"I have no wish to intrude on your relations with—with other men," he said, flushing with heat D'Arcy doubtless felt bloom beneath his fingers. "None of my business, obviously. But—"

"I'm not fucking Bell," D'Arcy interrupted flatly.

"Er…"

"And it wouldn't make any difference if I was. Nobody *cares*. Hang a moment; is that what you thought I was beaten for?" D'Arcy said, aghast.

"I— Whatever else would it have been for?"

"Because these past days, we've been *extremely* discreet," D'Arcy said sarcastically. "Especially that time in the dining parlour—"

"Oh, God."

"—with all the windows, and Vee—"

"I do recall it," Everard gritted out. "Thank you."

D'Arcy grinned. "Then I will enlighten you to other revelations. You two matelots may be uncommon in the year of our lord 1816, but nigh on the majority of these pirates are like-minded, Ever. That's half Varfolomey's infamy in itself, albeit written between the lines. *Have* you gone belowdecks of a morning?"

Even lit by blue moonlight, Everard was sure he was positively scarlet. "Well, yes—"

"And you a Navy man, too." D'Arcy chuckled. "Christ."

"I figured them especially loyal," Everard muttered.

D'Arcy collapsed into laughter. "Secretly Puritanical, these pirates. Extremely invested in maintaining the monogamy of a barely legal matelotage."

Everard hushed him. "You'll wake Vee."

"I shan't, as he wakes for almost nothing." D'Arcy pulled in close anyway, and whispered: "I'll fuck you off the weather rail, Everard, with all hands to witness. Then you'll see how much people care for it."

"Good lord. You will absolutely not—"

"Bent over the stanchion—"

"Then *why?*" Everard interrupted hotly. "If they don't care I was—stepping out, so to speak—why would they target you? In fact I'd rather thought—"

"Oh, no." D'Arcy sighed.

"Er."

"… yes?" D'Arcy encouraged, sounding resigned.

"That Vitaliy had in fact done something to remedy… well, the act of—er, claiming—it affords you much the same understanding…?"

D'Arcy stilled. "A man doesn't need an ulterior motivation to fuck me." All teasing had drained away from his voice; he sounded actually, truly offended.

Everard shifted away. "Of course not. But the situation…"

D'Arcy raised up on an elbow, leaning in and looming. "And Vee hasn't *claimed* me, publicly or not. Nor," he said, making a face, "do I want him to do so."

"But it was—don't you think it might have occurred to him it was—"

"If you say *convenient*, Everard Rubén, so help me—"

"Fine. Vitaliy's overture towards you came solely whenceforth behind his balls."

"Jesus Christ, the man hasn't got magic spunk. Sleeping here affords me nothing. For one, it's hardly unprecedented, and if you'd spent more than a moment speaking to any of the crew, you'd know—"

"Thank you, I don't wish to know," Everard said vehemently. "But then why would they not reattack?"

"Cannot this wait 'til dawn? It's three in the morning."

But Everard had already broached the impossible topic, and now it felt too large to be taken back into himself yet again. Wait 'til morning? If he did, it would bubble and fester.

"You do know why. By God! Does Vitya?"

"—Breakfast? Let a man get some porridge in him?"

"For he did *nothing*. Told me not to worry, as you did, but let me sit with it, day after day, while he knew. You both of you knew."

D'Arcy groaned.

"For that matter," Everard realised, "I believe he wouldn't have—have—with you—at all. In the first place. If that was the danger, the impetus. He wouldn't have even touched you. Don't you think?"

"You have him pretty well pegged, I daresay," D'Arcy muttered.

"He knew and yet he told me he would do nothing for it because of his *morals*. His principles. But surely, the only reason he would truly do nothing is because he knew it hadn't a chance of being repeated."

"Everard, I think maybe... later, on occasion Vee is awake—"

Everard sat up in the cot, threw off the sheets and D'Arcy's lingering grasp.

"Ev, what're you..."

Everard swung out, tromped round to the trundle cot, put both hands to Vitaliy's shoulders, and shook him.

"Jesus, Everard!" D'Arcy leaned far over across the cot and pushed him, hard, breaking his grasp; Everard stumbled backward.

Vitaliy awoke with a sharp, startled inhale, fists clutching the sheets tight as he hauled himself half-upright. "Wha—?"

"What in hell's wrong with you?" D'Arcy spat. He leaned to put a hand on Vitaliy's shoulder, rubbing vigorously.

"'S'aright, Vee, you're safe; it's only Everard being an ass. Breathe."

Vitaliy's eyes were wild, his breath gulping. He looked bewildered and… rather betrayed, if Everard was being honest with himself.

"Shh. Breathe," D'Arcy murmured. He glared up. "Christ, Everard, that was cruel."

"I…" God, yes. It had been.

"You told him," Vitaliy croaked. "But it is dark—what hour is it?"

"Too goddamned early is what." D'Arcy swung himself out of the cot.

"Half-three…" Everard glanced over. "No, four now. Told me what?"

He was surely an ass. But by the sound of it, also a righteous ass.

"It could not wait 'til morning, Lieutenant?" Vitaliy whispered. "I am so tired."

His quiet, weary voice knifed through Everard. Nonetheless:

"Told me *what*?" he demanded.

Vitaliy shut his eyes, his brow furrowing, looking more than anything else in pain as he sank back down into the bedding.

D'Arcy put his arm in Everard's and frog-marched him to the door. "I'll sort it, Vee. Go back to sleep, if you can. You," he said to Everard, "you are what needs sorting, God help me. Come with me. You don't deserve to breathe his air just now."

"But—" Everard didn't disagree, but he still wanted answers. He twisted round, resisting: but Vitaliy was already asleep, curled around his pillow, hair spilling like silken gold thread over bulky shoulders, lips pale. So beautiful it hurt, and *why* had Everard woken him like that?

D'Arcy dragged him through the companionway and onto the quiet weather deck, across to the bow, the forecastle, and there, as though he had just pulled Everard away from a fist-fight, he let him tug free at last.

"I'm not dressed!" Everard spat.

"I can't believe you did that," D'Arcy said, low and weary. "He needs every bit of sleep he can get, and not to be startled from it like we're back at war."

*Back at war?*

"We're pirates!" Everard clung to the rail and began to lose his breath. "When have we not been at war, pray? Anyway, how d'you… how d'you know about his sleeping?"

D'Arcy hadn't shared their bed for nearly long enough for that. There hadn't been any episodes recently. Unless Vitya had warned him?

"Don't you love him?" D'Arcy said fiercely, ignoring this. "You don't act particularly as though you do. But then"—he laughed—"you never have. The Navy got hold of you far too early."

Everard squeezed his eyes shut. There on the deck, they were so exposed—others would overhear, would *see*—he had hardly any clothes on. The Gulf breeze was warm, but lifted his hair from the root and gave him gooseflesh all over. How could D'Arcy know about Vitya's sleeping? Unless… unless.

*One other. Once.*

"Do you and he know each other?" Everard demanded. He clutched one arm round himself and shivered. "Have known each other previously? Is that what's to tell?"

But D'Arcy went on as though he hadn't spoken. "You'll be the luckiest goddamned fuck on the ocean if he trusts you to share his bed again, Ever." He put his face over his hands and groaned. "But he shall anyway because he's Vee and he *does* love you, you absolute self-centered donkey."

"I know…" Everard didn't know a single goddamned thing. "I know he does… *Please.*" His knees no longer seemed to work. He slid to the decking, bent his legs in front of him so he wouldn't keel forward. "I'll take my dressing-down as you see fit, and well deserved. But please, not out here in the air?"

D'Arcy eyed him with distinct sympathy, anguish, regret. Like it'd been his trust that Everard had shaken out of him.

"Fine," he spat.

To the hatch he went, slid down the ladder silently; he was still barefoot. Everard stood and followed, shaking.

The farther belowdecks they went, the trembling uneasiness receded in fragments, chipping away until Everard felt nearly his usual self again.

Nearly.

They made it to the orlop before D'Arcy ambushed him, a hand over his mouth and an arm thick around his chest. He flattened Everard tight between his stone-stiff body and the hatch's panelling. Everard was still too teary and startled to react; that was, until he heard the noises coming over D'Arcy's harsh, shallow breath at his ear. He gasped—D'Arcy's hand became painful over his mouth.

Fucking noises, somewhat distant. Slapping flesh, grunts and groans, several. A pause, laughter; more fucking noises. Several voices, encouraging, cajoling—more slapping—a vaguely familiar whisper, like scripture—

Everard fought the hand; D'Arcy released him but was still frozen against him. He put his head on Everard's shoulder and shook, just for a moment, trembling; then lifted his head and met Everard's wide eyes with teary hazel ones.

He pointed up to the third gun deck, to the right of Perran's workshop, where the carpenter's mates had slept before they'd gone aboard the *San Telmo*. The doors were solid for fireproofing, the panelling reinforced—there, they wouldn't be overheard.

Everard nodded. They slunk up the ladder once more, quietly as they could go.

As soon as D'Arcy shut the thick door behind him, Everard whispered, "Was—was—what was—was that—?"

"Absolutely none of your concern?" D'Arcy dashed away tears and glared.

"None of my concern," Everard agreed quickly. "Er… but a consensual none of my concern?"

"For fuck's…" D'Arcy sighed. "Yes. I… believe so. So far as I can… Yes?" He raked his hands through his curls, making them fluff every which way. "What d'you take me for, anyway, that I would stand aside if I thought it weren't?"

*Someone with secrets I can't conceive of.* "No," Everard said, rather patiently, all things considered, "I merely wondered if I'd have to back you against a half dozen pirates with fists alone."

"Oh, well, then." D'Arcy slumped into a bunk, sending a cloud of sawdust flying.

"So…" Everard hesitated.

D'Arcy groaned. "Christ, no, sod off."

"You really aren't…?"

"No. For the love of God, no." D'Arcy laughed, gave into desperate snorting, face in an elbow. "I don't know why it's funny," he said at last, sighing. "As neither of us is qualified to judge."

"Definitely not," Everard agreed.

The thought of that—they and Vitaliy, and everything that had transpired between them—sobered them both considerably.

Everard sat beside D'Arcy, hunching so he fit in the cot. He wove his left hand in the other man's, held it tight with the thumb.

D'Arcy groaned again, leaned away. "No, no, no. Should've stayed abovedecks, where we'd be overheard," he muttered.

But Everard wouldn't be dissuaded. Not now.

"What don't I know, Preston?"

# Twenty-Eight

I t was worse than Everard could've imagined.

"It had to be real," D'Arcy stressed, for perhaps the third time. "Real bruises, real blood—pirates are too known for their theatre and falsehood. They'd see through pig's blood and paint."

Everard clung to D'Arcy's hand and couldn't breathe. *Harder to leave a man alive than to kill him by accident.*

"No," he muttered, disbelieving. "Vitya… couldn't have." *It couldn't have been him. Gentle but ruthless Vitya—* "No."

"He enjoyed it about as much as I did," D'Arcy went on quickly. "Which is to say not at all. If that helps."

"No." Everard shook his head. "No, it doesn't."

"He asked if I'd broken anything, and I told him about my rib—from the *Wanderer,* you remember?—he insisted on avoiding it, though I told him you'd maybe see it and wonder…it seemed so conspicuous after…"

Everard jerked away, pushed his forehead into the heels of his hands, and keened. D'Arcy put a tentative palm on the curve of his back.

"No one else could do it, Ever. René knew—knows—but

she wasn't strong enough. No one else knew, not even Stephan. And it had to look like several men."

*Fists, boots, a belt or two. A strong arm around his throat, holding back his arms... One man.*

"But why? And *when...*" Everard gulped. "You weren't actually drunk, the day of the *San Telmo.*"

D'Arcy chuckled uneasily. "We-elll... as I had to look rather unconscious..."

Vitaliy, shaking after; Everard, comforting him, thinking it to be normal, commonplace battle shock. Vitya, lying to him, every moment of the past fortnight.

Everard moaned. "... *I* am going to be sick."

D'Arcy had anticipated this somehow, although they were at sea, and Everard had never, in his memory or anyone's, been sick at sea—he pulled a sawdust bucket close. Cedar and oak and fir shavings floated up into Everard's nose as he was thoroughly sick, and sneezed, and was sick again.

D'Arcy was there beside him as he shook. He pushed hair back from Everard's brow, carefully wiped his mouth with his handkerchief.

"I don't want—can't hear any more of how," Everard said weakly, after. "Only... why."

"All right," D'Arcy said softly. "To make a long tale short, it was necessary to keep Alarie's mounting suspicion off my back. He knows about Vee—that he's American, and up to his ears in it with Madison—but not me, and I'd like to keep it that way."

"Alarie knows... *I* don't know! What's to know?"

D'Arcy nodded. "I am—and have been—agent for the Americans. Occasionally the French."

"You *what?*" Everard stood abruptly, conking his head on the upper bunk, also accidentally stealing the handkerchief; he clutched it over his mouth in horror as he backed away. "Sodding—ow. Agent... *spy*. For how long?"

D'Arcy looked uncomfortable. He made to stand. "I'll wake Vee—"

Everard snatched away the handkerchief to enunciate. "*Sit down*," he ordered; D'Arcy complied. "How *bloody long*?"

"Since I'd met Vee. Thereabouts."

"Which was—certainly, that was York, three years ago?" Anger flared. "You were turned under my goddamn nose in the middle of war?"

D'Arcy shook his head.

"Then how bloody long ago!"

"Eighteen-oh-eight. Eighteen-oh-nine? I hardly remember. It was the West Africa Squadron in infancy. We were posted to the same frigate."

Everard staggered. "Vitya was a marine. And you—and he —and you— He was a marine!"

D'Arcy grinned weakly, scratched at the nape of his neck. "I like a red coat on a man?"

"Idiota, idiota, puto tontorrón. I am *such* the idiot," Everard said emphatically.

"Hey, now," D'Arcy protested, "slurs are uncalled for."

"Have you two been… this whole time?"

"No!" D'Arcy put up his hands and waved. "No, no, no. Not until"—he smiled crookedly—"the other night. I swear to you, Ever. Vee and I weren't— We were never suited, and just he and I in bed, it's… You maybe saw a bit of it. But he loves *you*; he'd do anything for you."

"Anything, except not put his fists to the face of the other man I love," Everard said bitterly.

D'Arcy's face worked, conflicted. "Everard, neither of us was prepared for the extent of your reaction. I'm sure if he'd known… hell, if I'd known…"

*They hadn't known I loved him.*

"I thought you were dead," Everard muttered, stunned and

shamed to his marrow. "Even if you'd just been my lieutenant… I'm responsible… Of course I would *care*."

"No, you aren't responsible," D'Arcy said firmly. "I'm sorry. It was really only bruising. The rest was feigned. And I was very drunk, which made it easier. Then"—he chuckled—"we both thought he maybe hadn't done enough. Especially when Stephan stayed vigil all of an hour."

Everard made a nauseated groan, put his hands over his face. "Enough? Please—it's too much."

"You're *not* responsible for it, Everard. And neither is Vee, not truly. You mustn't blame him. Blame me alone, if anyone."

*But how is that possible?* Everard thought. *It'd been Vitya's fists, his boots, his careful, meticulous touch.* Thanks to sharing combat with the man, Everard could see it there in his mind, just as well as he could not ever, ever imagine it. Vitaliy making a fist, drawing back—

Everard groaned, and was obliged to lean and be unexpectedly sick again, saliva and desperation the only things left in him.

D'Arcy reached an arm around, pulled Everard deep into his sturdy, warm shoulder. "I'm sorry," he murmured in litany. "I'm sorry."

So was Everard. Vitaliy would always weigh principles and ways against any one man's welfare, no matter whom that one man happened to be to him. The result, the goal was what mattered.

He knew this, had seen it borne out again and again; there was the proof.

Against D'Arcy's neck, Everard breathed in bitter almond, sea salt, the man's own sharp scent, and quietly went to pieces. D'Arcy squeezed him tight, as though they floated, vessel-less, on the open sea, and would be parted if he dared let go.

Eventually, Everard raised his head and asked, "Tell me how he turned you."

"The usual way," D'Arcy said, nonchalant; but the thickness of his voice gave him away. "In bed."

Everard managed a playful thump, straight onto the man's chest. "God."

"No, no. He didn't. Vee's good at speechifying his causes—I know you know because you're nearly as bad—but I was already a turn-coat in Philadelphia by that time. It was I who reached out initially."

This surprised Everard not at all.

"But… why?" Not why D'Arcy had reached out, spy to spy—he suspected that carried other implications he wasn't yet being told, besides that D'Arcy was sometimes irreconcilably reckless. "Why America?"

"Don't think that I harbour the same conviction Vee carries," D'Arcy warned, "I don't. There's only too much French in me."

Everard snorted.

"… too much romance and risk-seeking, too. I hated my father with a blistering passion." He shrugged. "What else would a boy need?"

"A survival instinct?" Everard put forth. "A distinct desire not to be drawn and quartered? Even sons of earls aren't spared in cases of treason—and the scandal… Do not you have a sister recently come out?"

"Last season, yes. Or perhaps two seasons. Three?" He paused. "The idea was not to get caught. And scandal"—he dimpled down—"Princey's accomplished that on her own. Went to an American ladies' school, you know, that's plenty. And even if she hadn't, I daresay my tying up and gagging a port-admiral already ranks pretty bad for society." He eyed Everard with mild suspicion. "You haven't ever asked after Little Prince before."

"I've a new understanding of what it's like to find oneself dependent, that's all."

D'Arcy pinched him. "Do you, now? Really? Christ, sometimes you're so offensive, it's almost endearing. No wonder Vee goes goggle-eyes at you. You're a challenge wrapped up in a pretty scowl—"

"I beg your pardon."

"—with a large prick attached."

"Hmph." Everard pushed away with a sniff. "I hadn't meant to be offensive. But tell me more of Philadelphia. It sounds awfully secretive."

"And shall remain so, I'm afraid."

This struck Everard as particularly unfair. "But—"

"No. I won't say, and Vee can't. Not under any circumstance."

"So, within this… secret strata… I am to understand you are his superior?"

"More or less," D'Arcy said cheerfully. "Did you think he called me Lieutenant because of you?"

"Yes, of course I had," Everard said, bewildered. "In irony. In jest."

D'Arcy smirked. "The world does ever turn around you."

"And what else would I have thought, pray?" Everard stood, and began to pace. "You were my first lieutenant four years, Preston. And so far as I understood, the bridge between you and he *was* only myself. Not some bloody Order of Bizarre Fellows."

D'Arcy chuckled. "Good guess. 'Tisn't that one, though, sorry. I'm teasing you," he admitted. "It was a perfectly reasonable assumption. But, Everard, I tell you this only so that you understand where the blame lies here. Vee didn't have a choice in this. I couldn't hit myself, and no one else could be trusted."

"Of course he had a choice. Still, we're speaking of the same man? Vitaliy Gray? V. Varfolomey, egalitarian, abolitionist pirate? That man takes orders from *you?* And fulfilled them for the sake of…" Everard gestured wildly, "… some unknown duty?"

"Again with the disbelieving!" D'Arcy said, but he grinned. "Orders as you and I were used to, they aren't. That's to say, they didn't come from me directly but were more to ensure an essential status quo that Vee's sworn to uphold. But he owed me more than a favor for York, and my not being discovered as spy benefits everybody involved in any case—"

Everard seized on that. York—where they had supposedly met Vitya? "York… when?"

"You do make a good distraction, Ever, even if you have a tendency to step in and tread over my plans at regular intervals."

Everard could only utter a weak "Have I?"

"Yes, though I can't fault you for it, since it's inadvertent. D'you know Vee abandoned me at the market that day?"

Everard's heart sank. "No?"

"He was my American contact. I had to get up at two in the morning and meet him again after; would you believe the nerve?"

"Two in the… I cannot believe you. No."

York. Where Everard *hadn't* been plucked straight from the crowd. Where Vitaliy hadn't made an extraordinary risk, hadn't taken really any risks at all; D'Arcy had been a sure, known thing to him, since they had… had already shared some kind of intimacy, unknown.

It made Everard just… an option. Distraction. Maybe a slightly intriguing one—Vitaliy hadn't feigned wanting him; he knew that much—but an option nonetheless.

"Of course you were worth it, but…" D'Arcy rolled his eyes. "Impulsive bastard."

Everard marvelled that there could be still so much antagonism between two men who'd had Everard between them—in every possible sense—for almost every night of the past week.

Was Everard just a kind of reconciliatory glue? A stepstone transition?

Perhaps he was merely in the way.

"What else?" he croaked. "What else have I… trod upon? Were you going to throw Vitya's court martial, in Kingston? Was that planned, too?"

D'Arcy stood, took Everard's hands gently in his. "No, I swear. That wasn't planned. That's not to say I would've let him hang—I would've done what I could once that blindfold came free and I saw who it was, even if he wasn't… yours. But that day was all *you*, Everard, every bit of it. Your bravery and selflessness and love. Yours."

Everard felt his brow furrow in his skepticism. "It wasn't but selfishness. Vitya didn't want me to have done it. Probably because it royally *trod upon* your… mutual what-have-you agenda. Mayhap you had him brought to Kingston specially, to free him yourself. Perhaps you have that influence. I don't know, because you haven't said the extent!"

D'Arcy let out a long breath.

Everard said, "D'you see? How can I possibly believe any of it?"

"Believe it if you can," D'Arcy said wearily. "I can't ask more of you. I don't know how to make you believe, as I can't prove it. But it's all true, I swear it. Vee will too, once he's more solidly conscious. And—we ought go see if he is by now, don't you think?"

"Not yet, no." Everard shook his head. "We've known each other seven *bloody* years, Preston. To think that even before York, you were turned. I cannot…"

He tried to turn away from D'Arcy's hazel sincerity, couldn't.

Every memory was suddenly in question. He wanted to go back, spin through, revisit; revise appropriately, if he could. He wasn't sure even his memory *worked* that way. It was extraordinarily faithful, but of a certain kind: a faithfulness to the one and only perspective he'd had to look through at the time. A tainted, hopelessly naïve perspective.

"I can see you thinking," D'Arcy said. "Your career was your own, Everard. Nothing I informed on directly affected you."

"That cannot be anything but a bald lie. It'd have made you a useless spy."

D'Arcy crossed his arms, hunched his shoulders. "Thank you," he muttered sarcastically. "Yes, well, it's true."

"Even the *Wanderer*?"

"Especially the *Wanderer*," D'Arcy emphasised. A tiny, hopeful twitch crept into the corners of his wavering smile. "Am I absolved?"

"Sant Jesús," Everard cursed vehemently. "I don't…"

Three years. Three years during which the other two had known not only each other but had shared knowledge, and values, and *bodies*—and, on top of all that, had shared some kind of secret so large that neither of them had been able to trust Everard's own intelligence and discretion and mutual damned values enough to divulge it.

Three years, leaving Everard out in the cold.

D'Arcy reached forward. "Ever."

Everard flinched back. "No. No."

*Oh,* he found. But he was angry after all. So very angry.

D'Arcy's smile dropped off his face. Hazel eyes flashed wide. He'd seen it too.

"Ever…" he pressed.

"Preston, I cannot."

"You can't… what?" D'Arcy laughed bitterly.

Everard couldn't look at him.

"So, you'll run," D'Arcy said, flatly revelatory. "Oh, my God. You'll leave. Run straight to Alarie. Won't you."

Everard couldn't see what else was left to him. They'd already expected it of him.

"I… Given the circumstances, what choice have I? I can't trust Vee, not after he's done what he did."

*His fists, his boots, his arms, restraining, bruising.*

"And yet you can trust *Alarie?* I told you it wasn't Vee's fault!"

"I don't…" Everard sighed. "Look, it doesn't matter; you plainly can't trust me. I am the last to know anything, it seems."

"Everard, that is wholly unfair! I'm being as forthright as I can—more than I should!"

"And Vitya trusts neither of us. Where does that leave us?"

D'Arcy pointed to the floor. "It leaves us here, on this ship," he said, and even stamped once; sawdust flew from beneath his foot. "Together, regardless." Then, to Everard's horror, D'Arcy's voice began to warp and thicken. "Will my letters even be read this time? Shall I even bother sending a one? Not every —" D'Arcy's voice broke entirely then. "Not everything can be said in a letter."

"Oh, Preston."

"I forgive too easily," D'Arcy went on, waveringly, "and you don't forgive at all. You want to know why I've kept this from you so long? It isn't that you couldn't keep the secret, or would or wouldn't defect from the Crown, Everard, it's this: the fear that you would *walk away* if I told you even a fraction of the truth. It's this that you've held anvil over my head. This, and the three years of utter and undeserved silence you put me through."

"So, you went and made my decision for me."

*I did not think you would ever want to be pirate,* it turned out, was just the same as *I didn't think you'd ever defect from the Crown. I didn't know you loved me.*

"Well, and here you are, making it." D'Arcy swiped at his damp face.

"I've apologised for those years already," Everard managed. "And we never… we never had an understanding, you and I."

"Horseshit," D'Arcy spat. "We've had as much of an understanding as men like us *can*. From practically the moment we met. Whatever else would 'Where you go, I go' *mean*? I said I loved you, put it straight at your feet—you merely chose not to acknowledge it!"

"You've never asked me for anything!"

"I hadn't need to. But it doesn't matter. Even if I had…" He nodded to Everard's right hand, the one with Vee's wide golden ring on the fourth finger. "…you'll abandon it regardless." He raised his chin. "Will you wake him to say goodbye? He deserves at least that."

Everard considered ripping the ring from his finger. Imagined handing it to D'Arcy, imagined his delivering it to Vitya.

No. He wouldn't be so cruel as that. Even more selfishly, he couldn't bear to part with the thing. Couldn't even think what goodbye would look like. No.

"He does," Everard agreed. "But I shouldn't wake him."

D'Arcy cursed viciously. "And I should've confessed all this when we floated in the middle of the goddamned Atlantic."

Everard nodded. "Maybe. That probably would have been best. Yes. I'm sorry." He began to back away, pull at the latch of the door.

"Jesus *Christ.*" D'Arcy stormed forward, collided with Everard, almost pushing him bodily into the door, stopping just before. "You goddamned bloody hypocrite." He grasped Everard by the nape of his neck, and shook him, forth-back, 'til Everard was stunned and limp like a hare, and they passed violent, sharp breaths between them.

Vitya would *never*—

But Vitya *had*—

*With D'Arcy's consent,* Everard thought dizzily. *His insistence. A claim of debt. An order, for the greater good.*

*Still.*

D'Arcy leaned in, halted. Leaned in again, halted. The faintest streak of ochre remained under one furious, wet-lashed eye.

"Preston," Everard whispered.

D'Arcy kissed him, not gently: like fighting. Kissed him like fucking, scrapes and biting, slippery impatient thrusts. Claiming.

Then he pulled Everard away and back, out of his grasp. Everard had to catch himself against the door.

"Go, then," D'Arcy breathed.

# Twenty-Nine

It turned out that when embarking on an unfamiliar vessel, en route to an unfamiliar destination, Why with Zero Persons was much, much lonelier than Why with Many Persons.

He thought of the last, painfully short glimpse of Vitya he'd had—the blond hair strewn over his beautiful, already-asleep face—and longed.

Xavier Mina was glad enough to grant him passage to Galveztown on his *Caledonia*. The days of the voyage passed slowly. Everard resided within a cloud of a strange, muted kind of disbelief at what he'd done, at the impetus for it. Nor did he understand why Alarie had wanted him in the first place, as he could not possibly stand as adequate replacement for V. Varfolomey, Romilly René, and their seven flotilla ships. Everard was just one man, one defector Navy captain out of a thousand, whose only distinctions were the Spanish fluency he'd been born to and a war injury that would've sent most into retirement years before. Frankly, he didn't see the appeal.

He had considered, many times, Vitaliy's comment about *ironclad assurance*, and wondered if Alarie was in fact snakelike enough to try to use their—previous, prior, anterior—connection to squeeze Vitaliy into compliance, secondhand; but he thought the fact that Alarie had reached out precisely when he and Vitaliy hadn't been speaking to each other made this unlikely.

And surely, Alarie knew—as Everard now did, too—that beneath Vitya's careful consideration lay a steel will. When his mind had set, he was unbending, unyielding, ruthless. No doubt the book he'd thrown at Alarie in the greatcabin had accompanied an insistence that no matter what happened to Everard in Alarie's care, Alarie would never have Varfolomey.

After all, hadn't Vitaliy proven himself, publicly and privately, quite unmanipulated in that way?

When it came down to it, Everard knew Alarie had merely settled for what he could. Lesser, but the best he could reach for, grasping at straws. Given his own life of late, Everard could sympathise.

But *had* jumping ship off the *Netley* to join a pirate meregildo felt like that? The best he could've reached for, under the circumstances? Desperation; helplessness?

No, it rather hadn't. Not at all. It'd been a dream, a marvel. Unbelievable circumstance, fate undeniable.

Not even dining daily with the serious, studious Xavier Mina could raise his spirits significantly; and this was including that the two of them in fact had a fair amount in common. Mina came from Pamplona, Navarra, a hop-skip from Catalonia and the mountain range shared with France. He was enigmatic, impassioned, frightfully young to have led an army at nineteen and spent four years in a French prison. He was black-haired like Everard, but short-statured, handsomer, with a square, boyish, small-mouthed face. And although they looked nothing alike, to Everard it was disturbingly like having a magic mirror placed before him: showing what could perhaps have been, had he not been pressed by the Royal Navy and moulded into a pseudo-Englishman. Had he been less of a coward.

It was painfully plausible, too. Two of Everard's four brothers had gone into the army themselves, another into the Armada. He knew nothing of their records or honestly even if they still lived, but suddenly, absurdly, he was tempted to ask after them, minuscule though the chances were that Mina had knowledge of any of them.

After a long roundtable discussion of the potential of México, democracy, the plain ugliness of Fernando VII and his turn to despotism—the particular sticking point for Everard being the monarch's dogged persecution of the free press— Everard pulled Mina aside and asked anyway. He'd no longer any reason left to hide his heritage. There, it was truly an advantage, to be a lynx among felinae.

"No," Mina said easily, "I have never known men by that name, alive or dead. Forgive me. And I think surely I would have remembered a family name so... half-English." He leaned back into his chair, crossing an arm over his lap, drink in his palm. "But I could inquire without too much trouble, if you'd like? There are liberales yet in Navarra." He smiled.

"No," Everard replied, "it was a passing chance. Thank you. I appreciate it."

"Not at all." He raised his tumbler. "La familia es todo."

"Cierto," Everard agreed. He looked down into his own wine, watched it swirl and make legs upon the glass.

His true family wasn't in Spain; they were all still aboard the *Sévère*. How long before he didn't know whether they, too, lived or died?

Good God, Everard realised with a start. That moment had, in fact, already come and gone. He didn't know. Four days the *Caledonia* had been en route to Galveztown, and they were set to arrive tomorrow; plenty of time for anything to have happened to the *Sévère*. Time for a hurricane to develop and strike, for another anti-revolutionary to overcome them, to shoot her through, for plague to wipe through… anything.

What had he done?

Everard stood. "Con su permiso," he muttered thickly. Receiving a raise of brow, a nod, and polite "Almirante" from Mina—who likely thought him suddenly grieving, and who wouldn't be wrong—he bowed, pushed his way through scores of hearty laughter and rapid Spanish syllables, foreign now to his ears, and fled.

# THIRTY

Galveztown *was* a sandbar: a beach surrounded by swampy, undeveloped wetland. But it was still land, and therefore Everard hated it on sight.

Evidence of frequent and recent wrecks floated all around them as they slowly approached: flotsam planking; rigging snagged in foamy sea-weed; the odd wave-tossed barrel. Through a borrowed glass Everard spotted palm trees on the distant mainland, some ripped to shreds on the beach, others steadfast and lonely; there were clumps of green-leaf mangroves with their white roots exposed on washed-away shores, and before these, a spotted, weaving carpet of marsh reeds and underwater grasses.

Within the bay itself, the water was infamously too shallow for anything larger than a canoe or light jolly—they'd heard Alarie himself, the fool, had wrecked a handful of ships in this same bay only weeks before—so the *Caledonia* and Mina's accompanying ships hovered in a vulnerable-feeling white-winged murder just outside the sandy peninsula. There were a handful of smaller ships already at anchor around the port:

these being what, Everard assumed, would soon make up his own fleet under Alarie.

Half of them had been lost, and the rest of them were a sorry bunch. He'd have gone so far as to call them ragged: small and two-masted at the largest, at least half of them needing careening; others were possessed of soggy, tearing sheets. The best-looking was one *Anemone*, the corsario slaver that Everard remembered had carried the Galveztonian marque—and slaves, humans, souls—to Louisiana and then Florida. All in the name of profit.

Everard lowered the glass, swallowing heavily. He remembered Louis-Michel Alarie, standing beside him at the rail of the *Sévère*, covered in expensive, masculine pink satin.

Profit for him.

*I have seen what motivates him.*

Money. Everard had thought Vitya meant *power, position, glory*; and he had surely meant those things, but primarily, he had meant Alarie was motivated by money.

Of course he had. What else drove the world but greed?

*All ideal, no practice.* Everard's convictions seemed more impossibles than ideals at the moment.

But why now? What had changed?

Throughout his career, he had upheld the brutality of authoritarian kings, obliged greedy admirals, endured tyrant captains, swept away officer injustices; all while telling himself he was different because of convictions and opinions he'd kept —for the majority part—private. Different because of a few anonymous essays, because of a handful of scratched cartoons mocking an untouchable man. Different because fucking other men had been the only thing he'd been unwilling to desert in his quest to become an unimpeachable, honorable, *English* officer of the Navy.

But he wasn't different. Not really. None of those things

had been active; none of them had changed him in any significant way.

Not even that last point; the thing he'd refused to let go, refused to think of as a flaw to be corrected. And perhaps he'd fucked—and *loved*—two men, and that was radical in itself. But he had never sincerely admitted or confessed that love, to the point that neither man even had been aware of his depth of feeling. Neither had trusted him with their true selves. Neither had had faith that Everard would, in fact, give up everything for that love, fight tooth and nail to keep what he'd found in them.

Because he hadn't fought. Hadn't given up anything. Had blamed them for inaction when it was inaction driven by his inadequacy.

No practice.

No; what *was* practice was what he was actively doing now, in this moment, with this decision he'd made to follow and support and uphold a man he didn't trust and didn't respect, who wanted revolution not for the sake of the people fighting and dying for it, but for the glimmering mirror that would shine the daylight of fame back upon him as gold and renown and legacy.

And in fact, it was with Alarie's first act as governor—that Everard witnessed, anyway—that the man immediately proved himself ill suited to leadership or respect.

He refused to let Mina's ships into Galveztown port.

The bay was too shallow. There was no other option for the *Caledonia* but to wait. Mina had his heart set on Galveztown, and Everard had nowhere else to go.

Fearing plague or worse, Everard sent a gig with a letter informing Alarie of his arrival, his answer to him in the affirmative. Yes, he would be his admiral.

No response, which stung Everard's pride, but less than he thought it might.

Mina sent one too, reminding Alarie of his commitments to México and his pledge to assist him. No response. Mina was infuriated.

Eight days later, Alarie relented, with no excuse more legitimate than he had too many mouths to feed already and that he was himself convalescent.

He received Everard in his tent as though nothing had happened. He was indeed convalescent, but seated upright at a desk regardless, a pillow behind him on the chair.

"Happy to see you, de Anglada. I knew you would change your mind." Alarie smiled handsomely. "Indeed, I had such confidence in you that I have written already to the American Congress: Galveztown is not only now possessed of a marshal, customs, port authority, and judges, but an admiral and admiralty court."

"Indeed?" Everard said. "All that?" he couldn't help adding. A week earlier, he had swung the glass over the smattering of shanty-like buildings on its east wing that made up Galveztown itself, and wondered.

"Yes. Now they cannot but recognise her sovereignty," Alarie relished. "In fact, I hope to hear from Washington by the end of the year."

Everard thought that unlikely, and not only because it was nearly December. If all of Haïti's might and beauty, their constitution and government and ideals, could not convince America to recognise her, what hope had tiny Galveztown, taken over by a disgraced white Frenchman with misplaced priorities?

"Is that not the Mexican flag flown outside?" Everard said pointedly. "The blue-and-white checkerboard?"

*Power, position, glory, money.* He saw it now. The man wanted all of it. He wanted to be a king.

"Of course," Alarie said, without a blink. "Sovereignty for México."

"Very good," Everard said; and then he saw his opening.

*Practice.* Maybe this was a step down the ladder from the careful, deliberate impression Vitaliy made on the world around him—several steps, even—but maybe he could also still salvage something from this.

"Surely American recognition will mean we must comply with the Act?" Everard asked.

Would it be so easy? As easy as insisting to Alarie that as his admiral, Everard would oversee no human transport, would issue no marques to slavers, would use his full authority to persecute those not in compliance with the anti-slave trade laws?

If V. Varfolomey himself could not consistently ensure such a thing from an ally, how could Everard ensure it of his direct superior? He had no true leverage but to walk away.

But Alarie was desperate, and thought of Everard as a path to the most powerful pirate in the Gulf.

"Oh, of course we will," Alarie said, offhand, as though it were nothing to go in either direction. "And have not I been doing so?" he challenged.

Everard gave him a steady, uncowed look. There was no possible way Alarie wasn't aware that Vitaliy knew what he'd been up to in his incarcerated absence. Vitaliy hadn't said exactly what for he'd fallen out with Alarie, but Everard knew it must have been something along the lines of violation of man's basic rights.

"Well, henceforth, we shall," Alarie went on, unperturbed and unashamed. "Neither I nor Mina could not get Haitian assistance without that assurance in writing, in any case; Pétion was adamant on liberation. As is right!" he added hastily.

Everard said nothing. He had already heard it'd been a crew of restless, slighted Haitians that had sent Alarie into his current convalescence; they'd become frustrated at Alarie's unfulfilled promises of corsairs and riches, had converged upon him and shot him—twice—then fled back home, taking three ships in the process.

Had he been here then, as admiral, Everard would've turned a blind eye and let them go right on by. A promise was a promise.

"When a gentleman gives his word, in trust and confidence," he said carefully, "there is no reason for assurance in writing."

A ridiculous statement; one always got things in writing. But as Alarie sat silent for a moment, blank-faced, shocked, Everard knew his meaning to have been perfectly understood.

"Precisely!" Alarie said, at last. "We are in agreement, de Anglada. Given recognition, we will comply with the laws. In the meantime, customs in New Orleans is quite amenable—"

"No," Everard said firmly. "Henceforth."

Alarie frowned. "The privateers…"

"I understand," Everard said, "that you wish me to condemn as prizes those vessels the fleet will bring into port, Governor."

Alarie's nostrils flared.

Beneath Everard's words floated this: *If you want any prizes able to come in at all…*

He didn't think Vitaliy would use the *Sévère* to exert force in that manner, but Alarie didn't know that. Maybe even feared that.

"You understand correctly, Admiral de Anglada." Alarie's gaze narrowed, dark and shrewd. "Indeed. Henceforth, then." He raised an eyebrow. "You know, I had thought you a bit of a different beast than our lion Vee. Despite your being his… mm, partner. But now I think your mint is just the same."

Everard said nothing.

It was plainly untrue, and thus simple flattery, no more.

"This is a good thing," Alarie emphasised, doubling down. "A good thing for me, and an excellent thing for Galveztown herself."

Everard closed his eyes. "Surely, Governor."

# THIRTY-ONE

F our Months Later
    ?? March, 1817
    Galveztown, Tejas, Republic of México (formerly Nueva España)
    29° 18' N, 94° 48' W

The most merciful thing Alarie could have done, Everard thought, was put him in a ship's prison hold bound for Spain. Or Cuba. Florida. Yucatán. After four months of being shore-side, Everard would've done anything to be on the water once more before he died, even if it meant being confined in a prison hold. Even if it meant that upon landing on Spanish ground, upon a last glimpse of the frothy blue sea's horizon, the soldados would take him out onto the beach to be shot. No trial.

But they hadn't. Everard wasn't important enough to be held by the Crown, to be made an official prisoner, earmarked for execution. Important enough to be a target for Jean Lafitte, spy for Spain—certainly. Important enough to be used as a bargaining piece between the bastard governor Louis-Michel Alarie and said spy for Spain—absolutely. But not to be put under the swinging focus of Fernando VII or his viceroyalty. Not yet.

Instead, Alarie's men—*Everard's* men, he would've said, hitherto—had left him there, in Alarie's earthwork hut of a fort, with feet fettered and hands manacled in iron. Alone but for the servant who, without meeting Everard's eyes, delivered just enough food and water every day so that he wouldn't perish.

Neither Jean Lafitte nor his brother were known to be violent men—at least directly—but they wanted him alive for something. Everard tried to shy away from thinking what for, but couldn't, because he knew precisely what it was—and knew it wouldn't work.

He merely wondered how long it would take for Lafitte to realise it too and give him to the Spanish to recoup his lost investment.

Xavier Mina, he thought, had been a friend enough that he maybe wouldn't have let Everard be held arrested without cause or explanation.

But Mina was two weeks gone now, back on the *Caledonia* alongside Alarie, with all of his men and his ships en route to southern México—including most of the men with whom Everard had got along quite well. Despite his reputation to the contrary, and indeed the immediate situation, he wasn't entirely friendless.

He shifted his fettered ankles. Just currently… alone.

Alarie, plain and simple, had begun an irrational campaign against any and all authority he perceived as threats. He'd tried to arrest his army colonel, Henry Perry, on the same day: an unwise choice, as Perry, unlike Everard, had loyal men who could fight and had fought back.

Everard had a dozen disconnected privateer captains with

loyalty to nothing but coin, and an unequal friendship with a Spanish filibuster obliged to the plans of rich American men.

In theory, he had Varfolomey, too—but of course, eventually, Alarie had seen through that, seen through Everard's posturing when Vitya had not brought the *San Telmo* or any other ships in support. Not that Everard had or would have asked.

Galveztown hadn't achieved recognition from America, in spite of their "navy," despite that the privateers were under strict orders not to touch any ships flying the stars and stripes, and they'd unilaterally complied. This had more to do with the two U.S. Navy frigates posted watch outside the bay than any orders. But New Orleans had got a new man in customs who let their unmarked goods in freely. Marques were issued in an orderly and official manner from the very same printing press Vitaliy had acquired—not the Stanhope, of course. Everard wondered if she were still bolted to the parlour floor, or if she had been broken up and sold.

Lastly, despite his threats and demands, Everard had not really been able to stop the privateers from plucking slaves from Spanish prizes and taking them straight to New Orleans. They saw dollars and nothing else. Everard wasn't Varfolomey, with a fleet and cannon and seductive wages and fat vanilla profits behind him. The Americans turned the other cheek, and so did Alarie.

More likely, Everard's betrayal had been motivated by nothing so heated as passion, or even strong dislike, but only cold silver. Lafitte had asked how much, and then all Everard had been to Alarie was an amount quite a lot less than his weight in Spanish coin.

He couldn't even say that this—being bargained over, being handed over in exchange for monies—was compared to being sold, because in truth, this was vastly more humane. In estimating Everard's price, whatever it had been, neither governor

nor pirate had ever considered Everard less than, as property only. His essential humanity had been maintained in their eyes throughout, by the color of his skin, that simple and thoughtless presumption, by his birth and speech and health, all informed by generations of wealth behind him. No matter how much he'd tried to refute them, redistribute his own.

The bargain had been a gentleman's agreement. V. Varfolomey wouldn't fold to it. It would only make him angry.

Well, perhaps sad for the loss of Everard himself, possibly, but mostly angry. Disdainful, that someone would try and sell his matelot for ransom—his mate, who'd abandoned him—that he would deign to respond to such a thing.

Everard imagined Vitaliy receiving the letter of demand, reading it, and throwing it aside in disgust. He laughed to himself, repositioned his manacles over his lap, and let his head fall back to the plastered log wall.

In fact, he thought, they couldn't have done more to repel Varfolomey.

# THIRTY-TWO

Everard had had four months—and then this past fortnight of imprisonment—to work it through his memory. Like beating a rug until the rays of sun shone clear of dust over it: with everything fallen away, he saw it plainly.

D'Arcy had implied to him that his beating had been to make Alarie believe him initially unaligned with Vitaliy. To confirm Alarie's assumption that D'Arcy was a weak-willed, drunken Navy defector. That had been successful, because despite his superior Navy record, D'Arcy had not been targeted by Alarie for Galveztown's admiralty; Alarie had seen him as a follower only, unthreatening. Definitely not a spy for anyone, not even the British. A sodomite only, led by a prick, or pricks: Everard's, at first, and then Vee's.

But if Alarie had a wasp's intelligence, D'Arcy was a hawk, snapping him up to fill out hungry corners. What he had really done was to highlight to the world how inured Vitaliy—V. Varfolomey—man and pirate, as one—was to manipulation. He'd said it was a favor for him, Vee obliging him, but it had been the opposite: D'Arcy had been upholding Varfolomey's reputation.

This was important, he thought. It meant someone significant in America knew Vitaliy Gray was V. Varfolomey and exploited that same reputation to their shared goals.

Whatever they were.

What D'Arcy had done in truth was counterbalance the effect Everard himself had had upon Varfolomey's identity. When Everard had made himself Varfolomey's proclaimed, advertised vulnerability, D'Arcy had threaded doubt through: *But false, everybody see?*

In this way he had protected Everard, too: from the very same hardship he was facing this moment. It had worked against Alarie, and probably would've done for longer, against others.

But then Everard had failed to take his pride in firm hand and had dangled himself deliciously before Jean Lafitte.

He understood now. Far too late; but at least he'd got there before his death.

If D'Arcy had come to Everard and said, *Hit me, bruise me— nothing permanent, I'll feign the rest—and in doing so you'll protect everything we've worked for and the one you love, too,* well… he might not have been able to go through with it, in the end, because it was D'Arcy, but he'd understand why one could do so, given a bit more distance of feeling towards the one being bruised.

And now they wanted Vitaliy—Varfolomey—to undo it all? To unravel everything for the sake of one man? He, Everard? Useless and worthless?

It was laughable.

The irony was that Lafitte *hadn't* had musket sights on Everard until he'd met him, hadn't known who he was to Vitaliy until Alarie had whispered in his ear what it meant for him to be there, at Alarie's disposal, as Alarie's port admiral. Hadn't heard a thing about the matelotage or the *San Telmo*. Lafitte had been lost in the wilds of Arkansas, surveying land with a French-Creole mapmaker friend. Alarie had known where he'd been the whole time, and yet had let Lafitte take the blame for the *San Telmo*, which of course had been his own doing. He merely hadn't counted on Everard not bringing her to make his navy flagship; had not counted on Vitaliy taking her on for his own.

It must've been the final blow against him.

The ultimate irony was, of course, that after accepting Everard's forced surrender as a token of good faith, Lafitte had since taken advantage of Alarie's absence and claimed Galveztown in the name of La Corona. He'd declared himself governor, and his men had declared for México.

Everard couldn't see how any of it—beyond Mina and his intentions—was tied to true revolution.

He saw only greed.

# THIRTY-THREE

On Everard's twentieth day of imprisonment, the rations slowed and became irregular. The Lafittes weren't violent men, and they didn't know Everard was accustomed already to fasting; but they knew how to slowly kill a man, knew exactly how long it would take for a missive to reach Varfolomey, how long it would take for a meregildo to make her way back this side of the Gulf.

And once they decided to withdraw water rations, no amount of Everard's being used to hunger would save him.

# Thirty-Four

It didn't matter. Everard was a naval man—would die a naval man despite the cursed earthwork currently surrounding him and the land beneath him—and many of those had died of thirst.

# Thirty-Five

The walls trembled. Everard raised his head briefly to see tumbling bits of dirt fall like pill-bugs from cracks shearing into plaster. Earthquake? A battle? He couldn't tell.

Then dizziness overcame him, and his head fell back. Vibrations in the earth continued beneath him, rattled his dried-out brain, staccato and rolling like cannon fire.

If this was what dying felt like, being taken up by the rumbling hands of the earth, then Everard didn't want it. Too much like York.

But maybe, if the wall collapsed entirely and fell inward, it'd be fast.

He closed his eyes.

Softer than bricks, at the very least.

# Thirty-Six

"Oh, Jesus."

A hand beneath his neck, threading into the dirt and hair at his nape.

*Of course* an angel would have D'Arcy's face—

"Everard," the angel breathed. "Everard."

Their hand blazed, hot as fire. A demon, then. Slightly more accurate.

Everard giggled. It came out as seizes of his chest, with no sound. His heart beat like a trapped bird.

There came an oath: buzzy, chopped-up syllables. Russian? A light source to Everard's left was abruptly blocked; he felt the impression of great weight upon the earth.

"He is beyond speech?" This voice was softer. "Delirious?"

"Little wonder. Everard, love, look at me."

Would an angel demand this of him? Surely there was no need.

He tried anyway, but to open his eyelids would be like parting a scar. He shook his head, had no idea if he was successful beyond a dizzy spin of black.

"No, no, it's all right, shh."

Wetness touched his parchment for lips, slipped over the rough crags of his tongue, into his seizing throat. It burned like a stab; he choked.

"Enough," the second voice said. "It will have to come in drips."

Then he was undoubtedly being lifted; he'd left his stomach behind on the ground and was too tired to pick it up.

Another curse, throaty this time, much closer. "I did not think they'd hurt him. He is skin and bones."

"He needs the sea, like a selkie." A hand trailed over the crust of his hair, down.

Everard felt a last rumble go through him, infinitely preferable to the earth's trembling: Vitaliy's quiet speech, doubled; vibration and sound against his ear.

"If he dies, Lieutenant, I am turning you in to the Navy."

"If he dies," D'Arcy said, "I'll go myself."

# THIRTY-SEVEN

The first words from Everard's mouth were inadequate. Far from worthy of the endless hours of dream and hallucination he'd put towards this moment: the one where he would awake to sparkling Gulf reflections upon pale blue panelling, feeling the push of waves beneath him. Home.

"Not again," he groaned.

But it didn't matter, because it wasn't real. It was illusion, like all the others.

"English!" D'Arcy gasped to his right, startling him. Then Everard felt his weight send them gently swaying in the cot. His mind was very good at recreating this feeling, which must have been what it was like to be in-womb, warm and contained, anchored in the back-and-forth rhythm made by his own gravity…

D'Arcy was still speaking: "—else? At least Vee gets a word out of ten from the Catalan. Go on, love, do."

Everard furrowed his brow. Go on? What more was he supposed to say? "I do apologise."

The hand at his cheek jerked away, came back.

"Christ, you're actually awake." D'Arcy laughed giddily. "Of course you are—only because I'm nearly about to go—"

"No," Everard corrected. "Not awake. 'S'not real."

"Oh, no, it's very real." Bristly, damp kisses fell over Everard's forehead, his nose, his cheek, his lips. "Missed you."

Everard wrinkled his nose. "Beard?" D'Arcy was one to get away with a bit of stubble, now and again, but never something so undignified as a beard.

"That's real too." His voice was thick.

Everard shuddered with sudden chill. More proof; the greatcabin was never cold in reality, not in the Gulf.

"—hates it too. But don't you move; I have to fetch Vee."

"Mm." Move? Everard was baffled. Even if he hadn't been fettered and manacled, he couldn't have moved from the dirt if twenty soldados had drawn upon him and demanded he do so. Too weak. They'd have to shoot him right where he…

… *Fetch Vee?* From where? Port-au-Prince? D'Arcy himself was a commonplace sight in his hallucinations—albeit *clean-shaven*—but Vitaliy's presence was too unbelievable for his brain to try and conjure.

But, gad, the sound of D'Arcy's heels on the deck seemed lifelike this time, so maybe it could.

"Don't," he tried to whisper, far too late; D'Arcy was long gone. It was useless, anyway, as the imagined Preston never stayed.

Although this time, D'Arcy had said he'd go… go where?

He slit open his eyes—milagro, he seemed to at last possess ones that worked as he bid them—and gazed up. The reflected sunlight was very bright around him, threads of wavering shimmer setting the weave of mosquito-net canopy sparkling. He watched it for a moment, waiting for the dream to fade and shift.

Nothing faded. Everard scowled.

The least it could do was make the time pass unfelt.

Nothing. Time crawled. A salted breeze pushed forward and sucked back the netting: once, twice, thrice.

Footsteps approached, heavy steps made with ordinary, serviceable boots, boots that wore through socks like wet paper cloth—

He shut his eyes quick.

"No" was murmured from the companionway, a single word jumping out from a muddled jumble of others. *Vitya.*

Everard's stomach lurched, and so too did the dream. His heart thumped hard. There he *had* been before, Vitya standing over his shot-through corpse, his beach-bleached skeleton, staring down impassionate—*Vitya.*

He held his breath. He needed to awaken now, even if it was to the earthwork fort.

"Matelot?"

Everard writhed, felt rather than heard his manacles clink softly. "Don't. For God's sake. Please go—I don't want to see the rest!"

D'Arcy murmured something wavering and short.

"No," Vitaliy said. "He is, I think. This…" His voice slid away into blur. "…nightmare-caught."

A hand pushed beneath his shoulder, lifted slightly, pushed him over, and then his world was sideways, righted, spinning; Everard's arm came from somewhere—unmanacled?—and caught himself from falling onto his stomach. Vitya's hand was there, too, holding him upright, rubbing between his shoulder blades, the too-thin flesh covering them.

"Holy God," Everard gasped, and coughed, and his eyes were open, and everything was solid again.

"Christ," D'Arcy said. "It worked."

Everard remembered—he *remembered,* and it was as real as this: every time Vitya slept on his back, he would shift and moan until Everard shook him awake. His terrified, surfacing gasps after sounded like the ones Everard was making now.

Vitaliy spoke, quiet and rapid.

"Matelot. You feel the linen beneath your fingers? You're here, in the greatcabin of the *Sévère*, and Preston and I are beside you. We are at nineteen degrees, fifty-six minutes north, eighty-six degrees, twenty-eight minutes west. It is April the thirteenth, 1817, and you are safe."

"April," Everard mouthed without sound.

That made sense. It wasn't outrageous. Shocking, but not outrageous; actual and precedented, nothing made-up but somehow rational, like Novemby-may the forty-second, or some such fairy nonsense. The coordinates too: somewhere southeast of the Yucatán; this checked out.

However…

"Imposter," he whispered. "Since when… d'you call him *Preston?*"

Vitaliy chuckled. He leaned and put his forehead on Everard's temple, weightless; his breath was warm and relieved on Everard's ear. "When he needs it."

"Which is often," Everard agreed, a little slurred.

D'Arcy tugged at his left hand, wrapped it in his own. "With you gone? Yes."

Vitaliy pulled away, not far; Everard fell backward, made a noise of discomfort. "Oh, God. I want…" Vitaliy leaned in to listen. "…I want very badly to not be lying down, please."

This was remedied, four hands pushing-pulling at him, Everard panting with effort and dizziness at the end of it regardless. He laid his skull back against the cot's headboard and squinted at his two men. Vitaliy looked just the same, handsome and concerned and faintly exhausted; D'Arcy, barring the silken-lashed hazel eyes, was practically a different man.

"They gave me up? The Lafittes?"

Vitaliy suddenly looked wary, fidgety, as though he strained against physical retreat from his side. He nodded once.

"After all that effort to starve me out?"

"Eventually. With some convincing," D'Arcy added, when it was clear Vitaliy wasn't elaborating. He snuffled at intervals, but his voice was hard. "Two hundred fifty guns of it."

"Two hun— *What?*" Everard, stunned, did the maths. That was the *Sévère*, the *San Telmo*, the *Enemistad*, three more of the eighteen-gunner brigantines, at the least, unless Vitya had prized yet another man-o'-war he wasn't aware of.

But that wasn't the point. The point was that not in a thousand years would he have thought Vitya would bring *one* ship for him.

"You did… You brought…"

But the *fleet?* The fleet *entire?* For one man? For him? He stared.

Vitaliy broke his gaze and bowed his head in profile. He returned the stare in little flicks, anticipatory, guilty, eager, like it scared him to see Everard watching him. One plush lip beneath the other, he seemed to be holding his breath.

D'Arcy was oddly silent, stroking at the palm of Everard's hand, no help at all in translation. Everard wondered deliriously if his new quiet was the beard's influence, and found that kissing aside, he hated it on those grounds alone.

"But *why?*" he exclaimed. He glared at D'Arcy. "Had you threatened to shoot him?"

D'Arcy laughed faintly. "*Ever.*" He shook his head. Put his face in his palm. "You're such an i-idiot."

Good God, Everard thought, bewildered. D'Arcy was crying again.

Vitaliy distracted him by lowering himself to the cot, a big cat settling down to curl round and sleep. He picked his way over, mindful of feet and knees and bone-thin thighs, and straddled Everard's lap, suspending his whole bulk carefully so that none of his weight touched down on aching bones.

Thankfully, those bones had not shrunk; the two of them still fit.

Vitya put his forehead on Everard's, put them nose to nose, and whispered. "You are mine, matelot."

Everard inhaled. "Yes." Agreement was pulled from him like compulsion.

Vitaliy's eyes were wide, and earnest, and so, so dark.

"Without you, I am dust. Nothing. A skeleton at the bottom of the sea." He stroked thumbs across Everard's cheekbones, where the skin still felt thin and raw, pressed lightly in the hollows beneath. "Did you know?"

"Reasonable," Everard said, nonchalant as he could manage; it was a hard thing, with one's mouth so close to Vitya's, breathing him in. He still could not believe he was awake and this was real. "I did rather save your life." Why the devil was talking so difficult? Was he still so weak? "You r-returned the favor."

"Only just." Vitya's hands threaded back, into Everard's hair, around his ears, causing gooseflesh to tremble up every-where in their wake. "Only just. But that's not what I mean."

Everard's heart skipped. "Oh?"

Vitaliy lowered his mouth and traced lips, velvet-soft, over Everard's. "Without you, it is nothing. Varfolomey. The *Sévère*. The fleet. I would risk it all again, the whole fucking thing. I would risk it to see you fully hale now." He pulled back. "It makes me unabashedly a villain—"

"Pirate," Everard corrected fondly; D'Arcy snuffed a laugh into an elbow.

"—but I would do anything for you," Vitaliy said. "Any-thing. I don't care what you have or haven't done. You could do whatever, go anywhere, love whomever you like. Regardless, you are *mine*," he said fiercely. "You do not need to be someone or do something in order to be worthy of my, or Varfolomey's, or anyone's love. Do you see?"

"Oh," Everard breathed. *Speechifying.* "Vitya. I shouldn't have left…"

"No, no. You tried to tell me, with the lieutenant." Tears rose in Vitaliy's eyes, and Everard panicked a bit, as two of them crying would soon mean three. "And I know now what you meant, that he is yours. I'm sorry. I didn't then. Truly. These hands"—his fingers twitched over Everard's scalp—"are violent ones. They must be. But not at that cost. Your cost. His."

"Vitya, I understand why you had to—"

"You are mine," Vitya said again. "So, to answer you with the truth: Preston didn't threaten me. He did not have to. We came as soon as we could. We *flew.*"

"And then nearly flattened Galveztown," D'Arcy said cheerfully.

Vitya shook his head. But he was smiling his tiny smile.

"We shot into the water—no casualties."

"There is generally a line," Everard agreed. "Murder is a good one."

"Generally," D'Arcy muttered.

"No casualties," Vitya said. "Except… almost…"

D'Arcy's hand on Everard's squeezed.

Except almost *him.*

Vitya pressed close again, breathed out shakily. "I understand now what I did to you then. The worst thing. And—"

"Vitya," Everard said. "It's done. It's past. Thank you for rescuing me. I love you. Kiss me, please."

Lips brushed his again, this time with the faint promise of a sweet, warm tongue. It was not nearly enough.

D'Arcy seemed to agree. "Vee," he groaned, in a shattering plead; Vitya drew back, leaned onto one hand, and, eyes closed, accepted D'Arcy's hand in his hair, his hard, frantic kiss.

Everard stared up. "Hell." He swallowed. Really, he needed his blood elsewhere than… "Did this happen… often?"

"You left us," D'Arcy said, at last, breathless.

"I— You— I did. But I… I regretted it from the second I stepped off the *Sévère*. And every day thereafter. Every minute. Every—"

"No," Vitya interrupted. "Not often."

He leaned and kissed Everard once more: a gentle transference of passion, no less powerful for its delivery.

"But yes," he murmured. "Don't leave us behind again, please."

# THIRTY-EIGHT

J une, 1817

Everard had tried everything.

Significant glances, meaningful brows. Early-morning advances, post-dinner suggestions. Even once—skirting danger, given he couldn't guarantee Vitya would be the first to walk into the printing parlour—his printing apron and nothing else.

But no.

Surely, Vitya's eyes went wide, huge in his face, darkened not just with kohl; his hands shook as he approached, every time. He'd sink to his knees and use those lips and sweetly, carefully take the edge off, or push pricks together and slowly drive them to it, any other number of blissful intimacies—so long as Everard was seated or lying or in no way moving or otherwise exerting himself. And it was all wonderful.

But Vitya would not fuck him.

Everard recognised that some men's preferences didn't

align with putting their pricks into arses—D'Arcy, a notable example, liked only the reverse—but Vitaliy was absolutely not one of those. He shared preferences with Everard, which was that sometimes he wanted to fuck and sometimes he wanted to be fucked, and they were usually fantastically well aligned—usually.

And he *wanted* to fuck him. There was no doubt.

But Vitya also had an iron will. Consequently, also an iron prick. Everard woke to it pressing against him, hot and pulsing and growing, and Vitya's hands pulling, pushing, clasping him close, his lips open and soft against Everard's skin. Every time, Everard gritted his teeth—for he would nonetheless keep his promise—and woke him, knowing it would mean the man would divert to hands and mouths and thighs or worse, retreat, would slide out of the cot with a soft final brush of a kiss and regretful murmur over his skin.

After weeks and weeks and weeks of convalescence and being fed and watered and being too weak to sit up without pillows and his joints aching from lack of movement, Everard merely wanted to feel *alive*.

And so thus he wanted, in particular, to be held down and fucked. He couldn't explain it, knew logically it meant nothing, but he wanted it, wanted Vitya heavy upon him, merciless, taking him apart, ruthless, gasping in his ear.

He tried being direct as he could bear, short of straight-out asking. When even finally asking, begging, pleading in the moment, failed just as well as anything else—a gentle, careful, trembling denial was his reward—he felt he had no choice but to enlist help.

Of course, then Romilly René, Vitaliy's close friend, crew advocate, enforcer, intelligence-extractor extraordinaire, was no help at all.

"Matelot," she said patiently, *scratch-scratch*ing into her ledger the take from the surrender of a Portuguese corsair, "I head an all-women company. So, I do not see why or from where you have gotten the expectation that I know the smallest thing about what makes a man's prick point up."

René, in addition to speaking loudly, liked to use her hands in emphatic gestures to underscore what she meant. Everard was grateful in this particular instance that she currently had both hands occupied, and that they were behind closed doors.

"Er—that's not quite the… issue. I only meant… perhaps that…"

He was sweating, suddenly acutely aware he was probably making a mistake but figuring any potential result would be worth it.

*Not quite how that works,* a voice told him. He ignored it.

"Since," he went on, "since you are yourself the fairer sex, I wondered if you might have encountered a point in your previous relations where—er, perhaps you found a man…" *Unwilling* didn't work. Nor *unobliging.* "… holding himself back?"

René looked up, expression blank, rouged lips parted. "Pardon? Relations? *Fairer sex?*" She wrinkled her nose. "What… do I do with this?" she murmured. "Vee and *myself,* you ask."

"Yes'm," he said quickly.

The eyebrows stayed high, but her expression had turned into slanted mockery. Vicious.

Yes, Everard had made a mistake.

She leaned forward. "Holding himself back… you mean in the sex."

Everard, scarlet, was nonetheless relieved that she'd understood. If she understood, maybe she knew—

René shook her head and muttered, "Cannot he piss himself in fear, like all the rest?" She signed the ledger page with a flourish, replaced the pen, and leaned back in her chair. "Why have you come with this, to me? You should not. One, you have no right to know what you ask about me. Or anyone."

"No. No, of course not. I see your point. You can of course turn me away—"

"Two, I don't think Vee would like you to say these things to me. Or anyone." She hummed. "Possibly your Fitzwilliam," she added thoughtfully. "Of course, he is not here…"

"Perhaps… perhaps not," Everard said hastily. "But I am fairly desperate—"

"Three, I do not want to shoulder this. Why must I?"

"Vitya said I ought do. Consult you, that is. More often. He trusts you. And I thought since you've had… er… relations… previously…"

She gave a brittle-sounding laugh. "Not like this, I don't think. For my profession—at which I excel—yes. Not this. But let me on one thing correct you. How to say again? Matelot," she said slowly, "I head an *all-women* crew."

Everard nodded, bewildered.

René rolled her eyes. "Mon dieu. All right. I have never with Vee. Ever. We have never. I am uninterested in the sex with men. Totalement. Especially with Vee." She shuddered delicately.

It hit him then. *All-women crew.*

"Oh," Everard said. "Ohhh."

René laughed, and Everard let the embarrassment douse him like spattering rain. No wonder Vitaliy had been so angry at his accusation. It had been mere jealousy; and, as it turned out, completely baseless, too.

Everard grimaced. "My apologies for the presumption. And the rest of it. You disliked me so that I thought—I assumed—"

She smirked. "You need not say le prétérit."

"Oh." Everard snapped his mouth shut. "Indeed," he made himself say. "I… All right. You make yourself quite understood." He bowed. "I'm sorry to have taken up your time, fleet master." He about-faced.

"Et alors! Wait a moment, matelot. We have come this far in spite of you."

Everard reluctantly turned back.

"I can assume you have never been with a woman?" she asked.

"Yes," Everard confirmed warily.

"Then you wouldn't know: we are generally not fragile."

"Indeed… no?"

"Pas non. Absolument pas." She shrugged. "But I have heard some men do forget it, time to time, and they get in their arses about it." She eyed him. "You think Vee finds you fragile, all the sudden? Because you had nearly died?"

Everard ducked his head. Was he not supposed to have been abandoning his cursed pride?

"Yes, I… I fear he must. But I am perfectly hale. Stephan says my heart beats as well as can be expected. I haven't felt the vertigo these two fortnights past. My weight is…" *Not ideal.* "… returning to its usual."

She looked him up and down. "You look well enough. Better than before. You are lucky to be alive."

"Thank you," Everard said. "I am."

René smiled. "Vee still wants you, matelot. I can say this without a doubt."

"I know," Everard said vehemently. "I *know* he does."

"Yes, otherwise, he would not keep you to your matelotage. You know him; he would set you free."

Everard agreed.

René said, "But you remember I said he and I are opposite? As is meant to be?"

"In authority. I understand that now."

"But also self," René emphasised. "Violence is my first option in most cases. I don't mind it, and often my crew and I do not anyway have the luxury of choice." She paused. "But Vee makes himself do violence only when he must."

"Though it sickens him."

René nodded. "For the sake of many, he will hurt another. But... hurt you, even accidentally, for the sake of himself? For his pleasure?"

"It wouldn't—"

"Even the chance."

"It's my pleasure, too," Everard muttered. "For God's sake, he's a bloody hedonist. My side of it ought count just as much. Surely he's realised."

René shrugged. She picked up the pen once more. "I think this is maybe what he forgot. Guilt is a powerful thing."

Everard thought this unlikely. Vitya had never been more focused on pleasing Everard, in every other way but the one. Probably, Vitya had just got it in his head to become a temporary martyr.

But this gave him an idea.

If his demands weren't enough, maybe he could tip the scales of rational hedonism. Put forth an empirical argument.

He just needed... help.

The *Enemistad* was due into Chetumal Bay two days hence. D'Arcy was due with her.

Everard felt those days as though they were weeks.

Vitya—absorbing into himself the guilt he felt about Everard's having to wake him in extremis nearly every morning—had most recently decided to abdicate the big cot and sleep in the trundle once more.

*Fine*, Everard thought. The man wanted his sleep uninterrupted, fine. Never you mind it was of entirely his own doing, and that he still woke rutting his mattress regardless of Everard's lack of presence.

If his plan to enlist D'Arcy's help proved unsuccessful, Everard thought he would go quite insane.

Two days.

D'Arcy hadn't gone strictly by choice. By choice, his letter said, he would rather be beside him in his convalescence—leaving quite a lot unsaid between the lines—but needs must.

Everard's rescue in Galveztown had been flown under Vitya's own American stars and stripes. The American brigs outside the bay had been perturbed by the *San Telmo* coming in flying their own—to say nothing of the *Sévère*—but left her alone at a message from Vitaliy.

Everard, not for the first time, began to see why three Crowns wanted Vitaliy—and not just the pirate Varfolomey—dead. A word from him, and two American brigs-of-war held their fire on a pirate fleet?

He also suspected D'Arcy and Vitya both had been understating their title of simple spy.

But that was a matter for another time.

With the Americans turning the other cheek, Vitaliy had, using the *San Telmo*'s massive guns and the *Enemistad*'s speed, brought Lafitte's privateers to their knees. He'd demanded Lafitte trade Everard for information on American interest in Florida—information that was vastly outdated and useless, he assured Everard later.

It had worked.

The *Anemone* had been the price of the pirates of the *Sévère* for taking the trouble of sailing into Lafitte's territory for the sake of one man. Alarie had left the *Anemone* behind, left her neglected, so she clearly wouldn't be missed, they reasoned.

Vitaliy had agreed. Everard wondered now to what else he would've agreed to get them to back him. He wondered if he would've agreed to nearly anything.

The other price had been that D'Arcy was obliged to then take the *San Telmo* and her prize north to sell in Boston—something about smoothing feathers for having defected from the Royal Navy before he'd had leave to from his espionage overlords.

Everard was selfishly glad he'd still been half-delirious when D'Arcy had initially gone, selfishly glad he'd been too sick to worry properly that D'Arcy would be caught and taken in as traitor. He'd worried enough as it was, until they'd had word.

But no; D'Arcy had been successful. It was only now that D'Arcy was returning on the *Enemistad*.

Now Everard paced the *Sévère*'s weather deck from sunup like a crazed man, amusing Vitya and every other crewman there was to witness. He only stopped pacing as the *Enemistad*'s gig finally, finally pulled up to the hull.

"Everard!" a familiar, dear voice called from beneath the rail.

"About time, Preston," Everard called back.

D'Arcy appeared, grinning, clean-shaven. He had a new contusion just above his left temple. His curls were ridiculously long and pirate-like. He looked wonderful and hale and—

He was helping a woman aboard.

Absurd. Women didn't climb the ladder—they were hauled in on chairs—but of course neither René nor her crewwomen abided chairs—

This woman was wearing shirtsleeves—with corset over— and *trousers*. She pushed away D'Arcy's hand like she resented it and shook out her half-queued, curly hair. She had instant sea legs, the steady and adaptive stance of a natural, and when she narrowed hazel eyes in apparent contemptuous survey of the *Sévère*, she resembled nobody so much as—

"Ever," D'Arcy said amusedly, suddenly before him, "you've looked less stunned when I pulled you out from bricks and harbour mud." He leaned in, peered close, and smiled. "But you look well enough for a kiss."

"Er—mmph."

D'Arcy pulled him in, arm around his waist, and did just that.

"There," D'Arcy said, with a sigh. "That done"—he steadied Everard on his own suddenly unreliable sea legs, and stepped back—"please be obliged to acquaint yourself with my youngest sister, Princey."

Said sister was glaring up at slightly frowning Vitya. He shot them an alarmed flash of a glance: the split-second panic of a man encountering someone else's responsibility and having no idea what to do about it.

Everard cleared his throat. "Miss Princey."

She spun to face him. "*Lady* Princey," the young woman declared archly. "At least to two-timing, polygamist bastards like yourself."

Everard stared. Somewhere behind him, Romilly René was cackling and muffling it—ineffectively—in her sleeve.

D'Arcy sighed again, rather less contented this time.

"Please, God," he muttered, "tell me there's been a recent rum take?"

René came forward and rescued them all, drawing Lady Princey away into her long-nailed grasp.

Another matter for another time. Everard was intent.

He put his fingers to his lips. "I think I can do you one better than rum."

D'Arcy's own lips drew up into a lopsided smirk. "Oho?"

Everard glanced over. Vitya was watching them steadily, eyes wide and knowing. But before Everard could make any sort of invitational gesture, Vitya flushed, ducked head and shoulders—a sort of nod, almost not one—and walked across the gangway to the *Enemistad.*

Away.

As clear as day.

Fine, then.

Predictably, D'Arcy did not require convincing.

"When, where, and how d'you want it, again?" he asked breathlessly. "Quite like that?"

Having been informed of the plan, D'Arcy had been enamored. So enamored he'd bent Everard over his desk in the greatcabin, removed his sapphire ring—*Because why not prove your point now? I know you can take it. It could be now. He could walk in any moment, he'll come in and see you spread for me, see how well you take it* —and had him then and there with his fingers, steady and fierce and fast.

Everard's head hadn't yet stopped spinning, but his heart still beat; he hadn't perished in extremis; D'Arcy was really very, very good.

Even if Vitaliy hadn't come in.

D'Arcy added into his ear, "Or something more drawn-out, perhaps?"

Everard groaned. "Get... off," he said clearly, "and give a man a moment."

D'Arcy straightened and complied, stepping back with a last swat and affectionate caress over Everard's skin; he didn't seem to want Everard to reciprocate. His boots clacked on the deck, and only then did Everard realise neither of them had earnestly disrobed.

It had been a long few months.

D'Arcy gave him more than a moment: he washed hands, tossed the basin water down the head, replaced it; then walked to where he'd thrown off his coat and rummaged in its pockets. Everard decided to make a night of the fading light. He cleaned up, shucked shoes and breeches and stockings, and sat in the armchair. The rest would bide. Vitaliy would return eventually.

He put his head back against dizziness. Even undressing was still a bit tiring. "Missed you, Preston," he murmured.

D'Arcy brought forth from his coat pockets two bright fuchsia pitahaya fruits and a small knife. He sat on the arm of the chair, cut the fruit and peeled it, then put a slice of it on the knife end, pushed it close to Everard's face.

"Eat."

Everard scowled at the white-fleshed, black-seeded stuff. "I do eat. Whatever happened to 'missed you, too'?"

"I said that a dozen times at least, three fingers deep." D'Arcy pushed the fruit closer. "But if you hadn't heard it, I suppose I can't blame you, poor, deprived thing, you."

Everard glared.

D'Arcy smiled tranquilly. "I don't mind doing what Vee won't. Eat, or I will call in Rob the cook with a full spread."

Everard ate. "Vitya's concern is silent," he accused, when he had chewed, swallowed, licked his lips. "And unforced."

D'Arcy gave him a look and put forth another slice. "Forced. Surely. Any louder with your assent, Ever, and Vee would've heard you on the *Enemistad.*"

Too true. Everard harrumphed and ate. It was a good pitahaya anyway, perfectly ripe and hardly bruised at all from being unceremoniously dashed onto old-growth pine. D'Arcy ate two of eight slices from both fruits himself; the rest he gave to Everard.

"He does ensure I eat," Everard said, feeling as though he must defend Vitya. "Only, he doesn't lob threats to do so. And he has done so since Galveztown. Along with… everything else involved in my convalescence."

D'Arcy nodded. "Of course." He squeezed Everard's thigh. "He loves you, and was terrified to lose you."

"I don't see why," Everard said lightly. "He wouldn't have let me do anything *but* survive, I think."

D'Arcy raised eyebrows. "Don't make light. He's quite aware how lucky we are you lived. Nothing doing with his will or anyone's. Except maybe yours."

"Speaking of his bloody will: Ought we discuss where, what, and when?"

Sable brows climbed higher. "Oh, you were speaking seriously?" Then they lowered in sheer Gallic disapproval. "Talk is one thing. A bloody exciting thing, I'll grant you; but I'm not going to ambush a man with the draw of a knife like that." He put up a restraining finger. "Much less a man with an arbitrary count of *yes*es he must meet to proceed in receiving fellatio. No, sir."

Everard was flabbergasted. He'd felt sure D'Arcy would agree, and then they'd just done what they'd done…

"But—what? *You* waited for his yes—surely, he won't mind! Given the number of times you and I—in his presence—" *His presence and then some*, he added mentally. *Under his touch.*

"I waited for his yes because I'm not suicidal," D'Arcy said, "nor a bastard. Come off it, Ever."

"Only that?"

"All right, and because I'm fairly fond of him, in spite of him. Because you love him. No, I shan't set him up against his consent."

"It wouldn't be—"

"Oh, no? Did he explicitly say he'd like to walk in upon us fucking, on the off chance?"

"Well—"

"Or set a date for it? Or—no, listen—did he, in reality, walk onto a different *bloody ship* at the first obvious opportunity for it? Hmmm?"

"He would never walk in *knowing*—" Everard paused. "Ah."

D'Arcy threw up his hands. "And thereupon we have reached it." He stood. "I'll fuck you even if he won't, Ever, but I won't manipulate him into doing so."

"It's not manipulation," Everard insisted, fairly horrified. "He isn't obliged to— The man likes *proof,* is all. If only he saw me—and you—"

D'Arcy looked him up and down. "And so you have it alrea—"

The door to the printing parlour crashed open.

D'Arcy spun, drawing his pistol from somewhere; Everard thought maybe the floor. By the time Everard could look round him, D'Arcy had cocked the thing, levelled it, and just as hastily pointed it to the floor again.

"Vee, what in *hell.* Warn a man."

By the looks of it Vitaliy hadn't even flinched being drawn upon: he was a man with singular intent. His pupils were huge, whites showing all around beneath careless rings of kohl, lips pressed so tight, they were ivory white. His blue stare flicked up and down, assessing the threat of his fellow spy, dismissing it.

"Loaded?" He was breathless like he'd run the length of the two vessels, and taken a turn rowing the *Birch,* too.

"Yes," D'Arcy said sheepishly. He shook his head and set the pistol down whence it came. "Always."

"I'm sorry," Vitaliy said, "for startling you."

"Not at all," D'Arcy said. "You'd do the same." He side-stepped out of the way so that Vitya's blue-hot gaze fell right upon Everard.

"Yes," Vitaliy said.

Another man might have mistaken Vitaliy's state for rage, or jealousy. Not him. No—Vitya was burning with sheer, untethered desire. After the past few weeks enduring its presence, Everard would've thought himself slightly more inured.

But he wasn't. Not at all. His mouth had gone dry, his lips numbed.

Vitya came closer, steps heavy and sure. Everard remained seated. Vitya had never used his bulk to intimidate him, and certainly didn't now. Furthermore, Everard wanted him. Like hell was he moving.

When Vitya was within a breath, he bent over the armchair, lifted Everard's chin. He placed trembling hands on either side of Everard's face, pulled him even closer.

"He's had you?" Confirmation, not accusation.

Distantly behind them, D'Arcy snorted. "Such faith."

"Er. Yes," Everard said.

Vitya kissed him, sudden, fierce, and encompassing. Everard moaned against it, overwhelmed. It was the first hard, thorough kiss Vitya had bestowed upon him since before Galveztown; the rest had been soft, cautious, sweet. The contrast was dizzying.

Vitya broke off, forehead on Everard's. "Good. I'm sorry. I waited as long as I could bear."

"You waited quite a bit longer than that!" Everard protested. If Vitya would only keep kissing him—Everard was tired, but surely he could be hauled to the cot and kissed some more—"You can't just pass me off, you know."

"I'm sorry," Vitya said again. "I trust the lieutenant. He is yours. And," he whispered, "I want too much. I want everything."

Everard shook his head. "You needn't have waited to come in, at least. Right, Preston?"

Best to have it out there, really.

"A-men," D'Arcy said. He was going round, locking the doors to the companionway, the printing parlour. All things considered, it was a smart move. Rather considerate. Forward-thinking. Everard dearly hoped it was forward-thinking. That there would soon be something worth locking a door for.

"I will keep it in mind," Vitaliy said, "for the future. Thank you. But for tonight…"

He looked up over his shoulder, found what he wanted.
Which… which…

*I want everything.*

Oh. *Oh.*

D'Arcy laughed when he caught Vitya's gaze. "Oh, hell. Really, Vee? Now? I should've gone, shouldn't I?"

Despite this declaration—whatever it meant—he sat at the desk and began to remove his boots.

"No," Vitaliy whispered. His eyes were back on Everard; it was like being in a corner, stalked and waiting to be eaten. "Your place is here, Lieutenant."

D'Arcy made a skeptical noise. "Happy to oblige, in any case."

"I beg pardon," Everard said, "But I am well and truly lost."

D'Arcy laughed again, slightly brittle. "He wants me as proxy, Everard." He removed his shirt, tossed it aside. "So he can wreck you. Without wrecking *you.* Yes, all right, Vee."

Vitya nodded his acknowledgment.

"What?" Everard exclaimed. "That's not… Is that quite fair? I don't need a bloody… proxy. And what… what d'you mean by *wreck?*"

Vitya didn't look away. He smiled.

What did he mean, indeed.

"In better world," Vitya said patiently, "I'd have you both. But I cannot. I have only this one. These circumstances. And you"—he pointed—"do not argue, matelot—you are still recovering. So. Do you want to watch me fuck him until he cannot stand?"

Everard stared. Behind him came a soft curse.

"I… *Jesus.* What a question, Vitya."

Of all the things they'd done… he tried to imagine it.

Vitaliy waited, slightly withdrawn, rapt but patient.

D'Arcy was muttering to himself and hauling drawers off

his hips like a resentful youth; the prick that sprang free was all man. The urgency of it seemed to find Vitya's question a foregone conclusion.

Everard swallowed.

"It is too much." Vitaliy withdrew more, expression shuttering.

Everard grasped frantically to keep him close. "No, no—it isn't. Yes. God. Do. Do fuck him. I'd love to watch that. I really would. If this is how you want it, please. Preston's said yes. He clearly wants it too. So yes. But—" He palmed his face. "Put— The sun's going?" he muttered. "Maybe put a lamp on?"

D'Arcy laugh-groaned. By now, he was lying on his back in the cot, and had a hand going steadily over his stand, up and down; his other hand was ringless once again, fingers deep inside himself.

Vitya smiled. "Good."

He kissed Everard once more, long and thorough, then pushed back and indeed lit a lamp—two lamps. He approached the cot, not even bothering to undress.

D'Arcy was naked to skin that glowed tawny gold in the lamplight. Vitaliy kept everything on except boots, undoing only his breeches fall. The contrast was thrilling, especially as he climbed up and knelt, shuffling forward, coat and stiff prick swaying alike with the movement of the cot.

"Ever?" D'Arcy croaked. He wanted confirmation.

"Yes, Preston. As long as you want it."

D'Arcy huffed. "Does it look like I don't? I want to know that *you* do."

"I want it," Everard said, roughly; and that was enough for both men.

Vitaliy straddled D'Arcy, and leaned in, hips forward, body covering body. D'Arcy gasped, and Vitaliy kissed him, as thoroughly and totally as he had just kissed Everard.

Had he seen the two of them truly kiss before? Everard

couldn't, couldn't remember, his brain was clogged screws and gears just then, but surely not; just as surely, the sight of it was seared into him forevermore.

In kissing Vitaliy, D'Arcy didn't fight or claim; he melted, groaned, and softly reciprocated. Did Everard look like that? Was D'Arcy playacting his place, mimicking Everard, or were his gasps truly, honestly sincere?

They looked sincere.

"Sweet," Vitya murmured, pulling back. "Like fruit. Both of you. You made him eat?"

D'Arcy scowled, only half-successfully. "Sod off and fuck me, Vee."

Vitaliy grunted, but he sounded pleased. Then he licked down D'Arcy's neck, the whole length of it, and bit sharply at a bare, shining collarbone; and proxy, Everard's arse, he'd never done such a thing in making love to Everard. This was all for D'Arcy, who liked a bit of sharp, who gasped and writhed now. "*Vee.*"

Vitya sat back and pulled fuzzed thighs wide; D'Arcy was pliant and moveable, undemanding, pending.

D'Arcy had said, *Just he and I together, it isn't.*

Everard whispered, "You're such a liar, Preston."

D'Arcy laughed, panting. "I tried," he said, sounding slightly strangled. Vitya had apparently decided D'Arcy's preparations insufficient; his fingers worked steadily inside, curving. "Thought it would hel— Oohh. Fu-uck, Vee."

Vitaliy shook his head, amused. "What did you tell him, Lieutenant?"

"That you aren't a very good…unh… lover."

"No, that isn't— *Preston.*"

Vitaliy laughed softly, unoffended.

"Well," Everard corrected, "he perhaps implied you and he were… incompatible."

Vitaliy raised an eyebrow that said, *Truly?*

"And said that you and he… hadn't. Since before York."

"Oh, yes," Vitya said. "That's true." He twisted his fingers, and D'Arcy bucked. "But before then…" He pulled his idle hand through his hair, smiled the tiny, knowing smile of a benevolent god. "Much, before then."

"Christ." D'Arcy clutched at sheets. "I think he's gathered. Vee, would you just—" He groaned, threw his head back, sheen on his top lip and all over, the day's stubble sparking in the flickering light.

"Yes. I will." Vitya glanced up once more. "How do you want him?"

Everard startled. "Hmm?"

"Ever," D'Arcy breathed. He raised a shiny hand and gestured in a way that'd previously meant, *Which way should he like to take him?*

"Oh." *Good God.* The options fanned before Everard in a spread—most of them memories of D'Arcy himself—impossible to choose from.

Almost. Luckily, the way he preferred to receive and the way D'Arcy did were the same.

"On your stomach. Arse—" He cleared his throat, "Arse up. Off the end of 'er. He'll want a steady base."

"Fuck," D'Arcy muttered; but he flipped, shimmied, stacked pillows, and arched, and— "C'mon, Vee."

Vitaliy climbed off the cot. He pushed knees wide, leaned forward, hands spreading, and sank in straightaway, no hesitation.

Then D'Arcy was his usual impatient self: he pushed back, writhed up, demanding, until Vitya put both hands on shoulders and pinned him, arms taut, and rasped, "No."

"Oh, lord," Everard said.

With an almighty breath, Vitya thrust once, brutally, sheathing himself totally. D'Arcy went boneless and shuddering; Vitya drew back and did it again. And again, and again, slow and powerful and merciless. Then, with D'Arcy panting and encouraging in whispers, he leaned, pushed up the sleeves of his shirt, flung the coat up out of the way—Everard staggered at the sight, at the reminder that he was meant to watch —and let himself to the abandon of thrusting.

And strangely, the most erotic part of it wasn't the actions, or the pants and the staccato groans D'Arcy made into the bedclothes, nor Vitya's taut arms, nor even the slaps of flesh on flesh as Vitya let him have it as hard as he could give it.

It was the trust. Trust these men were giving to each other, and to *him*. Him, Everard. D'Arcy gave his body over totally and completely, giving Vitya freedom to go as hard as he would for the sake of Everard, but without fear of actual harm. Vitya gave his utter abandon of dignity, held the weight of knowledge that D'Arcy could take it, gave the trust of that fact right back. *Safe. Safe.*

And both of them trusted that Everard could take it— would see it all and understand and want it and encourage it. *Safe.*

Everard stood—staying well clear of the back-and-forth of the cot, because Vitya was strong and the whole heavy thing rocked when he was like this, and God, he wanted that—and put his hand over D'Arcy's longer-than-regulation curls. They danced under the force of Vitya's thrusts, slipped through and caught on his fingers.

"Proxy, my arse," he murmured. "You sly dog."

D'Arcy slit his eyes open at him. They gleamed with mirth. "You—want—something—Ever—ard?"

"Hmm." Everard tightened his hand in silky warmth; D'Arcy groaned. "Besides to be precisely where you are?" He put a thumb to D'Arcy's lips, pushed just past. "Or perhaps here?"

Vitya cursed. His rhythm staggered, swayed, and then increased.

D'Arcy dropped his head on a moan.

"Oh, no." Everard held on tight to curls, pulled up gently; Vitya shallowed his thrusts accommodatingly. "You raise up and take it for me."

D'Arcy's eyes rolled. "Fu—u—uck. Like—to—see—you—here," he panted. "See—you—ta—a—ake it."

He dimpled, eyes crinkling shut in bliss; of course he had already seen Everard like this a fair few times. That wasn't the point. Everard leaned and kissed him, messily, 'til D'Arcy whimpered tellingly, and his prick looked urgent, valleying the bedclothes.

Everard let him go.

Vitya's eyes were dark, dark, dark. They shone with approval. His breaths had turned shallow, controlled.

D'Arcy arched, splayed arms, clutching, scrabbling for whatever he could reach: Everard's left hand was convenient. "Ho… oh-oh-ly *God,*" he groaned. "Vee—*Vee.*" His voice dropped low, into his chest, grunts drawn from the core of him, made up of the last bits of breath he could sustain. He was close.

Vitaliy was merciless, and wanting, and relentless.

"Ever," D'Arcy gasped. "Ever, Ever, I can't—"

Everard stroked the damp curls. His eyes were on Vitya, whose face was now set, determined, closed-eyed in concentration.

"Yes, you can. You must. I love you."

"*Oh.* Aarrgh." D'Arcy's shoulders bunched, sweat-slick and tense. His back arched, convex against the bedclothes, and the squeeze of Everard's hand became increasingly painful.

Everard leaned in. "You're the loveliest thing I've ever seen, taking Vee's prick like that. Did you hear him say it, Preston? That you're meant to be here? You. Proxy, my arse. Vee'll have you come on his prick, and then I will have both of you at once, and we'll see who's truly wrecked at the end of it."

That did it.

D'Arcy groaned, long and drawn out, and came, prick untouched.

Vitya cursed, throaty and muffled, clearly almost at his own breaking point. His teeth were buried in his lower lip, bright red splashed there and all over his face, but he held steady through D'Arcy's release.

When D'Arcy slumped, finally boneless, breathing deep and desperate the way he couldn't before, and Vitya had carefully, wincingly withdrawn, Everard spoke.

"Beautiful," he said. "Now me."

Vitaliy looked up, wild, disbelieving; his bitten lips parted, blood-red. *I want too much.*

"No," he croaked.

D'Arcy was semiconscious, still facedown; he stirred at this. "Mmn? No, what?"

"It's not too much. I meant what I said, Vitya."

D'Arcy groaned. "Pardon me, but even a corpse doesn't much like being spoken over." He clambered up, rolled over, and lay back, arm behind his head. He observed their standoff with heavy-lidded eyes. "Might as well give in, Vee. That looks fairly painful."

Everard felt a rush of triumph at being backed in this, at D'Arcy's support, though from his shocked expression, Vitaliy did not seem to like being outvoted.

Except that he *did* like to be outvoted. Most of all, he liked obliging Everard. At least he had in the past.

"Say no again, Vitya, and I'll leave it. But I meant it." He came close, almost close enough to kiss, and began to remove his clothing. "I want you to fuck me. You can't hurt me, I promise you. Be gentle if you must. Only, please."

Vitya watched him, wide-eyed. He swallowed. He didn't say no.

He did begin to take off his coat. And his shirt. And, slowly, shaking, everything else.

"Unf," D'Arcy murmured fondly. "You're a pair." There was a slick noise as he stroked himself; he was hard again, somehow.

Vitaliy glanced over with an impressed, half-exasperated look. "Again?"

"Think I can still stand," D'Arcy said cheekily. "And if you're wondering about the events just prior your timely interruption, well, ye of little faith, I used fingers."

Vitaliy's eyes went even wider. "Did you."

"So he'd be ready for you," D'Arcy said, significantly. Said fingers moved faster. "Next time, let's maybe confer about our plans? Using words?"

Vitaliy just breathed.

Everard climbed onto the cot. "I think this is working just fine." He knelt in the warm space between D'Arcy's knees. "Let me?"

"Let you… what? Hands, mouth, prick? Oh, you *were* serious." D'Arcy spread thighs accommodatingly. "Both at once?"

Vitaliy made a noise: a little gasp. A groan.

Everard said nothing, just lined himself up, watched D'Arcy's face as he pushed in. He felt incredibly hot and sensitive inside, lovely and soft and clenching.

"Christ."

Everard kissed him. "All right?"

"That bit of you hasn't changed. I'll say that."

"I've no plans to move much," Everard said frankly, apologetically.

"Thank fuck."

A hand touched his hip, traced softly up, and down again. Vitya, approaching.

"It will not take long," he murmured. Another hand came

up to D'Arcy's left knee, pushed it back, splayed him even wider beneath Everard. They both groaned.

The cot rocked as Vitya knelt behind and kissed Everard, soft and prolonged, on the nape. Everard felt his presence like fire, static cling, lightning striking the sea.

D'Arcy put hands on Everard's shoulders and grinned. "Shall I support you?"

Everard shuddered. "You may have to."


THE END

# Acknowledgments

This book, as most books, has been several years in the making. Thanks heartily extended toward:

Marith, Jo, Sam, and Kristen, who read the beginning rough draft far, far too long ago and gave crucial feedback. Marith - again - for being awesome and patient with me all these years as crit partner, even though I'm slooow. Lauren and Faye, whose enthusiasm gave me the courage to put this out there. (Several times over, including this last push.) Dee, for the sensitivity read and kind feedback. Richard, for the painstaking copy edit. (All errors that remain are mine!) Jan, for the stunning cover!

My agent, Cheyenne, for the spot-on insights and the unflagging enthusiasm for ~~D'Arcy~~ this book—throughout everything, including heartbreak—and for the iceberg of work we authors don't see. Handspun Literary, for being the best, most supportive agency toward me and also very many of my favorite authors.

The Loons (in order of Slack-joining, IIRC): Michelle, Lauren, Marianne, Ellen, Jillian, Margaret, Victoria, Rebecca, Katie, Ty, Ian, Matt, Casey, Faye, Carrie, and Mel—for all the things and especially the newspapers, across this book and others.

Mr. K, for telling me I'd be an author someday. Mrs. A, for driving me to high school writing competitions and sharing a love of *Outlander*. Mom, for everything, obviously.

My life partner, kiddos, and family: thank you all. I love you.

# About the Author

E.M. Caro is more at home in a restaurant back-of-house than in academia. They had the epiphany early on that becoming an author might, with luck and persistence, pay better than either—which is saying something. (Who does this for the money, anyway?)

Other than writing, they read—and then promptly forget—lots of dense and obscure non-fiction; stress-bake; rearrange the zone-5 perennial shade garden; and dream about taking time to learn woodworking and/or French.

E lives in the Midwest USA with one spouse and two kiddos. They can be found at www.authoremcaro.com, and, sporadically, on Instagram and Bsky.

www.ingramcontent.com/pod-product-compliance
Lightning Source LLC
Chambersburg PA
CBHW051506050726
47594CB00010B/3985